A SIN SO PURE

Book Cover Design by Maria Spada @mspremades.

Editing by Maddi Leatherman, EJL Editing @ejlediting.

Proofreading and Formatting by K. Morton Editing Services L.L.C. @kmortonedits.

1st Edition October 24th, 2024

Paperback ISBN: 9798990175310

E-Book ISBN: 9798990175303

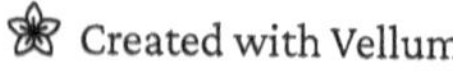 Created with Vellum

*For the younger version of me, who never thought she'd actually
finish writing a book.
You did it.*

CONTENT WARNINGS

This book is intended for audiences 18+. Please note the following content warnings before reading: sex, graphic language, graphic violence, murder, patricide, interrogations/mild torture, physical abuse (from a parental figure—flashback), shootings, guns.

THE COURTS OF FAERIE

The Unseelie Court

The Seven Unseelie Houses ("The Sins")
House Pride
House Wrath
House Lust
House Sloth
House Envy
House Greed
House Gluttony
The Unseelie Magics (in order of least to most rare)
Shadow-Walkers
Empaths
Soul-Stealers

The Seelie Court

The Seven Seelie Houses ("The Virtues")
House Patience
House Benevolence
House Charity
House Chastity
House Humility
House Temperance
House Diligence
The Seelie Magics (in order of least to most rare)
Light-Walkers
Shifters
Healers

MT. BRAMBLE
CASIMIR
THE UNSEELIE COURT
THE SEELIE COURT
ANNWN
AVALON
FAERIE
THE HUMAN REALM

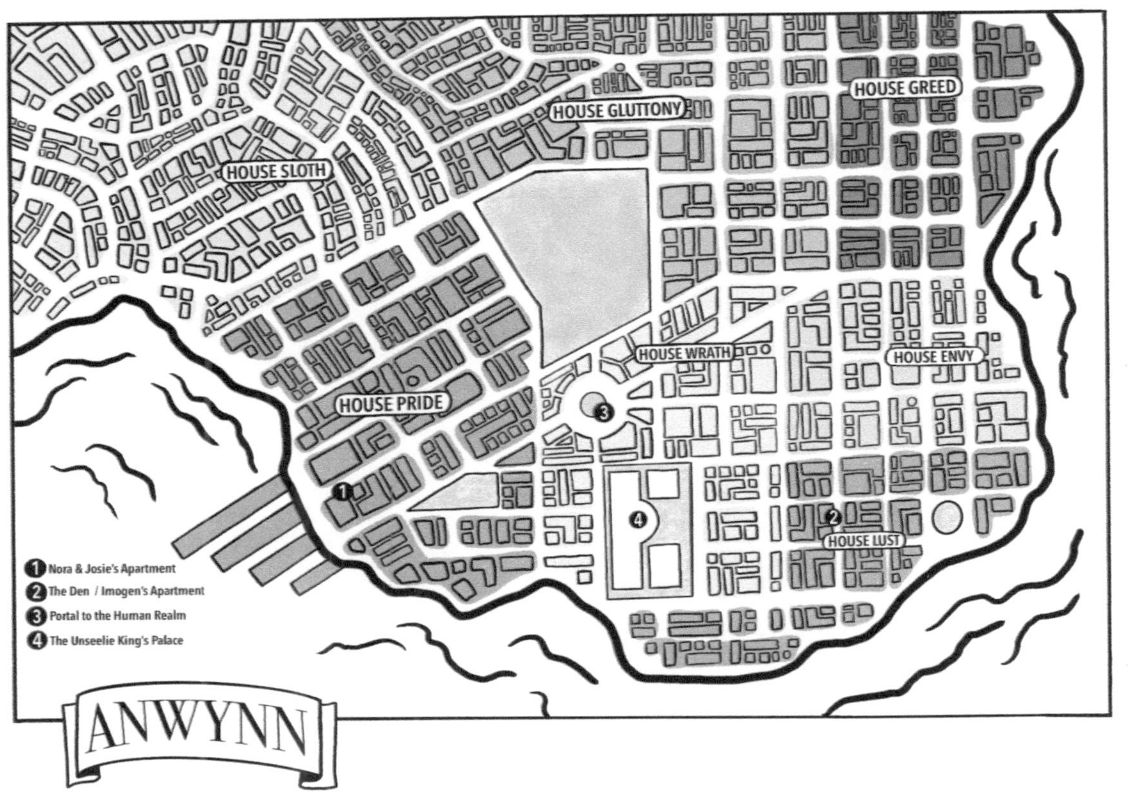

HOUSE GREED
HOUSE GLUTTONY
HOUSE SLOTH
HOUSE WRATH
HOUSE ENVY
HOUSE PRIDE
HOUSE LUST
1 Nora & Josie's Apartment
2 The Den / Imogen's Apartment
3 Portal to the Human Realm
4 The Unseelie King's Palace
ANWYNN

1
NORA

My mother said storms are omens of change.

There was one the night we discovered my magic and another the day my parents died; it seems fitting that one batters against the stained-glass windows tonight.

A strike of lightning flashes through the room, casting jagged shards of light along the oakwood four-poster bed that cradles Pride's sleeping body.

I shift in my seat, hugging one leg up to my chest as the other dangles to the floor, boot scratching back and forth over the hardwood like a heartbeat.

Is it beating in time with his? And if I stopped, would his heart stop too?

Could it be that simple?

My eyes narrow as they glide over Pride's thinning hair and the wrinkled lips that he licks whenever he knows something isn't going his way. His tongue darts out between each of his labored breaths, coating the chapped skin with a thin film that glistens before drying up again. A near-bloody crack rips down the center, so close to splitting open entirely.

I bite the inside of my cheek.

No, it's never that simple.

It will be a slow death. My adoptive father is too stubborn.

A crack of the storm rattles the windows at my back.

All fae go through the Fading if they live long enough. And Pride has lived a *long* time. Though, the gods only know he wouldn't think three human lifetimes were enough.

I reach into the bedside table drawer, pulling a small bottle from its hiding spot. The amber liquid sloshes against the clear glass when I twirl the flask by its neck. It's not unlike aged whiskey in color and scent, though its effects are vastly different.

Seelie tonics stave off the more obvious symptoms of the Fading—keeping a fae's mind sharp and steadying their stride until the end of their days. For the most part, Pride's gotten away with hiding his decline. But the Unseelie ranks can scent weakness like a bloodhound can a hunter's prey.

Pride hasn't left his bed for a week. For the past twenty-four hours, he hasn't woken from his slumber.

It won't matter how much of this tonic he downs when he wakes; it's obvious that his body is failing. And it won't be long before his mind goes too.

It's an inconvenience—of which I am left with two options.

I can let this illness run its course. Risk the stability of House Pride as we watch our leader fade and open the door for someone to question my place as his successor.

Or... I can end it now.

I should be more nervous, but when I search my gut for the throbbing ache of anxiety, I'm left with only calm in my belly. It may be coming about differently than I'd planned, but I've spent the last decade preparing for the moment when I'd take his place as Pride of the Unseelie.

I've waited patiently for this promise of power, yearned for the brand of freedom it offers.

My choice isn't a hard one to make.

And I know it's exactly what Pride would do if he was in my place. He's the one who taught me to be ruthless, after all.

My eyes narrow on the bottle's label, the cream parchment glued on the glass with chicken-scratch directions on it. No name, no company, just *3tbs 3x daily* scrawled in black ink.

Funny how such a tiny bottle could hold such immense value to the members of this Court. Of course, the catch is that Seelie goods are illegal on this side of Faerie.

I pull myself from the comfort of the leather armchair and perch on the sliver of bed at Pride's side. Sinking into the plush comforter, I keep one foot planted on the floor, grounding myself in place while I sit on the other.

Uncorking the bottle with a *pop*, I take a whiff and wince at the pure alcoholic stench before pouring a few drops down Pride's parched throat. It takes a second for the tonic's magic to kick in—it's not enough to get him up and walking, but enough that he soon sputters awake with a coughing fit.

Piercing pale blue eyes slide across the room with calculated precision, clocking their surroundings before meeting mine. Steely recognition frosts over those icy irises, like he knows this isn't a gentle bedside visit from a loving daughter.

"Nora."

Pride's voice is rough from disuse. He licks his chapped lips, smacking them together in a way that makes my own curl into a grimace.

"I'm sorry I had to interrupt your nap, but I have a rather important question," I say, holding up the tonic and giving it a little swirl. "I need to know how you got your hands on this."

Lightning strikes, spearing the low-lit room with shards of pure white; it's a stark contrast to the warm wood tones and amber sconces dotted across the walls. With the windows behind me, I'm sure I resemble a storybook villain, backlit and looming over Pride.

Thunder sounds not long after, the eye of the storm inching closer to us.

Pride's focus shifts to the bottle in my hand, greedy desperation tightening his features. He manages to lift himself into a sitting position, though his arms shake, and his nose scrunches in pain with each movement.

One trembling hand reaches out to me.

"Give me the tonic," he says. "I need a stronger dosage."

I place it in my lap, out of reach.

"Tell me who made it, then I'll think about giving you more."

A growl rips from his throat, rage pinching his brows. "You've always been an ungrateful child, but you know better than to disobey a direct order. Now, hand me the tonic."

"And I thought you'd have better sense than to bring banned Seelie goods onto this side of the Veil. It's one thing to use it while you're in the Human Realm. But here? What would Silas do if he found out?"

The mention of the Unseelie King has Pride's jaw clenching.

I flip the corked bottle, tossing it in the air and catching it like a baseball.

"Tell me who," I demand.

"The Seelie exiles. Some are healers," he says between bared teeth. "They need the extra cash."

I tongue my cheek. "For how long?" I ask.

I have my suspicions, but I want to hear it confirmed by him. The pieces of the puzzle I've long sought to solve are slow to fit together, but between bits of memory and this new information, the truth takes shape.

Pride chews on the inside of his cheek, a petulant frown marring his face.

If he was strong enough, he would have used his magic to take it from me already. But I've yet to see even a whisper of shadow come to his aid. Magic has abandoned him, and he knows *just* how helpless that makes him.

Especially against me; the realization sends a thrill down my spine. My magic is of a different breed. It *likes* to kill.

It thrums at my fingertips, impatiently waiting for my call to action.

"Do I need to resort to *discipline*, Pride?" I ask. "Your methods of parenting may have been unorthodox, but they did teach me exactly what I need to do to get someone to talk."

I clock the moment resignation softens his jaw.

"Your father helped me find a healer years ago," he chokes out, as if he's ashamed of his answer. "You know who."

My smile falls, but I quickly school my features into cold neutrality.

It doesn't change the past, but it's a comfort to know with finality. Someone else pulled the trigger, but Pride's greed loaded the gun that killed my parents.

"Thank you for your honesty. This will help greatly as I consider the next steps for our House." I pause, then smile. It's a fake, overly cheery kind of grin that drips sarcasm. "See? I can be grateful."

Twenty-two years ago, Pride saved me. He swept in, a false hero, and took an orphaned six-year-old in as his own. But I wasn't wanted in the way that a parent desires a child. I was a happy accident that fell into his lap. An asset he added to his collection. A tool to mold into a weapon that he could lord over his enemies.

I wasn't going to be that any longer.

Reaching across Pride's chest, I grab his hand. He tries to pull away, but I hold on to it tightly. He's not strong enough to fight.

It's softer than I thought it would be. I took my gloves off earlier as I had pondered this moment, wondering how they'd feel under my fingertips. He's played the role of father for two decades, but I've never once held Pride's hand.

I run my thumb over his knuckles; the clammy skin is pulled taught over his bones, nearly translucent over his protruding veins, and somehow paler than my alabaster skin.

Pride's body has gone tense. His breathing quickens with each passing second of silence.

I lean forward.

"For what it's worth, I don't enjoy seeing you like this," I say.

"I doubt that," he growls.

"No." I hum, pursing my lips. "I wouldn't say joy is the correct emotion to describe what I'm experiencing right now. It's something softer than that. Is this what being content feels like?"

Pride surges forward with what little strength he has left. "One day, they will realize—"

"No, no," I tut, quickly clamping my free hand over his mouth. "You don't get to talk anymore."

I meet Pride's furious gaze with my own determined one. Nails dig into my wrist as he tries to push me away, but it's a fruitless effort. His muffled protests vibrate against my palm, and I wonder if he has any regret, staring into the emerald eyes of the girl he raised.

"They will realize I am *exactly* what they need."

There's a knowing—an inevitability to this moment. It

never mattered how long it took; we would always end up here. It was simply a matter of *when*.

"I'm going to build a better Anwynn for our House. And I will be so much better than you," I promise, more to myself than to him.

I call upon my magic. It bubbles to the surface of my skin and eagerly flows from my fingertips into Pride. It seeps through his skin and into his blood. An invisible serpent, it slides through his veins at my discretion, taking its time on its journey to his heart. Veins and arteries clog and collapse in on themselves in its wake. And when my magic reaches his heart, it squeezes.

The organ falters.

It's a quick death, in the end.

His last breath catches on itself; it's not quite a gasp, but a stutter—the grinding of rusted gears coming to a halt.

Warmth slides over me, raising gooseflesh on my arms as I bask in my magic's satisfied hum.

I release Pride's hand; it lands with a dull thud against his chest. My own breath catches on my inhale, but on the exhale, relief sinks my shoulders. Closing my eyes and tilting my head to the ceiling, I let the sound of the storm wash away all my thoughts except for one.

Tomorrow.

Tomorrow I'll be Pride of the Unseelie.

2

NORA

The Human Realm is dull compared to Faerie; the vibrant autumn leaves are leeched to a mulled brown in the moonlight.

My hair whips around my face as we drive through the empty city streets. The open window lets the wind rush around us, carrying the acrid scents of automobile exhaust and hot garbage on its back. I breathe it all in, a smile toying at my lips—though I can't say the same for Wesley at my left.

His nose is scrunched in disgust, and his olive-toned hands are white-knuckled around the steering wheel as he navigates us to the meeting point.

It's not *all* that different from Faerie—at least *our* side of it. We can never quite paint a clear picture of what the Seelie do with their carved-out portion of the land.

Still, the murky river lapping at the city docks and the ever-present haze in the air would be enough to set any fae on edge.

Oddly enough, it's always felt a bit like coming home to me.

"You'll get used to it eventually," I say.

Wes's crooked smile is more of a grimace. "I don't know about that."

He doesn't come human-side as often as others in our House—we try to keep the younger members fae-side until they're more established within the organization. But with our planned expansions, he'll be spending more time here than ever before.

House Pride has always operated in both realms; we're the shipping moguls of Faerie, funneling human-made automobiles, guns, and anything else the upper echelon of the Unseelie Court wants across the magical border. Though our Court has been lacking one lucrative subset of goods for the last fifty years—anything that the Seelie can make.

"Pull over here," I say, pointing to an alley I recognize. "We'll walk the rest of the way."

Wes parks and turns the engine off; without the automobile's rumbling, the silence of midnight surrounds us.

We weave through a familiar path of empty cobblestone streets tucked between brownstones toward the shipping port on the east river. It's meant to be neutral ground for any fae who inhabit the human city, but I tug my gloves off and shove them into my trench coat's pocket.

Can never be too careful.

The city is always quiet at this time of night. The human speakeasies have closed their doors by now and any straggling revelers will be tucking themselves into their silk-sheeted beds. But there's something about the way my boots clack sharply on the flagstone sidewalk that sets my nerves alive. My pointed ears twitch as we stop under a flickering lamp post.

Two minutes pass where I scrutinize the shadows around us.

Of course, they're going to show up late.

I clear my throat.

"I meant to thank you earlier. For volunteering tonight," I say.

Wes shifts uncomfortably. "Just part of the job, right?"

I tilt my head, studying Wes's reddish-brown hair and the perpetual flush on his cheeks. It gives him a boyish appearance, despite being a fae of twenty-one years. His family has been a mainstay of House Pride for centuries, his dad being Pride's Second before me. And while Wes is still young, he shows great promise.

"Dangerous all the same," I say, a grin spreading across my cheeks. "Your eagerness is noted."

I reach a hand out, gripping his shoulder with a quick squeeze. His muscles tense beneath the fabric of his coat; he relaxes a second later, but the fear is still there, underneath. My people know the power that lies in my veins. But, despite their faith that I can control my magic and that I'd never hurt one of my own, their bodies can't help but react.

I don't blame them, though it tugs at something deep in my gut all the same.

The weight of my gloves bears down on my pocket, a reminder that—more often than not—they're the only reason I'm spared from too many moments like this. The gloves make people feel safe.

I release Wes's shoulder from my grip and refocus on the shifting shadows down the street.

"If this all goes well, I'll need you to step up for our House, yeah?" I say without meeting Wes's eyes.

"'Course, Boss," he replies.

The humming of the streetlamp intensifies, putting up a valiant effort to keep the darkness around us at bay.

"Good. Now only use your shadows if I tell you. Otherwise, stick to your gun."

Two Seelie exiles emerge from the darkness; the lamplight glints off the large guns slung around their torsos. They play a perfect pair of mobsters with their flat-caps, suspenders, and dress shirts pushed to their elbows. The only things that subtract from their attempt at intimidation are the glittering wings, akin to a dragonfly's, peaking over their shoulders. Seelie wings are so *fragile* compared to their Unseelie counterparts. And worse, the Seelie are always flashing them about.

It's *impractical*.

"Bit overkill with the machine guns, huh?" Wes murmurs at my side.

It is, but who am I to judge? Most fae don't have magic. They have to rely on human weapons in a fight.

The fae who *are* gifted with magic are split into two camps, just like Faerie. The Seelie are masters of healing, shifting, and light magic, while the Unseelie are masters of the opposite. We rule over shadows, minds, and souls.

We're meant to be an even match—opposites and equals, forever bound in a tireless fight for dominance. It's a war that Fate refuses to weave an end to, otherwise she risks upsetting the *balance*.

I'm not interested in balance.

I want the scales to topple over in my favor, for the waters to overflow in *my* cup. It's the mindset that's allowed me to rise through the Unseelie ranks, earn the trust of House Pride, and prove my worth as their new leader.

No, I don't want balance.

But I'm also not opposed to bridging the gap when it bene-fits me.

I step forward, leaving Wes to cover my back, and offer my hand out to shake.

"Welcome boys. Nice weather tonight, yeah? Not too cold for fall," I say.

They refuse my hand with matching frowns.

I sigh, folding my hands into my pockets.

So that's how it's going to be, huh?

"You going to hide in the shadows and let your grunt-men embarrass you, Jamison?" I pivot on my heel and call out to the night. "Or are you going to come out and get this deal done?"

"Forgive me if I've offended you already," a slimy voice echoes alongside sharp footsteps. "I wanted to make sure you were alone."

Jamison, the pseudo-leader of the exiled Seelie, steps into the light.

The Seelie Queen doesn't like ugly things, so she and her Virtues cast out their criminals rather than dealing with them. Why spend time and resources on prison and punishment when the Human Realm and us Unseelie can do that for them?

"We've been working towards this for months. Have I given you reason to assume it would be a set up?" I scoff.

With his slicked black hair, hip-first gait, and a gaze that slithers over the object of its attention, Jamison oozes a confidence that makes my upper lip curl into a grimace. I don't know what the Seelie Queen or her Virtues banished him for, but my gut says it has to be something depraved.

He needs to be knocked down a peg. And I won't complain if I'm the one that gets to do it.

At least he's smart enough to keep his wings tucked away. Wouldn't want them to be *accidentally sheared.*

He shrugs, scratching his nose. "Not particularly."

"Then stop wasting my time with theatrics." I don't hold

back my eye roll as I turn to his two grunt-workers. "Let's do this."

This time, they react, one of them throwing their gun over their back and retrieving a wooden crate. He drops it at my feet, and I nod to Wesley; he knows what happens next. Give them the briefcase of cash and count the merchandise.

Jamison's goons do the same, nodding to their boss when they see that every dollar of the fifty thousand is accounted for.

I tap my boot on the cobblestone as I wait for Wes, but his brows furrow as he counts the racks of clinking tonic bottles.

"There's only half here."

"Half?" I confirm.

Wes nods.

I look to the sky, wishing the stars could temper the frustration bubbling in my gut. But they can't.

My glare could cut through steel; it easily spears through Jamison's show of confidence, causing his slimy smile to waver.

"Are you stupid?"

It's the only reason he would stiff me on the first transaction. He must be an actual idiot.

Jamison laughs, but it's an awkward, breathy sound.

"Listen, Pride, I needed to make sure you were good for the money. Your Pa only ever ordered a month's supply at a time, and this case could easily heal a whole battlefield." His arms fold out in front of him in a placating gesture. "No hard feelings. Consider the extra cash a deposit toward your second order."

It takes me all of one second to rush forward and knock Jamison off his feet. My ankle sweeps behind his, hooking and pulling his leg off-balance, which makes it easy enough to push his chest to the ground. I pin him down with a knee in his gut and my hand around his neck.

At the same time, I pull my gun from its holster at my ribcage and train it on one of his lackeys, who steps towards us. The fae's gait falters, and I hear the other mutter a curse at my back. When I tilt my head over my shoulder, I see Wes with his gun pointed at the third Seelie's head.

Smart boy.

An ice-cold smile frosts over my lips at how we got the three Seelie frozen and helpless in seconds.

I slide my hand up from Jamison's neck to his jaw, squeezing indents into his cheeks with my fingertips.

"Don't fuck around with me, *Jamie*," I say. "You won't enjoy the aftermath."

His throat bobs as he swallows down his fear.

I'm sure Pride handled business with Jamison differently—with secrets and hush money and third, fourth, and fifth chances because he's the only supplier we have access to.

But that's not how I handle business.

You get two chances. That's it. In that way, I'm worse than my predecessor.

I turn Jamison's head left and right. I could kill him in seconds with ease. My magic wants to. It's a rabid dog inside my chest, barking to be let out.

Unfortunately, the fact remains that he *is* the only supplier. And it'd be a shame to lose this business before we even start it.

"Next time, you'll give me triple the product at no cost. Or there will be a promotion opportunity for your grunt-men over there. Understand?"

Jamison nods with a high-pitched squeak.

I pat his cheek twice and stand, holstering my gun.

"See? How easy was that?" I smile. "We'll be in touch for the next drop off."

I start towards the car, knowing Wesley is following by the sound of his heavy footsteps behind me.

"Happy anniversary, by the way!" Jamison's voice echoes into the night.

It doesn't sound like the other well-wishes I've gotten all day, it's more of a veiled warning from a petty man.

If he's trying to shake my confidence, it won't work.

I walk into the chilled night without a second glance at the Seelie behind me. Endorphins from the fight pump a dangerous high through my veins, turning my steps into bounces.

A year ago, I killed Pride and took his place.

I've never felt so free.

Happy anniversary, indeed.

I'm not two feet into our main fae-side warehouse before my Second is scolding me, but I wouldn't have it any other way.

"I thought *I* was going with you as backup," Josie says, matching my brisk pace towards my office. Her short dark brown hair, expertly waved and tucked behind one ear, bounces with each step. "So, color me surprised when Claude tells me you took the Cadillac and drove off with his *little brother* before I even got to the warehouse."

"Half brother," I correct.

A frustrated groan rumbles from her throat.

"Wes offered, and he needs more experience. So, I thought, why not? I didn't think it'd be a big deal," I say.

"It's not, but you still need to *tell* me."

"Mhm."

"It's a matter of House security—"

"Of course."

"And not to mention your safety—"

"Yes, Mother."

"*Nora*," Josie sputters, stopping mid-stride. Her arms flop at her sides with a defeated sigh.

"*Josie*," I mimic back to her.

Of the two of us, I've always been the one more likely to jump without looking or to ask for forgiveness rather than permission.

Like right now.

"You forget who you are," she says.

"I'm Pride of the Unseelie."

"That's not what I mean, and you know it."

Her jaw feathers, the warm beige skin rippling as she physically holds back her frustration.

Shit, she's serious.

My shoulders soften at the concern swirling in Josie's deep brown irises.

I grab one of her hands, curling my fingers around hers, and squeeze. She doesn't flinch; she squeezes mine back, a silent understanding passing between us. Josie and I are the same in the ways that matter. Both orphaned young and taken in by the same cruel and power-hungry fae, we're sisters in all but blood and name.

"I'm fine. Wesley is fine. Everything is *fine*."

"I know," she sighs. "I just worry."

My lips twist into a playful pout as I swing our joined hands.

"But I don't pay you to worry."

"You don't pay me enough to *not* worry," she huffs and

wriggles out of my hold. "It seems to be a hazard of being your Second that I have yet to find a way to avoid."

"Maybe you should meditate. I've heard that helps with anxiety."

"Oh, *fuck off*, Nor."

She may curse at me, but her full lips curve into a familiar smile.

"It's all going to work out for us, Joze. This brings us one step closer to what we're after." I jab my thumb over my shoulder. "Can we please go to my office and get this meeting started?"

Josie snorts, walking backwards with her hands perched on her narrow hips.

"I see how it is. You want to ditch us for Imogen."

A flash of blond hair framing full freckled cheeks has me biting my bottom lip.

"Can you blame me?"

Josie laughs, shaking her head as she opens the door to my office.

"No, I can't."

It had taken longer than I anticipated for Wes and me to drop the tonics off at our human-side warehouse before crossing back into Anwynn. We had to use the main portal since we drove, which takes forever between the travel logs and Wrath's security checks. Between that and my inner circle taking an entire *hour* to review their weekly updates, I'm all too quick to slam our smuggled trophy onto my desk and finish this meeting.

And as much as Josie likes to poke fun, the whole team is joining us at the Den for drinks tonight; I *know* they're all itching to let loose as much as I am. Especially since I'm the one who's paying.

They sit three across on the other side of my desk. I study them in the silence, waiting for their reactions.

Josie stares at the tonic with her unreadable poker face. With her ability to peer into people's minds—a rare empath gift—she's the most calculated and reserved of my advisers.

Claude leans back in his chair, which is much too small for his bulk, and scratches the dark stubble on his chin. His reddish-brown hair is cropped short, the color much like Wes's and their father's before them. He's not gifted with magic, unlike his brother, but he's loyal and knows the ropes.

Hattie, on the other hand, broadcasts every thought and feeling that crosses her mind without restraint. Her head bobbles in disbelief, her white-blond curls bouncing around her neck. Wide, downturned doe-eyes, which are perpetually smudged with mascara on the bottom lash line, blink once, twice, then—

"Is that what I think it is?" Hattie asks. She looks to Claude, then Josie, then back to me. She inches forward, eyes nearly crossing as she inspects the amber liquid through the glass. "I thought it'd be more... glittery. Bein' magic and all."

Josie snorts. "Do you sparkle when you shadow-walk?"

Hattie pouts, her pink bottom lip jutting out. "No. But I wish I did. I'd look like starlight."

Meanwhile, Claude reaches forward, grabbing the bottle and inspecting the label.

"Go on, take a whiff," I say. "It's nasty stuff."

He pops the cork and sniffs, immediately coughing at the industrial-strength healing tonic.

"How do we know it works?" he asks.

I pull my dagger from the holster at my ribs—one side holds my gun and the other my knife. The leather straps wrap my weapons around me like an armored cocoon. I flip the blade so the sharp metal rests against my palm and hold the handle out to Claude.

"Go on."

His shoulders stiffen, but he nods, pulling the knife from my grip. He makes to slice his own forearm, but I cut him off.

"*No*, not yours."

I push one sleeve up and jab my arm at him.

His chocolate-brown eyes meet mine with a sheen of confusion; my predecessor was the type to let others take pain for him. Claude is still learning that I am not.

He nods, then grips my palm with one hand, slicing a line across my outer forearm with the other. Blood quickly wells at the open wound.

I grab the tonic, quickly throwing a shot back. Grassy, herbal notes mixed with rubbing alcohol hit my tongue. Then, the telltale tickle of magic rushes over my arm, dulling the cut's sting and stitching my skin back together.

Josie hands me a handkerchief and I wipe away the pooled blood from my forearm. It takes a few swipes to rid my skin of the red streaks, but once I'm done, my skin is as clear as it was before the blade touched down.

"See? Works perfectly fine," I say. I grab the knife and clean that too. "Claude, you'll be in charge of distribution when the time comes. Usual vendors should work. Bring Wesley along with you too. He should learn the routes."

"About Wes." Claude clears his throat. "He was askin' about his clipping the other day."

I freeze midway in working the handkerchief over the blade, ice filling my veins.

"I'm proud of you." The words are foreign on Pride's tongue, but they are spoken nonetheless.

Blood runs down my back; twin rivers of red bracket my spine. These are wounds that will scar, ones made with iron blades crafted specifically to mark our skin with proof of our clipped wings.

I clear my throat, shifting at the phantom pain that slices between my shoulder blades.

"I thought I made myself clear that while clippings may be a part of our history, they will not be a part of our House's future."

"But, Boss, it's tradition—"

"If Wes wants to prove his worth to me, he can find another way of doing it. Understood?" I say, my tone laced with ice.

Claude shuts his mouth, a good little soldier.

"Yes, Boss."

"Good. Hattie? Any updates on the paperwork? Then we can head out."

She nods, her curls bouncing with the action. Pulling a folder of papers from a bag at her side, she places them on the desk in front of me.

"These are the permit applications you asked for. They were hard to dig up, being fifty years old, but the library had a copy from old imports that I was able to get my hands on."

I pick up the folder and leaf through the pages. The paper is old, yellowed, and stiff between my fingers. I catch a whiff of musk as I rifle through them, and a tingle of excitement works its way through me at the scent. It's a prickle of anticipation that has me biting my tongue.

"Do you really think Silas will approve this?" Hattie asks.

Then she whispers, "Wouldn't it be easier to sell it on the black market?"

"Silas would find out within days. This is bigger than human drugs." Josie shakes her head. "It's better to go to him first. If we follow a semblance of protocol, get people excited about the product, it puts pressure on him to concede. Otherwise, it's likely he'll squash the venture without a second thought."

I snap the folder shut, flicking it back on the desk.

"Then we're all in agreement. I'll bring the proposal to him tomorrow at the Sins meeting." I look each of my inner circle in the eye as I grab the bottle from the desk and tuck it into my coat. "You're all to keep quiet about this until then. Got it?"

Three nods have me smirking.

"Then let's get going. We've got a lot to celebrate."

3
IMOGEN

The night is ripe with mischief.

Waves of heady arousal and glittering joy crash over me as I step into the Den, which means there's *just* enough debauchery going on in my bar.

I stroll between champagne towers and giggling patrons, shooting soft smiles at those who turn my way. When one of the servers passes me, balancing a platter of fresh drinks on one shoulder, they nod. It's a silent signal for me to follow.

Pivoting in their direction, my heels click on the black-and-white tiled floor. Our band's crooning saxophone and plucky piano fade to the background as she leads me to the back corner, far away from the active bar and dance floor. Here, in the corner, warmly lit by a bronzed overhead sconce, three gentlemen sit in a booth. With their sharp black suits and leering smiles, I immediately clock them as Royals—distant cousins and courtiers of the king.

Unseelie Royals always have this *air* about them. Even fae without magic like my own can sense the way they exude a specific brand of unearned confidence. They think because they're related to Silas that they run this city. They think because they don't belong to a House that they sit *above* the Houses.

But their food is grown on Gluttony's fields, their money is held in Greed's banks, and their guns, cars, and shiny human oddities come from Pride's supply chain. They're watched over by Wrath's soldiers, and they're housed in the flats Sloth builds. They enjoy entertainment provided by Envy, and their secrets are kept by my House.

Sure, Silas is the king and the most powerful fae on this side of Faerie. And he may keep the Seelie out with the shadow veil he erected fifty years ago. But they're delusional if they really think they have more power than the Sins.

Still, appearances must be upheld.

"Gentlemen," I say. "How are we tonight?"

The server deposits their drinks and doesn't linger, leaving me with the three men.

"Lust," one purrs, his yeasty beer-breath wafting across the table. "You are ravishing tonight. But that's expected."

My magic balks at the slimy smugness radiating from him. He *genuinely* thinks he's being charming. His leering is anything but.

"I heard you were hosting a celebration tonight for a certain special guest, yet they haven't made an appearance," another pouts.

My lips stretch into a tight smile.

"You know how Pride is. She's a busy woman," I say.

"She's been Pride for a year and hasn't attended any of our functions," the third Royal chimes in over a sip of his cocktail. "Rude, if you ask me."

"They say she's a real femme fatale," the first slurs. "I want to judge for myself."

"You two are close, right, Lust? Can't ya' help a guy out?" The second smirks.

It's not as if Nora would give these men the time of day, but the thought of their slimy gazes gliding over her makes my jaw tick.

I dig deeper into my magic as I lean forward, placing both hands on the wooden table, and infuse compliance into my speech.

"You know I don't do favors for *free*."

My magic slides over them with ease, a hazy sheen of intrigue glazing over their irises.

"Tell me, boys, what are you most afraid of?"

"Spiders—I absolutely can't stand them."

"Of losing myself to the hysteria of the Fading."

"That I'll die alone."

Not all empaths have the strength to use compulsion; it's not as subtle as reading or manipulating emotions, but it has its uses. Secrets are an often overlooked and underutilized currency. House Lust has collected them for ages, though I have yet to cash any of them out since taking over four years ago.

Still, I can't help but play with these three a bit. Nora must be rubbing off on me.

I break the hold my magic has on them; the effect is instant, the three men shaking away the haze with awkward chuckles.

"I can't believe I told you that," one says with red-laden cheeks.

"You and your party tricks, Lust," another chuckles, scratching at the stubble on his chin, but his laugh doesn't quite reach his eyes. "We should've known better than to ask."

"Yes, you should have." I smile.

It's a fake, plastic grin, but they can't tell the difference, so their tense shoulders fall, and their embarrassment fades.

"Pride actually called earlier," I say, biting my bottom lip as if I'm fighting with the decision to tell them. Their eyes light with excitement. "They moved the celebration to Gallagher's. It's less of a trek to Envy's clubs from there. If you leave soon, you might be able to catch her on the way out."

Smiles shine all around.

"I'm gonna put in a good word for you with Silas," one says, rapping his knuckles on the tables.

"You're sweet." *I'm going to vomit.* "I'll see you gentlemen next time, yeah?"

I wink and turn on my heel, hearing their glasses slam to the table and the squeak of their suits against the leather booth as I walk away. It's not until I'm through the throngs of patrons and at the edge of the dance floor that I let out a snort.

Idiots.

Something inside me preens at having sent them on some wild-goose chase. Meanwhile I wait, secure in knowing Nora is not at our other bar, nor will she be at any point tonight.

No, she's coming here—to *me.*

Bouncing on my toes, I stand watch in the space between dancing fae and the u-shaped bar at my back.

The lights are dim in this half of the bar; chandeliers dangle from the vaulted ceiling at different heights, setting the room aglow with warm amber. It's bright enough to see the person in front of you, but dark enough to let you enjoy a spark of anonymity. With the band plucking a rousing beat from the raised stage, the dance floor is a sea of sparkling sequins and fluttering tassels, roaming hands, and sweaty bodies.

The energy of it all is overwhelming in the best way.

I give people a place to be free, and my body tingles from

the high of my magic. It urges me to join in the revelry, to get lost in it.

The lead singer croons into the microphone, red-stained lips nearly kissing the metal. Cream feathers frame her body, her wings out and on display for everyone to see. Most fae keep them tucked away—my own included. There isn't much need for them anymore. With trains coming to Faerie over a hundred years ago and automobiles now more common than not, wings aren't practical for our modern world.

But that's opened the door for them to become something *more*, transforming from a practical piece of ourselves to something sensual and intimate.

Why have them out nowadays if not to impress, seduce, or intimidate?

The singer onstage somehow does all three, the feathers ruffling against her bejeweled green dress, not unlike my own with its high square neck, low draped back, and swishy skirt. Though the one I wear is a simple silk—I wanted something a bit lighter than beading and fringe tonight.

"Had fun with the Royal pricks?" a deep voice calls.

I spin, spotting Leo, my Second, behind the carved wood bar. His coarse curls sit perfectly coiffed atop his head, only a few shades darker than his brown skin.

I roll my eyes as I slip onto one of the unoccupied leather stools. It squeaks as I swivel towards Leo, and I make note to fix that later.

"You saw that?" I say.

"I see everything, Mo."

Leo smiles, revealing the cute little gap between his two front teeth. He signals to one of the bartenders, then points to me, silently ordering my usual.

"More like you love to stick your nose in everyone's business." I snort.

"You've got me there," he says. "Though I'm not eager to stick my nose near *them*."

I click my tongue. "Better start preparing yourself now, Leo, because dealing with all of those idiots is your future."

His wide nose scrunches. "Not unless you plan on dying anytime soon. I'd like to see you live a long and healthy life, please and thank you."

A twinge of something that's not quite guilt pinches my stomach. It's not that the idea of spending the rest of my life as head of House Lust is unappealing… it just wasn't the original plan.

My chest tightens. Taking over the business side for my family was never the problem. It's the rest of it. The position of Lust was supposed to be my brother's, not mine.

I bat the somber thoughts away.

"It amazes me how they can still think Nora and I are *close friends*. I'm 90 percent positive they've seen us kissing in this bar," I say.

"I mean, you are *technically* close friends." Leo crosses his arms as he leans his elbows on the bar, muscles flexing underneath the rolled sleeves of his button-down. His lips twitch as he tries to hold back his smirk. "Maybe their definition of friendship includes orgasms."

"Then I'd *love* to see what their friendship looks like after a few drinks," I say, sarcasm dripping off each word.

Leo laughs, but it quickly fades to the background as my senses home in on *her*.

She's a beacon to my magic. Her emotions are silent compared to the patrons who are feeling so *loudly*. She's a black hole in a sky of stars. It's not quite a nothingness, but an absence of emotion caused by her mental shields being fastened tight.

There are no cracks in her defenses. No lock to pick. Just a door welded shut.

Gods, I want to break down that door.

The crowd parts for her like she's a god, both feared and desired.

It's not only the threat of who she is—a soul-stealer, whose magic can kill with a touch—that sets fae on edge. It's the sharp cut of her cheeks, the cold glint in her eyes, and the night-black hair set in perfect waves to her collarbone that merge together to create something *more.*

Beauty and brutality. Pleasure and danger. She's a study in dichotomies.

I'm so unbelievably fucked.

Leo snaps in front of my face; the apples of my cheeks flush with heat.

"Drinks are ready," he says, pushing a glass of white wine forward from a line of four drinks.

One for each of us—me, Leo, Josie, and Nora. The bartenders know our orders by heart.

I down a few gulps, the fruity fragrance filling my nose as the cool liquid slides down my throat. I shoot Leo a glare over the rim, daring him to comment at my rapid consumption. He doesn't, but there's that devious spark cloying at the edges of his brown eyes.

Leo's attention flicks over my right shoulder. A second later, there's warmth at my back. Lithe arms draped in billowing white silk reach around me. One gloved hand grips the bar to my left and the other grabs the crystal glass of whiskey on my right.

"Lust."

Nora's hot breath tickles my ear. Gooseflesh spreads on my skin like wildfire on a drought-ridden land. The flush consumes my cheeks and neck.

"Pride," I say, tilting my head towards hers.

We're so close our lips could touch.

But neither of us leans forward, both of us relishing in the tension that lives in the space between our bodies. We stay suspended in this moment, the rest of the world a blur of color and static sound around us.

"How are you?" she asks, voice thick as honey.

"Can't complain now that you're here," I whisper. "Happy one year, by the way."

Nora steps back, smirking over her glass. The loss of her warmth feels like a punishment, but she knows that. This is how it is between us: a push and pull.

She hums, reaching forward with her free hand to finger the end of my hair. She wraps a blond strand around one finger, twirling the golden wave so that it gives a delicious tug at my scalp—not enough to hurt, but enough to tease.

"You wore your hair long."

I shrug. "Didn't feel like curling and pinning it short today."

"I like it."

"I'm also doing fine. Thank you for asking, Nora," Leo interjects.

My cheeks somehow get hotter as the bubble around the two of us pops. But Nora laughs, leaning over the bar on both forearms to match my Second in a standoff that's all too familiar.

Leo isn't angry; this is just how they are.

"Hi, Leo," Nora drawls.

"I fucking hate parallel parking. Especially now that every Tom, Dick, and Harry has a car. Next time, you're driving, Nor." Josie sidles up to the bar, to the right of Nora.

"I told you we should have come with Hattie and the boys," Nora mutters into her drink.

"Yeah, but then I can't leave whenever I want." Josie pauses and leans around Nora to shoot me a dimpled grin. "Hey, Mo." Then, her attention shoots to Leo, her brows knitting together. "Why are you behind the bar?"

Her fingers tap on the bar with nervous energy.

Josie's always like this, fidgety around so many people. Some empaths love it, the rush of emotion from crowds—others get overwhelmed. Josie is the latter.

She's a different kind of empath. One that doesn't just sense emotions, but can hear thoughts too.

"Don't worry, I was just helping out during the big rush. I can still be your wingman on the dance floor," Leo teases.

He hops over the bar with ease, peacocking his strength for the patrons around us, but nearly knocks over our drinks in the process.

How many times have I told him not to do that?

"Thank goodness." Josie snatches her cocktail off the counter, taking a sip and humming when she finds it satisfactory. She jabs a thumb at Nora and me. "These two are no help."

"Hey, I used to be an excellent wingwoman," Nora says.

"*Sure.* But then you two started fucking, and now your poor Seconds are nothing but chopped liver," Leo says.

Bold, Leo. Bold.

Nora shoots him a glare that could shatter glass, but Leo throws his arm around Josie, unaffected. "C'mon, Josie, let's leave before they start pawing at each other."

Josie snorts, waving goodbye as Leo guides her to a booth across the bar where the other members of House Pride gather. Only the ones closest to Nora and Josie were invited, so it's an intimate affair.

Nora sets her glass down on the bar top and turns. She leans back and perches her elbows on the lipped edge. Digging into the pocket of her wide-leg trousers, she pulls out a cigarette and a silver lighter. I'm entranced, watching her mouth circle the bud of the cigarette. She holds it there, hands-free, while she clicks the lighter on. The flame flickers as the tobacco burns, smoke curling around her teeth.

I never enjoyed the bitter tang of smoke until I tasted it on her.

She pulls the cigarette back between two fingers, a red stain is left in the wake of her lips. And when her eyes meet mine, I quickly fall into their depths, an anchor plummeting into the emerald sea. Nora gives me the tiniest smirk—the kind that screams of *knowing* someone, that speaks to a secret that's just ours.

She touches me with her gaze; I never thought a look could be tangible before.

"Did everything go okay tonight?" I ask.

She huffs, smoke unfurling from her nose like a dragon.

"It's been handled."

Annoyance pricks at my skin at how I can't tell if that's a good thing or a bad thing.

"Another human raid?" I ask, needing the specifics.

"No."

"But something *did* happen?"

She takes another drag of her cigarette and watches me watching her. The silent stare off ends with a sigh parting my lips.

"Fine, don't tell me," I say. And though I don't mean to let it, my frustration slips into my tone. My jaw is tense as I whisper, "Is it wrong for me to care about your safety?"

"You know it's not that."

I do know.

And I still don't like it.

We may be friends—more than friends—but we're still

both House Heads. And that comes with holding our own secrets. On top of that, she's said how bloody the Human Realm can be. She doesn't want to bring that on this side of the Veil.

My gut twists as white hair and black eyes flash in the back of my mind.

"You didn't invite the other Sins?" Nora changes the subject, crushing her cigarette into the glass ashtray on the bar top.

"I know you well enough that if you had to see Wrath's face outside of work..." I let the sentence trail off. She can fill in the blanks.

She laughs, deep from within her chest. "Yeah, he's not my favorite."

The man's picture should be listed in the dictionary under the definition of asshole, yet he somehow charmed his way into our king's good graces.

Finishing the last dregs of my drink, my gaze is drawn back to the dance floor. The band sings a steady, sultry beat. A warmth simmers in my belly as I let the dancers' intoxicating emotions flow through me.

"Dance with me?" I ask.

"Don't I always?"

The air between us crackles with frenetic energy.

A beaming smile lights my face, and I launch us forward, gripping her gloved hand. We move deeper through the sea of sweaty, drunk, high-on-the-prospect-of-sex fae.

When we reach the center, I twirl, lifting our hands in the air, swaying to the music. As we turn and touch, my skin becomes flushed with desire. And even with our hands intertwined, there's far too much distance between us. The leather gloves rub my skin the wrong way, despite them being worn down and softened by time.

I know why she wears them; how many times have I felt, firsthand, the fear that lingers around others when she walks past? It lessens when her hands are covered.

But I'm not afraid. I don't think I ever have been.

As if she can read my mind, she slips them off.

Finally.

The burn of her skin on mine sets my nerves alight, and I want nothing more in this moment than to catch flame. I can see it in her half-lidded gaze too, the hunger. The soft pads of her fingertips glide across my spine, the touch featherlight as she pulls me close. Our breath mingles, but neither of us closes the distance. She traces the edge of my dress; the drape hangs from the thin straps at my shoulders and scoops low on my back.

I hum, a near purr rumbling from my throat, as I look up at her. She's not that much taller than me, but the difference still has my head tilting back.

A slight frown slants Nora's lips as she fingers the silken fabric at my waist.

"Do you not like my dress? I picked it out just for you," I tease.

I let my own hands wander. Gliding up her shoulders and to the back of her neck, my fingers mindlessly tangle in her hair.

Nora's frown flips into a smirk.

"It'll look better bunched around your waist later."

Giving into temptation, I lean forward to take what I want. But Nora pulls back, twirling me. One of her arms bands around my waist, pulling my back to her front, while the other traces senseless patterns up my hip as we sway together.

"Don't tell me you're not wearing any underwear, Imogen."

"Okay. I won't."

We both know you can't wear any with this kind of dress. Tights, sure. But where's the fun in that?

Nora groans; the vibration rumbles through her chest and right to my core. She drops a kiss to my racing pulse.

"You're trouble," she murmurs against my skin before releasing me.

We go back to dancing with our hands intertwined. The band's tempo rises to match the beating of my heart and, like before, the distance between our bodies is a punishment. But it's one I'll gladly endure if it means her coming back to my bed tonight.

We've always teased each other. It's a give and take, this addicting little game. One where we draw out the tension until it snaps under the pressure of our hunger. It's soft touches stolen at midnight, starved kisses in dark hallways, roaming hands, and whispered promises.

So, we dance. And we order second, third, and fourth rounds of drinks. And we giggle as we people-watch until last call rings. We join Leo and Josie and their other friends from House Pride in their booth, and our asses stay firmly planted in our seats as each one of them leaves.

Then it's just us at the deserted bar together, taking turns drinking straight from a bottle of wine. And when I try to sneak a kiss again, she denies me, whispering that we should go upstairs instead.

4
IMOGEN

A girl bursts from the dorm in a storm of tears, anger and heartbreak pulsing off her. I stumble out of her way, watching her run down the hall before turning back to the door. But as my hand touches the doorknob, it bursts open a second time, one of our classmates pushing past me to follow the crying girl.

"Agnes, wait!" he yells.

"Jeeze," I murmur, nudging open the already ajar door, ready for a third person to appear.

But I push inside without incident. The party is unfazed by the couple's outburst as I squeeze around my classmates. Some are already smoked and falling into revelry, while others mull about and chat.

We had our last class today; our graduation ceremony is this weekend.

I sidle up to Earl, the classmate who's hosting today's celebration, in his small kitchenette. He's one of the few fae who live in the university's dorms, having moved to the city for school from a small village out west. Most of us live at home, our parents not wanting us to live with members of other Houses, lest we get too close to our rivals.

"What happened there?" I ask, nodding my head to the door.

Earl doesn't miss a beat. "She caught George in the bathroom with Myrtle."

I grimace.

"Yeah, I made the same face," he chuckles. "Drink?"

"Please."

We're quiet as he mixes me a quick cocktail. It's far too strong and sweet, made with cheap liquor and mixers I'd never pair together, but it'll do its job.

I take a second sip, larger this time, and my lips twist into a puckered mess. A shiver racks my body.

Maybe I should have offered to do it myself.

"Nora's playing cards with the others, if that's who you're searching for," Earl says casually. He doesn't meet my eye, busy fussing with his makeshift bar. "They're at the dining table."

I shoot him a side-eyed look.

Nora and I had one class together our first year. From there, our friendship flourished. We're both the daughters of House Heads; there's a kinship there that I haven't found with many others.

And there's something else, too, niggling deep in my gut, when it comes to the heir to House Pride.

"You're far too observant for your own good," I say. "You sure you wanna stay in House Sloth?"

He laughs. "Not really my choice, is it?"

I shrug. "I could pull some strings with my mom."

Earl pauses his mindless organizing, looking up from the

bottles to meet my gaze. "I'm not an empath. I don't have magic."

"Don't need magic to have good intuition. Or working ears and eyes."

I quirk a brow, trying to convey my meaning with as few words as possible. I'm not as good at this as my brother, despite our comparable magic. Conor's always been a natural at working a room. I got this far with lots of practice and lots of failure.

"I'll think about it," Earl says.

"Good. Door's always open."

I pat his shoulder, leaving it at that. My mother asked me to make friends in different Houses while I attended school, but I can see Earl being more than a convenient asset. He's a good guy, and Leo likes him too.

I make my way to the dining table. Despite the dorm being relatively small, it takes longer than I'd like to walk the thirty feet, having to field hellos and congratulations from our classmates.

Finally, I face the circular dining table where there's an animated game of cards going. Leo's clearly winning, his pile of poker chips mountain-high compared to the others. The only one even close to him is Josie. Even Nora only has a measly three chips left, while the others at the table only have one each.

Nora ups the ante, throwing another chip into the pile. The others groan, tossing their last chips in one by one. Leo snickers, not even trying to hide his lopsided grin. My magic picks up the dejected slog of loss radiating from the few guys at the table; it's only a matter of time before whatever money they bet is swept into Leo's pile.

But when they all drop their cards, it's Josie who has the winning hand. She swipes the chips into her pile, making her an even match with Leo. The others groan, shoving their chairs back and moving on to nurse their wounded pride with alcohol.

"That's not fair," Leo cries, pointing at Josie's cards.

"You're getting too cocky," Josie tuts. She taps her temple. "Remember who you're dealing with."

"Oh, you little cheat," he growls. It's all in good fun though, his gap-toothed smile never wavering. "You said I couldn't use my magic, but you're using yours?"

Josie shrugs. "I said not to influence anyone's emotions, not that you can't read them."

Our friends bicker back and forth as I slowly round the table. All the while, Nora watches me like a hawk. When I pause behind her, I lean forward and speak softly into her ear.

"I don't think I've ever seen you lose this bad."

She snorts, tilting her head towards mine. "I knew early on it wasn't going to go my way."

"So, you tried to get the others out to help Josie?"

"Don't tell Leo."

"Oh, trust me, I won't. He's a sore loser."

I straighten and her gaze continues to track me. Her head tilts up, while mine tilts down, my hair creating a blond barrier on either side of the two of us. Her lips quirk, the action making my throat bob with nervous energy.

"Want to leave?" I ask.

"Didn't you just get here?" she asks in turn.

I shrug. "I meant the poker table. I saw some others playing backgammon by the couch."

"I'm tired of playing games."

"We can watch."

Nora contemplates for a moment, then, a switch flips. She pushes her chair back, throws her last chips onto Josie's pile, and takes my hand in hers.

"You better take him for all he's worth," she says as she pulls me away.

"Good luck!" I say.

"Mo, you traitor. You're supposed to be on my side!" Leo calls after us.

I giggle as Nora leads us to the living area. The music coming from the gramophone is louder here; a soft but peppy jazz croons from the brass horn and wooden box where a record spins.

We stop in front of an armchair where an underclassman sits, intensely focused on the backgammon game being played on the coffee table.

"Get up," Nora orders.

"I was here first. Go find your own seat," the under-classman scoffs. His attention lazily shifts from the board game to us, and when his eyes land on Nora, they widen. His whole body goes still, and his mouth gapes open.

Nora cocks a perfectly penciled-in brow.

"Maybe try that again," she says, the threat clear in her voice.

She doesn't need to repeat herself, because the boy is up and out of the chair before she can even finish the sentence.

"Sorry about that," the underclassman fumbles. "I was going to grab a new drink, anyway." He pauses, glancing down at the full glass in his hand. He quickly throws it back, coughing when it goes down the wrong pipe. Then, he squeaks out, "Do you two need anything? Actually, let me go get you something anyway."

He scurries away, but Nora's already over it, simply sitting down in the chair with the grace of a queen. She tugs my hand, pulling me into her lap.

Okay... not going to complain about this seating arrangement.

"You scared him shitless," I whisper. "You need to be nicer."

"Not my fault everyone thinks I'll murder them if they look at me wrong," she says. "Let me take advantage of it when I can, Mo."

"But if you'd let me tell people you don't *actually* want to murder them, then maybe..." I drawl.

"Don't make promises you can't keep, Imogen."

Nora had opened up to me, slowly, over the past four years. I've gotten tidbits, small pieces that fit into a larger puzzle that's taking shape. Like how she's a patron of the city orphanage and makes sure the kids have all the clothes and school supplies they need. Or how she saved a classmate in House Envy when they were mugged on the street, all to swear them to secrecy about it after the fact.

People assigned the role of monster to her the second she stepped into society. She thinks she has to live up to that expectation forever. I disagree.

"I've said this before, but one day I will break down that wall you've got up," I say, tapping her nose with my pointer finger.

She scrunches up her nose, but I see the way she has to fight off her smile.

We settle into watching our classmates play their game. At one point, the underclassman comes back with fresh drinks for us—of which Nora deposits onto the end table without either of us taking a sip. Instead, she leans further into the velvet armchair, pulling me closer to her warmth. I'm angled in such a way that I can lean my head in the crook of her neck while still seeing the board game. Nora's arm wraps around my middle, gloved fingers dancing circles over my dress. And even with two layers of fabric separating us, the touch still raises gooseflesh.

Breathing in the heady mix of smoke and vanilla wafting off her skin, I fall into a peaceful trance. It's a slow build, the way my body reacts to her ministrations. We've sat like this before, under the guise of there not being enough seats—a silly excuse to touch each other.

Some think I'm being foolish, getting close to someone of high rank in another House, let alone a *soul-stealer*.

But I know there's nothing to fear if you aren't doing anything wrong.

My hands stay folded in my lap, centimeters from where her free one rests, motionless. It takes minutes, or maybe longer, but I inch my hand closer to hers until my pinky brushes the soft leather encasing her thumb. Her fingers tense, then relax as I twine ours together.

I mimic the swipe of her thumb on my waist with mine on her palm.

Her face tilts to mine. Our noses brush.

Nora's eyes shine like the brightest jewels, the warm light reflecting a multifaceted depth within them.

They flick down, darkening.

My tongue darts out to lick my bottom lip.

Her fingers dig into my side.

My breath stutters.

She leans in. I close my eyes.

Then we're crashing together.

She tastes of smoke and whiskey, and it reminds me of a winter night spent near the fireplace. Her lips capture mine in a kiss that's softer than I thought it would be. It's thrilling, but not frantic. She doesn't rush the way she explores my mouth.

She savors it.

My lips are cherished by her tongue.

Our kiss doesn't end as we explore each other. It's nothing crazy—*we're still in the middle of a party*. But Nora doesn't stop her hands from dropping to my hip or gently brushing over my breast when they travel up to bracket the back of my neck. And I certainly don't stop mine as they weave into her hair. It's smooth as silk between my fingers, and I relish the way she hums when I grip it at the root.

"Imogen."

I rear back from Nora, breaking the kiss. My lips are puffy, parted in shock as I blink up at my brother.

Conor stares down at us with a knowing smirk. His arms are crossed against his wide chest, though one hand comes up to cover his twitching lips as he clears his throat, clearly holding back laughter.

Nora's hands protectively pull me closer—if that's somehow possible.

"You're out past curfew," he says.

My head whips around, my body twisting in Nora's lap to peer at the clock mounted to the wall.

"Shit," I say.

I scramble off Nora's lap and realize the party has almost entirely died down. It's an understatement to say we lost track of time.

I guess no one wanted to interrupt us.

I don't blame them, based on the way Nora's shooting daggers at my brother, but Conor doesn't seem fazed. In fact, his blue eyes glint with mirth as they take in my rumpled state.

"Can you give me a minute? I'll be right out," I say, pushing at his chest and hoping he gets the hint.

I'm not being subtle.

He ignores me, focusing on Nora. He shoots her one of his signature grins, and I swear I hear the other girls in the room sigh wistfully in response. I may be Lust's daughter, but Conor is her heir, and he looks the part with his flawlessly styled blond hair and pressed suit that fits him to the millimeter.

Nora isn't as googly-eyed as the others, though.

"Good to see you outside of work, Nora," he says.

"Same to you," she says. Her eyes flick between me and my brother. "Imogen asked you for a moment alone, no?"

Conor chuckles with his tongue in his cheek.

"That she did," he says. He turns, raising his brows at me. "I'll be outside."

I wait until he's halfway to the door before I speak again.

"Sorry," I whisper to Nora. I twirl my thumbs together, suddenly a fumbling, awkward mess. "I'll, uh, see you around?"

She smirks. "Graduation's this weekend."

"Oh. Right. Yeah. Graduation," I say.

Where the fuck did all that confidence from before go, Mo? Get it together.

"You should probably get going," she says, ticking her head towards where my brother holds the front door open, waiting for me. She does a terrible job at holding back her playful smile. "He won't like me keeping you any longer past *curfew*."

I groan a curse; she chuckles.

Nora stands and gently presses a kiss to my cheek, but she doesn't pull away. Her lips come to my ear, whispering, "Have a good night, Imogen."

"Goodnight," I murmur, basking in the feel of her cheek against mine.

Then I'm out the door, pushing past my brother and hoping that he's not using his magic. I don't want him to pick up the swirling mix of awkwardness and arousal still coursing through me. I fortify my mental shields, padding them with imaginary materials so that none of it can slip out of me.

Though I imagine the deep red blush blooming on my cheeks betrays my embarrassment enough.

Conor's footsteps and laughter follow me down the hall.

"Ma said to make friends, not lovers, Mo," he says, like it's some kind of joke. But his tone doesn't hold any cruelty, just the teasing lilt of an annoying older brother.

At least he didn't try to threaten her like he did my last girlfriend.

Conor catches up to me and tries to wrap his arm around my shoulder. I bat his arm away once, twice, then give up when I realize *he's* not going to give up. He envelops me in a protective embrace as we walk through the city streets, leading us back home.

"And I promise I won't tell Ma you're stuck on the heir to House Pride."

5
IMOGEN

I wake to the soft rustling of bedsheets.

She always leaves.

Nora's arm shifts under my neck, but I twist, not daring to open my eyes, and burrow my nose in the crook at her collarbone. My legs entangle themselves with hers; I'm a leech to her warmth, to her presence.

"Don't go yet," I groan. "The sun isn't even up."

Her soft chuckle shakes us both. "It is. And I have to."

Cracking open one eyelid, I confirm that the early morning sun is, in fact, peeking through the curtains. It casts golden-orange stripes across the bed.

We do have the monthly Sins meeting tonight, but that isn't until the evening.

"What's another five minutes?" I say, snuggling closer.

Our bodies are two puzzle pieces that fit together. We're not quite naked; Nora's still wearing her undergarments and my nightshirt's ridden up. The matching pants in my silk sets never seem to stay on when she comes over, so my legs are beautifully bare.

Her sigh puffs over my forehead.

Nora twists, bringing us nose to nose. In the process, her thigh rubs against my sensitive core, pulling a groggy moan from me. She tries to pull back, but my hips follow hers, chasing that glorious friction.

"Stay," I say.

It's an order and a plea.

"Another five minutes, huh?"

The huff of her soft laughter brushes the shell of my ear. I can hear the smirk in her words. Her hand that's wrapped around my waist wanders, tracing circles over the crest of my hip and down the lush side of my thigh. The smooth pads of her fingertips play with the lacy edge of my nightshirt.

"You're being *greedy*, Lust. Did I not leave you satisfied last night?"

Gooseflesh rises on my arms.

I brush my lips against hers. "Use my real name when you're in my bed."

"*Imogen*," she chides. Her fingers slide under my shirt, grazing over the soft flesh of my tummy, then lower, playing at the waistband of my underwear. "Open your legs for me."

Fuck. Is it possible for a voice to make you come?

I'm quick to comply, giving her easy access to my core.

You'd think I *would* be satiated after last night. But I'm not. I never am. My body is to her like a moth is to flames. It's a dangerous thing, giving into her touch, and I can't help but beg to burn.

Nora's lips capture mine, rough and seeking. She's desperate, thirsty as the desert is for rain in her ministrations. Her tongue licks the seam of my lips, and I yield with a moan, our tongues dancing steps we've memorized. My hands find purchase on her shoulders, and my nails dig into the skin there as she rubs circles over my covered core. She's relentless, keeping a steady pace despite the way my hips buck against her hand.

She concedes to my body's begging, finally slipping her hand underneath my lace underwear and into my heat. Her fingers quickly find the spot that makes me fall apart, and they curl over it repeatedly, all while her thumb strums at my clit.

And *just* when the pleasure is about to crest over that hill, Nora pulls away. My lids snap open to find her devilish eyes studying me as she actively denies me release.

"That's five minutes."

Before my mind can process, Nora hops from the bed with a maniacal laugh.

"You're such a tease," I growl, grabbing a pillow from behind me and throwing it at her. "You can't do that."

She dodges, her snickers growing into cackles as she scurries towards the bathroom. But before she disappears past the archway, she turns, a smirk dimpling her cheeks.

"Yes, I can," she says. "You said five minutes."

Then sucks her fingers into her mouth, licking them clean.

I can't help but bite into my bottom lip at the sight.

Nora's fingers exit her mouth with a *pop*. She winks and, without another word, disappears into the bathroom.

Moments later, the shower spurts on, steam quickly billowing from the cracked door.

I pull one of the pillows left on the bed over my head, letting loose a groan.

Maybe I should've stayed asleep.

But would waking up alone, again, have been any better than this?

I throw the pillow to the other side of the bed.

No. Waking up alone would have been worse.

At least now she has to look me in the eye as she leaves before breakfast.

Kicking the covers away, I get out of bed. I don't bother changing into full day clothes yet—the clock arms stand at a measly six and ten. I wrap myself in a velvet robe instead. Pulling the knot tight across my waist, I pad around the room, picking up our clothes from the night before and draping them on to the bed.

If I hid her pants, would she have to stay?

A half smile tugs at my lips at the thought.

No, she'd probably ring Josie to bring her a spare and then be on her merry way.

When I lift Nora's coat and hang it over my arm, something heavy within its pocket hits my hip. Reaching into the folds of the wool trench coat, my fingers curl around a glass bottle.

Is she carrying flasks with her cigarettes too? Jeeze.

I drop her coat on the bed with the rest of her clothes and shuffle over to the window for better light. I examine the bottle, squinting to read the handwritten label. Popping the cork, I take a whiff and nearly gag.

Definitely not any liquor I know.

Once I have the cork secured in place, I flip the bottle. My brows shoot to my hairline as sunlight reflects on the small, raised icon stamped into the glass.

A pair of wings, but not feathered. A four-pronged butterfly.

Seelie.

Shit.

The water cuts off in the bathroom, and the curtain rings squeak across the shower rod. I jolt at the metallic scrape, dropping the bottle onto the ground. It rolls across the floor and under the bed.

Double shit.

There's no time to dive under the bed for it.

Instinct has me scurrying to my vanity. I sit and busy

myself with straightening the messy pile of makeup that I left last night before spritzing myself with some perfume.

Rosy floral notes tickle my nose and calm my jolted nerves.

Nora steps from the bathroom, wrapped in a towel that does nothing to cover her lean legs. She spots her clothes laid out on the bed and her brows furrow.

"You didn't have to do that," she says.

I shrug, watching as she tosses the towel into the hamper and pulls on her clothes. Everything is a shade of black or white; cream undergarments that match her skin, a white blouse, and black pants. I imagine her closet is completely devoid of color, though I'd love to one day find out.

We never go back to her place.

My stomach twists. It's a yearning that I've been battling more and more often when it comes to the woman before me.

Finally, Nora pulls on her jacket. When she smooths down the front, patting her pockets, she pauses. Her observant eyes scan the floor in one slow swoop, the line between her brows deepening.

"Everything okay?" I ask.

"I'm fine."

She does another pass around the room before scratching her head.

"Actually," she says, slowly. "I had a new product sample." She holds her fingers apart. "A flask about yay big. I didn't take it out last night, did I?"

My tongue turns to cotton in my mouth, but the lie still slips over my tongue with ease.

"Not that I remember. We did drink a lot."

Nora lets loose a snort.

"That we did." She visibly shakes away her confusion. "I must have left it at the warehouse."

She walks to me, reaching out with a now-gloved hand. It

grazes over my cheek, a tender touch goodbye, though, her eyes beget no emotion.

Any cracks I might have made in that fortress of hers last night are now repaired and sealed.

The yearning in my gut spoils into hurt.

"You know that you can stay," I offer.

"I can't."

"Can't or don't want to?"

"I have things that need to be done before the Sins meeting."

I sigh, turning to my vanity. I busy my hands with my makeup again, putting each tin of rogue and mascara in its rightful place this time.

Nora's eyes meet mine in the mirror, a thin line spearing down the center of her brows. If I could sense what she's feeling, understand why she needs to run from me, then maybe I could choose the right words to convince her to stay.

"We can do something after," Nora says.

She crouches down and presses a kiss to my cheek.

Then she's out the door. And not once does she look back.

We're going over architectural plans for a new bar in the eastern block when Leo gives me *the look* for the third time.

My eyes flick from him back to the papers and then to the backbar. After Nora left, I had fished the tonic from under my bed and tucked it there, hidden between bottles of liquor. I've been stewing about it ever since.

Do I bring it up to her? Say I found it under the bed when I was cleaning and act none the wiser?

Do I ignore it completely? Dump it down the drain and toss the bottle in the trash and hope it's not something important?

Each hypothetical scenario has me gritting my teeth, embarrassed at how I was snooping.

I thought I was done with that.

I draw my attention back to the blueprints clutched tightly between my fingers. The lines and numbers on the page blur together; focus eludes me, and the heat of Leo's stare isn't helping.

The papers land with a *smack* onto the counter.

"Alright. What is it?" I ask.

His brows fly to the top of his forehead. "What?"

"That look. On your stupid face." I wave my hand at him. "Either knock it off or tell me whatever it is you're thinking."

Leo purses his lips, running a hand over his cropped curls.

"You're really milking the suspense here," I grumble, reaching for my drink.

When Leo had silently poured a glass of my favorite wine earlier, I hadn't complained. Alcohol at noon sounded like an excellent idea to cure my emotional hangover.

"You know I don't try to get into your personal business," Leo says.

My snort almost makes me choke on my wine.

"Uh-huh," I say, wiping a small dribble that's escaped the corner of my mouth.

"I said *try*—doesn't mean it works." He tries to hold back a guilty smile. "But I have to ask..."

My gut sinks, knowing exactly where he's going with this. It's the same conversation every time. Leo thinks he needs to fill the shoes that my big brother left. What I *really* need is for him to trust that I can figure my own shit out.

"Did she stay for breakfast this morning?"

My neck heats involuntarily at his question. I rub at it, hoping the action will hide the blush.

"I don't think this is an appropriate conversation," I say, clearing my throat.

"Mo." Leo levels me with *the look* again. It's that of a concerned friend—the one that screams of an impending intervention. "Fucking her is one thing. And I get it. She's attractive. But it's been years."

"I'm intimately aware of how long we've been fucking," I mutter.

Years—*plural*—sounds worse out loud than in my head.

Leo shakes his head and rounds the table. Shifting into the seat at my side, he scratches his stubble before speaking again.

"I don't need my magic to see that she clearly *likes* you. But I wouldn't be your friend if I didn't point out that there's something off about it all. How long are you going to wait for her to give you more than her Friday nights? I don't want you getting hurt."

I grind my teeth together; they've got to be shaved smooth with how tight I've kept my jaw the past six hours.

"You don't have to worry about mending a future broken heart, Leo," I snap. "I'm a big girl. I know what I'm doing. And, as I've told you many times before, I'm perfectly capable of separating sex from feelings."

But that's a lie, isn't it?

I silently curse the Gods.

"I know the past few years have been an adjustment, and Nora's been an easy crutch. I get it, truly. You weren't the only one whose life changed from that crash," he says, sighing. "Just think about what it is you want. And consider whether she will be able to give it to you in the long run."

Then he stands, gathers the blueprints from the table, and disappears behind the bar into his office.

I hate it, but my Second is right.

What is it that I *really* want from Nora? I could list a million specific things, but it can all be encompassed in one word: more.

It's that simple.

But at the same time, it's too fucking complicated.

We're both the leaders of our Houses and that comes with responsibilities that will *always* complicate relationships—let alone those with someone from another House.

And I know Nora well enough to understand that her House comes first. Her *family* comes first.

I could be her family too...

My head falls into my hands, and I let loose a frustrated groan. I just need to get through today. Then I can talk to Nora and get it all out there so there are no secrets.

My thoughts drift back to the tonic.

Shit. I have to deal with that too.

I don't know how long I sit there, palms squishing my cheeks and nails digging divots into my forehead, before a powerful presence slithers into the bar. The hair on my arms stands on end.

"Rough morning?"

The Unseelie King's voice is sensual without trying to be— a rich and melodic siren's call.

It makes me squirm. And not in a good way.

He had to show up today, didn't he?

I silently curse the Gods for their terrible timing.

I steel my shoulders as I twist in my seat, tossing the smirking bastard a glare.

The last black tendrils of shadow dissipate around his feet, the only visual sign of his magic fading into the ether. He's pulled it back, but his power still radiates off him in waves. His magic is as deeply rooted as the eldest tree in Faerie and as vast as the ocean.

Silas casually leans against the bar, legs crossed, hands tucked in his fitted suit's pants pockets. His white hair is cropped short on the sides, the top longer and pushed back from his forehead—though a stray piece hangs loose and brushes the top of his brows. He raises those brows, patiently waiting for a greeting.

"Your cousins keep embarrassing themselves in my bar," I say in lieu of a hello.

He pulls a hand from his pockets to wave in the air. "They're idiots."

I have to hold back my eye roll.

Clearing my throat, I ask, "What can I do for you, Your Majesty?"

Silas pushes off the bar, stalking towards me. Lean muscles carry him silently across the space between us.

"It's been a couple of months. I figured it was time for a check in on our favorite new addition to the pack, given the first meeting of the last quarter is tonight," he says. His lips purse. "I guess she isn't considered new anymore, is she? One year already under her belt as of last night."

My stomach drops.

When Nora first took over House Pride, Silas asked me to spy on her. I refused at first. But then he threatened Leo, and I found myself stuck.

I tried to feed him common information, things anyone could find out if they dug deep enough. But Silas has an empath's instinct, and he's far from stupid. He knows when I hold back and swiftly reminds me of what's at stake. Not that I've ever had anything of note to share. Until today.

Silas drops into the chair across from me.

He took the throne at only eighteen, crowned fifty years ago after his parents were killed at the Winter Solstice celebration between the Faerie Courts. He's ruled with cruel precision ever since.

"So…" He smiles, sharp and cold. "Tell me what's new."

I hold back a bitter laugh. It's comical, actually. I've been a mess all morning over Nora not giving me more of her heart, yet here I am about to report about her to Silas.

The hypocrisy is not lost on me. Guilt swells in my gut as a result.

I lick my dry lips, contemplating if I can keep what I found this morning as it is and should be: a secret.

"You're hesitating. I thought we've been over this, Lust," Silas says. His head turns to Leo's closed office door. "You have such little family left. It'd be a shame to lose more of it because of a little guilt."

"You'd kill him here? Right in front of me?" I seethe. It's the first time I've tried to call his bluff, the roiling emotions in my belly fueling the words.

His lips twitch. He's holding back a laugh.

"No. But accidents occur all the time. Your mother and brother, for example," he says. "When you upset the wrong people, things happen."

My throat tightens. I know that Silas wasn't the one who caused the crash that killed my family and Leo's mom, but the principle is the same.

My eyes flick to the backbar on instinct. But his eyes follow, and a smile curves his lips.

He knows he's got me.

I curse internally, shoulders sagging as I push up from the table.

"Give me a second."

Am I a coward to give in so easily? Maybe. But I can't stomach the alternative.

I hate myself for it.

Silas watches me, his irises are twin black voids tracking every step as I grab the bottle from the liquor shelf.

"There's nothing new that you don't already know," I say, glancing away from his intense stare as I place the bottle on the table. "Except for this."

"What is it?"

"I don't know."

Silas scoffs, as if annoyed that I'm telling the truth.

"There's a crest on the bottom," I say begrudgingly.

He flips the bottle, tracing over the imprint of the Seelie wings, a hum sounding from his closed lips. Then, he turns the bottle upright, pops the cork, and sniffs—though he isn't nearly as affected by the smell as I was.

"Interesting," he murmurs.

He dips his finger in, coating the tip in the amber liquid, and lifts it to his mouth. He smacks his lips while staring narrow-eyed at the bottle. Then, he grabs my glass of wine, throwing it back.

His face sours.

"That is far too sweet for my liking," he says, pointing to my empty wine glass. Then he points to the tonic. "And that has a terrible aftertaste."

I have no idea how to react to that; I blink at him with a slack jaw.

He's insane. That could've been poison.

"Stop looking at me like that. It's just a healing tonic."

I snap my jaw shut.

How does he know that?

"Well, with that out of the way," he drawls as he stands,

pocketing the tonic in his suit. "One more question and I'll be out of your hair."

He stalks over to the empty dance floor, head tilted towards the rafters. Devoid of patrons, our voices echo. The sterile house lights cast everything in harsh shadows.

"How is she?" he asks.

"*How is she?*" I repeat.

"Yes."

It's such an open-ended question. *How is she?*

"Why are you interested in her, anyway?" I ask. "She's proven herself capable as Pride. Exceptional even, given everything she's already done for her House."

It was unbelievable, actually. Nora and Josie stepped into their roles seamlessly, taking over with grace and a kind of ambition I could only imagine having. Not only are they expanding their businesses, but I hear the rumors—I know they've put an end to clippings. Now, the barbaric House Pride tradition that they had to suffer through won't be forced on anyone else. I've seen the scars on their backs—their change is a blessing.

Nora's got a pure heart. She might be violent and dangerous, but it's there, underneath all the layers of bravado.

But he knows all this, as I do. I've told him as much from the start.

"I keep tabs on the Royals and the other Sins, but you don't ask about them in such detail. What's different about her?" I ask.

He's got an infuriating, lopsided grin plastered across his face when he shrugs. Smoky tendrils of shadow curl around his body. But as they swallow him whole, he leaves me with an answer.

"Call it a gut feeling, Lust. There's something more there that you're not seeing."

6

NORA

Early is on time. On time is late. And if you're going to be late, you might as well not show up.

It's a rule that was hammered into me by Pride, but one that's proven to be true—and more importantly, *useful*—as I've navigated the political ring within the Unseelie Court.

Being early means you have the opportunity to be settled in a space before others, to claim it as your own, so that everyone else is the "other."

Alternatively, it could mean spying something not intended for your eyes. Imogen taught me that one.

My thoughts flitter to my morning with the blond. Her amber eyes had a sad, disappointed sheen about them when I was leaving.

It made my insides twist.

It's not that I don't try to bask in the warmth of an early morning embrace. I do try. But it only lasts a minute before my skin starts to itch as we lay tangled and still.

It's the stillness that always pushes me from the bed, the silence too loud for my mind. Her gentle breath becomes a clock ticking down to the alarm. Thoughts cloud the edges of my vision: the pressure of the moment, the intimacy of it, the *knowing each other* that comes with waking together—it becomes too much.

And so, I sneak away when dawn wakes me. I slip from her bed before she can be roused from slumber. At least, I *try* to.

She's an addiction as much as my cigarettes are. I can't quit her, nor do I want to. But her side effects are something I don't know how to treat.

And *then*, as if to make my morning worse, I thought I lost the tonic sample.

When I got to the warehouse, Hattie talked me off the ledge. My inner circle played a game of he-said-she-said until they finally let me know that I apparently gave it to Wes to bring back amid the chaos of the party. An event of which I have no recollection of.

Then again, what do I remember from last night other than the flashes of Imogen's smile, her delicious moans, and the taste of wine mixed with her honeyed flesh on my tongue?

I must have been drunker than I thought last night...

"You okay?" Josie asks, ripping me from my thoughts.

She walks in pace with me as we step through the quiet halls of Silas's palace, an old castle-like structure that sits in the southern sector of the city. Our heels clack sharply against the marble floor: a mosaic pattern of black and silver stone that blends right in with the updated interior of the building. Silas is a monarch who keeps up with the times, a fact that provides me with a glimmer of hope that he'll accept my offer today.

I shake my head.

"I had a weird morning."

"*Oh-kay,*" Josie drawls.

"I'd rather not talk about it right now."

Josie might not be able to read my thoughts without me opening my mental shields for her, but she knows me well enough to sense my discomfort. She holds her tongue.

We stop outside two artfully carved wooden doors, the entrance to the formal meeting room, and Josie hands me a file folder containing our permit application.

"Kill 'em dead," she says.

I snort. "Would make things easier, wouldn't it?"

Her head teeters back and forth. "Depends on who you ask. I'll meet you in the usual spot afterwards."

Josie takes her leave, heading to the private lounge where all the Seconds wait. It's their own kind of meeting, where they can size each other up or get intel, but in reality, Josie will shoot the shit with Leo for an hour.

I rest my hand on the gilded doorknobs and push, the metal ice-cold on my fingers.

The room is already set for eight, with water carafes and crystal glasses placed at each seat. Silver candlestick holders are topped with thin candles at the table's center, lit and dripping black wax. My fingers graze over the tops of the overly large chairs as I circle the table. Carvings that match the entry doors curve along the crest of the seats, extending down the arms and ending in small black cushions on which to rest your wrists.

I bank around the head seat and my nose twitches at the crisp musk and smoke scent imbued in the upholstery. It's reminiscent of an old book near a fireplace.

Three chairs line either side of the long table and another caps the head opposite Silas's seat, which is reserved for the eldest Sin, Sloth. The rest are fair game, though there is an unofficial seating chart we abide by.

As if on cue, the doors swing open, and Sloth hobbles in. He carries a cane with him, a gnarled piece of wood that is about as ancient as him.

Fae age gracefully; even on their deathbed, most look no more than a human sixty.

Sloth is an exception.

With long gray hair and wrinkled walnut skin, his near four hundred years is obvious.

I walk across the room and pull Sloth's seat back—the seat that Pride sat in before him—gesturing for the old man to sit. He huffs as he walks over, cane smacking against the stone floor with sharp *fwacks*.

"Always working, hm?" he says, a thin smile on his lips.

"You know I never turn off the charm."

Sloth is as crotchety as elders come, the traditional take-no-shit type who is long past his days of ambition and refuses to give up his seat. He's not unlike the former Pride in that regard, except he hasn't shown any noticeable signs of the Fading.

Most of the younger Sins tolerate him, but I enjoy his company. I like to think of him as an uncle of sorts.

I perch in my own seat, which is directly to his right, when the door opens and in walks Envy. The candlelight glints off his glossy black hair like an oil slick.

"Sloth," Envy says in greeting, giving Sloth all of two seconds of attention before gliding into his seat across from me. He unbuttons his red velvet suit jacket and lounges back into the chair, taking up far more space than he needs.

"Pride," he says with a feline smile, stark white teeth shining. His hazel, mono-lid eyes roam over me, from my chest up to my face. When he reaches my deadpan glare, his smile falters. "Warm as ever."

"To you, at least." I snort.

Envy waves a hand, and his glass fills with liquor. The cups are ancient relics that fill with the desired substance of the holder, created before magic was so structured. He gulps a finger-full down and sniffs, the alcohol singeing his sinuses.

"Do we think this one will be fast or not?" Envy asks, licking his lips. "I have a date at eight downtown."

I roll my eyes.

"It'll take as long as it takes. You should know better than to make plans. Especially for the first meeting of the quarter."

"I hate to admit it, but she's right, Envy," a deep voice croons from the doorway. "Don't want Silas to question how serious you are about your position."

I turn my head to meet the fiery red-brown eyes of Wrath. His sandy-brown hair is pushed back from his forehead, the hairstyle accentuating the sharp angles of his cheekbones and jaw. Akin to his House title, Wrath is ruthless. He took his House seat from his father by force, rather than waiting for the man to die of natural causes.

He sits in the seat at Silas's right.

Gluttony and Imogen stroll in together, chatting quietly. Gluttony is in a white dress that contrasts the deep brown of her skin; it cuts a sharp V on her torso and flares out into batwing sleeves. Her waist is cinched with a diamond encrusted belt, giving the businesswoman that old-money air.

They part ways. Gluttony heads to her seat next to Envy; meanwhile, Imogen takes hers next to me.

"Hi," she says.

"Lust," I say.

Her lips twist at the use of her title, even though it is the standard for these meetings. It's a sign of respect, but I've learned I can use it to tease her too.

"How did earlier go?" she asks.

Imogen grabs her glass, which immediately fills with wine, and takes a sip.

"Earlier?"

"With work?"

"Oh." I blink. "You know Hattie. Always a whirlwind when she's on shift. We were training someone new, and they were off put by how much she shadow-walks."

I hold back a wince at the way the newbie screamed every time Hattie appeared out of nowhere. It wouldn't be so bad if she didn't purposefully *try* to scare people when they worked.

"So, you really did have things to do," she says slowly.

My shoulders stiffen, and I reach into my pocket to pull out my cigarette case and lighter.

"Yes, I did," I say, lighting the cigarette and shoving it into my mouth.

But did I *have* to be there for their training? No. Hattie could have handled it herself. It's just close enough to a lie to make me feel a twinge of guilt about it.

I lean back in my chair and let the smoke unfurl around me. Imogen watches, caught in her own trance as I tap ash into my empty glass. Silas's staff never set out ashtrays.

"Pride, put that shit out. No one wants your secondhand smoke here." Envy pops our bubble of privacy with his whining. "Some of us are trying to make sure our complexion stays wrinkle free until at least two hundred and fifty," he continues, head swiveling between the other Sins for agreement.

None are too keen to join his quest. I roll my eyes at his usual dramatics, taking another unbothered drag.

"Look at Sloth." Envy points at the old man, and Sloth quirks a brow. "If you keep chain-smoking at these meetings, we're all going to be wrinkled like him in fifty years."

My lips thin into a cold smile, that petty little part of me coming alive. I stand, my chair scraping against the marble floor when I push it back. Leaning forward, I bring the cigarette to my mouth. Tucking it between my red-stained lips, I inhale.

And then I exhale.

Right into his face.

I drop the cigarette into his drink for good measure. It makes a short fizzle and bobs in the liquid. He blinks down at it, then up to me, shock written all over his face.

I shrug. "I was done anyway."

Sloth lets out an unfiltered cackle while Envy stutters. Even Gluttony snorts into her drink. As I sit back down, I catch Imogen holding back her laughter from behind a manicured hand.

Imogen is quite pretty tonight—like she always is—but the purple jewel-tone dress she wears compliments her golden hair perfectly.

I'll make it up to her tonight.

Orgasms fix everything.

Greed saunters in, clearing his throat as he steps through the door, demanding all our attention. And at last, we are seven.

I glance at the clock on the wall: eight minutes past six.

He's late. Again.

"Don't tell me I missed all the fun?" Greed quips, the lilt of his posh accent turning the words up at their ends.

Greed is the only Royal among the House leaders. While technically related to Silas, his family is too far removed to be considered a contender for the monarchy. However, that doesn't stop him from carrying the self-importance of a king.

"We were only getting started," Gluttony says, still recovering from her laugh. "You missed Envy making an ass of himself. Again."

"So, nothing new," Greed says. The candlelight shows off

the warm tones in his brown skin and highlights the sparks of gold in his eyes.

Greed's body freezes when he sinks into his chair, a reaction to the chill that cuts through the air.

The Unseelie King has a habit of making you feel him before you see him. He's a cold front sweeping across the land. Shadows collect in front of the double doors, a mass of writhing snakes from which Silas's form materializes.

My eyes widen a fraction at the bright white wings that extend behind him. They are only visible for a moment, but they are a stark contrast against the shadows. His wings bristle, shaking off a dusting of snow before dematerializing.

In a few sharp steps he is across the room, suit jacket unbuttoned by deft, pale fingers, and lounging in his seat.

Silas turns to Greed.

"You were late."

I hold back a snort.

Greed's eyes narrow at the same time he shoots Silas a blinding smile. He ruffles his curly black hair as he speaks, as if he's trying to distract from the disdain shining in his eyes.

"My apologies, Your Majesty. It won't happen again."

"See that it doesn't."

Silas intertwines his fingers, leaning forward on his forearms with a vulpine grin. His eyes, twin night skies, trace over each of us with precision.

They meet mine last.

"Let's get started, shall we?"

The meeting flies by as it normally does—going, by seniority, through each House's monthly status reports. Silas is mostly quiet as each Sin talks, only speaking when he needs to. And after listening to forty-two minutes of other Houses' business, it's my turn.

I clear my throat, pulling out the papers of my proposal.

"House Pride's standard operations are running as usual," I say. "However, there is one new proposal I would like to discuss today—"

Silas raises a single hand, cutting off my speech with only a movement.

"I want to stop you right there, Pride," he says. His mask of indifference has melted into one of cunning, like a cat who's caught a canary. "A little bird brought to my attention a concerning fact about your recent imports from the Human Realm."

My stomach drops as Silas reaches into his suit jacket and pulls out one of our Seelie tonics. He places it down, the glass refracting the candlelight into a spatter of rainbows across the room.

How did he get that?

My thoughts run fast and swift through my mind, carrying with them a slew of emotions. I catalog the last twenty-four hours, scouring over every interaction. The tonic. The Den. Imogen, this morning. Wes—who was carrying a tonic this morning, *human-side*, not in Faerie.

It all leads me to one harrowing conclusion.

My eyes cut to Imogen, whose back is ramrod straight and eyes are trained on the bottle. Her lips are parted in shock. But it's her eyes, which are laden with guilt, that have betrayal cutting through my own shock. I'm so, *so* stupid.

I knew I didn't leave it at the office.

My tongue runs over my teeth as I push all my muddled

thoughts and inconvenient emotions away. I lock it all away, falling into the practiced persona of Pride to get me through this conversation.

"If you would have waited about thirty seconds, I would have gotten to that," I say.

"So, you're not denying you brought Seelie goods across the Veil," Silas says, eyes narrowing at me.

Envy whistles. "Busted."

"Zip it, Envy," Imogen snaps.

"I'm just saying what everyone else is thinking," Envy whisper-yells.

Ignoring them, I slide my folder across the table.

"I have all the permit applications right here. Before you interrupted, I was going to walk you all through my proposal."

Silas's white brows knit together, and a frown tugs his rosy lips down as he flips through the papers. He'll find everything in order, including a prepayment for taxes. I knew if I was going to do this, I had to stack the odds in my favor.

"That bottle is simply a sample. Risky, I know. But all great business decisions require a level of risk," I add.

"So, you *don't* already have a stockpile of these healing tonics?" Silas asks.

"*Nora—*" Imogen whispers a warning.

"*You've done enough,*" I snap back at her before returning my attention to Silas. "No, I do. However, I have them stored human-side. Where you technically don't have jurisdiction."

"That's bold of you," Silas says.

"Some would argue it's smart."

He points to the bottle on the table. "This wasn't smart."

"I've already explained that. And I don't take kindly to being scolded."

That pulls a snort from him. "It's only scolding if you've done something wrong, Pride."

"Have I?" I challenge.

"Done something wrong?"

"Mhm."

There's a beat of silence where the tension in the air grows thick. But then, a white-toothed grin spreads across Silas's face. It's not one that eases any of the nerves firing up and down my spine, it's one of devilish intrigue.

"Tell me why," he demands.

My throat bobs.

Why *what*? Why would I take the risk? Why healing tonics specifically and not something else?

Or is it deeper than that—why work with the Seelie at all? And how does my gut already know that he means the latter?

Josie's going to kill me.

"I've never been anything but honest about my intentions for my House or the Court when you've asked, Your Majesty," I say, letting the words run slow and sweet like honey off my tongue.

And it is the truth.

One thing that was abundantly clear from my time shadowing Pride during his tenure with the Court is that you don't lie to the king.

Half-truths and omissions are fair game, sure. But I've heard the stories of those who betrayed Silas's trust—or at least tried to swindle him for their own benefit. Their lives didn't last very long, and their deaths didn't sound pleasant.

It's like he can taste them in the air, the lies.

"And I believe you," Silas murmurs, almost in annoyance. "Which is part of the problem," he adds under his breath. "So, I ask again, why?"

"I want more power than all of them," I say, jabbing a thumb at the other Sins. "And I see this as a perfect opportunity to take that. The fact that it'll help the common folk and the upper echelon alike simply sweetens the deal."

There's a beat of silence where he searches my face.

"But there's more," he adds.

I huff a laugh.

Intuitive bastard.

"There's always more," I say.

Silas glances around the room, as if remembering that there are six other people listening to our conversation. He clears his throat.

"You aren't allowed to bring any more across the Veil until your permits are fully approved." He gathers the papers and neatly places them back into their folder. Relief sags my shoulders. "And they *will* be approved, provided that I have full access to your operations going forward."

"Pardon?"

"I think we'll be excellent business partners, Pride," he says, that sly smile on his face once again. The man runs through expressions as quickly as Envy goes through girls. He nods to the door, dismissing all of us. "I think we're done here."

The room is a cacophony of chairs scratching against the floor as the Sins depart.

"And Pride," Silas calls before I exit. "Do keep me updated."

As soon as I step from the meeting room, the measly control I have on my emotions breaks, and rage pumps through my blood. I'm seething and spiraling, and I need to *get away*.

"Nora!"

My pace is rushed, my hands shake, and my boots clack sharply against the floor as I turn away from the exit and tread deeper into the palace. I know this feeling well, the overwhelm. It's worse this time around, and I need to put distance between myself and Imogen before I say something cruel.

"Nora!"

Josie always says my words are punishing when I'm like this—when my heartbeat is in my ears and my chest is caving in. She says that I should try to walk away, get a clearer head, rather than fall prey to my anger.

But Imogen follows me still, and I fall into the red-tinged haze anyway.

"Nora, *please* wait."

I whip around as we turn a corner, a growl ripping from my throat.

"What the *fuck* was that?" I point over her shoulder.

She jolts back a step, mouth parted. I don't think she's ever heard such vitriol in my tone before. I tend to keep this side of myself far away from her.

There's a reason for that.

"I just want to ex—"

"No. You don't get to talk right now, Imogen. I thought you were better than the rest of them," I seethe.

There are a few feet between us, and our voices echo in the empty hall. I take a step forward.

"Since college, you've kept your House business to yourself. I was fine with that. I don't tell you everything either. But that's because it's bloody business that you *shouldn't* have to hear about. I didn't realize you kept quiet because you were rattling secrets off to Silas behind my back!"

"I haven't been rattling secr—"

I cut her off with a huff of sardonic laughter.

"I'm not an idiot, so spare me. It's clear you're just as much a sellout to Silas as the rest of them."

My words are pointed, aimed to hurt. They land their marks, each one hunching Imogen's shoulders more than the last. And I don't hold any of them back.

"I *knew* something wasn't right this morning, but Hattie said she saw Wes with one, and *he* said I gave it to him—which I'm now realizing means he tried to sneak one for himself, *that stupid little shit.*"

I groan and shake my head, a physical attempt to break the spiral I'm headed down. I turn my attention back to the woman in front of me, lips curling into a sneer.

"Did you have one of your staff slip it from my coat while we were dancing, or were you the one to do it?" I ask.

The accusation has Imogen pulling her shoulders back, a determined glint filling her eyes.

"No. *No.* I didn't take it on purpose. It fell out of your coat and rolled under the bed, and then Silas showed up before I could tell you and—"

"Before you could tell me?" I snap. I step forward again, closing the distance between us. She takes a step back in turn and her shoulders hit the wall. "I *asked* if you saw it, and you lied to my face. Why wouldn't you tell me right away?"

Imogen scoffs. "Because me saying '*Hey, I found illegal substances in your coat. What's up with that?*' right after I caught you trying to sneak out would have gone over *real* well."

"It would have been better than Silas blindsiding me."

The tension between us buzzes as I cage her in against the wall. The position is familiar, one we've been in too many times before. My eyes fall to her lips; they're puffy from her nervously biting at the skin there. I'd usually be capturing them in a kiss—I *still* want to capture them in a kiss.

Instead, I meet her gaze. I stare into those golden globes as

I systematically shut down my emotions. I wrangle every drop of lust pumping through my veins. My shock and my hurt go too. I lock them all in tiny boxes in the back of my mind, despite the fight they give me for doing so.

I only leave my rage alone.

And then I land a final, cruel blow.

"I'm damn lucky I was prepared with a proposal and that Silas seems so interested because otherwise I'd be screwed. I'd probably be dead. And it would have been *your fault*."

Her mouth twists into a pained expression, and her amber eyes glow with gathering tears. She tears her gaze away, unable to meet my eye; the action douses the burning flames of anger within me, leaving my insides as steaming, bitter ashes of betrayal.

I can count the number of people I trust on one hand—Josie, Hattie, Claude—a chosen few. I *had* thought Imogen could be included in that list. We've been friends long enough, and we had whatever this *thing* was between us.

Unfamiliar pain stabs my gut. It's the kind of foreboding ache that alludes to future regret.

I try to ignore it, erecting another wall around an inconvenient emotion.

A numbness takes over me.

"He's been having you spy on me," I say. Not so much a question as a statement of her duplicity.

Imogen swallows on her nod.

"How long?" I ask.

Quick footsteps approach from behind us.

"Hey, Nora, we have a problem," Josie says beside me.

I hold up a finger. "I need a second, Josie."

I grasp Imogen's chin, pulling her face to mine. I force her to look me in the eye.

"How long?" I repeat.

"A year," she says softly, voice breaking. "I *had* to."

"You don't *have* to do anything you don't want to, Imogen."

Releasing her, I pace backward. I rub my leather-clad fingers over my jaw, hoping to release some of the tightness there.

"I'm really sorry to interrupt whatever is happening here, but we need to leave," Josie steps into my line of sight. "We have a situation human-side."

The look of concern on her face has dread dropping in my stomach.

Shit. That isn't good.

I spare a glance at Imogen, and it only serves to scramble my insides more, a toxic mix of emotions that curdle my blood.

"Go," Imogen says.

I sigh, pulling myself together. I turn my back on Imogen.

"Let's go. Fill me in on the way," I say to Josie.

I start down the hall.

"Sorry, Mo." I hear Josie say behind me.

I should stay, say something else to Imogen, but I don't have any more words.

7
IMOGEN

"Lover's quarrel?"

The hair on my neck stands on end at Silas's voice echoing down the hall. When I turn, he's there smirking, with his hands in his pockets and one leg perched against the wall.

I frantically wipe the few escaped tears from my cheeks and quickly make for the exit.

"Politely, Your Majesty," I seethe as I storm past him. "Fuck off."

His laughter bellows through the air, trailing me home. And like a ghost, it haunts my dreams that night.

It's the same scene, over and over again. Slightly different words may come out of Nora's mouth with each iteration of our fight, but they're all as hurtful as the truth. It's a varied verbal lashing, courtesy of my subconscious, that always ends the same: with a replay of Nora's eyes breaking with betrayal.

Those bottle-green irises crack before me, shards of sea glass scattering between us. They cut me with their disappointment.

Because she *cared*.

The realization hits me in the night, as I toss between sweat-soaked sheets and bouts of nightmares.

I rerun the exact moment she decided she *wouldn't* care anymore. The way the emotion drained from her features and hid away, taking shelter behind all the carefully constructed walls in her psyche. She retreated, started building those defenses back up far too easily. Much too fast.

She's not wrong to pull away. I know I fucked up, but I didn't even get a chance to explain. And then she left.

Everyone always leaves.

I tug the sheets up to my chin and burrow my face in the pillow. It's cold and wet under my cheek, having caught my stray tears. I wish for my brother, who used to hold me on nights like these, when the world became too much and things fell apart. But even he left me too.

He left and will never come home. Would Nora be the same?

Curling into myself under the covers, I pull my knees to my ribs, and I pray that sleep grants me mercy.

8

NORA

The brownstones on this street stand silent in the dying light, five levels of red-brown brick mourning the loss of their tenants.

They're identical, save for the little numbered plaque next to their doors. But we don't need to search for number 88-2B. It's clear by the broken window on the first floor of the building which apartment we're headed to.

I nod acknowledgments to the two guards standing watch at the front steps.

Sad eyes blink back at me.

Each step up to the front door is heavier than the last, my shoes weighed down by the thought of what we are walking into.

A family slaughtered. Another daughter alone.

There's a sickening familiarity about it all.

Josie had gotten word while we were in the Sins meeting, and instead of interrupting—as if taking care of my people could ever be an inconvenience—she waited until I was halfway through my burning rage with Imogen to pull me away.

I rub a hand over my jaw when I reach the last stair. I made a mess of things with Imogen earlier. And during the car ride here, I found myself yearning to fix that.

If there's anything left to fix.

How fucked up is that? She's the one who betrayed me, and I still want to forgive her?

It's got me off-kilter. My consciousness isn't fully grounded in my body, rather, it's floating alongside it, precariously tied to the weights at my feet. I'm surrounded by a cloud of disorienting emotion, but I wave it all away. I push it deep down in my gut where all my other bullshit lives. Because these feelings are inconvenient and shutting them down is the most efficient way of dealing with them.

Because family comes first.

"Windows were broken from the inside," Josie says. "With no other signs of a break-in."

"So, either they let the person in, or they used magic."

She stands at my back, watching with careful consideration as I make my way through the apartment.

My gut says she thinks I'm going to break.

I won't. Not again.

But I'm becoming less and less confident with each step that I'll leave this place whole.

Glass cracks under my boots as I freeze in the doorway of the kitchen. My heart beats a fraction faster at the scene in front of me.

I'm a trained killer. I've tortured my fair share under Pride's direction. I can handle blood and broken bones and the distinct stench of death.

This is somehow more disturbing.

The room is a tornado-swept mess—the cabinets are

thrown open, the shelves swiped clean, and their contents broken across the tile. The two bodies are centered in the room: a pair of lovers staring, unblinking, at the ceiling.

I step over the mess and crouch next to the Halverson's bodies.

Their skin is pale, ashen from the blood that's drained from their veins. A dried red river flows from their throats and into a halo around their heads. I can only hope they were blessed with a painless death, but my heart knows otherwise.

It's the terrified expression that's frozen in their eyes that unleashes something dark and twisted inside of me, a monster thirsty for revenge.

They were under House Pride's protection, working for us on this side of the Veil because we promised they'd be safe in doing so. They were under my care, and I failed them.

The crackling of glass signals Josie's arrival in the doorway. She leans against the wooden frame—it's a casual movement, though her stiff shoulders and tight jaw are anything but.

"Their daughter was upstairs when it happened," she says. Her head shakes as she takes in the sight for herself. "The girl hid, but not before..."

She doesn't need to finish the sentence. *Not before she saw.*

"Claude is keeping her at the warehouse until we're ready to bring her back to Anwynn."

My head bobs up and down, a never-ending nod, as I try to reel in my body's response. But my deep breaths don't do anything but fan the flame roaring in my belly.

I was already on edge when we got here, unmoored and quick to anger.

My attention snags on the wife, who lies closer to me than the husband. Her eyes are a bright green, similar to mine. And similar to my mother's. I blink away the memories flashing at the edges of my vision; instead, I try focusing on the way her arm is stretched out towards me, reaching towards the cabinets. It's purposefully pointed to the ruined kitchen cabinetry. And to the only cupboard that's still closed.

My hand is steady when I reach for the handle; the hinges squeak as it swings open. It's empty, save for a single folded piece of paper.

My fingers grip the note with white knuckles—the corner of the off-white cardstock creases under the pressure of my thumb. I flip it open and my stomach drops. In an elegant black script is a single sentence.

Happy anniversary, Pride.

The already taught wire grounding me in my body snaps.

Whoever did this, *knows.*

"Josie, I need a minute."

"Nora—"

"*I need a minute alone.*" I meet her caring eyes and silently beg her to listen. My next word comes out as a command, but it's a desperate plea. "*Now.*"

She's seen me at my worst, and yet, I still don't want her to see this.

Josie's face is pinched in pain as she nods. "You get five minutes, and then I'm coming back in here."

And then she's gone. And I'm left alone with my grief.

It's all-consuming, worse than I've experienced in years. My skin is hot and itchy, the air around me thick. My body acts on autopilot, doing anything to numb the overwhelm. The wall meets my fist, again and again and again. I barely register the pain of my knuckles splitting open beneath my gloves.

Unsatisfying.

My magic batters against the cage of my ribs. Its displeasure at not having an outlet is apparent.

Soon, I promise it—I promise myself.

This isn't the anger of a broken mind or a broken heart.

It's the anger of one that knows, with certainty, that there is retribution to be paid. For the sins of the past. And of the future. Because things like *this*—this massacre—is just the beginning.

I know this. Josie knows this. We've seen it all play out before firsthand.

She watched the memories like a motion picture years ago, the same ones that are clouding the edges of my vision now.

They have broken free of their cages, and I can't stop them.

9
NORA

The rain battering the kitchen window doesn't drown out the sound of my parents arguing in the living room. They think I can't hear them—maybe because of the storm, or maybe because I'm supposed to be eating the peanut butter sandwich that they gave me. But the bread is stale, the walls of this old house are thin, and their voices carry through the sheetrock whether they mean for them to or not. I can't help but listen.

"Evelyn, we should leave," my father says.

"Pride's coming, Adam. We have to have a little faith," my mother replies.

"And if Patience finds us before then?"

"Then we fight. What other choice is there?"

Silence. Did they stop talking?

I slip from the kitchen chair, tiptoeing on the tile until I can peer into the living room.

The room is mostly empty, my parents having barricaded

the front door and windows with whatever furniture they could when we arrived at the safe house last night. Or was it this morning?

We've been moving a lot. It's always dark when Mama pulls me from bed, and we can never bring much with us. I couldn't even bring my stuffed cat.

She said we can't cry about it because we'll be in a better place soon.

The sky's been crying for me; for days, a storm has grieved everything we left behind.

"It's a good sign, Elenora," she had told me as we trudged through puddles last night. The water had soaked through to my socks, making every step in my Mary Janes squelch. "Storms are omens of change. This one means that we'll be back in Faerie soon."

The sound of my father pacing back and forth pulls my attention. His hand runs over his jaw, scratching the short beard that's grown thick over the past week. Where Papa is jittery, Mama is still. She sits on the lone armchair in the room, only her eyes sliding back and forth to follow Papa's pacing.

"We could run. Try another human country across the sea. They wouldn't bother trying to follow," my father says.

"You don't know him. Patience *will* follow." My mother sighs her frustration. "We agreed that this was the best option. It's a fair trade since Pride needs—"

A loud pounding sounds from downstairs and my parents freeze.

A moment goes by, barely a second, where nothing but the rain pattering against the windows can be heard.

Then another loud crack. The sconces on the wall flicker before going out. Now, the only light comes from the moon and stars, casting my parents as silhouette puppets.

"Mama?" I squeak, revealing myself from behind the doorway.

"Shit," my father says. His eyes glaze over. They always do that when he uses his magic to calm me down. "They're angry."

My parents share a pointed look before my mother nods.

Papa shrugs off his jacket with a heavy sigh, revealing a chest holster with two guns strapped to his side. He takes one out and inspects it, sharp clicking noises ring as he spins the barrel. Whatever he does, the gun must quickly pass his inspection, because he hands one to Mama before coming over to me.

He grips me tight; the faint press of his lips on my forehead is a butterfly kiss, fleeting and full of love.

"Love you, baby girl," he whispers against my hair.

"Love you more," I reply on instinct.

It sounds like a goodbye, but I don't know why.

He releases me, rounding the corner as another pounding comes from the floor below, the thunder before lightning strikes.

"Come, darling." My mother takes my hand. "We're going to get you settled upstairs, okay?"

But before we can reach the landing, a stark white light flashes, filling the house. Mama reacts faster than me, falling over me as rain crashes over us—no, not rain, glass. It cuts my hands as my mother shifts us into a sitting position.

I blink hard as the multicolored static filling my vision clears and my mother comes into the picture. Her mouth moves, but no words come out. My ears *pop*—

"—Elenora, honey, are you okay? Can you hear me?" Her voice is hoarse with worry, and when I nod, her shoulders sag. She wipes my cheeks, pressing a kiss to each apple, and I realize that I'm crying. "Thank the Gods. Okay. Baby, I need you to go hide so I can help your father."

Dazed, I look down and see blood.

"Mama," I whisper, reaching out to grip her thigh where there's a deep gash of red.

"Shh, baby," she coos, though I can see the pain in the way her smile cracks over her words. "I'll be fine, but I need you to listen to me, okay?"

"I can't leave you," I cry. "I can help you. I'm strong."

Her emerald eyes, mirrors of mine, shine with unshed tears.

"No baby, you can't," she says with the firm tone of a mother's conviction.

No. I know that if I focused hard enough, I could help her. I could save her. Something inside of me tells me it's the truth.

She pulls me to her chest; her heartbeat soothes my panic, if just for a moment.

"Evelyn!" I hear my father call from the living room.

My mother kisses the crown of my head.

"You need to go hide," she says. "I love you."

"Love you more," I whisper into her chest.

Again, it sounds like a goodbye when it shouldn't.

Mama pries me from her chest and pushes me back toward the hall we came from. She stands, careful not to put much weight on her wounded leg. The cut has stopped streaming blood, but she sways before steeling her spine.

"Go," she orders.

And with one last fleeting look back at my mother, I run to the kitchen and climb into the cupboard underneath the sink.

I hide.

And I wait.

And I listen to the gunfire.

And I watch from the small crack in my hiding spot as my parents rush into the kitchen, followed by our attackers.

Then there's red and my parent's eyes staring up at the ceiling, unblinking.

The scene keeps playing in my head, over and over again. It fills my eyes with fresh tears—the way my mother begged and pleaded with the white-haired man.

"Where is she, Evelyn?" he snarled into my mother's face. "Disgraces like you don't get to keep younglings like her."

She spat in his face, cursed his name, and then he ran his knife over her throat.

How could he do that to her?

"Come out, come out," the man croons.

He rips the doors from the pantry cabinet's hinges and spills the shelved contents onto the ground.

"We will find you," he growls, taking his anger out on a bag of flour. Chalky, white plumes of flour waft at his feet. "You're making it worse for yourself by staying hidden. Our little soul-stealer."

He continues down the line of cabinets, and I freeze, terror seizing my muscles.

He will find me.

He will take me.

Will I be like Mother, covered in red?

My breaths are panicked, erratic. I clutch the wooden walls so hard my nails chip.

And then he's there, ripping at the cabinet door—my only protection stripped away.

"There we are, Elenora," he growls, and reaches inside to drag me from the depths of my hiding spot by my dress.

His bright green eyes glow as lightning flashes behind him.

But the Gods must have been angry he found me because

the windows burst apart and another storm of shards, rain, and bullets fall over us.

I hear him curse, and he drops me. I tumble to the ground and throw my arms in front of my face, blocking the wet glass from piercing my eyes. When the chaos subsides, the white-haired man is gone, replaced with a rush of men in black suits with big guns strapped across their chests.

My body shakes, and I crawl towards the only comfort I can think of seeking.

My mother's eyes are open when I reach her; open and glazed over like frosted glass, the emerald color leeched of its brightness. I paw at her round cheeks, her plump lips, her roman nose—but they are all cold. I cry into her chest, but there is no heartbeat to soothe me. Tears flow down my cheeks again, but I don't try to wipe them away.

"All clear." I hear someone say behind me.

"Check the perimeter and look for anyone else while Boss talks to the girl," someone else says.

"Shit, Adam," another whispers. "What did you get yourself into?"

Their conversation fades into the background. I don't know how much time passes before a pair of shined black oxfords step into my line of sight. As I am racked with my sobs, I peer up at an older man with the sharpest blue eyes I've ever seen.

He's wearing a crisp gray suit, and his fingers toy with the button of his jacket, a jet-black stone set in silver glinting on one finger. He doesn't blink as he crouches low and tilts his head with scrutiny. I freeze under his gaze, cowering from the power that radiates from him.

One devil fled, only to be replaced with another.

A saccharine smile spreads across his lips. He looks like the bad guy in the book I read at school.

"Hello there. I've heard a lot about you from your father, Nora," he says. "My name is Pride."

10

NORA

"I'm going to kill him."

I brush my gloves off on my trousers, plaster dust streaking across the black fabric.

"What? Who?" Josie asks when I step from the kitchen.

She pushes off the wall she was leaning against.

"The one who did this," I say.

I walk past her, needing to get out of this brownstone.

"Okay. Yeah. Agreed." Her footsteps quicken to keep pace with me.

"Right now. I'm going to kill Jamison."

Once I'm out the front door, I hop down the last two steps and make a beeline for the car. The boxy black Cadillac idles at the curb, white-rimmed wheels waiting to deliver me to my vengeance.

"Woah, woah, woah." Josie manages to get in front of me, raising her hands as if she can placate me with a gesture. "Why do you think it's him? This could have been a burglary gone wrong."

"We both know that it wasn't."

"Sure. But we need to think before taking action," she says. "Preferably, in a rational way. Why do you think it's Jamison?"

I toss the note at her. She catches it before it can fall to the pavement.

"Because he said this to me yesterday. Bastard was probably pissed I knocked him on his ass after he tried to cheat me."

"Okay, I can buy that. But what about the rest of it?"

"Rest of what? We go and we off him. That *is* the rest of it."

"Nora," she deadpans.

"*Josie,*" I mock.

"If Jamison did this, then he knows about that night."

"All the more reason to kill him and be done with it."

"You're not listening," she growls. "How does he even know about what happened to your parents? Why would he taunt you with reminders of that? Especially for something as small as last night's slight."

"Because he's an asshole trying to make a point? Men have done worse for less," I snap, trying to push past her. But Josie shoves me back with more strength than you'd think she'd have, given her slim stature.

"Stop being dense and think!"

Her voice is full of frustration, but her tone does its job, making me pause. The world, which was blurred around me, only showing me the one directive, comes back into focus. My head swivels, taking in the empty street around us.

"Okay," I say. I take a deep breath. "Okay."

I'm sorry. I project the thought from my mind, knowing Josie will hear it, and will feel the sincerity in it. *Can we finish this in the car?*

She doesn't answer, just opens the passenger side door and sits on the front bench.

I round the car, popping into the driver's seat. It roars to life when I turn the ignition key, the engine vibrating the entire vehicle. I put it in gear, and we sit in silence until we've driven through the portal and are back in the safety of Anwynn's streets.

"Anyone who was there that night is long dead. I made sure of that years ago. Outside of Pride himself, of course," I say, turning down a one-way street that leads us back to our apartment building.

"You're *positive*?" Josie asks, her brows furrowed as she stares out the window.

"You've scraped my memories over and over again yourself —did I miss anyone?"

Josie lets out a sigh. "No."

"So, unless Pride told someone, which he *wouldn't*," I say. "Then there's only one answer to your question."

She fills in the blanks. "He's working for a Virtue."

"Not just any Virtue."

Josie stares at me, but I keep my attention on the road. "You really think Patience is pulling the strings?"

"What we saw is too similar for it not to be."

A beat passes between us as we pull to a stop in front of our building. The valet waits patiently outside my door, but I don't get out of the vehicle, leaving it running.

I think the stakes of it all hit us both at the same time.

"We need to be careful with how we handle this," Josie says.

"I know."

"*You* need to be careful."

"I know."

"So, where do you want to go from here?"

I start packing away my own doubts. Compartmentalization is a skill I learned early on. Unfortunately, emotional regulation didn't click as easily.

As I have proven many times over today.

"First, I want all families stationed human-side moved back to Anwynn."

"What? That'll push back the timeline on our new shipments by—"

"That was an order, not a suggestion," I cut her off. "You asked me to think and act rationally. I will not needlessly risk more lives until we know more about the situation."

I'm not an empath, but I can feel the subtle approval radiating off her.

"Okay," Josie says. "I'll handle that transition personally. They won't be happy, though."

"I'd rather they be pissed at me than dead."

We get out of the car, slamming the doors shut and tossing the keys to the valet.

"And we're still paying Jamison a visit," I add as I hold the building door open for Josie. "Someone needs to pay for the lives lost, and I think he needs a reminder that Sins are scarier than Virtues."

I can't sleep.

My dreams are plagued with memories I'd long since banished but can't fully exorcize from my consciousness.

Nothing some tea and a cigarette can't fix.

I'm nursing a Black Cat, the tobacco a bitter companion on my tongue as I wait for the kettle to boil, when Josie shuffles into our shared kitchen.

We each claimed half of the penthouse suite in one of the apartment buildings our House owns. The kitchen and dining room split the floor, giving us both a neutral ground to coexist and privacy when we need it.

"Can't sleep?" I ask.

She rubs at her eyes before waving at her head.

"Migraine," she says.

I hum. Josie gets them often. A side effect of always having to engage with her magic—otherwise, she'd be bombarded by a constant stream of people's thoughts.

"I'll make you a cup, then."

I pull an extra mug from the pantry, along with the bag of loose-leaf tea. The kettle whistles, and I pull it from the burner, clicking the flame off. I throw the portioned bag into the pot to let it steep and bum out my cigarette. The blackberry aroma quickly overtakes the room.

"Are *you* okay?" Josie asks. She's taken up her usual spot in our breakfast nook, plump cheek balanced on her hand.

"Define okay," I chuckle.

That pulls a sleepy snort from her. "Adjective. Satisfactory but not exceptionally good."

I huff a laugh, leaning back against the counter, and pull my silk robe tighter around me.

"I'll be fine. Today was just... a lot."

"Are you going to tell me what happened with Imogen?"

I turn with a sigh, worrying my lip as I pour us each a portion of tea. I drop a cube of sugar into both mugs and add a splash of cream to mine before bringing them to the kitchen table.

Josie blows on her tea as she waits for me to answer, steam dancing off her cup in little twirls.

"We were arguing."

She quirks a brow over her cup as if to say *Yes, I know that already. Please continue.*

"She told Silas about the tonic."

"Ah." Understanding fills her warm brown eyes.

"Yeah."

"I take it Silas wasn't too happy with you during the meeting today? Though it couldn't have been that bad considering you walked out alive."

"You could say that." I take a sip, letting the scalding tea burn my tongue. "Actually, I need to make a few calls. We need to take him with us to see Jamison."

"What?"

I wave my hand. "I'll fill you in with Hattie and Claude tomorrow."

"Okay." She hugs her mug with both hands on the table. "Back to Imogen, then."

I groan, head hanging back.

"She snuck behind our backs and nearly cost us this deal. And, apparently, this wasn't the first time. Silas has been using her for information on us since I took over." I lick my tea-stained lips. "Not like we have much to hide when it comes to business bu—"

"But this was the one thing that *could* have ruined us," Josie finishes. "Bad timing."

"Terrible timing." I sniffle, the steam wafting up from my mug making my nose runny. "I shouldn't feel like my stomach is going to fall out of my ass, but the look in her eye when I yelled at her... it's bothering me."

An elongated sigh slips from Josie's lips. She weighs her words before she speaks.

"Hearing she did that, I'm definitely hurt. But I don't think Imogen would betray our trust for nothing. There's gotta be a good reason." Josie stares into her tea. "Did she say why?"

"We didn't get that far before you pulled me away." I circle the rim of my mug; the ceramic burns my fingertip, but I let it. "Does the why even matter?"

"That depends."

"On what?"

"The right why could ease your guilt."

"I don't feel guilty. *She* betrayed *me*. I'm angry."

"*No.* I think you *want* to be angry. But instead, you feel remorse 'cause you're stuck on her," Josie says, expertly uncoiling my unsaid thoughts. "And that complicates things. Especially if she has a good reason to back up her actions."

Stuck on Imogen... I scoff internally. That's a terrible understatement. Ever since she walked into my class ten years ago, I've wanted her.

Could I quit my addiction to her?

I chew the inside of my cheek, thankful for Josie's patience as I search for the right words.

"I don't know where to go from here," I admit.

Josie's head bobs back and forth, lips pursed. "If you care about her, or even just value her friendship, then the first step is to ask her why. Then maybe apologize. Then talk about your fucking feelings for once."

My head drops to my forearm on the table with a groan. "I hate apologizing. It makes me feel weak."

Josie laughs. "You apologize to me plenty."

"That's because you're the one person in Faerie who is right more often than me." The words are mumbled into the wood. "And I hate you for it."

"You don't hate me."

"No, I don't."

I peer up at my best friend—my sister—and give her a soft smile that only she's ever seen.

She squeezes my forearm.

"I'm going to have to talk to her too. Hash it out. But as for the trust part, try to give her some credit. It's hard enough being your friend. I cannot imagine being your girlfriend,"

Josie snorts. "I'm sure you'll think of some way for her to gain it back. Just like I'm sure she'll be willing to entertain your antics *to* gain it back."

"Like a test?"

"I was thinking more along the lines of inviting her to dinner, *talking to her...* but a test could work too."

A beat passes between us before we both chuckle into our tea, sad little smiles dancing over our teeth.

"I still need to think about it," I say.

"It's okay to take your time."

"Thank you, Josie."

"You're welcome, Nor."

And then we sit, each refusing to leave the other. Hours pass, the moon says its goodbye, but Josie's shoulder doesn't stray far from mine. Her presence is a quiet comfort.

Sometimes, you just need to not be alone.

The window teases a purple-pink morning sky, and taxi exhausts pop, the world moving forward while we sit still.

11
IMOGEN

I t's been two weeks.

Josie came to see me only a day after my and Nora's fight.

She wanted to know what happened from my point of view. But I couldn't say it all out loud, so I held out my hand and opened my mind to her.

The calloused pad of her palm slipped across mine, and I let her see it all. The first time Silas came to me, every time I tried to argue against him, and every time I gave up because he threatened the last family I have left.

"I'm disappointed, but I get it," Josie said with a sigh.

"I'm sorry," I replied.

"I know," she said, pulling me into a hug. "I forgive you. But Nora's forgiveness will be harder to earn. I think she wants to, though. She's a mess by her standards, Mo."

"Should I go to her?"

Josie shook her head. "No, she needs to see you on her own time. And some shit has gone down that we need to deal with first."

When she said that, I was given a spark of hope. But that

hope has dwindled as I've sat alone with my guilt, night after night.

Is this how ten years of friendship—and four years of whatever else this is between us—ends? Do I have to mourn a relationship and a friendship at the same time?

I go back to wiping down the mountain of glasses stacked in front of me. The monotonous task keeps me busy behind the bar. But not even the revelry of the Den can help my mood; Leo keeps casting concerned glances at me as he works the room.

I could go help him—*should* go help him. But the thought of whispering influence in people's ears, of busying myself with the nonsense of cheating scandals and who ditched the last soiree, makes my stomach turn.

No, I belong back here. Where I can ensure every crystal glass shines as brightly as the jewels around my patrons' necks.

It's also the one task that allows me to indulge in my memories uninterrupted. It seems I'm a glutton for punishment, as I can't help but recall the night that led me here.

So much has changed since then.

I don't want Nora and Josie to change too.

4 YEARS AGO

"Don't fuck up tonight."

My mother stalks past me in her highest heels. Her long embellished gown, which should be glittering, barely shines in the dark of the Den.

The bar is only lit by a few houselights that dangle from the rafters. Somehow our construction team had forgotten the essential feature in their rush to finish the build. Leo and I had rolled up our sleeves and put on our electrician hats for a grueling eight hours trying to install them ourselves.

The three we managed to hang are working by grit and a miracle alone.

We have someone scheduled to come fix them all tomorrow; unfortunately, that doesn't do much for our opening tonight. The one saving grace is that it doesn't affect our patrons, only our prep and closing staff.

I continue wiping at the rocks glass in my hand, making sure there's no fingerprint smudge to be seen. Every detail needs to be perfect.

"I know how to run my own bar, Ma. I've been doing it for a while with Gallagher's," I say.

My mother rifles through her purse, pulling out her lipstick and reapplying it in the reflection of the mirrored shelves behind the bar. Her blond hair is styled similar to mine, fussed and pinned into perfect ringlets that make a fake bob around her collar.

"That's true," she says with a smile. She might sound like a hard-ass on the outside, but it's her way of showing affection. She saves the charm for her marks. "But this is different. If all goes well, this can be a main hub for your brother to exchange information with other Houses."

Gallagher's is a small, hole-in-the-wall-pub. House Lust has owned a few within our territory, but the Den will be the first of this size and caliber. It has the potential to attract the rich and powerful from every House.

We're the smallest of the seven Houses, and after watching Nora and Josie push House Pride forward, I figured expanding our patron-facing businesses would benefit us. I also wanted a project of my own, something to prove that the spare heir to House Lust could be as capable as the firstborn.

Access to more funds means more power. And it didn't hurt that the staff can be empath spies, as my brother had pointed out to my mother.

He doesn't mean to steal the spotlight from me. Conor sparkles as brilliantly and naturally as a star. I'm more akin to the gas lamps lining the street. My light is a softer, warmer glow. It's hard to compare us.

"Give her a break, Ma. She'll be fine," my brother calls as he exits the bathroom.

Conor runs his hand through his blond hair—the three of us are a golden trio—before hopping behind the bar. He steals the glass I was cleaning and pours himself a shot of vodka. I roll my eyes as he shoots it back.

I jab my thumb at him while turning to face my mother.

"Yeah, I might not be mister perfect over here, but I have some things going for me."

My mother laughs. "You said it, not me."

"You're not going to disagree?" I say with mock outrage.

"You're a little green, Mo," Conor snickers, wrapping one arm around me and pinching my cheek between his fingers. "You need to work on keeping your emotions to yourself if you want to take over for me one day."

"And what makes you think I want to do that?"

"Because I don't want to sire any crotch-goblins. Therefore, next in line is you."

I bat his hand away as the front door opens with a rush of spring air. In walks Leo and his mother, my own mother's Second.

"That's our cue," Conor says.

He pulls me back into his side by brute force. Conor is a lot taller than me, and I fit under the crook of his arm snugly.

Squeezing me tightly, he shakes me back and forth. It's a silly little habit he developed when he was little to annoy me.

I might grumble at his antics, but I secretly love them.

"We should be back by one," he says, releasing me. "So hopefully, I'll be able to catch last call to celebrate with you."

A genuine smile spreads across my teeth. Conor knows how much this means to me—even if a lot of the operations are being hijacked by my mother and him.

"I'd love that," I say. "Don't get too smoked at the Royal's mixer though. I know they're not your favorite."

"Are they anyone's?" Conor murmurs, tone dripping with sarcasm. "See you later, Mo."

Then he's gone, hopping back over the bar, slapping Leo on the shoulder.

"Leo, watch over my little sister, will ya?" Conor says.

"Like she's my own," Leo replies with a laugh.

Conor leads our mothers to the door, swiftly opening it for them. He's a picture of the perfect gentleman, exactly what he was raised to be. I lean against the bar, waiting for a goodbye from my mother, but it doesn't come.

And as the door swings shut, I call out, "Bye, Ma!"

"Bye, baby!" she yells, not even peeking back.

The door closes.

The opening goes well; the bar is busy, and patrons are happily drunk. The band is a hit, and the dance floor is packed like a can of sardines. There are folks from every House present, and the houselights Leo and I installed never fall from their precarious perches.

All miracles in their own right.

And when midnight strikes, the front door opens again. My magic tunes into a dead frequency—a radio station playing static instead of the music of emotion. Her black hair bounces around her chin as she strides through the maze of patrons, eyes locked on where I stand behind the bar.

"Imogen."

Nora settles against the bar to my right, leaning over on her elbows. She's changed out of her standard uniform of dress pants and a blouse tonight, opting for a simple black dress. It is plain compared to the rest of the flapper-like frocks donned by the women on the dance floor, but the silk shines just as brightly against her pale skin.

"You came," I say, mouth ajar.

"Of course, we came," Josie says from my left. I twist to see her beaming, dimpled smile. "We couldn't miss this."

"We would have been here earlier, but I had to deal with Pride," Nora says, rolling her eyes. "You know how he is."

I know as much as they'll tell me, which isn't much, but what little I do know is nothing good.

"He didn't want you to come here?" I ask.

"No, he doesn't care about that," Nora says, waving a gloved hand in the air. "He wanted to lecture me about making smart choices now that I'm his Second. As if I don't already have Josie to do that."

"Hey—"

"I'm kidding. I love your lectures, Joze."

"Well, if you love them so much, why don't you listen to them?"

My grin somehow grows wider, my body buzzing with pride, happiness, and love for my friends. It all swirls together, a mix of emotions that bubbles up into tears. I swipe them away before anyone can see, Nora and Josie still bickering like an old married couple with me in the middle.

"You okay?" Josie suddenly asks.

I nod. "I'm just happy."

"Good," she smiles.

"Your brother around?" Nora asks.

I narrow my eyes at her. "Why? You want to ask him to dance?"

Her nose scrunches. "No. More like I want to make sure he knows he's not stopping me from dancing with you."

An excited shiver runs down my spine. Nora and I have this tension between us, one that's only grown stronger since the fateful night we first kissed. We've been tiptoeing around it ever since, having been pulled apart by our House duties.

Even so, a collision feels inevitable.

"He and my mother won't be back until later," I say. "So, you don't have to worry about him for the time being."

Nora and Josie share a glance, dual devilish grins spreading across their cheeks.

"Excellent," Nora says.

"Then it's time for you to stop working and enjoy your success a little," Josie says, reaching a hand out for me. Then she adds with a wink, "We already cleared it with Leo."

"He gave me a hard time. The man got two bits out of me before I realized he was playing us," Nora grumbles.

I let loose a cackle. "He made you play cards to give me the second half of the night off?"

"Yeah, I should have known better, given how good he was in college. But he knows how to push my buttons," she says. "He always planned to force you into some fun at the end anyway. Thoughtful little fucker."

"Either way, let's go dance," Josie says. She taps her fingers on the bar top, a nervous tendency I've noticed when we're in public places. "And maybe grab a drink first."

We each down a shot of liquor, and then I follow them through the throngs of people, falling into the elation around me.

And when the clock strikes one, then two, and my family

doesn't show, I don't even notice, because I'm wrapped in Nora's arms.

They don't come home.

They didn't even make it to the party.

When I'm finished cleaning all the glasses, my staff promptly kick me out from behind the bar. They did it politely, handing me a glass of water and pointing to the empty barstool at the far corner of the u-shaped counter.

I grumble about being able to help with stock in the back, but they shake their heads and remind me that I'd already done that yesterday.

They're trying to help, in their own way. They know I'm tired of sitting in my apartment, sulking. But they also know I'm not ready to be working the room.

So, I sit at the bar, my finger circling condensation around the rim of my water.

I'm so consumed by my thoughts that I don't notice her presence at my back until her arms are reaching around me on both sides.

"Lust."

Her hot breath tickles my ear, my spine shivering on instinct. My breath catches in my throat when our eyes meet over my shoulder.

"You're here."

"I'm here."

I blink. "Why?"

"I want an explanation." Her eyes dart down to my lips. "So, I came to talk."

"Oh."

Time slows as we sit in this moment, our breathing in sync.

Nora shifts, pulling away from me and sitting in the empty seat to my right. The night has slowed, the bar empty given the late hour. The slow croon of the band has stopped, the musicians packing away their equipment. The staff have disappeared to the back room.

We're alone.

"I'm sorry—" I say.

"—I shouldn't have reacted the way I did," Nora says at the same time.

"What?" Shock jolts through me.

Nora clears her throat. "My words and tone the other day. They weren't kind. And I want to apolog—"

"I forgive you."

"I didn't even say the words yet."

"You don't have to. It hurt, but I can't argue that your anger wasn't justified," I say, maybe too quickly. Nora is not the type to say it out loud. Actions are her language; the fact that she came to talk at all speaks volumes. "You're not the one who needs to apologize. I've wanted to—*need to*—make sure you know how sorry I am. I just didn't know if you wanted to hear it."

She sighs, resting her chin on her gloved hand. We're huddled close together, leaning into each other like two lovers.

Our bodies don't get the message that we're fighting.

"I'm still pissed," she says tentatively.

I nod.

"But I want to hear why," she finishes; the words are slow and gritted out between clenched teeth.

"Josie came to ask why too," I say.

"I know."

"Did she tell you?"

"I want to hear it from you."

I nod, looking down at my hands. They tremble, clenched together. I bite my bottom lip, tugging at the raw skin there.

"You remember when my brother died?"

"Yes," she says. And while I'm still staring at my shaking hands, I know her brows furrow from the question in her tone.

"It wasn't as simple as an automobile accident," I say. "Some Royal got upset that my mother had dirt on him. The party was a set up and their crash was planned."

Nora's huff of laughter is cynical. "Greed?"

"I'm sure he helped. The party was in his territory that night," I say. I clench my hands harder, nails digging into my palms as the anger about that night fuels me. "Silas threatened that a similar *accident* would befall Leo if I didn't answer any question that he had about you."

I tilt my head up, and we stare at each other. Both of our jaws clench as the seconds tick by.

"I can't lose him, Nor," I say, my voice breaking. "And I'm sorry. You know how racked with guilt I've been keeping this from you? But he's family. He's *all I have left.*"

I don't stop the tears from falling. It might not be fair to cry, but it's the first time I've said it all aloud. And it's too much.

I've spent four years suppressing my grief and this is my breaking point.

"There's no one who will beat me up about it more than myself," I say. "But the worst part is that I realized I can't lose you guys either. Josie held me as I cried at their funeral. You stocked my icebox and pantry so I would have something to eat as I figured out how the hell I was supposed to run my House. You both guided me through my sorrow. Leo's too. You were there for us because you knew what it's like to lose your parents."

I wipe at my cheeks, my hand coming away sticky with tears and stained pink from my blush.

"Silas forced my hand. He made me choose. But I don't want to choose anymore," I say. "You guys are my family too. I just didn't know what to do. I was stuck."

Nora sighs. It's one of defeat, where all the angry tension in her shoulders dissipates.

"Look," she says, scrubbing her hand over her jaw. "I don't want to, but I understand."

She swivels in her seat, staring up at the back bar. I follow suit, the mirror reflects the two of us between bottles of liquor.

"When I think about it logically, if the roles were reversed and Josie was threatened, I'd protect her the same," she says. "But I also would have tried to find a way around it. I wish you would have told me. Josie and I could have helped."

"I realize that *now*." I huff a dead laugh. "But he's the *king*, Nora. Don't be foolish."

"Silas isn't invincible," she says. "Kings are only strong because of the pieces that surround them."

I shake my head. "Life isn't chess."

"Isn't it?" she asks. "Pawns and Houses. Knights and Sins. Kings and Queens." She shrugs. "They all sound pretty similar to me."

We lapse into silence, both leaning on our elbows and staring at each other through the mirror. We keep falling into each other's gazes out of habit, unable to stop the collision before it happens.

We've always been like this.

It happens slowly, the way her eyes can't help but run over my flat hair and the dark circles under my eyes. The few tears that fell have already dried up, their tracks tight on my cheeks. Nora's eyes land on my lips and darken.

She's probably noticed how chewed up they are; the metallic taste of blood blooms on my tongue as it darts out to lick over the ripped flesh.

"I told him off after you left."

Nora blinks out of her haze. "Silas?"

"Yeah."

"Good. He deserves it for being a nosy prick," she huffs. "Promise me, if he comes to you again, you'll tell me."

"I promise." I don't even have to think about it.

"And you'll politely inform him that if he has questions, he can talk to me directly."

"He won't like that."

"I don't care what he likes. I only care about you."

My head tilts down, heat rushing to my cheeks. Nora's hand enters my view, landing on my knee.

She squeezes.

"Part of me wanted to cut you out. But the other part, the one I can't ignore, can't let you go because of this. I've known you too long, gotten too close," she says. "I don't give second chances, Mo. But I want to give you one."

She rubs her thumb over my knee, back and forth. We sit still for a moment, each focused on the place where we're connected.

When Nora speaks again, it's soft and vulnerable, barely a whisper.

"You know I'm not good with this stuff."

This stuff. Relationships. Intimacy.

"But," she says, searching for the words. "I want to try." A finality steels her voice, and my heart soars. She clears her throat. "I would like for you to join me for dinner on Sunday."

My head snaps up. "But you never invite outsiders to family dinner."

I swear I see a tinge of pink bloom on her cheeks as she glances away. "Josie thought it'd be a good idea."

"She's a smart girl, that one," I say, quiet and dumbfounded.

"So, you'll come?"

I don't have to give it a second thought. "Of course, I'll come."

"Good," she says, then stands.

"You're not staying?"

Nora shakes her head, a fierce divot forming between her brows as she adjusts her long wool jacket. Autumn is waning, and soon we'll all need to don our winter caps and scarves.

"I have some things I need to handle tonight," she says, buttoning the jacket.

I narrow my eyes at her. "You're not going to tell me any more than that, are you?"

This elicits a real smirk from her. "No."

She steps into my space. Her eyes fall back down to my ruined bottom lip, full of restrained hunger; she reaches up and tugs at it with her thumb, the leather scraping against it sweetly.

"You need to earn the right to details again," she says.

Gooseflesh spreads down my arms.

"I like the way this looks," she says, thumbing my raw lip again. "But I want to be the one to do it next time."

"Okay." The word is hushed against her glove.

Then she leans down and places a chaste kiss on my cheek, as if she can't help but leave her mark on me.

"Goodnight, Imogen," she says.

"Goodnight," I murmur.

The burn of her kiss sears me, but I hold on to the pain. It's a comfort that I take to bed—a reassurance as I drift asleep that maybe we can rebuild what's broken between us.

12

NORA

I'm not surprised when I walk into my home office and see the Unseelie King sitting at my desk.

Silas pokes at the perfectly lined pens next to my typewriter, nudging them out of order with a ringed finger, as if he knows it'll make me twitch. His silver-white hair is cropped shorter on the sides than usual, freshly cut by the barber. A few strands hang loose and brush the edges of his brows.

I imagine he does it to unnerve me—sitting where I should be, invading my space, and making me stand in front of him like I'm a guest in my own home.

It's something I would do, though I think the repercussions of me sitting on Silas's throne would be very different.

The Unseelie King does what he pleases, which I respect. Even if my approval of *what* he does is up for debate.

"Your Majesty," I say in greeting.

He doesn't acknowledge my presence at first, but when he looks up, it's easy to understand why the humans often mistake us for demons; rimmed with dusty white lashes, Silas's near-black irises contrast the rest of his pale features.

It's unnerving to be the subject of his attention.

"Nora," he greets with a slow smile, leaning back in his—*my*—seat. His tone is rich and deep in the way that the cliffside sea is: deceptively beautiful and utterly dangerous. "I got your message."

I pull off my coat and hang it on the rack next to the door.

As I walk towards the twin leather chairs that sit opposite my desk, I jab my thumb over my shoulder.

"Want a drink?"

"I already helped myself to one." He salutes me with a glass of whiskey that emerges from a swirl of shadows and into his waiting hand. He inspects the glass. "I didn't think your taste ran so close to your predecessor's."

I recline in one chair, leather-clad fingers gripping the armrests.

"I don't entertain enough to warrant buying anything new, and now I'm used to it."

Silas snorts, eyes glinting as he takes in my poised position in the armchair—relaxed back and ankle crossed over one knee.

A standoff of sorts forms in the silence between us. One where he expects me to fold under his gaze, to trip over myself to win his favor, or fall in line as a good little soldier he views the Sins to be. Because that's what we are to him. Pride taught me as much; he hated how he was pressed beneath the Unseelie King's thumb, free to do whatever he pleased *except* for when Silas said otherwise.

It isn't freedom at all, only the illusion of it.

I've never operated under the assumption that we're anything but chess pieces for Silas to position across his checkered board. My only goal is to be freer than a pawn, a rook, or a bishop.

I want to be as free as a queen. And as powerful.

So, I wait.

I called him here, but that doesn't mean I'm not curious as to what he has to say. What questions he'll ask. How he'll handle the way I push him and if he'll call me out on it as he did at the Sins meeting.

What can I get away with in private?

He breaks the silence first.

"Taste for liquor aside, you are quite similar to the former Pride," he says. The words sound thoughtful on his lips. He's considered them carefully. "I had my suspicions when you came into the position, given the rumors on how you handled business under him. But it was never quite clear, the vision of who you were going to be as the new Pride. Like you were blurred around the edges, and I needed better focus."

Silas stands and rounds the desk. He perches on its edge, not quite in front of me, but slightly to my left. It gives me the impression that he wants to be close enough to intimidate, but not *too* close.

He crosses his oxford-clad feet.

The stance is threatening in the way that only casual power can be—all subtleties and grave mistakes before you realize you've stepped into a trap.

I cross my arms over my chest, my fingers wrapping around my biceps defensively. Suspicion roils in my gut.

"Is it clear now?" I ask. "Who my version of Pride is?"

Silas cocks his head. The move is akin to a fox, black eyes studying me to decide whether I'm predator or prey. I am careful to keep my face a blank mask of indifference, but there's something in the way he examines me that sends pinpricks up my neck.

"No, you've still got me baffled." He smiles, and for a brief moment, it reaches his eyes. He sips his drink with a playful shrug. "Which means either you're going to do great things for this Court or very bad things."

"Is that why you had Imogen report to you?"

"I struck a chord there with you two, huh? Can you blame me for wanting to get to know more about the first soul-stealer born in a millennium?"

"I didn't realize I was that special."

My sarcasm is thinly veiled. Pride had beaten the facts into me early on: the last soul-stealer had died years before he was born, and I had to claim that mantle seamlessly. Failure to do so risked more than just embarrassment.

"And it's nothing we can't move past," I add, but forgo the details. I don't owe him anything where Imogen is concerned.

That's between me and her.

He huffs, almost surprised.

"I underestimated your loyalty to her." Silas sets his glass down on my desk before clapping his hands together. "Now, tell me why you called."

"You said you wanted to be updated on my business venture."

"Yes..."

"So, I'm updating you," I say.

I've talked Josie through how I wanted to approach my plans for Jamison with Silas a hundred times over. Our suspicions of who is pulling the strings behind the curtain complicates things. How much can we risk Silas knowing?

"We're headed across the Veil tomorrow to handle a... misstep by our Seelie supplier."

"A *misstep*."

I hum. "And I thought it wise to fill you in on the context beforehand, so you're not surprised."

Silas regards me with caution before saying, "Go on."

"Do you know of the circumstances that led to Pride taking me in?" I say, the words forming carefully on my lips.

I remind myself that Silas has a bloodhound's instincts. It's as if he can smell the lies as they're spoken, and I'm not willing to divulge every detail of that night. I don't think I ever will be. Even Josie hasn't heard it from my lips directly. Instead, she peeked into my memories when we were seven, an instant bond forging between us through shared trauma.

"Orphaned young, but your talents were noticed, so you were brought under his wing. It's not an uncommon story, especially for your House," Silas says, lips tucking into an unamused frown. "I assume you'll connect the dots as to why this is relevant?"

"My biological parents weren't caught in the crossfire of some raid on House Pride. We were targeted. They came to our house human-side, and they killed my parents." The words are thick on my tongue. I don't tell him that they came for me, to take me to Avalon like I was some kind of prized mule. "Well, one specific Seelie killed my parents. And he got away."

It takes a second, but I can see the cogs turning in his head, the questions forming on the tongue that now pokes the side of his cheek.

"*There's always more,*" Silas chuckles as he quotes my words from the Sins meeting back to me. A single dimple forms in his left cheek with his smug smile. "Let me guess, whoever orchestrated the murder of that family is also the man who killed your parents?"

My lips part into a scowl. "You already knew?"

"It's naive to think I wouldn't assign someone else to watch over you after the other day," he says. "But don't worry. It wasn't one of Lust's lackeys."

I shake my head. "If you already knew about the attack, why didn't you say so?"

He snorts, pushing off from the desk and heading to the window. "You're cute when you're confused."

And then it clicks. My face falls into an accusing glare.

"You're testing me."

"I wanted to see if you'd be honest with me of your own accord."

"Did I pass?"

"Are you still breathing?"

When my eyes darken in their glare, he laughs—but I know by the glint in his obsidian eyes that the threat behind his humor is very much real.

"I'm glad you called me rather than doing something rash on your own. Wrath owes me fifty dollars—he thought you'd kill them right away. *I* figured you were smarter than that when it came to Faerie's other half."

Doesn't mean I won't still kill them.

I stand, stepping around the desk to reclaim my vacated chair. His hawkish eyes follow me as I sit. The leather is still warm and malleable from his body heat. I jerk open the bottom right drawer, pulling my revolver from its home along with its cleaning kit.

It's infuriating, the way this man is one step ahead of me.

I empty the cylinders; the bullets laced with iron clink like wind chimes as they hit the desk. Then, I set into my nightly routine, cleaning the barrel and cylinders with a bristle brush and cloth that I dip into solvent. My nose tickles as the stench of the cleaning solution fills the air. I should have the window open while I do this, but I need to still the sudden frantic beating of my heart and routine is the easiest way.

Today has been trying. The past two *weeks* have been trying.

Slowly, I regain my composure.

I move onto polishing, making the metal shine under my

fingertips. Silas's eyes narrow on the movement, but he doesn't comment on it. He waits. Minutes pass, and he is silent as I work.

"You speak as if you know me, yet you claimed confusion not ten minutes ago," I finally say.

"I gather data and make assumptions," he says. "I believe we share a lot of the same values, which makes me think you'd handle the situation similar to me. But sharing qualities does not equate to *knowing*."

"And what is it you think we share? The King and a Sin. I'd say they're quite different," I say. I keep my eyes on Silas as I reload the gun.

"Loyalty to our people. A sense of responsibility and the desire to protect. To shield them from the worser fates out there." Silas says this casually, as if he's ticking boxes on a list. "It's why you killed Pride."

My fingers pause on the barrel as it clicks back into place. I bite the inside of my cheek and set the gun down.

"I don't see how—"

"Let's be clear, he was a pain, and I was happy to see him go." He waves his hand in the air as if it's common knowledge. "You didn't kill Pride because you wanted power. You replaced him because you wanted to protect your family, and that's the only way you knew how."

My head starts to shake before he even ends his theory.

"You're wrong."

"Am I?" Genuine curiosity tints his voice, sensing the truth within my words.

"They're one and the same to me. Power is protection."

"And I'd say they're opposites. One is rooted in selfish greed and the other rooted in selfless love."

"Love, at its core, is selfish."

Silas hums. "Maybe. But you would have to be in love to know for sure."

He saunters as he closes the distance between us. When his knees are inches from mine, he plucks my gun from the desk. Inspecting it, he rolls the cylinder, clicks it back into place, and points the gun at me.

My breathing stops as I stare down the barrel.

Then he twirls it—so fast the metal is a silver blur in the air—and the handle is facing me. I'm quick to try to pull it from his hand, but he holds onto it with a viselike grip.

Silas leans forward, anchoring one hand on the desk chair as he peers down the sharp slope of his nose. He studies me as I've studied him; both of us carefully logging the tightness of our jaws and the way our lips twitch in the silent stare off.

His pupils dilate. His sigh is a breeze on my lashes.

"Send me the details for tomorrow," he says. "I look forward to seeing you in action."

13
NORA

A chill seeps through my coat, numbing my back. The cold metal of the passenger side door vibrates, and the smell of gas fills the air as the engine rumbles to life.

"See them yet?" Josie asks, popping her head out the window.

I told Silas to meet us at sundown, but he has yet to arrive. The sun is past the horizon now, the sky a mottled bruise of black and blue. The streetlamps have been lit, peppering the pavement with amber specks.

"Yeah, how much longer, Boss?" Hattie chimes from the bench in the truck bed. "I'm friggin' freezing back here."

"I told you to wear a thicker coat," Josie says.

"I thought you meant for the walk human-side! I didn't realize we were taking the friggin' truck."

"What's with you and the word *friggin'* all of a sudden? Are you too broke to pay into your ma's swear jar?" Josie teases.

I snicker as they dive into a heated argument, but my attention is drawn to where the shadows slither together, creating a void from which two men step from. I bang on the truck to stop Hattie and Josie's bickering.

"We've got company, ladies."

Silas is bundled in a three-piece black suit, topped with a black wool coat that hangs open, revealing a lining of blood-red silk. His nose and cheeks are already rosy from the cold, giving life to his pale skin.

"You're late," I say.

Silas shrugs as he saunters over. "Can a king *be* late?"

I ignore his question and point to Wrath. "Why is he here?"

"Wrath is my security."

"I have security."

"Not crown-appointed security," Wrath clarifies, mouth downturned in a perpetual scowl.

His eyes narrow as he scans over me and the truck, taking stock of our surroundings. Wrath's posture is stiff, uncomfortable even, but I know beneath it all, he's a snake poised to strike. House Wrath trains the Unseelie militia, and I know he graduated top of his class—how else would he have overthrown his father?

"Fine. Just don't get in our way."

I pop open the car door and get in.

"Where are we supposed to sit?" Wrath asks.

"In the back with Hattie. Hattie, say hi." She waves through her shivers. "We're picking up everyone else on the other side of the Veil." When they don't move, my eye twitches. "Get in. We don't have all night."

Wrath sputters, but Silas laughs, draping a familiar arm around the grump and shaking him.

"C'mon, Wrath, play along. I'm the one who wanted to come, after all."

"Alright, listen up."

I glance at each person gathered around the back of our truck. My core team—Josie, Hattie, Claude, and Wes—plus a few other lower-tiered soldiers from House Pride stand, waiting for my instructions.

Silas and Wrath, on the other hand, are like two children in a candy shop, eyes wide, and their attention half on me and half on the human city.

Most fae never cross through the Veil, including Royals and Sins alike. House Pride is the only House with daily dealings human-side.

It almost makes you forget that the air is different here. It's thicker, slower to fill your lungs. The sounds of this realm are subdued, the colors muted, like an old oil painting or a piano-plucked tune played with the dampener pressed.

I snap my fingers twice, pulling Wrath and Silas's eyes to mine; the former has the decency to look embarrassed.

"I want Claude and the others to hold the perimeter while Hattie runs reconnaissance. Once she's given the all clear, Josie and I will take lead. No one is to kill without explicit orders." I pause, waiting for questions. My people know to speak up if they need. "Wes, I want you to practice putting up a shadow-veil around the building. Let people in, but don't let 'em out. I don't want anyone fleeing before I'm done. Everyone savvy?"

"Yes, Boss," Wes says. The rest nod.

"Good," I say, then tilt my head towards the dilapidated building down the street. These Seelie exiles have taken over an abandoned boarding school and turned it into their head-quarters. "Hattie, you're up."

"Finally," she sighs, shucking off her coat. "Hold this will ya'?"

Hattie throws her coat at Wrath. He catches it with a bewildered expression, and—surprisingly—doesn't immediately toss it to the ground. He watches, befuddled, as Hattie pulls dual daggers from the sheaths at her side and disappears in a cloud of shadow.

Then, he turns to me, eyes accusing.

"You just said they aren't supposed to kill anyone," Wrath says.

Hattie appears behind him in a flash of black.

"Doesn't mean I can't have a little fun with 'em first," she cackles.

She disappears again, and I swear I can see a hint of pink flush Wrath's cheeks in the dark.

"Let's go," I say, rolling my eyes and leading the group towards the building.

It's easy, securing the property.

Once Hattie confirms their numbers, Wes releases his magic and a black shadow encases the perimeter of the old brick building. A few of the Seelie try to shift, buzzing by us as bees and birds, but they can't get past the wall of inky darkness. Jamison's men may carry big guns, but it's clear that they lack the magic to overpower us, the precision to shoot us down, and the organization to out-maneuver us.

Soon enough, we have the Seelie disarmed and corralled in what used to be the front lobby of the building. Water-stained brick surrounds us on three sides, and the doors, covered with shadow, stand at our backs. My nose twitches at the mildew stench lingering in the air as my men secure the last of the Seelie.

Silas and Wrath linger in the background. They watch our

operation with hawk-like stares, and every few minutes, they whisper in each other's ears.

They follow Josie and me to Jamison's office, the wooden floors creaking with each of our steps. Josie nods at the guard Hattie placed outside the door, and he relieves himself of his post. She pauses with her hand wrapped around the handle, glancing back at Wrath and Silas.

"How is this going to go?" Josie asks.

I might not be able to hear her thoughts like she can mine, but I know her well enough to parse the true meaning of her words.

Are we letting them see this? Her eyes ask for confirmation. *You trust them?*

"We'll handle it like normal," I say.

Then I open my mind to Josie so she can hear my thoughts. *They'll see what they want to see. I'm not worried right now.*

Josie nods.

I level with the two men. "Are you two staying for this part? I can't promise it won't get ugly."

"I wasn't lying when I said I wanted to see you in action," Silas says. He pokes at Wrath's cheek with one finger and Wrath bats it away. "And he's stuck with me. We'll be good. I promise."

Silas shoots me a brilliant white smile that has me sighing as I open the door.

"You've been warned," I mutter.

It's familiar, this part.

How many times had Josie and I entered a room exactly like this on Pride's orders? I find myself slipping deeper behind my protective mask, accessing the well of apathy in my chest.

"Pride," Jamison leers when we enter, twisting his sinewy frame our way.

His gaze tracks over me as he licks at his cracked and bleeding lip. A gift from Hattie, I'm sure.

"I wasn't expecting a visit," he continues, as if this is a simple, last-minute drop-in on our part.

Josie huffs, circling behind him. Jamison shifts in his seat, smoothing his hands over his thighs, but otherwise keeps his composure.

We'll fix that.

"Yes, well, there's been an incident that warranted me making a house call," I say, striding to the two wooden chairs that sit opposite his desk.

"Oh?" he says. "What can I help you with?"

Playing dumb? I project the thought to my Second.

Josie's nod is subtle, but I clock it.

Shucking off my jacket, I hang it over one chair. Next, I pick at my gloves. They are the softest black leather and tug easily from each of my fingers; I go finger by finger, pulling one hand free and then the other. They land with a soft *smack* on top of my coat.

Then, I turn the empty chair around and sit down. My legs are splayed wide as they straddle the seat, and my arms cross over the seatback.

I lean forward.

And I wait.

Most would get right to it—the questioning and the torture. But I've learned to savor the edge that silence brings to the air.

My tongue flicks out over my bottom lip. I can taste it on my skin, the anticipation, the question in his gaze as he scans over my soft smile and cold eyes—*what is she going to do?*

A bead of sweat trails down his face, that leering smile faltering. A single drop splats onto his desk.

"Do you remember what I told you a couple weeks back?" I ask.

"Um…"

"*Don't fuck around with me, Jamie,*" I recite. "*You won't enjoy the aftermath.*"

"I don't know what you're talking about."

"I think you do. But it doesn't matter what either of us thinks. It's about what you know. Up here." I tap my temple. "Did you order a hit on my people?"

Jamison's face goes pale as he sputters. "Of course not!"

I peer up at Josie, and she shakes her head. She steps forward and places a hand on the back of Jamison's neck.

His mental shields must be stronger than we anticipated. Josie rarely has to use physical contact to get inside someone's head; usually she can pick the mental locks from afar. But sometimes she needs a stronger connection to break through.

"I wouldn't lie. It'll only make her mad," Josie says, leaning over his ear.

Jamison's wide eyes flick to Silas and Wrath, who stand silently at the door.

I sigh, getting out of my chair. Josie anticipates my movements and pulls Jamison's chair backward so I can get in his face. The metal wheels squeal in protest.

"Nuh-uh, keep those peepers over here." My fingers press indents in his cheeks as I turn his face to meet his eye. "They're not going to help you."

It's almost too easy, our method.

Pride perfected it when we were young. Pair a rare empath with an even rarer soul-stealer and most people crack under the pressure—whether that pressure be from fear or pain.

When I was eighteen, I learned that my magic didn't have to kill instantly. I could draw it out if I wanted. Make them feel every second of their death. I've only gotten more precise since.

Now, I don't *have* to kill them once I start using my magic, though it's much harder.

My magic pricks at my fingertips, searing through the nerve-endings on Jamison's skin. It weaves excitedly between the muscles and bone in his jaw. I don't control fire, but I can match the sensation of his skin burning off, the layers of flesh breaking apart under my hand.

Death is a wicked kind of magic to wield.

"This is bullshit," he groans.

"This is business, babe." I smack his cheek, teasing him with a moment of relief when our connection breaks. But I'm back at it the second our skin reconnects. "Now tell us who killed my people."

"They sent two of the goons from outside," Josie scoffs.

"And was it you who ordered it?" I ask, though Jamison moans through his pain.

He doesn't have to answer. He just has to listen to me and let his mind think of the answers. Josie will pick up the rest.

"No," Josie says.

"Then *who*, Jamie?" I growl. "How did you know to place their bodies like that? Why did you leave the girl alive?"

The questions tumble from me without warning. Under my cold mask, my rage churns in my belly, my magic goading it from its place between my ribs. They swirl together, my fury and my magic, a volatile cocktail.

My magic wants me to stop wasting time and—

"Nora," Josie whispers.

Our eyes meet over Jamison's shoulder, and I instantly let go of his face, my magic pulling back with my hand. Red blotches of molted flesh score across his cheeks and arms. Blood seeps through his clothes, turning his white shirt crimson. He groans, head lolling to the side.

I went too far.

Shit, sorry, I think.

Josie shakes her head, a soundless response of *it's okay.*

She steps away from Jamison, back straightening.

"We've got our answers. We can go."

"And?" I ask.

Josie hesitates before speaking. "A Seelie man came to them months ago, after you first agreed on a deal. He had green eyes and white hair. And he offered them a pardon if they did as he asked."

His name, Josie. I need you to say it out loud. Silas will find out either way.

"Only a Virtue or the Queen can pardon a Seelie exile," Silas says, appearing at my side. "Which one was it?"

Josie works her jaw.

"Patience," she says.

It's not a surprise to me, but Silas goes eerily still at the name. His posture turns rigid, and his face contorts with icy rage. He quickly schools his features into indifference, but he wasn't fast enough to hide the reaction completely.

How very interesting. What is our king hiding?

"This one doesn't know more than that." Josie points to Jamison. "In his eyes, they were given instructions and completed a job by their superiors."

I clear my throat.

"Thank you, Josie. I have one more question and then we can be done."

I push past her and crouch near a groaning Jamison. I smack his face twice, shocking him out of his pain-laden nap. Already, his skin is stitching itself back together, his cheeks striped with fresh pink scars.

"Hey, bud. I need to know which of your goons are the healers," I say. "We still have a deal, and you owe us product."

"N-none of them. I'm the only one making the tonics," he says.

"Excellent. Makes this much easier knowing I'm not jeopardizing the supply chain."

I smile. It's a shark-toothed grin.

My fingers slide against the slick column of his throat, and I relish the feeling of my grip tightening over his pulse; I don't care if I get blood on my hands—they're already stained red beneath the skin.

"If Patience comes to you again asking for a favor, you will tell him no. If he comes offering penance or pardon, you will tell him no. You're not Seelie anymore. Despite your magic and despite your wings, you're *nothing* to him. You're now *my* asset." I pull back, staring deep into his vulnerable eyes. "And if you ever feel inclined to assume otherwise, let today be a reminder that I am *so* much worse than him."

I leave him, brushing past Josie and Silas and Wrath. Their footsteps follow me, the pitter-pattering drizzle after my storm.

"Which two of them?" I ask once we reach the lobby.

No one needs to ask what I'm talking about. Josie simply points to two Seelie—the thugs that met with Wes and me.

I lift my gun and shoot.

Two sharp *pops* echo through the room, punctuated by two dull *thumps* on the concrete floor.

A sliver of satisfaction rolls through me, but it doesn't quell that thirst for vengeance. It's a hollow kind of victory, knowing I've only taken one step towards the real subject of my revenge.

14

IMOGEN

When Nora said family dinner, I figured it was an intimate affair with Josie and a few select members of her inner circle. What I did not expect was an entire floor of her apartment building to have been converted into a sprawling dinner hall.

"Thank you for coming," Nora says.

She didn't say much as we waited for the elevator. And what she *has* said as the metal box slowly lifts us to the tenth floor has been far too formal. There's only an inch of space between us, but it feels like I'm wading through an entire ocean as I lean to the left, bumping my shoulder into hers.

"Of course," I say. An awkward beat passes, marked only by the groan of the elevator coming to a halt. "Is it bad that I'm nervous?"

"Don't be. Everyone loves you."

"They haven't even met me yet."

"The only one that matters is Josie, and she likes you more than me."

Nora shrugs as the doors slide open. She leads the way,

striding off the elevator with sure steps before spinning on her heel. Nora looks me up and down, her lips twisting like she doesn't know if she should smile or frown.

"Trust me," she says.

Little butterflies flutter in my belly.

"Okay."

I step out of the elevator and the doors close behind me.

My steps immediately falter.

Nearly two hundred fae fill the space, multiple generations mulling around two rows of farmhouse tables pushed together. Nora grabs my hand—she doesn't intertwine our fingers—and pulls me through the throngs of people. At each turn, they vie for her attention.

"Boss, glad you made it this week."

"Frank. How are the girls?"

"Eh, you know how it goes. Can't ever say no to nothing with 'em."

"Good luck with when they get old enough to realize they can take advantage," Nora snickers.

"Yeah, I know. Irene and I are in for a doozy."

"Hey, Pride, make sure to have the lasagna tonight. Nan made her special sauce," another man, younger than the last, speaks through a mouthful of bread.

"Thanks for the gouge, Chester."

"I got ya, Boss," he says with a wink.

"You're in for a treat tonight then," Nora whispers my way. "That woman may be pushing five hundred, but she still manages to whip up enough food for an army every Sunday."

Her hand tightens around mine, the leather of her gloves soft against my palm. She pulls me to three empty seats at the center of one table.

"Sit," she says.

She doesn't introduce me to anyone seated around us, but I

don't think she needs to; recognition dilates each one of their pupils when they glance at our linked hands.

Those to my left smile and say a quick hello, then turn back to their own conversations. Everyone keeps their distance now that we're seated, but I'm still overwhelmed with the warmth of it all—the joy and respect radiating from each fae in the room. They're genuinely happy to be here.

"Are Hattie or Claude coming tonight?" I ask.

"Not tonight," she says, running her gloved hands over her trousers. "Josie should be here soon though."

Nora pours me wine from one of the bottles scattered across the table. Then, she fiddles with her napkin, resetting it on her lap a few times until it's laying *just right* over her thighs.

"Is everyone always so..." I drawl, not finishing the sentence.

I can't quite find the right word, but my meaning must translate because she finishes the thought for me.

"Normal with me?" she says, one brow quirking up. "No. It's the one time that I ask for status to be checked at the door. For everyone."

"I'm surprised they go along with it."

"It wasn't a hard sell. I was one of them before I was Pride. Grew up alongside them." She grabs a piece of bread from one of the baskets on the table, dipping it into a plate of olive oil and herbs. "Sometimes it's nice to slip back into being Nora. Even if they don't call me that anymore."

My lips twitch with a sad smile. Being a Sin's daughter always kept me separate from everyone else, but becoming one? That solidified a divide between me and my peers that couldn't be crossed—that they didn't want to cross.

Except for Nora and Josie, of course.

"I can understand that."

Nora's hand lands on my knee and squeezes.

"I know," she says.

We were lucky to find each other when we did. Nora and me, Leo and Josie—the four of us are a rare bunch of perfectly matched friends.

Younglings burst from the kitchen doors to a chorus of cheers; the teens, clearly conscripted into being servers, roll their eyes, while their younger counterparts beam crooked smiles. Large, round serving dishes full of pasta and seafood are dropped in front of us along with basket upon basket of fresh bread. Inhaling deeply, the scent of melted butter and roasted garlic makes my stomach growl.

"They've got you running with the younglings again, Wes?" Nora asks, snapping me out of my food-induced haze. "When you're done, you should join us."

The fae stands between our chairs, ruffling his red-brown hair. He doesn't look much younger than us, though he's on the lankier side. He's got his shirt rolled to his elbows and is wearing a stained apron tied around his waist.

"I figured I'd help Nan out. Like I told you the other day, she's been complaining about her joints." He leans in close to whisper, "Thank you for letting me keep that tonic. I've started slipping a drop in her tea at night. I think it's working." His smile turns nervous as he leans back and pats at his belly. "Also, I can't say helping out in the kitchen is completely self-less. I get to be the taste-tester."

Nora pulls apart a loaf of still-steaming bread, dropping one piece onto my plate and popping another into her mouth.

"Well, the offer still stands." She smiles, and it's the softest tilt of her lips I've ever seen on her. "Or you can go tell your grandma thank you for me."

"Of course. Will do," he says, turning away.

"Oh, and Wes?" Nora calls.

"Yes?" He jolts to a stop, wide eyes turned our way.

"Good job the other night. I'm adding you to the guard rotation human-side."

His smile is tight-lipped, rosy cheeks getting redder at the praise. I'm still watching the door swing back and forth when Nora speaks again.

"That's Claude's younger brother. Half brother. Their dad was a cheating bastard, but their moms raised them right." Nora begins serving herself food off the many platters. "He made a stupid mistake recently, but he cares about his family. He's overall eager to prove himself. And he's powerful. I don't want him falling through the cracks."

I nod, understanding.

Rising in the ranks of your House can hold a level of danger, bringing you closer to the powerful players in the city, Royals and Sins alike. But there are a thousand worse ways a kid can get lost, tied up in the wrong kind of trouble.

"So, you've taken him on as a protégé?"

She hums, her head bobbing from side to side. "He has potential."

"You care for him."

Nora's knife pauses mid-slice in the pan of lasagna. Her brows knit together.

"Yeah, you could say that," she says. "He reminds me of me."

"I think it's sweet," I say.

She doesn't respond, her attention trained on her knife stabbing into the layers of pasta, cheese, and meat. Her tongue darts out to lick her bottom lip, then her eyes dart towards me with a devious glint. A flirty mask slides over her face.

"You're sweet," she says.

"Charming," I snort, but my cheeks still heat.

She's in a good mood tonight. Hope tickles my gut.

I serve myself, using the tongs to deposit a heaping portion of the garlic and oil pasta with clams onto my plate. Nora cuts me a slice of the infamous lasagna and another piece of bread, telling me to use it to sop up the extra sauce.

We fall into a peaceful silence as we pass the family style dishes back and forth, filling our plates—though it's less of a silence and more of a lull in conversation. The room itself is quite loud, a symphony of forks and knifes scraping against ceramic and little *oohs* and *aahs* over mouthfuls of pasta. They are the sounds of contentment, so different from the overly animated screams and giggles I'm used to at the Den.

It's a new kind of intimacy to bear witness to.

I like it.

A child runs past us, hair whipping wildly around her face and arms tightly clutched around an entire basket of bread. Right behind her are her siblings, screaming for her to slow down. My chest shakes with restrained laughter—how many times had Conor and I chased each other around our mother's apartment like that when we were little?

As I twirl spaghetti around my fork, a curiosity finds itself on my tongue.

"Do you want kids one day?" I blurt out.

The blood drains from Nora's cheeks.

"What?" Nora sputters, nearly choking on the pasta in her mouth.

She coughs, face turning red as she pats at her chest. When she finally clears her throat—and after guzzling down half a glass of water—she takes a large steadying breath.

"Um. No. I don't," she says. "Why do you ask?"

"I was curious," I say. I twirl the rest of the pasta onto my fork and pop it in my mouth, swallowing down the garlicky goodness alongside a dallop of disappointment. "And the way you were with Wes before."

"I'd be a terrible parent," she says quickly, stabbing a piece of shrimp onto her fork. She waves it at me accusingly. "I think the food is making you see things."

"Oh? Is special sauce code for something else?" I tease.

"Wes's nan is definitely spiking it with *something*," Nora mutters, popping the shrimp into her mouth.

"If garlic and butter are drugs, sure." I take a sip of my wine, the burst of fruity flavor complimenting my meal. "Though I have to say, I'm offended you haven't brought me to one of these yet. I've been missing out on stellar home-cooked meals all these years?"

Nora dabs her mouth with a napkin before setting it atop her finished plate.

"Like I said before, it was—" she's interrupted by a body falling into the empty seat at my side.

"Hey, Mo," Josie says, an exhausted smile on her face. She looks all kinds of rumpled, shirt wrinkled and flyaway hairs framing her face. She licks her lips as she deftly fills her plate with the scraps left from the meal. Her brown eyes, ever watchful, spy me from her periphery. "Glad to see Nora finally took my advice. You two hash it out? You good now?"

"Um..." My mouth pops open and my eyes cut to Nora. "I think so?"

She takes a second to answer, but I note the moment she commits to my forgiveness fully: her shoulders pull back, her eyes glint, and her red lips pull into her signature smirk.

"We're good."

The crushing weight on my heart lifts.

"Good," I say softly.

"So, our standing Friday nights at the Den can resume? Leo and I were worried you two wouldn't make up, and then we'd have to go to Envy's clubs." Josie fake gags. "As if I want to be Leo's wingwoman at a dance club."

"The Den has dancing," I argue.

"Not the same kind of dancing."

"I thought Leo was *your* wingman," Nora says. "He better be doing the job right, since he stole it from me."

"Does he help with my anxiety until I'm two drinks in? Yes. But after that, I'm good. I'm not eighteen anymore, Nor." She shoots us both a look that says we're both being idiots. She taps her temple. "He just likes that I can tell if they're into him."

"But he's an empath," I say. "Can't he tell for himself?"

"He says it's unethical for him to use his magic like that."

"Leo's unfairly attractive, and women throw themselves at him completely sober. I say you ditch him, and I take my rightful place back at your side," Nora says, utterly serious.

"Excuse me," I mock outrage, hand on my chest.

Nora throws up her hands. "It's simply a fact that he could pull anyone attracted to men."

"We do have an above-average looking friend group," Josie says through a mouthful of bread.

A beat passes between the three of us before we burst into laughter.

It's easy for us to fall back into our friendship.

"Actually, speaking of Friday night. We have Gluttony's opening this week," Nora says, pointing at Josie with her fork.

"Oh yeah, I almost forgot with everything else going on." Josie throws her napkin onto the table and leans back in her chair. Josie's smile lights up her face, round cheeks prominent and squishable with two little dimples. Where Nora is all sharp angles, Josie is rounded. "We have a whole table reserved. You should come, Mo."

"Sure," I say. "I didn't realize Gluttony and you were close?"

"Not so much that we're close as we're experimenting on some new business deals." Nora's nose scrunches. She leans her forearms on the table, cocking her head and shooting Josie a conspirator's glance. "Josie over here took lead on the project, sourcing goods for Gluttony's chefs."

"It's a whole human-fae fusion concept," Josie says, red tinting her cheeks. "Utilizing rare human ingredients and pairing them with Faerie staples."

"Why didn't you say something sooner?" I reach over and squeeze Josie's knee. "That's amazing."

"Thanks, I'm quite proud of it."

"I never realized you were so creative. You've been holding out on me. You should help out with our expansion."

The kitchen doors fling open again, revealing younglings carrying bottles of dessert liquors, coffee, and platters over-flowing with cookies and pastries.

"Only if you want me to," Josie says.

"Why wouldn't I want you to?"

She shakes her head. "I don't know."

"Then it's settled," I say, lifting my glass. "To the first of hopefully many collaborations between our Houses."

Our glasses clink together, ringing out little chimes as Wes drops a plate of dessert in front of us that makes me salivate. Flaky golden pastries shaped like clam shells sit at the center and cookies line the edge. Some are sprinkled with pine nuts, some have thumbprint dips filled with jam, and others are dipped in chocolate. But all of them smell like butter and sugar and all that is good in the realm.

Nora taps my shoulder, and I'm once again jolted from a food-induced stupor. One of her black brows is cocked in amusement.

"What?" I ask.

"I asked if you will join me upstairs for dessert?"

I eye the platters of pastries, then her. I have to blink a few times before it registers that I'm *not* imagining the way her eyes darken with hunger.

"Only if I get a pastry after dessert," I tentatively tease.

"I already asked that someone bring some up for us," she says, a dangerous lilt to her words. "Though I'm not opposed to partaking in both kinds of sweets."

Josie snorts as both Nora and I shove our chairs back, the legs scraping against the floor and drawing the wide-eyed attention of those around us. But Nora doesn't pay any mind, simply grabbing my hand and tugging me from my seat.

And like so many times before, I find myself being pulled upstairs by Nora—but this time we're not drunk, not stumbling, and the voice at the back of my head is blissfully silent.

15
NORA

I'm tired of denying myself.

The fire crackles low, casting an ethereal yellow-orange glow across the wood-slated walls as I push her through the door.

Once it's shut, I crowd her against it, pulling her mouth to mine. It's been too long since I've tasted her—two, three weeks maybe? The longest time our bodies have been apart in years. Our lips dance together, tracing familiar steps. Imogen hums into my mouth, opening so sweetly for me.

I pull back, but only enough to let us catch our breaths. Her amber eyes glitter, flittering around the space and taking in every detail. She gasps, her gaze stalling over my shoulder.

"Gods, Nora," she says, mouth agape. Her tongue darts out, swiping over her bottom lip. "A wall of swords?"

She ducks under the cage of my arms, scurrying over to the wall behind my desk, which does, in fact, have a number of swords and daggers mounted on it. They shine in the soft light, silver and steel glinting with our reflections. Imogen runs a finger over the edge of one blade, shivering at the sharp and cold metal.

I follow, stopping behind her. I snake my arms around her waist, tugging her back to my front; warmth surrounds me, and it's not from the fire that crackles under the mantel.

"Be careful," I whisper in her ear. "I don't feel like playing nurse and giving you stitches tonight."

"You couldn't kiss it better?"

My lips nuzzle into her neck, placing kisses on her pulse. "Not my specialty, I'm afraid. And I've been told I have terrible bedside manners."

Imogen snorts, turning in my embrace. Her fingers dig into the small of my back, keeping me just as close as I hold her. She leans in for a kiss, but I keep our lips from touching with one hand anchored at the back of her neck, fingers curled in her hair.

"I need to tell you something," I say.

"Okay..."

I take a steadying breath, inflating my chest with the courage to be vulnerable—to be honest. I heard Imogen out, I understand her reasons, and I believe her when she says she won't betray us again. And that means the only way to move forward —to bridge the gap between us—is to *take* a step forward.

I hate it when Josie is right.

"You remember how my parents died, yeah?"

She's heard the gist of it before, not all the details.

Imogen's blond brows knit together as she nods, attention firmly locked on me.

"The man who killed them is back. And he's targeting House Pride."

Her face goes slack; she's a perceptive woman, hearing the unsaid details between the lines.

"Josie had mentioned something happened," she says. "Are you okay?"

"A family was butchered, but they spared the child. A daughter." I clear my throat, not able to look Imogen in the eye. Instead, I'm met with my own reflection, split in half by the blade behind her. "That part was a clear message to me. So, we struck back. Silas knows, and it has since become a more complicated matter."

"Oh, Nora. I'm so sorry."

Her hands run over my neck and shoulders, they graze over my cheeks, thumbs swiping at nonexistent tears. She's trying to comfort me, but she doesn't realize I'm not sad about it.

I'm furious.

Even more so after we got what we needed from Jamison, and Silas explicitly forbade us from taking any next steps in retaliation.

"I know that things haven't been... easy between us lately. But even if you doubt me as a lover, I'll always be your friend. If you need help, all you need to do is ask."

Imogen runs her fingers through my hair, nimbly finding the point where my neck meets my skull and rubbing with her thumb.

I sigh, my forehead falling to her shoulder.

Fuck, why is this so hard?

"It's difficult," I say, running my nose up her neck, drinking in her rose scent. "To let you in."

She must know there's more coming, because she stays quiet and continues to rub my neck. A sign of reassurance— that she hears me.

I place another kiss on her pulse, lips lingering on the soft skin there. I need to be close to her heartbeat; the steady *thumps* are a calming rhythm.

"You scare me."

"Why?" she asks.

"Because of how viscerally I reacted the other day."

I pull back, not enough to let her go, but enough that she can press her forehead to mine. I close my eyes, focusing on the way her nose brushes up against mine.

"If I let you in, it means I can lose you," I admit.

It means I'm weak.

Her hands bracket both of my cheeks.

"Have you not already let me in?"

"Not completely."

Her sigh brushes over my lips, a soft and warm spring breeze.

"Do you want to be with me?" she asks.

My brows furrow. "What kind of question is that?"

"An important one, to me."

Her lashes flutter, her gaze settling on my chest, as if staring right through to my heart.

"Yes," I say.

I think that's what this yearning in my gut means.

"Then don't hold back," she says. Her smile is soft, a mere wisp of a cloud spread across the bright sun.

I huff. "That simple?"

She leans forward, giving me a quick peck on the tip of my nose.

"That simple."

My tongue swipes over my lips, licking up the remnants of her past kisses. I search her face like it's a map that holds the answers to the universe. In turn, her eyes darken to the deepest amber.

"I waited a long time to hear that from you, you know," she adds.

"I don't know if I can give you more than this—or what we had before. But I find myself wanting to try," I say.

Her lips purse, as if pondering how my words taste. Then she nods.

"As long as you're trying, I'll have patience," she says. "I really like you, Nora."

I smirk. "Yeah?"

I push on her waist, walking us backwards, until Imogen is pressed against the mounted swords on the wall. She sucks in a short gasp. Her hands fall to my waist, gripping at my blouse when I lean into her neck again, nipping at it, unable to help myself. She has such a pretty neck, a blank piece of paper that I want to ruin with black and blue ink, the pen my teeth and tongue.

"I'm starting to wonder if you're a vampire, not fae," Imogen laughs.

"Funny," I say, admiring the mark that now blooms on her skin where my teeth nibbled. I pull away, fisting her hair. Her head tilts back. "You told me that if I need help, all I need to do is ask. Take this as me asking."

I'm not the type to spill my heart; I could go blue forcing every word past the lump in my throat. Or I could open up to her like *this*.

Bodies have a language of their own.

"Stay," I whisper the word into the shell of her ear.

"What?"

"Stay with me tonight. Here."

Imogen's breath hitches in her throat and then she's crashing her lips to mine with a fury.

I've tasted nothing sweeter.

I release her hair in favor of hiking up her dress. It's liquid silk, the way the fabric sluices over the curves at her hips. My fingers find Imogen's damp heat beneath her underwear, and I circle her with a feathered touch. She grinds into my palm, desperate for more contact.

I take my pleasure from Imogen's moans, the vibration of her body pressed against mine runs straight to my core. My fingers leave her clit and slide through her slick; she writhes when I dip one finger inside of her.

Capturing her whine with my lips, I pump my finger slowly. I continue until her pussy clutches my finger, but I don't push her over the edge. She lets out a frustrated growl.

It's clear she doesn't want to be edged tonight.

I lift my head and our noses brush as I stare into her half-lidded eyes.

A shiver racks her body when I pull my finger from her core and bring it to my mouth. I lied before. There is nothing sweeter than *this*, the taste of her coating my tongue.

My lips curve into a smug smile.

"Be a good girl, and get on the desk," I say, stepping back.

She lets loose a breathy laugh.

"You got it, *Boss*," she teases.

She doesn't move right away. Instead, she reaches for the zipper at her waist. Her dress is quick to pool at her feet, a puddle of scarlet silk, leaving her bare except for the lace that wraps around her hips and between her thighs.

Something possessive and dark rouses in my gut.

"Get on the desk," I repeat, letting it hang as a threat between us.

Imogen smirks before slowly pulling off her underwear. She drops it into the pile of fabric at her feet and brushes past me to hop onto the desk. She said I was a tease, but she's the embodiment of torment, perching there with her legs spread and offering me a perfect view of her needy cunt.

"Coming?" she lilts.

I am across the room in seconds.

My fingers find purchase on her ample hips while my head dips down, my tongue darting out and circling one pebbled nipple. Imogen's hands immediately grip my hair. It stings, the way she uses it as leverage to press my mouth tighter to her chest, silently begging for more.

I bite down on her breast before sucking and flicking my tongue, giving her exactly what she wants. And when she's writhing again, hips grinding on air and searching for friction, I let my fingers return to her core, plunging two into her.

"Fuck," Imogen curses.

I laugh into her chest, peppering kisses down from her breasts to her navel.

I drop into my desk chair, rolling it close so I can lean forward and brush my tongue over her clit. She flutters around my fingers at the stimulation—so I apply more pressure by sucking on it. *Hard.*

Her fingernails dig into my scalp, and her whimpers fill the office, spurring me on. I curl my fingers, pulsing them against the spot that makes her fall apart.

Imogen comes beautifully around my fingers; she rides my mouth through her orgasm, muscles taught and throbbing as they grip me.

And when the final aftershocks recede, her entire body melts. Her back arches, and she purrs a satisfied hum.

I pull back, licking my lips clean while drinking in the sight of her.

Imogen's a rumpled mess compared to the composed beauty the rest of the world usually sees. I'm the lucky one, I realize, that gets to see her like this: laid out on my desk, leaning back on her hands. I get to see her with puffy lips and a heaving chest as her lungs desperately clutch to oxygen. *I* get to see her bask in the aftershocks of the orgasm *I* gave her.

In this way, she is utterly *mine*.

Her long lashes flutter against her flushed cheeks as she gazes at me with primal satisfaction.

I reach up and pluck at one of her still hard nipples. A shocked yelp turns into an exasperated laugh as she grabs my hand and pulls it away from her chest. Intertwining her fingers with mine, she lifts our joined hands to her mouth, kissing my knuckles.

Once. Twice. Three times.

I hum.

"I shouldn't have done that," I murmur, and her body freezes. I smirk, letting my eyes capture every detail of the woman before me. "I'm never going to be able to look at my desk without thinking of your sweet cunt now."

The relief is instant—the drop of her shoulders and huff of laughter filling the room. She bats my hands away.

"You can't say shit like that, Nor," she sighs. "*Fuck*. You scared me."

I snort, unable to hold my own laughter back. We lapse into silence, and I rest my head on my forearm that drapes over her leg. I mindlessly trace patterns on her milky thigh.

I glance up at Imogen. With her hair a golden halo and skin flushed pink, she's the picture of salvation.

Imogen shivers.

"I want to stay," she says, running a gentle hand through my hair.

I close my eyes and sigh.

"Good. Because you know I have a sweet tooth, and I'm not nearly done with dessert."

"And what about *my* dessert?" she teases, knocking her knees into me playfully.

I huff, forehead dropping to her soft thigh before biting it. She squeaks as if she's been tickled, jumping from the desk right into my lap. Both of us laugh as she pulls my lips to hers.

It's a languid kiss, our tongues slow dancing to our calmed heartbeats. And when our lips part and Imogen kisses her way to my ear, she sets my nerves alight.

"But seriously, I want one of those cookies."

16

IMOGEN

When morning breaks my slumber, the sun peeks through the slatted wooden shades, illuminating the still and sleeping Nora. Her long lashes dust over alabaster cheeks, and her bare skin glows under the streaks of sunlight, her ribs expanding with each easy breath she takes.

It's progress, seeing her like this.

My body hums with newfound peace. All the weight I've been carrying for the past year has disappeared—and while I know there's a long road ahead of us, we both took a huge step last night.

The fact that she didn't kick me out as dawn broke is proof enough.

I bite my lip, fighting the smile that wants to spread across my cheeks.

Closing my eyes, I try to lull myself back to sleep, snuggling under the covers and into the warmth of her embrace. But minutes pass and I only get more and more aware of my surroundings. Rest runs away from me, swift and elusive.

I slip from the bed, making sure to tuck the quilt over Nora;

my fingers graze over the raised twin scars running down her back. They bracket her spine, reaching from between her shoulders to just above her waist.

I've never asked about them, but I know, like the rest of Faerie, how they got there.

It's well known that House Pride has a history of shearing its member's wings as a sign of loyalty. To cast away your own ego and choose to serve the *family*. The former Pride had shrunk the practice to only his inner circle, but that didn't make it any less barbaric.

My spine tingles as if my own wings are shivering at the thought.

Tea. I am in urgent need of some tea.

I steal a robe hanging from the back of Nora's wardrobe and wrap the soft black fabric tightly around me. The last thing I need is for one of House Pride's staff to see me prancing around naked.

Nora's living space is situated one level above her office, with one half of the penthouse floor belonging to her and the other to Josie. In a series of interconnected rooms, her bedroom leads into a small dressing area with a wardrobe, dresser, and mirror.

I patter past the bathroom, with its black tiled floors and large clawfoot tub, in which I immediately picture Nora soaking, bubbles clinging to—

Tea, I remind myself. That's what I'm searching for. Not fantasies of kissing Nora in a bubble bath.

I hadn't caught all the details of the apartment last night, having been pulled straight to the bedroom by the ravenous woman before I could get a good look. But entering the main living area, I'm struck by how distinctly *Nora* it is.

Dark and inviting, but not overly personal, the walnut

shelves, green wallpaper, and brass sconces play perfectly with the well-worn couches and musty smell of leather-bound books. Windows line the far wall, overlooking a small bar cart full of crystal decanters. Emerald-green velvet couches and armchairs sit before the fireplace, same as in her office. Below the intricately carved mantel, a fire crackles low, mere glowing embers.

But my gaze catches on what's mounted above the mantel—my arms wrap around my waist, and my heart drops into my stomach.

Wings.

A pair of *Seelie* wings.

They are spread wide, a four-pronged pair that shimmers a near-translucent green in the morning light. The upper wings are edged in a thick line of black that curves and thins as it crests the lower edge of the wings. At their center, the darkest black, like an ink spill, spreads. Matching eyespots sit at the center of each lower wing, and trailing at the bottom, the wings taper and curl in on themselves like ribbon.

I'd seen depictions of them in books, renditions in childhood faerie-tales, but never in person. Though, this one is different from the old picture books. They were always lighter, brighter, thrumming with life.

These... aren't.

It's odd. I may be an empath, but the emotion swirling in my gut evades me. It's not quite awe, and it's not quite sadness.

"Snooping for secrets?"

I jolt, spinning around to find a smirking Nora leaning against the room's archway entrance. She's donned her own robe, the same crow-black shade as her hair, though it does little to cover her long legs.

"No," I say defensively.

A lightning bolt of nerves strikes me as I worry that it *does* appear that I'm snooping.

Her smile only grows as she launches off the molding, prowling toward me predatorily. She catches me, arms wrapping around my waist, and gooseflesh spreads over my skin.

"No?" she asks.

"I was searching for a kettle to make some tea," I squeak. All my muscles are tight and taut, stiff in her arms.

"Relax," she says, and my body responds in kind. "I was just surprised to wake with half my bed empty. You're the one who is always begging *me* to stay for cuddles."

"Oh."

Her nose runs up the side of my neck, stopping under my ear where she plants a kiss.

"Good morning," she adds, laughter coloring her words. "Your heart is racing. I didn't mean to startle you."

I huff, letting myself melt into her embrace.

"I was more surprised by the decor."

Nora hums, her arms tightening around me a fraction. Her face is still sleep-rumpled, indents crisscrossing on her cheek from her pillowcase.

I spin in her embrace, my back pressed to her front, and stare up at the pair of wings.

"What are they?"

"Wings." I feel her shrug at my back.

"I can see *that*. I meant are they—"

"Real?"

I hum, leaning my head back on her shoulder. Without my heels, she's able to peer down at me. Her jewel-toned eyes search my face, for what, I don't know, but a sadness darkens them all the same.

"They're the wings of a Seelie I killed for Pride," she says.

"Why would you keep them?" I ask.

Our words have become quiet, hushed. Suddenly, our voices ring too loud in the room.

Nora's throat bobs. She brushes a stray piece of hair behind my ear; the tender touch pulls a flush to the apples of my cheeks.

"They're a reminder of what's at stake if I fail," she says.

"Fail at what?" I ask.

Her eyes narrow, flicking back to the wings as if a memory is replaying behind those gemlike irises.

"Anything. Everything."

A beat passes between us.

"Did you do it yourself?" I ask.

Nora clears her throat. She shifts, though she keeps me in her embrace. I can tell she's having trouble getting the words out, so I wait for her.

Slowly, with intention, they fall from her lips.

"Pride cut those. But others..." she trails off. "He had me take over clippings once I turned eighteen."

"He had you doing that all through college?"

"He thought it important for me to build respect within the House."

Respect. I hold back a scoff at the word.

There is a difference between respect turned from fear and respect that is earned.

Pride clearly had a tendency to lead with the former.

"Including Josie's?"

Nora sighs. Her lashes flutter with memories I can't see as she presses her forehead to mine.

"No. I didn't shear Josie's wings. But I was there, holding her hand. And she did the same for me."

For the first time in ten years, I sense a small tendril of emotion slip past her mental shields—a deep-rooted grief sinks my gut.

As quickly as my magic picks the feeling up, it's gone; the emotional void around Nora swallows it whole.

A pounding on the door has me jumping out of Nora's embrace. Even Nora flinches, muttering a curse. Her brows pinch together as she opens the door, revealing an equally sleep-rumpled Josie.

"What's wrong?" Nora asks, back immediately straightening with concern.

"Hattie's downstairs, freaking out…" Josie's eyes dart to me and quickly back to Nora, pink rushing to her cheeks. "I think it best for you to hear it from her yourself, but shit's gone down human-side. Again."

<h1 style="text-align:center">17</h1>
NORA

I would be lying if I said it didn't hurt when I turn the corner and see the burned carcass of our warehouse. All our hard work over the past year reduced to smoking rubble.

The large paned glass windows are blown out from the fire and are now shimmering, deadly confetti scattered on the street. Once a brilliant red brick, the face of the building is scarred with black where the flames licked, like necrosis spreading over flesh.

It'll need to be gutted, but the building seems to be salvageable based on the whispers of the authorities gathered around.

So, there's that, at least.

I watch the response team scour the rubble from the sidelines. The rope they put to block pedestrians hits my hip every few seconds in the breeze, which carries with it the bitter scent of burned metal and charred wood.

The human authorities are well paid to keep their eyes off our business, but this will be harder to sweep under the rug than a few dead bodies. Still, my people have jumped into action as they were trained to.

"They're not as shaken as I thought they'd be, given the circumstances," Imogen murmurs, scanning over the few members of House Pride who are chatting with Josie and the police.

When we heard the news, she'd demanded she come with us, wanting to help in what ways she could. I didn't have the nerve to say no.

"Especially Hattie."

"Hattie's a survivor. She doesn't fear death in the same way others do," I say.

My boot taps against the pavement, my impatience physically overwhelming me. I had told Josie I'd let the professionals assess the damage first, but it's been a half hour. I've given them enough time.

I lift the rope barrier and step into the rubble.

Hattie had acted swiftly when the flames broke out during the shift change, using her magic to transport as many as she could from the building. She was hacking up half a lung and covered in soot by the time she made it to our apartment in Anwynn, but she'd been successful in getting everyone to safety.

She'd had a furious glint in her eyes as she described what happened to us, one that I'm sure I've been wearing since the words hit my ears.

Was I grateful no one was hurt? Yes. Of course. It could have been a terrible tragedy otherwise.

But was I also pissed that we lost hundreds of thousands of dollars' worth of product? Also, yes.

"Ma'am, you can't go in there." A human fireman steps in my way. "It's not safe."

"This is my building. I'll do what I like," I say with authority.

"I'm sorry, but rules are rules," he says, puffing out his chest. His thick mustache hides his mouth, but I can tell he's frowning. "Let the men do their work."

I smile, sweet and saccharine. "Step aside."

"What she means is, *please*, step aside." Imogen appears at my side, gripping my arm. I'm hit with the force of her magic, and it nearly makes me stagger. Pride had me trained against compulsion since I was young, but there's no denying she's as powerful as they come. "*We want to take a quick peek. We won't be long.*"

Of course. Not long at all.

I have to focus to shake away the yielding thoughts that her magic spurs. Meanwhile, the fireman's eyes glaze over and he's nodding, waving us forward with apologies. Then Imogen's pulling me along, shooting a cheeky grin over her shoulder.

"See? Told you I could help," she says.

I shake my head. "I had it handled."

"Sure."

I tug Imogen to a stop. "How many times have you been on this side of the Veil?"

Her expression falters, confusion twitching across her features. "Not many."

I cock a brow. She huffs.

"Okay, only once with my mother. And I didn't even get out of the car."

"I have been here over a thousand times. They may be humans, Imogen, but this realm isn't a playground. Don't forget that."

She nods, and I let go of her hand as we head into the disfigured building.

I forgo the warped metal door, opting to climb through the blown-out window to its left. Glass and charred debris crunch under my boots as I help Imogen over the edge.

It's quiet inside, like the soul of the building has left its body. The only sounds are the small crackles of rubble as it cools, the final fissures of the blaze taking shape. I expect rage to bubble up from my gut, but it doesn't. I'm the same as the warehouse: a shell with a gaping emptiness inside.

What was once red-toned brick is now black. All the vibrancy that lived here is charred and burned and *ruined*.

A third pair of footsteps join ours.

"It's me," Josie calls from behind us. She comes to a stop at our side, hands on her hips and murmuring a curse.

Then I hear a groan.

My head whips from side to side, trying to locate the sound. But there's nothing but burned rubble.

"Did you two hear that?" I say.

"What?" Imogen asks.

I hear it again, low and aching.

"That," I say, stepping deeper into the building. "There's someone still here."

"Not possible. Hattie got everyone out that was on shift," Josie says, but panic is laced through her tone.

The moans are louder now, and Imogen gasps, confirming I'm not alone in hearing them. The three of us curse, following the sound.

"Help me," the person cries. "Please."

The air is thicker, still smoky and warm, the deeper into the building we go, but we push through. I spin in place, the moans right next to me, but there's no one in sight.

And then I see it. The air wavering, a slight shimmer within the dust and smoke that curl around us. The Seelie illusion breaks, and where a pile of burned boxes once stood, a man lies, red and bloodied burns marring half of his body. Beyond the burns, recognition flares—

"Jamison?" I say, dropping to his side while Josie protectively shoves Imogen behind her.

"Shit! Is he okay?" Imogen squeaks.

My magic perks to life at the sight of him, tickling my fingertips under my gloves.

"This is because of you," he groans through barely parted lips.

Now that I'm closer, I can see his skin making an attempt to stitch itself back together. But it's far too slow to quell the bleeding. Even the strongest healer would need help with wounds this extensive.

"I told him no," Jamison moans. "He didn't like that."

I glare into Jamison's one good eye; I recognize the fear shining there.

This was a challenge.

A lump forms in my throat as I scan the rest of the room, acutely aware of our surroundings. My gun is out of its holster before I know it.

"He said you don't get it both ways. You can't keep prete—"

"Nora, what are you—"

Imogen's yelp echoes in the space alongside the single shot to Jamison's head. His body slumps against the rubble, blessedly still.

"Why did you do that?" Imogen screeches.

"He was going to die anyway. Think of it as a mercy." My nose twitches, the smoky air starting to tickle my sinuses. "We should leave. We're probably being watched."

"What do you mean, *being watched?*" Imogen snaps, eyes wide. "You just killed someone."

I sigh. Imogen knows what I've done—had to do—but it's

much easier to hear about it and rationalize my actions than to see them in person. While Imogen's not squeaky-clean, her sins are far different from mine. House Lust may be full of spies—they may bribe or blackmail Royals—but they don't deal with the true, brutal nature of our kind.

Lust doesn't deal in death. But House Pride and House Wrath do. So does the Unseelie King.

Maybe I should have had Josie take her away before I pulled the gun out.

"He was Seelie," I say, even and steady. "The man I told you about before?" Imogen nods, jaw tight. "He was with him. So, trust in my judgment that he *needed* to die."

Though Josie stays quiet during our exchange, her lips twist, betraying her judgmental thoughts—she knows I didn't *have* to kill him.

I just didn't want Imogen to hear what he had to say.

"Everything is fine, but we do need to leave, okay?" I say.

"Yeah," Imogen says, straightening her spine. "I've never seen someone die before."

"First time for everything, yeah?" I whisper, but the joke doesn't land. I press a kiss to her cheek and turn to Josie. "Get her and the others home. I need to pay Silas a visit."

18

NORA

Silas's office is eerily clean.

Not a speck of dust lines the bookshelves, and each piece of decor is perfectly curated to fit the moody aesthetic; the black walls and dark wood furniture certainly help with that too.

I sink into his desk chair, fingers drumming mindlessly against the arm. The taps are dull, the leather of my gloves muting the sound.

I'm honestly surprised his staff let me in here alone, but based on the lack of papers—or even a pen—this space isn't often used.

The door finally opens, and Silas enters.

His steps falter when he notices where I'm sitting. A huff of laughter escapes him as the door creaks shut.

"Pride. Nice of you to stop by," Silas says. He leans back against the door, shoving his hands in his suit pockets. He's forgone the suit jacket today, only wearing a fitted gray vest over a striped dress shirt and slacks. "Though I do recall already scheduling a follow-up to discuss what happened the other night…"

His eyes rake over me, narrowing when they land on my serious expression.

"What happened?" he asks.

"Patience got pissed we played with his toys. Then he torched my warehouse, and my supplier got caught in the crossfire." I smile, but it isn't sweet. It's that of a wolf. "So, I figured it prudent to inform you."

Silas's lips part on an *o*.

"That's an unfortunate turn of events. And so soon," he says, slowly.

"Yes. Unfortunate. That's a good way to describe it."

"Did anyone—"

"Die?" I finish for him, brows hopping to my hairline. "Not from our side, luckily. Your Royal buddies will be out of their favorite imported champagne for a while, though."

Silas stalks across the room, coming to a stop in front of his desk; he leans forward, both hands spreading across the ebony wood.

A moment of silence passes between us.

I'm the one who breaks it.

"I told you what I wanted. And now you fully understand the stakes. So, the question is, are you going to give it to me?"

"What about what I want?"

"What *do* you want, Silas?" I lean farther back in the chair, crossing my legs. "It's not clear to me. Don't you want a little taste of revenge?"

His white brows knit. "Why would you think that?"

"Because Patience killed your parents too."

Silas's head tilts, a strand of white hair falling to the side. "And how do you know that?"

He didn't deny it.

"I didn't, actually, until now. Just had a hunch based on how you reacted to his name the other day."

Silas laughs; it's full-bodied and fills the barren room. He rounds the desk, squeezing between me and the wood. I push the chair back as far as it can go, but there's little room with the bookcase at my back.

He hops onto the desk, long legs dangling in front of me. We're far too close for my liking, but I don't back down. He's trying to intimidate me, and it's a challenge I'll meet head on.

"You're quite perceptive," he says.

"It was a skill learned out of necessity."

He tilts his head, studying me like I'm some kind of anomaly. "Tell me, have you ever experimented with your magic?"

I shake my head. "What does that have to do with anything?"

"It's unique. Rare. Unstudied." The words sound savory on his tongue. "Little is known about soul-stealers. The other day, you tortured that man without killing him. How?"

The question takes me off guard. "I ask."

"You ask?"

"My magic. It enjoys killing, but I don't always want it to, or need it to. So, sometimes I ask it to go slow. It works so long as the wounds aren't too deep when I pull back."

It's second nature by now, though, with how much Pride made me practice treading the line between life and death.

"How curious." Silas's black eyes sparkle. "And you've never tried to delay death? To kill *after* you've touched someone?"

This time, it's my turn for my brows to knit. "It doesn't work like that."

"But have you ever tried?"

When I don't respond, he takes my silence for a no. Silas smiles; it's that of a fox who's cornered his next meal.

"I don't *want* a war, Nora." The use of my name and not my title has gooseflesh rising on my arms—and not the good kind. "But you are right in that I've developed a hunger for vengeance. You'd think fifty years would have quelled the bloodlust. They say *time heals all wounds*." He bites his thumb on a sardonic laugh. "The elders are either lying or I'm just not that good of a man."

"It's probably a bit of both," I say. "Coming from experience."

"You don't think of yourself as a good person?"

"Never have."

"And why is that?"

I purse my lips. "Because it's not true."

Silas hums, considering my answer. Then he says, "Stand up."

"Why?" I narrow my eyes.

"I'm the king?" He rolls his eyes, and it's nearly playful. "Because I don't want to look down on you when I ask my next question."

Begrudgingly, I stand up. I'm bracketed by his legs, and even though we aren't touching, the heat from his body seeps into me. It's far too intimate a position.

"Do you want to kill a Virtue with me?"

My magic perks, writhing between my ribs; I have to take a deep breath to settle it inside me.

There's only one real answer to his question.

"Yes."

"Then here are my terms."

19
IMOGEN

I hang off Leo's arm with a vice grip—I had forgotten how the cobblestone side streets uptown do *not* cooperate with heels. He doesn't hold back his laughter as I hop along on my toes, trying to avoid the deadly cracks between stones.

"Couldn't you carry me the rest of the way?" I beg.

"Nope. You did this to yourself," he says. "You must suffer the consequences."

I groan. "I'm making Nora drive us home."

"Why didn't they pick us up, anyway?"

"Because I wanted to run something by you before we get there," I say.

"Oh-kay," Leo drawls the syllables out. "Maybe a better time would have been before we left the Den, and you weren't fighting for your life?"

"Yeah, well, hindsight, right?" I huff.

"So..."

"Right. This is where I'm supposed to tell you what I wanted to talk to you about."

My throat is tight and my body jittery as I gather the nerve to get the words out. It's funny, we joke about succession all the time, so you'd think it'd be easy bringing this up. But I need him to understand that, this time, it's not a joke.

It hit me the other day, after Nora and Josie escorted me back to Anwynn. I had collapsed on top of my quilt, my soot-smudged shoes dangling off the bed, uncaring if the chemical campfire smell I carried home seeped into the sheets.

Going from such sweet contentment to walking through the burned rubble of their warehouse—seeing Nora *shoot someone*—had me staring at the ceiling of my bedroom for hours.

Suddenly, I was thirteen again, spacing out and replaying how I fucked up my first kiss over and over. Except I wasn't thirteen, and I was replaying how my girlfriend killed someone in front of me.

I knew her hands weren't clean. She had never *lied* about what they had to do under the former Pride's reign, but it hadn't really *clicked*.

I chose to be a Sin four years ago. To continue my mother and brother's legacy because that was what they would have wanted. I always knew there was a certain level of danger that came with this position, but I thought I could avoid it if I kept my head down. If I didn't ruffle any feathers, it would be okay.

Then Nora became Pride and Silas came knocking at my door. Some deranged Seelie is burning down Nora's warehouses. She's killing people in turn. And I've found myself at the center of all the shit I tried to avoid in the first place.

As I was lying there, staring at the blank ceiling, so pure and white, an inkling of doubt crept into me.

Did I choose to be Lust because I wanted it? Or did I do it because I was grieving, and it was the last thing I had that belonged to my family?

Leo's advice from weeks ago had haunted me as I stared into the untouched plaster.

Think about what it is you really want.

"What are your thoughts on filling in for me at some upcoming Sins functions?" I ask.

I want to ease him into this conversation.

"Sure, anything you need," Leo says quickly. But then he peers down at me with concern in his deep brown irises. "Why? Is something wrong? Are you sick?"

A snort escapes me. "No, I'm not sick. But I don't want you to agree because you think you *need* to—"

"I know I don't have to do anything I don't want to with you, Mo."

"Good. Because I think it's time you step up more."

"Oh?" He smiles. "Am I not doing a good enough job running things as your Second?"

"The opposite," I laugh. "I've finally taken your advice to heart. I've been thinking a lot about what I want out of life. To see what happens if I take a step back, focus on the bars like I was supposed to before the accident. And let you take the lead."

His heavy gaze weighs on me, but I keep my eyes focused on the cracks and crevices at our feet. It takes two of my steps to keep pace with one of his.

"We'll take the transition as slowly as you need to feel comfortable," I add with a laugh. "No pressure. You know?"

"If that's what you want."

This time I meet his eye and give him a smile, albeit a bittersweet one.

"I think so. But I'll keep you posted if that changes," I say. "So, you should be on your best behavior when we see Glut-tony tonight."

Leo nods, eyes swimming with a whirlpool of emotions. I

lost my family that day, the same as him. Life looks different from what we both had planned the night the Den opened.

We turn our attention back to the street, me focusing back on our feet and him guiding us around a stray pedestrian.

After a moment, he chuckles.

"Does that mean things are going well with Nora?" he asks.

I smack his chest, though it doesn't have much power behind it.

"This is about me." My lips twitch, holding back a smug smile. "But yes. I think things are looking up."

Leo's laughter bellows between the buildings as we turn a corner and stop before a crowd gathered outside Gluttony's restaurant.

"Oh, Mo. You're fucked."

"Yeah. I really am."

Throngs of fae wait in line to use the elevator for the restaurant; the entrance is a small room at the base of the building used to ferry guests up to the top floor. Lit by two brass sconces, the plaque labeling the restaurant features delicate script and detailing around the edges.

When it's our turn to step into the elevator, the attendant closes the safety barrier for us and presses one of two buttons on the panel. The doors close on their own, then the elevator jerks into action, raising us stories into the air.

The first thing I notice as we step out of the metal cage is the view. Three of the walls are floor to ceiling windows, overlooking the park and showcasing the sprawling city skyline. It gives the illusion that we're gods floating in the clouds, looking down upon the little fae scurrying around the city like ants.

It's still light out, but the sun will dip down soon; I imagine it'll crest over the horizon with grace, painting the sky a beautiful wash of colors as we watch on.

Leo tugs me to the hostess, a thin, sharp-boned woman with her hair cut into a short bob.

"We should have a reservation under—"

"Lust!"

I'm cut off by a cheerful voice. My head whips to the side to find Hattie waving at us from a table near the far windows. Nora sits to her left, beside an empty seat, shaking her head.

"Actually, I think we're set, thank you," I say, pointing to the half-filled table.

I don't wait for the hostess to reply before I grab Leo's hand and pull him towards the group. He quickly takes the empty seat next to Josie and across from Nora while I slip into the one between Nora and the windows.

"No Claude tonight?" Leo asks, noting the empty seat opposite Hattie at the other head of the table.

"He and Wes had promised they'd do dinner with their nan a while ago," Josie says.

Leo unbuttons his suit jacket and leans back in his seat like he owns the place.

"They should be here to support you," Nora grumbles.

"It's fine." Josie waves her off. "I've got you guys."

"I'm glad you invited us," I say. "This place is fancier than I thought it would be."

I take the cloth napkin and drape it over my thighs. It's a deep ruby-red that compliments the amethyst shade of my dress. I curated my outfit to impress tonight; the heavily embellished gown reaches my ankles, and my hair is curled and pinned into a low bun.

The rest of the table is also dressed more formal than usual. Josie is wearing a dress tonight, a deep teal that suits her warm tan skin, and Nora has added a matching suit jacket to her blouse and trouser set.

Nora fingers the beaded fringe that serves as the sleeve of my dress.

"This is cute."

"Not sexy?" I pout.

I'm teasing, but I don't think she realizes since her brows knit in concerned confusion.

"You're always sexy," she says, like I'm speaking nonsense. "Do you not enjoy being called cute?"

"Of course I do. I was teasing."

"Oh, okay. Good."

Things have still been a bit awkward between us, but I wasn't lying to Leo when I said they were looking up.

"You're pretty cute too," I say.

"How is it that you two got even more sickeningly sweet after your latest relationship woes?" Leo says, adding a fake gag after.

"You're just jealous because she doesn't like dick, and you can't find anyone as good as her," Nora says smugly. "No offense, Hattie."

"None taken. If I was attracted girls, I would have a crush on Imogen too," Hattie says, nodding her head emphatically. "I know a catch when I see one."

Leo sighs dramatically, steepling his fingers and leveling a serious stare at Nora over them.

"Mo is basically my sister. And I have never *once* thought about her sexually," he says. He takes a dramatic pause, giving each of us four girls an individual glare. "However, if you know someone with a figure like hers, I will not say no to an introduction."

I lock eyes with Josie across the table, both of us trying—and failing—to hold in our laughter. It dominoes into all five of us filling the room with the cackles of our amusement.

"On that note…" I snag the menu off the table. "What is everyone thinking for food?"

"I recommend anything with truffle in it. Those were my favorite dishes during testing," Josie says.

"Eh, I don't eat mushrooms," Hattie says, nose scrunching as she picks up her menu.

"Then don't order a dish with mushrooms." Nora rolls her eyes. "Simple."

Leo buries his face in the folds of the menu. "What about drinks? Did you three order before we got here?"

"I told the server to get us a bottle of white faerie wine," Nora says.

"No champagne?" Leo asks, popping his head over the fancy cardstock. "I thought this was a celebration?"

Nora, Hattie, and Josie all go awkwardly silent.

"Unfortunately, there's going to be a champagne shortage for a while." I grimace.

"What? Why?"

"Seelie bastards is why," Nora mutters under her breath.

She reaches into her pocket to pull out her cigarette case and lighter, deftly setting light to one and tossing the lighter onto the table. It lands with a dull *thunk* against the thick tablecloth.

"Josie, why don't you pick out a bunch of your favorites and we can all share?" I say. "I'm fine with anything, and I trust your judgment."

Pink flushes her cheeks at being singled out.

"Okay. Yeah. I can do that," she says. "The rest of you good with that?"

Resounding *yeses* sound from the table, and we fall into easy conversation. Soon enough, our food is served and my nose tickles at the indulgent smells. Butter and sage waft up from the dish in front of me, while the dish in front of Leo steams with spices. Josie explains where each dish's human ingredients were sourced from, and we all listen, enthralled by the passion in her voice.

As we finish the dinner course, the lights dim around us. A singular light falls on the small circular stage at the center of the room, and Gluttony struts onto the platform. She's glowing in a batwing gown of glittering gold with deep swaths of her brown skin peeking out from the dips at her chest and back. Her hair is slicked into shiny finger waves, and she's dripping in jewels.

"Thank you all for coming tonight," Gluttony says into the standing microphone on stage. "I hope you all are enjoying your meals so far."

Gluttony pauses; patrons clap and yowl and whistle, all of us already buzzing from the atmosphere and alcohol. My own cheeks flush—between the two bottles of faerie wine we've guzzled down and the stray touches Nora places on the skin between my shoulder blades, I can't help but feel warm.

"Now, I want to introduce a very special guest who is going to perform for you all... Miss Venus Day!"

Applause erupts as the well-known singer joins Gluttony on stage. Her skin is a shade lighter than Gluttony's but just as warm-toned.

"Thank you, Gluttony." Venus's deep velvet voice flows through the microphone. "I'm excited to sing for y'all tonight. Boys?"

Three musicians step up behind her, taking their places with the instruments on the stage—a piano, a standing base, and a drum set. Gluttony quickly waves a goodbye, and the room is filled with smooth riffs and gentle jazz.

"She stole Miss V from us!" Leo says, lips pressed into a flat line as he glares at the singer who does a weekly set at the Den.

"She's a singer, Leo. She needs to book other work. We only hire her for Saturday nights," I say. "Plus, Gluttony's clearly not letting her have her wings out. That'll differentiate us enough that it won't matter."

He's utterly miffed when he realizes I'm right, sinking into his seat like a sulking child.

"Maybe I'll book her more often," he mumbles.

Two shadows fall over our table, the air crackling with electricity. I look up and find the Unseelie King and Wrath, smirking and frowning respectively.

"Evening, ladies," Silas says. His head tilts pointedly at Leo. "And gentleman."

They're backlit by the sunset; the orange glow glints off the silver piercings lining Silas's ear and his ring-clad fingers. Meanwhile, Wrath resembles a demon, his warm sandy-brown hair glinting molten amber in the light.

I stare daggers at Silas, though his attention is focused solely on Nora. Her knuckle brushes over the vertebra of my neck, a silent, soothing gesture that she repeats.

"Your Majesty," Nora greets begrudgingly.

Silas tsks. "Do we need formalities tonight? We're all here as friends of Gluttony, celebrating her success."

"We always need formalities," Wrath mutters. His red-brown eyes cut across the room, uninterested. He can't even be bothered to be near us.

So why come over here, asshole?

Silas waves Wrath's comment away, pulling out the empty chair at the end of the table and sitting down.

"I did hear House Pride had a hand in our meals tonight. So, I wanted to come over and give my compliments."

He looks expectantly at Nora, but she gives him a deadpan glare.

"Why are you staring at me?"

"Because you're Pride?" he drawls.

"This was my Second's project. You can direct your congratulations at her."

Nora's lips twitch upwards as the table registers that she's issued the Unseelie King a command, however small. We wait, all on edge, to see if he'll follow.

All the while, her thumb strokes up and down my neck.

Silas lips part, forming an open-mouthed smile. Slowly, he turns to Josie—who freezes under his searing gaze—and speaks.

"You did an excellent job," he says. "You should be very proud."

"Thank you, Your Majesty."

"Are you two together?" Hattie calls across the table. Her cheek is smooshed against her hand, her head tilted, and her brows are knit over curious eyes that flick between Silas and Wrath. She waggles a finger from her free hand at Wrath. "He's always hanging off you like a shadow."

The table goes still, preparing for the Unseelie King to reprimand Hattie for speaking out of turn. But Silas laughs, the deep ocean waves rolling over us.

"Ha! No," Silas says. "He's more of a grumpy, over-protective, older brother who I can't get rid of—"

"I'm only two months older than you," Wrath grumbles, pulling a golden pocket watch from his suit.

"—wait, why do you ask?" Silas asks. He and Hattie chatter back and forth like two happy squirrels.

The rest of us watch, dumbfounded.

Leo leans into Josie, whispering, "What is happening right now?"

"I believe he is trying to build friendly rapport with the group," she whispers back.

"Ah," Leo says. "Why?"

Silas snaps his fingers, and Josie and Leo jump to attention. He's got a smarmy, closed-lipped smirk on as he drawls, "It's rude to talk about people when they're right in front of you."

Leo's eyes widen and cut to mine. I cock my brow as if to say *get used to it, bud, this is your future.*

Wrath's hand comes down on Silas's shoulder, his sturdy grip apparent by the wrinkling of Silas's suit. He doesn't say anything, but a quick shared glance between the two men is all Wrath needs.

"It seems my carriage is going to turn into a pumpkin, and I've got to get this grandpa home—it's well past Wrath's bedtime." Silas gets up, gently pushing his chair back into place. Then he throws his arm around Wrath with a cheeky salute. "See you Monday, Pride."

Wrath shoves Silas's arm off his shoulder as the two retreat across the room.

"I would not describe him as a grandpa," Hattie murmurs, biting her bottom lip as she makes googly eyes at Wrath's back. "Maybe a daddy, though."

All four of our brows snap to our hairlines.

"Hattie!" Josie nearly chokes on her wine.

"I'm usually all for that, but with him?" Leo gags.

"What? Wrath's hot." When she realizes we're all staring as if she's gone absolutely mental, she has the decency to look embarrassed. "Not that I would pursue someone from another House without explicit permission and enthusiasm from our fearless leader."

"Uh-huh," Nora deadpans.

"Wait, what did he mean by 'See you Monday?'" I ask.

Nora winces, pulling her hand away from my neck. She grabs my hand instead, intertwining our fingers.

"Don't be mad."

"I feel like that statement does the opposite of what you want it to do..."

Nora scratches her cheek. "I have to go on a research trip with the two of them on Monday. Our king has decreed that my magic must be studied."

"Why would I be mad about that?" I say.

"Because it's Silas?" Nora says.

Okay. Fair. I don't want her spending more time with that dangerous asshole than necessary.

"Where is this research taking place?" Leo asks for me, tone laced with suspicion. "I'm assuming somewhere not in the city?"

"I don't think so. He didn't say," she says. Then, with a grimace, she adds, "And I don't know how long I'll be gone."

"*Ah.*" I'm finally getting a sense of where this conversation is going.

I pull her hand into my lap, cradling it with both of mine. I glance around the table, and with a subtle tilt of my head, our three companions suddenly find themselves all needing to use the restroom.

When we're alone, I ask, "What is it that you're worried about?"

Nora chews on her cheek, not meeting my eye, obviously uncomfortable with talking about this here. But the other night she asked me to help. And pushing her to explain her worry is a part of that.

"I don't enjoy the idea of leaving you for that long after, well, you know."

After she murdered a Seelie in front of me?

"Do you think I'm incapable of protecting myself?" I ask pointedly.

"Of course not. But there are larger threats at play—"

"Things are no different today than they were two weeks ago."

She glares at me, but there's no ire in those gemstone irises, only concern. "I would argue differently."

I tilt my head, tracing over her pointed features. "Are you nervous?"

"Why would I be nervous?"

"It's just strange that Silas is doing this now, rather than when you were younger." I don't need to add the rest of the context—*why do this after he had me spying on her?*—she knows. "And let me be clear, I don't like it. But after everything, I know you wouldn't agree to spend time with him without a good reason."

Nora nods. "He's being cagey about it, but I'm curious about what information they have on my magic. It could change things human-side."

It could help her protect her House.

"Okay," I say.

"And it seems he didn't trust me before." Nora runs her finger over the rim of her crystal glass.

"But you think he does now?"

"Well enough." Nora shrugs, but the look in her eyes holds a darkness I can't place. She takes a deep breath, letting out a languid sigh. "I don't want to talk about him anymore. I want to enjoy the rest of the night with you and our friends." Then, a devilish smirk spreads across her cheeks. "I should be home by Solstice though."

"Oh yeah?" I say slowly, following her train of thought.

"Mhm," she hums. "And I can think of the *perfect* present to unwrap when I get back."

We laugh, fingers still intertwined, and the colorful notes spread warmth through me.

"Are you sure you don't want a ride home?" I ask Leo.

He waves me off.

"It's good. Hattie and I are going to one of Envy's clubs," he says, arm slung around the tiny blond.

"We want to dance," Hattie says with a little shimmy.

"Alright," I laugh. "Be safe, then."

"Thanks, *Ma*," Leo snickers. But before I can smack his arm, Hattie shadow-walks them out of the lobby with a giggle goodbye.

Nora comes back from settling the tab and pauses. "They already left?"

"Apparently we are too boring for them," I say solemnly.

Nora chuffs.

"Josie should be back from the restroom shortly. Why don't you wait for her while I grab the car from the valet?"

"Okay."

Nora places a kiss on my cheek before hopping into the elevator.

The metal doors slide shut; they are elaborate golden panels that contrast the dark jade paint on the walls. I run my hand over the cool metal, tracing the filigree designs, both geometric and floral at the same time.

It's not more than a few minutes before I feel a presence at my side.

"Hi," Josie says.

"Hi."

A beat passes between us as we both stare at the elevator.

"Everything will be okay, you know," Josie says, sticking her hands into the pockets of her coat.

"Why do you say that?" I ask.

Josie shifts next to me, and I know that if she didn't have her mental shields locked tight, I'd catch a whiff of embarrassment floating off her. She doesn't look at me as she speaks, instead analyzing the elevator doors as if they're the most interesting thing in the world. I shouldn't judge, though; I was doing the same thing.

"You seemed concerned when Nora mentioned her trip." Josie shrugs. "I wanted to reassure you. I know Silas isn't your favorite."

I tilt my head at her, a smile tugging at my lips. She still doesn't meet my eyes. "Reading my mind?"

"No, your shields are ironclad. I can just tell."

"Empath's curse," I commiserate, earning me a delicate snort from Josie.

"My mother certainly thought so," she says. "She thought it a burden for me to know everyone's business. Would've much rather had me wield shadows like them."

I turn toward Josie in earnest, leaning my shoulder into the framing of the elevator as I cross my arms over my chest.

"She wasn't an empath?" I ask.

"Neither of my parents were."

"Strange."

"My father thought as much, with such an uncommon gift. I'm confident that if I wasn't his spitting image that he would've thought my mother cheated," she says, though her tone is laced with fondness, not spite. "Then my grandmother got loose-lipped on her deathbed and dropped the big family secret: she had a fling with an empath before my dad was born. Pretty sure that conversation aged him a century."

I laugh. I can only imagine how that kind of conversation would have gone.

"Sorry, didn't mean to say all of that," Josie adds, pink rushing to her cheeks.

"Don't apologize. I like hearing about your past," I say. "I can tell there's a lot of love in your House despite the bad bits."

"Bad bits" is an understatement, but it feels wrong to refer to their traumas as anything more after such a nice night.

Though, I'm filled with the urge to reassure Josie that she *can* talk about those things with me. Good or bad.

I pick at the beading on my dress.

"When I stayed over the other day, I saw the wings on the wall," I say, and Josie's back stiffens. "Nora told me about what Pride made you guys do. You know I'm here for both of you if you ever want to talk about it."

She gives me a tight smile. "Thank you. But they're not my stories to share."

The hall grows quiet, as if speaking of him has caused the ghost of Nora's predecessor to fall upon us. Josie's gaze lands anywhere but on me, tracking the wall and catching on the elevator panel. She lifts a delicate finger to point at it.

"You know you didn't hit the button to call the elevator up, right?"

"I didn't?" I ask, feigning surprise, though I know I never pressed the button. She jabs it for me, the little down arrow lighting up under her touch. "It's a good thing you got here in time to help, otherwise I'd be stuck."

She laughs. It's a warm chuckle that wraps around me like a hug.

Maybe I did need her reassurance after all.

Sliding the deadbolt into place, I flip the bar's house lights on and shuck my jacket off. I had offered Nora a nightcap, but she declined, needing to prepare for her trip.

My fingers brush over my lips, puffy and swollen from the toe-curling kiss she'd left me with, whispering promises that she'll see me before she leaves *and* make up for her absence tenfold when she returns.

The difference between now and two weeks ago is staggering.

With light feet, I twirl across the empty bar, skirt fluttering around my ankles, humming one of Miss V's riffs.

"You two are cute."

"*Fucking Gods—*" I drop my jacket as I nearly jump out of my skin.

I scan the bar, searching for the intruder until my glare lands on the signature white hair of the Unseelie King.

"You're always showing up when you're not welcome, you know that?" I huff, bending down to pick up my jacket and drape it over the bar counter. "That is twice tonight."

Silas's deep chuckle echoes in the empty space.

I approach him, shoulders taut and pulled back as I stop at the edge of the table. Silas lounges in one of the VIP booths, one arm stretched across the back, fingers tapping a chaotic rhythm on the leather. Ice clinks in the whiskey glass that he twirls on the table.

"Helped yourself to the top shelf?" I ask. "Didn't drink enough at Gluttony's?"

His responding smile is cloyed, an all-too-sweet falseness shining up at me.

"Wrath says I shouldn't overindulge in public," he says.

"Does the Unseelie King always listen to his subordinates?" I ask, a lightning strike of confidence pushing me to test him.

My hands come to rest on my hips; the Unseelie King's eyes

—pupil-less voids in the dim light—flick between my hips and the other end of the booth. An unspoken order that I ignore.

"Sit."

The one word wavers my confidence; devoid of all amusement, his voice commands obedience. My hands drop back to my sides, and I slide into the booth across from him—then the playful spark in his eyes is back.

"I don't mean to offend, Your Majesty, but I will *not* be—"

"I came to apologize," he says. My breath catches in my throat when he cuts me off. "Not about using you for intelligence, that is my right as king and part of the vetting process for all who come into power here. But I do hold a *minuscule* sliver of guilt for causing any trouble between you and Pride. I won't be asking you about her any longer. We've come to a mutual understanding."

My lips twist. "Why didn't you say that when we saw you earlier?"

"I didn't think it was the proper place for this conversation."

"Okay."

"Well?"

I blink. "Pardon?"

"Do you accept my apology?"

I give him an awkward, tight-lipped smile. "Consider it behind us."

"Good."

My skin grows clammy as we sit and stare at each other.

"Are you going to leave now, or did you need something else?" I ask tentatively.

His white brows hit his hairline, and I swear I can almost make out a hint of pink on the apples of his cheeks. Silas throws back the last sips of his drink before gracefully getting up from the booth. He pauses, tapping the table with his ringed knuckles, shadows curling around the appendages.

"I hope you can find it within yourself to think of me as more of a friend than a king going forward," he says, slowly disappearing into the inky tendrils. "If things progress the way I think they will, then we'll all be seeing a lot more of each other."

20
NORA

The wind is brisk, a sharp whip against my cheek.

I wait outside the iron-spiked gates of Silas's palace, realizing that autumn has begun to pack up shop, and winter is rounding the corner with a flurry.

My nose gets a brief reprieve from the cold as I flick on my lighter, the flame burning through the end of the cigarette I've got pinched between gloved fingers. The sharp scent of smoke usually calms me, but lately, it's been a reminder of the burned rubble we left across the Veil.

In some moments, it's a good thing, like fresh coal thrown into my fire, but in others, it's a heavy weight on my shoulders.

"Silas will arrive shortly. I suggest you finish that before he gets here," a deep voice calls.

I close my eyes, already feeling the migraine pinch across the side of my skull. A fake smile spreads across my cheeks.

"*Wrath.*"

"Pride."

Wrath doesn't smile back as he greets me. I don't think he

was partial to me before I came into power, but afterwards, it became clear I'm not his favorite.

He isn't mine either.

His steps are silent as he approaches, dressed in his standard three-piece black suit with a gray wool overcoat—much like mine—and a flat cap to match. It's all freshly pressed; straight creases cut the center of each leg of his trousers. Even his oxfords shine as they peek out from the hem of the pants.

I take a final drag of my cigarette before dropping it on the pavement and stomping it out with my boot. I barely smoked through a quarter of it, but Wrath isn't Envy, and I can't push him the same way I can the other Sins.

Luckily, we aren't left in awkward silence for long. Shadows merge together in the empty space before us, silky tendrils of night that are tangible enough to skim your hand through.

"Evening," Silas says as he materializes from the darkness.

Silas is dressed even warmer than us, with a fur-trimmed jacket over his suit. It's an interesting choice in outerwear, but it matches his personality. He claps his hands together, the sound a muted thud given the leather gloves he wears.

"We don't have much time to waste. There's a storm coming."

I peek at the sky. There's not a cloud in sight.

"Storm's on the other end," he says, as if he can read my mind. He turns to Wrath. "You good?"

Wrath nods before grabbing my suitcase and disappearing into a swirl of shadows.

"You may be sick after this," Silas says.

The six words are the only warning I get before Silas's hand falls on my shoulder, and I'm thrust into the void.

Darkness swirls around me, a hundred shades of night that I never knew existed. I've been shadow-walked plenty of times before, but there's something different about Silas's shadows —something dangerous lurks within them.

As quickly as I was plunged into it, I'm yanked out, tripping over my feet and blinking at the bright white landscape. A wet chill soaks my knees and forearms.

Snow, untouched and sparkling, surrounds us for miles, blurring into a mass of white-dusted evergreens and mountains whose peaks are hidden by clouds.

"You'll have time to gawk at the views later. Follow me," Silas says from behind me.

I stand, whacking the snow from my legs and coat. Silas is already striding through a path cut in the snow and leaving me behind.

He calls over his shoulder, "It's a short walk from here. Apologies for the trek through the snow, but there are ancient wards around the area that block us from landing too close."

Snow crunches under my boots as I follow, the cold already soaking through the leather. Ahead, a shadowed cavern yawns open in the side of the mountain; its entrance is unnervingly black, and I recognize the telltale shimmer of magic.

"You brought me to a cave?" I deadpan. "This isn't the creative end I assumed you'd think up for me, Your Majesty. I have to admit I'm disappointed."

He laughs—a throaty chuckle that echoes across the mountainside.

"You continue to surprise me with your honesty," he says, wiping an unshed tear from his eye. "And please, call me Silas." He sweeps a hand out in a grand gesture towards the cave. "Welcome to Mount Bramble, where the berries in spring are delicious and Court secrets are plentiful year-round."

Passing through the outer barrier of the cave feels akin to traveling between the realms. The magic clings to me like glitter, a faint dust that shimmers before sinking into my skin. The inside of the cave is surprisingly warm, the air thicker here than outside. The shadow barrier keeps heat in as much as it keeps people out. The rounded walls are smooth, and my leather-tipped fingers drift over the gray rock as easily as they would marble; it's as if someone shaved and polished them.

Our steps echo as Silas leads us down the natural hallway.

When we reach the end of the path, punctuated by a set of large iron doors, Silas turns to me.

What kind of stronghold has he brought me to?

"What lies beyond these doors is accessed by only a select few members of the Court. I hope you will use the utmost discretion about what you see here when we leave," he says with a seriousness that strikes my gut.

"I understand."

Like a child, his mood shifts from serious to carefree in an instant. He shoots me a mischievous smile.

"Now to show you all the goodies," he says and throws open the doors.

They open to a large underground cavern.

No, that doesn't do it justice.

The right word escapes me as we step onto a small landing that overlooks a vertical tunnel carved into the mountain stone. It stands maybe fifty feet wide and five stories tall, with three going up and two going down from our vantage point.

At the top of the cavern is a massive, pointed skylight. Made of large panes of stained glass, it paints a rainbow of colors across the neutral-toned stone canvas. Below, the bottom of the circular cavern hosts a few round tables. A handful of fae sit there, studying next to piles of thick tomes. Behind them, rows of bookshelves continue under the cover of the lowest level.

My head shakes at the sheer size of the place.

"How?" I whisper.

"Generations of stubborn Royals committed to their contingency plans," Silas quips from my side. "Myself included."

He leaves it at that and leans his back against the railing, arms crossed. The position makes him look like a puffed-up cat, with the fur-lined coat collar pushed up to his chin.

Part of me has the sudden urge to push him over the ledge.

Would he shadow-walk himself to safety? Or would he spread his wings and glide down to the lowest level?

Maybe he'd simply fall to his death.

Silas studies me studying him, the corner of his rose-colored lips twitching up.

"Come," he says, pushing off from the ledge. "I'll show you to your room. Your bag will be there already."

We turn towards the stairs and climb up the stone spiral. My blood unfreezes, and warmth seeps back into my flesh. I unbutton my coat, shuck it off my shoulders, and tuck it over my forearm.

"Everything better be as I packed it," I mumble under my breath.

"Wrath may be thorough, but he isn't a thief," Silas chirps in front of me.

We climb past the first level, then the second.

"Will we be seeing much of him during this trip?"

"He is integral to what I have planned for us, so prepare yourself to be in his presence more than you're used to," Silas says. He peers over his shoulder with a glint in his obsidian eyes. "Robbie really is much nicer than he seems. We'll get some liquor in him, and he'll loosen up."

I blink.

Is that Wrath's name?

I imagined him as more of a Bartholomew, or something equally stuffy. *Robbie* is a child's name.

"I didn't come here to drink and make friends," I say.

Silas tuts, "Don't be such a grouch, Nora."

We crest the third landing, turning down a narrow hall. It's lined with burning torches, rather than electric sconces, which cast the space in flickering shades of amber.

I guess they can't fit an entire mountain with electricity.

We stop in front of a wooden door, carved with swirling lines that knot together in symmetrical patterns.

Silas shucks his jacket off, revealing a sharp pin-striped charcoal suit. He reaches into his pocket and pulls out a metal key, holding it out to me.

"This one is yours. I'm next door and Wrath is one past mine," he says, pointing down the curved hall.

I take the key and our fingers brush, though they're both covered in winter gloves. He doesn't flinch. He simply lowers his hand back to his side, unfazed.

"Get settled, then meet us at noon for a debrief in the library. It's on the bottom level with the big green doors," he says. "You can't miss it. But even if you do, each floor is a circle, so you can keep walking till you pass it again."

"Understood," I say.

I expect him to leave, but he remains, waiting like a puppy who's expecting a treat. My lips stretch into a formal, tight-lipped smile.

If he thinks he's getting my thanks, he'll be sorely mistaken.

"I can manage from here."

Silas frowns at my dismissal of him.

"If you need anything, you can give either one of us a knock. There aren't Royal staff here, just a few of Wrath's security, the scholars, and a cook who *only* cooks. So, everything else is on us," he says. I give him an awkward thumbs up, and he snorts. "See you in a bit, *neighbor.*"

I wait until his steps fade around the curved hall to enter my room. Locking the door behind me, I toss my jacket onto the small table situated in the entry and sink into the nearest chair. It's a wide-back lounger upholstered in rose-pink velvet placed next to the hearth.

With a passing glance, I scan the room I've been given. It's small, but cozy. The ceilings are low and made of rough-hewn stone. The walls are decorated with pink-toned tapestries, likely to keep the space warm, and the simple four-poster bed sits in the far corner with pale fabric tied to each post. A dark archway stands next to the bed, leading to what I assume is the washroom.

I pinch the bridge of my nose, then sigh at the failed attempt to block the pounding against my skull. I'll have to take a hot shower, if this place even has running water, to dull the pain before I head back downstairs to meet with Silas.

His behavior unnerves me—the way he regards me as a friend in one moment, then casts out commands in the next. It alludes to a game that only he knows the rules to.

Our deal requires us to place faith in one another, to share each other's secrets. It's a risk on both our parts.

The reward will be worth it. That is, *if* I can keep the two of them close enough to help with Patience, but far enough away that they don't notice the cracking mortar holding together every half-truth I've ever told.

When I walk into the library, my nose is assaulted by deep notes of mildew, dust, and cedar. It's a distinct mix of scents that I expect from an ancient cavern that books call home.

My gloved hand skims over the leather and clothbound tomes as I glide through the rows searching for Silas and Wrath. I turn a corner and exit the circular maze of books, stepping into the open area at the center of the mountain complex.

Silas stands over a round table scattered with papers and pictures while Wrath lounges in a chair next to him.

"Ah, Nora, good. You didn't get lost," Silas says, quickly glancing my way and waving me over.

His attention falls back to a photograph on the table, silently pondering it and scratching his jaw. Wrath glares at me, not hiding his distaste for my presence. Both men have gotten rid of their outerwear and suit jackets; watch chains dangle from their vest pockets, though Wrath's is gold and Silas's silver.

The scratch of a chair against the stone floor echoes through the library as a man gets up from the table next to ours. He slides his reading glasses into his pocket and walks away with a book tucked under his arm.

It registers that Silas didn't clear out the library. A few others linger between the shelves and at the tables, all dressed in similar black robes.

"Who are they?" I ask, nodding to the few fae with their noses tucked between the pages of their own books.

"Researchers," Wrath answers.

My lips tip into a frown. He doesn't continue.

"Not going to elaborate, are you?"

A smug little smirk spreads across Wrath's face. He stays silent.

"I know we believe Patience to be the same man, but I am curious..." Silas taps the photograph on the table. "Do you recognize him?"

I lean on the edge of the table, peering over the photos.

One is an ancient sepia-toned square of a young woman with hair cropped into a flouncy pixie cut. She's mid-laugh, her head thrown back and mouth open wide, and behind her, you can barely make out the faint outline of translucent wings. Underneath her photo is a simple label scrawled in ink: *Oonagh.*

The Seelie Queen.

Below her photograph is a group picture with her and seven others at a banquet, all holding up glasses of wine and spirits and dressed to the nines. It's a mix of men and women, but some of the faces are crossed out with large black x's.

A weight settles in my stomach, the dropping of an anchor in the sea.

Though the photo is grainy, I can make out a few details: a smile that doesn't reach his beady eyes, a suit that's of an older fashion, and two-toned hair, a clear sign of aging.

He's younger in this photo than I remember him to be, but the sharp nose and cheekbones are the same as the day he ruined my life.

Patience.

Where did they get these photos?

It's a silly thought, because we weren't always cut off from the Seelie Court. I know the stories from my father. The two Courts were far from friends, but we still had customs where we joined together as one realm. Such as the Solstice celebration in late December, when fifty years ago, Silas's parents were murdered and he cemented our realm's divide.

"This one," I say, tapping on his face.

This man tried to steal me from my parents, and when he failed to do that, he killed them. Now, he continues to poke and prod at my life as if it's some kind of plaything for his amusement.

I am one person, but the lives of my people are not toys to be played with.

"See, I told you," Silas says to Wrath.

Wrath grunts.

"Where did you get these photos?" I ask.

"This library holds records of both Courts going back thousands of years," Silas says.

A ghost of a smile graces his lips, and his eyes focus on the wall of books behind us, as if they're replaying memories he can't pull away from. It's a look I've seen in the mirror a hundred times before.

"My parents were excited when photography was invented. They documented most of the Solstice events they attended and any other Court functions they thought worth preserving." His smile grows. "And some that probably weren't worth preserving. There are boxes of pictures from my youngling days in storage. Ones that should never see the light of day, let alone be discovered by a curious researcher wandering the archives."

"You should keep them somewhere else then. Or burn them," I say.

"He craves the attention too much to do that," Wrath mumbles.

Silas whacks him on the back of the head, causing Wrath to mutter an *ouch*.

"Well," I drawl. "Now that we know we're talking about the same man, what's the plan?"

"Patience is old guard," Wrath says, crossing his arms over his chest. "Been in power longer than the queen. It's a miracle he's still active in any capacity, but we can't underestimate him."

"He's a *very* strong healer. And like his House's title, he doesn't shy away from playing the long-con. He's smart, perceptive." Silas's vulpine eyes slide over me. "Same as you, Nora."

I avoid meeting his gaze, instead I watch my fingers tap dull *thunks* against the wooden table.

"Again, where does that leave us? Stop being vague."

"Our plan only works if we get three things right." Silas points at me. "Number one: you. You're our sniper. We just need to refine your shot."

"Meaning?"

"Use your magic to plant the seed of death within him so that it blooms *without* your presence."

I shoot him a deadpan stare.

"Like poison?"

"Yes, but even poison leaves a trail. Your magic won't." There's a devious little tilt to his lips. "*If* we manage to do it right."

Silas paces around the table, one hand behind his back and the other holding up two fingers.

Such a showman.

"Number two. We have to figure out a way for you to touch him without him realizing."

"I'm a decent pickpocket, but if he's as smart as we think, he'll see the sleight of hand from a mile away," I say.

"Which is where I come in," Wrath says. He's got a dead-eyed, shark-toothed grin plastered across his face. "I'm working on a solution. I hope you're not too attached to those gloves."

"Not particularly," I grate between clenched teeth.

"And that brings us to number three. You and Patience need to be in the same room." Silas plants both hands on the table and leans forward, tongue in cheek. "If we can check off one and two within the next four weeks, then number three won't be an issue. That part is on me."

"This is my final formal warning that I don't think it's a good idea," Wrath says, standing. His spine cracks as he stretches, arms raised above his head and head bobbing to the side. "I think we have a good thing going. Is it truly worth the risk?"

The two men have a silent standoff, silently communicating much like Josie and I do. A beat passes between them, then Wrath heaves a defeated sigh.

"Fine," he says, turning away from both of us. "But don't be pissed when it blows up in your faces and I say I told you so."

21

NORA

Silas holds up a single finger, stopping me from following Wrath out of the library.

"Stay right there," he says.

He points to Wrath's vacated seat and disappears into the maze of shelves. I slide into the seat with a sigh, tilting my head up at the rainbow skylight. It doesn't take long, but Silas returns hugging a stack of ancient tomes. He lets go unceremoniously, and they slam onto the table.

A plume of dust puffs out from the books.

Silas huffs, waving away the dust, and leans on the stack with one hand propped on his hip.

"Now that we're all briefed, I have more important things to do than to spoon-feed you a millennia's worth of Unseelie history." He flicks the cover of the first book in the stack. "I suggest you start with this one."

"I'm sorry?"

"In two days, we'll begin practical training, but before that, I think it's important that you know more about other soul-stealers. May help quicken the process—"

Practical training? Does he have a bunch of criminals to line up for me to kill?

"—this one is a *riveting* compilation of biographies of documented Unseelie with your power. Their lives all pretty much end in pitchforks and fires though, so maybe skip over those parts."

Silas shivers at the last part, nose scrunching up, as if reliving a horrible memory.

"You want me to study," I deadpan.

"Exactly." He taps his nose.

"Will there be an exam?"

"Ha. No." Silas's laugh is a quick, hearty burst that echoes in the cavern. "I've already read all of these and think it might help you figure out how to manipulate your magic in such a way."

He pulls away from the table, plastering on that cheeky smile again. Silas's mood and expressions shift with the wind, easily flowing into one another in a way that's impossible to predict.

"Have fun!" he chirps.

He's whisked away by shadows before I can get another word of protest in. Resigned to my fate, I heave a sigh and shuck off my gloves. If I'm going to be forced to read history books, then I want the parchment between my bare fingertips.

I'm loath to admit it, but it's a smart strategy. Had I known about these resources earlier, been able to learn about how others harnessed this magic...

I shake the thought away. It's no use fantasizing about an idyllic childhood. Pride had forged his own training methods for me; they were unorthodox, but they worked.

How many times had he brought me into a barren room, the concrete floor forever stained with red-brown splotches, and shoved me towards a "traitor" restrained at its center?

How many times had he told me my magic was a mercy compared to what he would do to them? How many times had he slit a man's gut open, made me watch their entrails spill onto the floor, and told me that their deaths didn't have to be gruesome?

Guilt was how Pride convinced me to use my magic as a child. Because my touch didn't *have* to hurt. I didn't *want* it to hurt. That is, until I became desensitized to the violence.

Cruelty is learned, and I took to it quickly.

I scrub my hands over my face.

I don't have time for guilt. It does nothing for me now.

Relaxing into the chair, I slide the first book from the stack over to me and flip open the cover. And then, I read.

Hours pass before my eyes burn, much like the funeral pyres of the late soul-stealers I've come to learn about. It seems that even thousands of years ago, the Unseelie Court was still wary of those who wield death so freely.

My migraine had faded to the background with the distraction, but it's back with full force, an incessant pounding of a pickax through the left side of my skull.

I may be driven, but I know when I've reached my limit.

It reminds me of grade school, when studying for a test; after a certain point, the information doesn't stick, and it's better to sleep and start again in the morning.

After I say my goodnights to the fae researchers still studying away at the other tables, I don't rush back to my room. Instead, I explore, letting all the information I learned tonight sink into my being.

Not one of the ancient fae in the books I'd read had the ability to control the methods or times of death. It was always touch-and-die. *Poof.* A quick lightning strike.

With each word, my gut sank deeper upon the confirmation that I am what I thought long before Pride took me in: an anomaly.

"You're special, Nora. That's all."

My mother's words hadn't comforted me the stormy night my magic revealed itself, and they don't comfort me now.

I stroll through each of the circular levels in the complex, mapping out the rooms and exit points, the latter of which are few. Every exit corridor leads back to the main entrance Silas had walked me through earlier.

A bit of an operational security issue, if you ask me.

I stop by the kitchen and snag some bread and dried meats from the cupboard to hold me over until the morning. When I finally get back to my room, I barely strip off my clothes before I fall into plush bedsheets and drift into a fitful sleep.

The next day isn't much different, with not one Silas or Wrath sighting as I stay holed up in the library. Though, after I snag a late dinner, the cook whips up a special tea for the pain thrumming in my skull.

I startle awake on the third morning to someone pounding on my door.

Sucking in a ragged breath, I take stock of my surroundings: the fresh but soft linens under my fingertips, the natural stone walls draped in tapestries, and the blessed absence of my migraine. Sunlight peaks around the curtains of my window overlooking the mountainside.

The knocks continue, followed by Silas calling my name in a sing-song voice.

"Nor-ra!"

"Gods, give me the strength to deal with this man all day," I whisper.

I murmur curses under my breath as I rub the crust from my eyes with my palm. Yawning, I throw a dressing gown on over my underwear and head to the door. I crack it open, but only as much as I need to wedge my face between it and the doorframe.

"What?"

Silas lifts a golden apple to his mouth and bites, the crunch of his teeth piercing the crisp flesh loud in the empty hall. Juice gathers at the corner of his lips; he catches the budding droplet with a swipe of his tongue.

"You slept through breakfast," he says.

"Okay."

"So, I brought you an apple."

"*Okay.*"

He holds a second apple out with his other hand, this one bright red. I don't reach for it. I don't have gloves on and neither does he.

"I could have gotten something myself on the way down."

"Yes, well, I can't have you training on an empty stomach. It's no good for either of us if you're hungry and stoking thoughts of murder." Silas shakes the hand that holds the spare apple as if to say *Hurry up and take it. I'm waiting.* "We want this experiment to be successful, no?"

With a huff, I stick out my hand, palm open and facing up. Silas's eyes narrow on my outstretched hand, puzzled brows knitting above them. Then, the confusion drops from his face. A smug smile creeps onto his lips, like he knows I don't want our hands to touch.

He does realize I could kill him, right?

Silas drops the apple into my hand and backs away. He twists and saunters down the hall, waving his mangled apple core in the air over his shoulder.

"See you in half an hour."

I close the door without replying, tossing the lock into place. I rub the ruby-red apple on my dressing gown, polishing the skin until it shines.

I imagine I'll see a lot of red today, whether it be in person or in my memories.

Lifting the fruit to my lips, I bite.

Turns out, Silas did, in fact, have a bunch of criminals lined up for me to kill.

He leads me past a red door on the first level of the complex, which opens to a large training room. Half of the space is crowded with mats and weights that have been pushed to the side. In the far corner, there's an elevated mat for sparring, roped off like a boxer's ring.

The other half of the room is cleared of all equipment; instead, a row of fae sit chained to chairs, iron shackles wrapped around their hands and ankles. Their clothes are in varying states of distress, stained and ripped in several places, and their hair is unkempt and greasy.

"Don't worry," Silas says. "They were all pulled from the Royal prisons by Wrath and were execution bound within the year. Rapists, mostly, and a sprinkle of those who killed a Royal and didn't clean up the mess. So if you're worried about post-murder guilt, you shouldn't be."

"Do I look like someone who'd feel guilty?" I ask.

My jaw ticks, and I study the chained fae with a new light. Their mouths are gagged so they can't do more than growl in our direction, but their eyes flare with the hatred burning in their souls. I'm confident that if any of them were given the opportunity, they'd slaughter both of us in a second.

"You don't have to convince me," I say, rolling the sleeves

of my black blouse to my elbows. My movements are methodical and quick. I'd dressed for efficiency today, a simple shirt and slacks. "My conscience was stained black years ago."

I pace along the line of criminals; the *clack clack clack* of my boots, a metronome cutting through their snarls. The skin at their wrists and ankles is rubbed raw and blistered from friction with the iron.

Stopping at the end of the line, I pivot on my heel, turning to Silas.

"How does this work?"

He stands a ways back from me with his arms crossed. Not bothering with a suit jacket for this, he's dressed in a similar fashion to me, with simple pin-striped slacks and a white button-down. In their crossed position, his arms bulge against the golden sleeve garter that circles each bicep.

"Well, what did you learn during your studies?"

My lips downturn at the corners. "Didn't you explicitly say no when I asked if you were going to quiz me?"

"Do you always need to answer questions with more questions?" he says. And though a dimpled smirk dusts over his cheeks, I can hear the threat in his tone.

He wants me to take this seriously.

I am.

"A soul-stealer by the name of Emmet B. Mara used the Black Death as a cover for his experiments with magic on humans. He kept detailed journals of his methods, which included attempts at manipulating the circumstances of death."

I recite the facts monotonously. It's another one of Silas's tests; *everything* seems to be a test to him.

"And?" He motions for me to continue.

"And while he was unable to produce his desired results, he did find that his magic reacted poorly to forced commands." I take a breath and a step forward. "Meaning that soul-stealer or not, he hypothesized that the relationship between magic and the fae who wields it is an equal partnership rather than that of a master and servant."

"So, how do you figure you're managing it when he and many others before him could not?"

"I ask it nicely?" I shrug, the half-truth slipping out easily. "I told you as much when we made our deal. My magic knows what it wants. It *wants* to kill. To pull the breath from someone's lungs. To hold a heart in a tight grip and squeeze. To separate flesh from bone. All I've done is convince it to savor the process."

Silas's dark eyes search my face, scanning over it like he's seeing me for the first time. Then he nods.

"Start on the right, going left," he says, pointing to the criminal chained beside me. "Aim for one minute and we'll work our way up to the two-week delay needed to avoid any kind of suspicion from the Seelie."

I swallow the lump that forms in my throat and nod.

And then we get to work.

22

IMOGEN

I'm lost in the grind behind the bar, high off the steady trickle of joy I pull from the room. My skin is flushed and my blouse sticks to my back, damp from running back and forth between patrons and the stockroom. I twirl, bouncing to the band's upbeat music as I return two bottles of liquor to their respective homes on the shelf.

It's good to be back.

A violent shiver shoots down my spine, the distinct rush of arousal pushing past all the other emotions. My head snaps to the couple at the end of the bar, who are deep throating each other's tongues.

I smack the bar with my hand when I reach them, two firm *whacks* that has the couple turning my way with glazed expressions.

"Dance floor, back hallway, or bathroom," I say, pointing in each direction. "But not at the bar. Other people need these seats to wallow and drink in. Got it?"

They share a dazed glance with each other before one mumbles and pulls the other towards the bathrooms. I snort, taking a moment to watch them retreat before getting back to work.

Two more fae take the open seats, and I grab their orders. As I place down the pint of beer and cocktail, a tanned hand rises above those at the other end, calling me over. As I get closer, a smile grows between my cheeks.

"What are you doing here?" I ask, eyes scanning Josie.

She's leaning forward on the bar, the butterfly sleeves of her simple green dress fluttering above the wood. She tucks a strand of her dark brown hair behind her ear; today, the straight strands cut a sharp line across her mid-neck. It's shorter than normal—she must have gotten a fresh cut.

It's a cute look on her.

"I figured I needed a night out. Blow off some steam," she says with a shrug.

I place one hand on my hip and cock a single brow. "Yeah?"

"Mhm," she hums. Josie's head swivels, observant mahogany eyes making quick work of scanning the room and everyone in it.

"Okay," I snort. *She's a shit liar.* "Nora asked you to keep an eye on me while she was gone, didn't she?"

She scrunches her nose, and while she doesn't say it out loud, I know I'm correct.

"I can handle myself, you know," I say.

"I know. She knows that too."

"But."

"*But.*" Josie rocks her head from side to side. "You know how she gets. And why can't I do both? View it as an excuse to hang out like we used to."

I scoff, though excited butterflies float in my belly at her words. I don't think we've spent time alone together since college.

Another patron flags me over, and I give them a nod that I'll be over in a second.

"You mean when we were reckless twenty-somethings with too much to drink and too much to prove?" I say.

"Yeah, except now you're old." Josie clicks her tongue with a snicker.

"I am *not* old," I gape, my hand coming to my chest in mock distraught.

"You're almost thirty," she says. She keeps a straight face, but her eyes sparkle with mirth.

"Thirty is *not* the new three hundred," I say. "And you two aren't that far behind me." Under my breath I add, "Stupid cutoff for school pushed me into the younger year."

"Oh, I know. But soon we'll all be geriatric. The younglings will wonder when the Fading will catch up to us."

We burst into laughter; hers sounds like wind chimes made into music.

"Excuse me—" the same patron calls from my right.

I give Josie a sorry smile and rap my knuckles on the wood in front of her.

"I'll grab you a drink when I'm done with this one."

An hour passes. Between me making drinks for other patrons and Josie sipping on hers, we chat; it's easy, not needing to keep the conversation going long or with any kind of seriousness. Just two friends poking fun at each other and catching up.

It's nice. Simple. Uncomplicated.

Work dies down, the main rush complete. Fae are buzzed from their drinks and craving the respite of the dance floor. Josie and I are huddled over the bar, people watching, when we spot Leo's gap-toothed grin pop up among the partygoers.

"He's really working the room tonight," Josie says.

"Yeah, he's doing good."

"Why is it him out there and not you?" She asks it inno-cently, but those watchful eyes peer into my soul from over the edge of her glass.

"Why do you need to know?" I tease.

"Because I'm curious."

I turn, grabbing Josie's wine of choice from the icebox and pour her another drink. The faerie wine sparkles in the dim light, a maroon whirlpool that I get sucked into.

I haven't told anyone about testing out a transition of power with Leo yet. It's not common for a Sin to pass on the role while they're still alive. It's even less common to pass it to someone outside of the familial line, though it's not like I have any biological family left.

"Sorry, I didn't mean to pry," Josie says, pulling the glass from my hand and taking a large swig.

I shake off the strange trance.

"You're fine," I say. "We're trying something new."

"If you say so, Mo."

Josie's warm eyes dart to the dance floor as a fresh song plays. Excited screeches sound from the gaggle of women jumping up to dance; it isn't a new hit by any means, but there's something about the Charleston that gets alcohol-laden patrons moving.

A ghost of a smile parts Josie's lips.

"You should go dance," I say, wriggling my brows. "Enjoy your *night off.*"

"No. No way," she says. "I'm no good at dancing. Especially without everyone else to shield me."

"It's not about being good, it's about having fun."

She takes a tentative breath, eyes flicking between the dance floor and me.

"Should I?" she asks.

Her cheeks and neck are flushed red from her drink. She's

tipsier than she's letting on. I lean forward to whisper with her conspiratorially, the devious part of me curious to see if I can egg her on.

"I think you should."

"I don't know."

"I'm not going to force you, but I promise I'll whisk you away if you make that big a fool of yourself. *Which you won't.*"

She nods her head, lips pursed in contemplation. Finally, when her eyes meet mine, they shine with determination.

"I think I'm going to go dance."

"Great," I say with a goofy smile.

"Okay." Josie nods as she stands. She wipes her hands on her dress. "I can dance. No problem."

I tap the rim of her glass. "Liquid courage."

"Right," she says, downing the rest of the drink.

A shiver runs down her whole body as she swallows. Slamming the empty glass on the counter, she turns and heads into the throngs of people. Giggles pour out of me as I watch Josie get wrangled into a group of dancing girls; bright grins spread across all their flushed cheeks.

I lose track after a while, but she doesn't leave the dance floor after the first song—or the second, or the third. Seemingly adopted into the gaggle of single women, I leave her to her fun.

After an hour passes and she hasn't come back to say goodbye or get another drink, worry wriggles in my gut. I know she can handle herself, but—

Jeeze, where else did I hear that one tonight?

I refocus on drying the glass in my hands.

Actually, Josie's the most capable of all of us when drunk; I laugh to myself as a college memory flashes in my mind. Some guy wouldn't stop hitting on her after multiple rejections, so she knocked him out cold. It was the three of us out that night

—she, Nora, and I—early on in our friendship and years before any of us were Sins or Seconds.

Still, that little tickle of nerves bounces around my gut.

When the clock strikes one, and there's no Josie to be found, I go check the back hallway where the bathrooms are.

As I turn the corner, I collide with a lean body.

We each go to steady the other, her gripping my waist and me her biceps. Josie's hair is a rumpled mess of flyaway hairs and her lipstick is smeared.

We both freeze.

"Hi," she squeaks.

"*Hi,*" I say.

We both let go of each other; she steps to the right, and I mirror her, then it happens again, but this time we both go left.

"Sorry," I snort.

"It's fine."

A deep pink flush spreads up her neck, this time not from alcohol. She glances behind her, nervously.

"Are you okay?" I say slowly.

"Yep."

"Are you sure?"

"Mhm," she hums, but it's too high-pitched.

I stare at her, trying to stop myself from smiling because I think I know what's going on—and I'm not letting her leave without telling me.

"Why do I not believe you?"

"Because you like to pry when people's answers don't satisfy you," she blurts.

Her hand immediately covers her mouth. A muffled *oops* sounds from behind her fingers. I huff, not knowing whether to laugh or rage.

"I don't know how to respond to that."

"Don't say anything, just forget it," she waves her hands

around my head like she can magic away my memory. "There. Forgotten."

Oh, she is *drunk*.

It's at that moment that a fae woman stumbles out of the bathroom door—a bathroom that is a *single stall*—adjusting the string of pearls around her neck.

"Excuse me," the woman says as she scurries past, casting Josie a sheepish glance.

I didn't think Josie's face could get any redder, but it does.

A devious grin spreads slowly across my lips.

"Did you have sex in my bar's bathroom?"

"I would never," she says. "I'm far too responsible to do something like that."

"It's okay if you did," I tease, trying to hold back my laughter by biting my bottom lip. "Plenty of people do it."

Josie groans, shuffling over to the wall and banging her forehead on it.

"This is embarrassing."

"No, it's not," I say, quickly walking over and rubbing small circles on her back. "It's perfectly normal. You know how many times Nora and I fucked in there?"

"Ew." She casts me a disgusted glare from her periphery.

"Okay, maybe not the best example to have chosen."

Josie groans. "I needed a distraction."

My hand stings at her back, my magic taking in the sharp pinpricks of her stress. I pause in my ministrations.

Josie *never* projects her emotions.

"Joze—"

"It's been a lot. Dealing with, you know, *everything* lately."

Her frustrated groan vibrates against my fingertips, and my gaze softens on her. Josie's the kind of woman who keeps her worries to herself and, at the same time, takes on everyone else's.

It's a wonder she's so composed all the time, honestly.

"Are you sure that you're alright?" I ask.

"Yeah, I am." She tilts her head to the side. No tears well in her eyes, but a sadness shines there alongside the drunk haze. "Sorry. This is weird."

"Don't apologize. I told you I'd whisk you away if you needed. The offer wasn't limited to dancing," I say. "You want to crash upstairs? I baked cookies earlier and can put on a pot of tea once I'm closed out down here."

"No, I couldn't do that—" She launches from the wall, a red mark on her forehead where it was resting against the brick.

I roll my eyes.

"I'd be glad for the company. I've been having a rough go of it too. I'll tell you about it. I could probably use your advice." I cross my fingers over my heart. "Honest."

Josie nods, and I send her upstairs with my key before helping Leo and my staff close the night out.

When I go upstairs an hour later, Josie is already asleep, one arm hanging off the couch and the other thrown over her eyes. A half-eaten cookie sits crumbled on the table next to a full glass of water.

I shake my head. She's going to wake up with a hangover for sure.

I grab a blanket from the basket next to the couch and drape it over her. Josie stirs, a deep sigh filling her chest. I freeze, hoping I don't wake her, but when her lashes flutter, I know I've failed.

Sleepy brown eyes squint up at me, little crow's feet dancing at their corners.

"Caught me," I whisper, dropping the blanket over her.

"Hey," she says, yawning.

Josie sits up, blinking away her nap. She's got this tiny pout when she glances at the coffee table. My lips twist, holding back a giggle.

I don't think I've ever seen sleepy Josie before.

"Scooch," I say, pushing at her legs.

She pulls them up to her chest and under the blanket, allowing me room to sit. I throw my legs up on the table and let out a breath, sinking into the cushions.

"I didn't mean to wake you."

"And I didn't mean to fall asleep," Josie counters. "Downstairs all closed up?"

"Yep."

"Nice."

"Yeah."

A beat of silence passes between us.

"Sorry, again." Josie winces.

I shoot her an incredulous look. "Josie, I do *not* care. You can crash here anytime you need."

"Duly noted," she says.

"So. Do you want to talk about before?" I say tentatively.

Josie shifts, curling up on her side and staring at the half-eaten cookie.

"I know I told you everything would work out okay the other day, but I think I was trying to convince myself too," she says.

"Why? What's got you so worried?"

She shrugs one shoulder.

"I keep thinking about the girl who lost her parents. And the warehouse. We've only been in charge a year and shit's gone sideways. I'm not doing a good enough job protecting everyone."

"There are some things out of your control," I say. "You and Nora are doing the best you can, given the circumstances."

"Nora's on her own warpath," Josie sighs. Her lashes flutter, slow and heavy. "And this Virtue knocking at our door? He's not a good man, Imogen."

"Is any man good?" I joke, but she doesn't laugh.

"You know they're planning to kill him, right?" Josie asks, yawning.

My body goes still.

"What?"

"That's why she and Silas are off training together," she mumbles. "Two orphans set on hunting their fucked-up uncle."

Josie rolls over, head tilted up on the pillow, her eyes closed.

"Wait," I say, my mind still catching up to her words. "They want to kill a Virtue?"

Silas cut off contact with the Seelie years ago. How the hell are they going to kill a Virtue who lives in Avalon?

"Revenge is a sin so sweet they can't help but want a taste," Josie says, yawning for a third time. "And I don't know. I imagine they're figuring out how to do it as we speak."

Shit.

I didn't realize I was projecting my thoughts out to her. There's just something about having Josie in my space that has my guard dropping.

Her eyes open, and those deep brown irises, as wise as the earth, stare right through me.

"So, what's the deal with you and Leo?"

I shake my head, jerking away from Josie's gaze at the change in subject. I pull my legs to my chest, resting my chin on my knees, the thick fabric of my work trousers scraping against my skin.

"The past couple of weeks kind of put things in perspective," I say. My right hand fiddles with the tasseled hem of the blanket. "What Silas had me do, what everyone expects of me as Lust? It's different from what I thought it'd be."

It's a much crueler reality than I expected.

Josie hums. I spare a quick glance and note she's closed her eyes again.

"Are you thinking about passing on the title?" she asks.

"It feels like the right decision. But I'm worried about what everyone will think." I purse my lips. "Do you think we learn to live our lives for those we love and, on the way, forget to live them for ourselves?"

"I don't know if I understand..."

"It might be easier to show you," I say, holding out my hand.

Her eyes open, the deep brown swirling with shock.

She might have poked through my memories when I needed to explain the shit with Silas, but it's not something you make a habit of—offering your mind to someone.

"Okay," she says.

Her nimble fingers thread between mine; her warm palm heats my cold one as they press together.

I show her every doubt I've had. I show her the hundred times Conor reminded me that I was next in line after him. I show her how hesitant my mother was when I brought up the idea of the Den and how proud she was after Conor explained what the bar could do for our House. I show her how little I cried for my mother when she died. And how I could bottle all the tears I shed for my brother.

Her passing didn't hurt nearly as much as his. I'd been brought up to equate my mother's death with Conor's ascension. Her death always meant his dream would be realized.

But they both died in that crash, and I alone remained to pick up the pieces they left behind. I was twenty-five and forced to make an impossible decision while I grieved: take up my family's legacy, my *brother's* dream, or leave it for the vultures to devour.

I pull my hand from Josie's.

"Do you understand now?"

"Better than before. But, Mo, I've never lived for anyone but myself."

So she doesn't get it, not really.

"What about Nora?" I ask, tilting my head so my cheek is resting on my knee.

Josie's brows pinch together. "Nora's different."

"How so?"

"We lost our families young and only had each other. We chose to forge a path together. You had a mom and brother to follow," Josie says plainly.

"But you *both* still followed in Pride's footsteps."

"This life is all we've ever known. To want anything outside of that..." she trails off. "I don't think it's ever crossed Nora's mind to not climb the ladder of power. For me, it's a matter of keeping the one sister I have safe. But I know, in here —" She pats over her heart. "I've chosen that for myself."

I chew my lip. "I see."

"That is all to say," she says on a final yawn, falling into slumber. "Don't talk yourself out of happiness, Mo."

23

NORA

My frustrated growl rips through the air when the fae slumps over in his chair, dead. It's been days of this bullshit, and I have the bodies to prove it. Seven, in fact, sit as sunken statues in front of me, still chained to their chairs.

Wrath's lackeys take them away every night, replacing them with fresh faces each morning. They've all blurred together—the men and women, the clawlike nails and bared teeth, the curses spat onto my skin as I grip their pulses and squeeze.

My fingers press divots into my own cheeks, circling the hinge-point of my jaw. It does little to stave the ache radiating there or the one in my chest.

My magic is writhing and impatient, turned bitter by our asynchrony. It doesn't know how to do what I ask of it, nor do I know how to guide it.

"I don't expect you to get it on the first try." Silas shrugs.

"It's well past the first try," I snap.

Five days of me trying—and *failing*—and Silas has sat in the same chair the entire time, watching all my mistakes. He's so nonchalant, straddling the backwards chair and leaning his chin on his crossed forearms.

"Try the last one, and then we'll take a break," he says, unfazed by my frustration.

"Fine," I say, voice rough as gravel.

I plant my hands on my hips and close my eyes.

Taking in a deep breath, I coax my magic to the surface. It's a snake coiled tight in my gut, refusing my summons.

Please.

It's been a one-sided battle with myself.

I take another breath. In through the nose, hold for a count of four, then out through the mouth.

If I focus hard enough, dig out the root of the issue, then I can unearth the solution. Tackle it the same as any other problem in my life.

I can fix this.

I can fix this.

Why isn't it working?

I work backwards; the facts track across my mind in little lines of text, running across the splotchy darkness behind my closed eyes.

My touch kills.

When I touch them, my magic seeps into them and then it deals damage, and they die.

My touch is the vessel of magic between us. It allows my magic to enter them—

My eyes flick open.

That's it.

Every time I've used my magic, I think of it as an extension of my touch. When I break that physical connection, the magic breaks too, and since my intention *is* to kill, every test subject before me has died.

But maybe, if I think of my magic as an extension of my soul and try to leave a piece of *that* in them... it could work.

Plant the seed of death so that it blooms without your presence.

"I'm going to try something different this time," I say.

The prisoner shifts in his bindings as I approach. Ignoring his struggle, I place my hand on his. My touch is featherlight over his fist as I coax my magic to my fingertips. But instead of it sweeping through his body like a storm, I encourage my magic to mark him. I ask my magic to leave a piece of itself in him, a tattoo on his soul.

I pull my hand back and nothing happens.

But I can feel it thrumming inside him. And yet, he doesn't die. It wraps around his heart, tucking itself between the veins and arteries. Seconds pass and my excitement builds. The tension grows inside me, a taught wire of magic stretching between me and the prisoner before me.

It's strange, to be connected like this to another person.

Sixteen, seventeen, eighteen, nineteen...

Hold fast. Not yet.

The wire snaps, the connection between me and the prisoner breaking, and with it, my magic flows back into me. The fae sputters, heart seizing as my magic wreaks havoc in its departure.

He slumps in his chains.

Letting my frustration get the best of me, I kick the chair holding the dead fae in front of me. The chair tips over, toppling the body onto the ground with a dull *thump*. An irritated growl tears from my throat.

I couldn't even make it to thirty seconds.

Half success may be just as bad, if not worse, than complete failure.

Maybe I need to think of it as an infusion, rather than a mark, like how my mo—

"I don't know why you're kicking the man when he's already down," Silas chirps from behind me. He snaps his silver pocket watch closed, the metallic *click* piercing the air. "Twenty seconds. That's excellent."

I pin him with a glare.

"It's really not," I say.

His lips twitch with bewilderment as he takes in my tense shoulders and clenched jaw. And then he laughs. *Laughs.*

"You are truly something else," he says. He twists in his chair, stretching. His back cracks with the action.

"Don't be facetious."

With a sigh, Silas levels with me. "Look, I get it."

"Do you?"

"You can't fail."

I scoff, pacing towards the door.

I need a smoke.

"Don't scoff at the truth," he calls. "You know that if you fail, then you may bring war on your house, your friends, and your lover. If you fail, you put everything you've ever worked for at risk. But worst of all, *what good are you?*"

I freeze, gooseflesh spreading over my forearms.

"What good are you if you're not constantly performing well? Being the best? *Succeeding?*" He hisses the word like it burns his tongue. "What value do you have then?"

A beat passes where my feet are frozen to the floor; my heart is a frantic beat in my chest as his words hit their mark. I turn my head, Silas's white hair a spec in my periphery.

"I'm done for the day," I say, and though it comes out in more of a whisper, my words echo between us. "Meet me in the library tomorrow morning. I have an idea, but I need more information."

My neck prickles as I leave, and as I close the door behind

me, I peek over my shoulder, finding Silas staring thoughtfully in my direction. Recognition swirls in his black irises.

Does he think he's found a kindred spirit?

If so, he's mistaken.

It's then that I decide I don't like the feeling of his eyes on me.

24

NORA

"**P**ull everything you have on healing. I'll grab us a table."

"Do I at least get a *'please, Silas?'*"

My footsteps come to a halt, and I shoot Silas a glare.

"Seriously?"

I would get them myself, but it would take hours of searching through the rows of shelves. They're ten feet tall and twenty rows deep around the entire study area. Silas, on the other hand, knows exactly where each catalog lives.

Silas shrugs, spinning so he walks backwards between the bookshelves, forcing me to follow. A playful smile tugs at his lips—I've quickly learned over the past week that Silas is a trickster and a brat wrapped into one. He doesn't discriminate with his jabs, subjecting Wrath, the staff, and me to his antics.

"I've been bored. Wrath is holed up in his workshop until all hours of the night, and you only hang out with me when you're killing people."

"This isn't sleepaway camp."

"I mean, it could be," he says.

Silas stuffs his hands in his pockets; his sleeves are rolled up to his elbow, putting the matching tattooed gauntlets that circle his forearms on display. Over the past week I've studied the designs. They're a swath of black linework florals, which seemed an odd choice at first, but they fit him.

"If you're so bored, shadow-walk back to Anwynn."

"Security risk, going back and forth too often."

"Then I don't know how to help you," I say. I stop at the fork in the bookshelves. Turning left goes deeper into the stacks, while turning right leads to the open center of the library. I heave a sigh. "*Please*, will you gather all the books on healing you can find?"

He beams.

"I'll be right back."

It's not long before we're both hunched over stacks of ancient tomes. The downside to Silas having cut off formal contact with the Seelie means that everything in the library is out of date.

A few hours pass with our heads tucked between yellowed pages.

Silas huffs a frustrated sigh, pushing his book away. He's been screening books for me, passing on the ones that may be relevant and tossing the others aside.

"Is any of this making sense to you?" he asks.

"Huh?" I ask, only half paying attention.

I finish the sentence I'm reading and put my pointer finger on the period, marking my place. It's a transcript of an ancient healer's medical journal. Most of the entries are tonic recipes, lists of herbs and solvents, but every couple of pages, there are notes scrawled in the margins.

Don't force it. This one needs time for the magic to settle with the herbs. Make sure they're fresh. Magic connects with the spark of life.

Our magic isn't finite. Don't be afraid to part with a piece of it.

Some make more sense than others, but they all read like a teacher advising their student. They're personal, and I wonder who this journal belonged to before it ended up here.

The entries on infusing tonics don't relay the knowledge I had hoped for. But at the end of the journal, where my finger presses into the page, I find what I'm searching for. It's an entry on tethering—a technique for healing long-term ailments, where the healer establishes a lasting connection between them and their patient. The cursive instructions have my lips tilting upwards.

We're dealing with the bodies, not souls. Hearts, not minds. Remember that your magic can only do so much to bring someone back from the edge. But if you tend to it like a garden, with intention and persistence, their resolve will grow—and with it, your connection.

It will be strange at first, the tether. Unlike tonics, you're not truly parting with a piece of your magic. It's not a gift, but an active lifeline between you, your magic, and your patient. It is a constant draw on your power to keep the connection flowing. Over time, it will settle in the background, but don't lose sight of it for too long. If you do, it'll fade away.

Emotion is the root of our magic. The urge to heal, to save, is tied to that. Therefore, fluctuations will test the strength of your connection.

Tethers are fragile things.

My hand cuts off the rest.

My gaze flicks up and Silas gestures to the open book in front of him.

"This isn't how magic feels. When I use my shadows, it's not a separate entity to carve away at—it's an extension of myself. A fifth limb."

"Maybe it's just not what magic feels like for *you*."

He tilts his head at me. "And it does for you?"

"My magic..." I search for the right words. I hadn't realized it before now, but the way I was taught to use my magic is different from the way it flows through my body. "Think of it as a second soul that I can manipulate. It's part of me, but it also isn't."

"How strange," Silas murmurs. He fiddles with the small silver earring dangling from his lobe. "I wonder why yours is so similar to theirs."

I drop my gaze back to the journal. "Death and life are two sides of the same coin, are they not?"

Silas's lips part, but he's cut off by Wrath's voice calling through the stacks of books.

"Ah, good. You're both here."

Wrath appears seconds later. I sigh, giving up on keeping my place and shutting the book. I want to reread the whole section over anyway.

"He has emerged from his cave!" Silas says, giving Wrath a cheeky side-eye. "Nice of you to finally pay us a visit."

Wrath's expression is less than amused. "I have a prototype ready."

He drops a bundle of fabric on the table, sheer and black, right over the book in front of me.

"What's this?" I ask.

Silas leans forward, eyes glinting with delight.

"Those," Silas drawls. "Are your new gloves. Right?"

He looks up at Wrath, to which Wrath nods.

"Try them on," Silas commands. There's a wicked edge to his excitement.

I quickly shuck off my leather gloves. Then I pick up one of Wrath's, and it unfurls, hanging long and glossy between my fingers. I pull it on, though it scrunches around my forearm, fighting for space with my blouse. These sleeves were not made to pair with elbow-length gloves.

I rub the fabric between my fingertips; they're like no fiber I've touched before, as if air and silk were woven together.

"They'll appear and feel like real gloves, but there isn't any actual separation between your skin and who you touch. So be careful," Wrath says, a glint of pride in his eyes as he explains.

My brows knit together as I examine the dark fabric.

"How?" I ask.

"Shadows. It took a while to realize the answer was simple." He holds his hand up and a twirl of inky black dances between his fingers. "If they can be corporeal one moment and not the next, if I can mold them into barriers and use them to travel across great distances, then why can't we apply the same logic to something more mundane?"

I flex my fingers, and the fabric shifts over my skin. It's subtle, but one minute they're real and the next they don't exist at all. As if they're merely a shadow on my skin.

"I have to admit, it's quite genius," I say.

"Thank you." Wrath bristles under the praise. "They're connected to my magic, so I'll know when to phase them in and out."

The gloves vanish, dissipating into fading tendrils of shadow around my fingers.

"Will you teach me how to do it too, Robbie?" Silas asks, staring up at Wrath with wide puppy-dog eyes.

Silas has developed a habit of using both our given names. And while it still makes me uncomfortable, I can't help but chuckle at how I'm not the lone victim of his larks.

Wrath's frown deepens. "Fine."

"Oh, we also need more people to test these out on," Silas adds.

"You ran out of prisoners already?"

"Mhm."

Wrath levels me with a glare. "You're going through them

too fast. At this rate, the Royal prisons will be empty, and we'll have to go catch Seelie exiles."

"Oh, that's a good idea. We should test it on some Seelie," Silas says.

"It wasn't meant to be a suggestion. That's a huge security risk, bringing one here."

"I don't think it matters." I cut the two of them off as I stand, tucking my book under my arm. "The next test will work."

Wrath held up his part of this plan. Now it was my turn to prove myself. Between the knowledge tucked in this book and the power simmering in my gut, I have everything I need.

25
NORA

That night, I'm plagued by dreams.

They're nightmares that could be memories or memories that could be nightmares; they all blur together. Even when they're smattered with inconsistencies, they're too close to the truth.

I'm carried across the house, one arm banded around my back and another under my bum. I latch onto my mother's waist with both legs.

Her footsteps change from thuds on the stair-runner to clacks on kitchen tile.

She puts me down, and I'm surprisingly steady on my feet.

"Elenora, darling?"

Hands caress my face; thumbs brush over the plump apples of my cheeks.

"I need you to talk to me, baby. What happened?" My mother's voice is soft but tense. Her hands try to pull my face to meet hers, but my neck is stiff. My gaze is rooted to the ground, where my black Mary Janes and white socks butt up against her knees. "Can you look at me, Nora?"

I blink, and I'm not looking at my shoes, but the blank eyes of my nanny staring up at me. I blink again and the world is back to patent leather, tile, and the fabric of my mother's moss-green dress.

A door slams shut, and wet, heavy footsteps follow.

"What's wrong?" My father's voice rings in the room. "I came as fast as I could."

My mother holds me, cradling my head to her chest.

"I'm sorry. I know I'm not supposed to call the warehouse unless it's an emergency. But I didn't know what to do," my mother whispers. "Her magic came in."

"Is it not the same as—"

"No," my mother is quick to cut him off. "Go upstairs. You'll see."

My father curses under his breath. I don't know how long it takes, but soon enough, he's back in the kitchen.

"It'll be fine," he says to my mother. "Don't tell anyone else. I'll take care of the rest."

My father's rough hand strokes my cheek, much like my mother's did moments ago. It's still damp from being out in the storm, but it isn't cold because the warm tickle of his magic spreads from his fingertips. It makes my shoulders un-scrunch and fall away from my ears.

Everything was so loud inside my head, but now it's dulled.

"Nora? Darling, are you okay?"

I look up and into the green eyes of my mother, then to the soft reassuring smile of my father. Suddenly my cheeks are wet, and my father wipes them off.

"I didn't mean to," I squeak. "W—We were playing a game, and when I lost, I got mad and then—"

"It's okay, baby girl," he says, and he repeats it to soothe my crying as I'm pulled into his tight embrace. "Take your time and tell me slow."

"I was mad and then I felt weird. In my tummy. And then I

touched her and—" The sob gets caught in my throat. "I didn't mean to do it. I didn't mean to."

"I know." My father's large hand strokes from the crown of my head to the nape of my neck. "I know you didn't mean it."

I don't know how long we sit there, on the cold kitchen floor, with my father running his hand over my hair and hugging me. At some point we move to the couch, and I'm pulled into my mother's lap.

They whisper comforts in my ear, trying to soothe me, but I can't pull my stare from my hands.

I am unable to move, frozen with fear. My hands are sticky and red.

Why are they red?

The scene shifts, and I realize it's not fear, but helplessness swelling within me.

A lash of leather slices my forearms. Straining against the iron cuffs around my wrists, I bite back a groan.

I can't show my pain. I can't let my shields fall. That's the only way this ends.

But I can feel her magic in my head; it doesn't hurt, but it's strange. An entity that's other sliding under my skull.

My gaze locks on a ten-year-old Josie; while her stare is perfectly blank, every time the leather strikes my skin, her fingers twitch. It's her tell.

The red welts heal over only to be replaced by two more.

While she hasn't been in the chair, she's been at the mercy of Pride's tests for as long as I. She knows she's lucky she doesn't need to train her mind. She's already powerful enough to break past his shields if she wanted to—though she hasn't told him that.

She told me, though.

We keep each other's secrets, Josie and I.

At night, we sneak into the kitchen and steal leftover bread from supper, toasting it over the hearth in my room. Sometimes, we hide in the room next to Pride's office, and we press our ears to the vents, straining to hear what he says to the other Houses. We're too young to be included—we haven't passed our test of loyalty yet.

And once, even when Pride told us not to, we showed each other our wings. Hers were black as night. The feathers were soft as velvet under my fingertips.

She didn't want to touch mine, but that's okay.

We pinky promised we wouldn't show anyone else. We were sisters then. Not by blood, but by choice.

Josie shakes her head, and Pride sighs. Fatigue weighs me down, my eyelids heavy, but I can't lose consciousness, or this will go on longer.

"I can still get past," Josie says. "They fall as easily as blowing down a tower of cards."

"Nora," Pride scolds. "You must learn to keep your mental shields up and strong."

"I'm trying." My voice is hoarse from screaming.

"Try harder," he says. And strikes again.

Pride thinks that if I can manage blocking Josie while in pain, no one could ever break through my barriers.

Hours later, when it's done and I've passed to his satisfaction, I slump in my bindings. My lids fall closed—I have no strength left to keep them open.

Josie comes closer; I'm lifted from the chair and cradled in tiny arms on the cold floor.

Josie holds me.

I know she thinks that tears will come, but I have no tears left to shed. Especially not for myself. I'll let the sky pity me, cry for me.

I didn't choose to go down this path, but I choose to walk it now.

The scene shifts, the hazy world of memories and dreams tilting around me.

The scars on my back tingle—the phantom pains berate me.

I blink; this time, I'm not in my body. I watch on, a ghost haunting my own memory.

I don't see two ten-year-olds cradling each other in a dank concrete cellar, but two sixteen-year-olds, kneeling side by side. They're too young to be sacrificing such an intimate part of themselves for the trust of one man.

"You wish to pledge yourselves to House Pride?" he asks. His voice echoes through the cellar, an ancient rumble. "Once you do this, your loyalty to this House will be absolute. You will tie yourself to House Pride until death."

Josie's lips move, then mine utter the same pledge, though I can't hear the words. The dream is silent save for Pride's voice, deep and cavernous.

My wings are pierced through with iron. Blood runs down my back, twin rivers bracketing my spine. These are wounds that will scar; the iron blades mark us as survivors.

I scream when he hacks at my back—I don't mean to, but the pain is blinding. I see white, my whole world a blank piece of parchment.

Josie grips my hand, and I grip hers, nails digging divots into her palm.

And when the wounds have clotted and my back is bandaged, I stand on shaky legs. I glance down at Josie, and she stares up at me. She nods and closes her eyes, at peace with her decision, with our promise to each other.

I try to tune out her screams, but their song is carved into me like a record. Trace over the dips of my scars, and you'll hear her cries in harmony with mine. They are the same track, the same haunting melody.

As they bandage Josie, I stare at my hands.

I will never be able to wash the red from under my fingernails.

It's always there, an invisible brand. No matter how many times I soap and scrub, it never disappears.

I toss and turn under sweat-dampened covers. Each wink of sleep is as restless as the last; behind my lids, hours pass, but for my body, it's only minutes between each hellish memory.

At one point, I crack the window, hoping the mountain chill will soothe my heated skin and save me from my nightmares.

It doesn't work.

There are no telephones here, so I bat away the brief thought to ring Imogen—she'd probably still be awake, closing out the Den at this time of night. I opt for the next best thing: a cigarette and a cup of tea. One soothes the body, and one soothes the soul.

The mountain is quiet as I pad through the halls, the smooth stone cold on my bare feet. My steps are near silent but still manage to echo against the rounded ceiling.

When I reach the kitchen door, I pause, hearing soft murmurs and laughs on the other side. Pressing my ear to the door, I try to make out the low mumblings, but their voices are muffled. I don't wish to interrupt anyone, but it *is* nearly three in the morning.

If they wanted privacy, they could have retired to their rooms.

I push open the door and freeze.

The kitchen is small but still large enough to fit a long wooden prep table with two benches on either side. Silas and Wrath are huddled over two half-empty bottles of whiskey at the head of the table, drunk off their asses.

A wet stain on the wood shines under the warm candlelight, the evidence of one, or both, of them having spilled some of their drink.

They both turn towards me as the door hinges squeak shut; Silas's cheeks are flushed pink, while Wrath's neck flushes a deep tomato red.

I curse under my breath, more to myself than at them, but Silas hears me, his attention turning my way.

"Nora!" Silas says, far too loud for such a late hour. I flinch at the sound, turning my head to see Wrath wince.

Silas murmurs a sorry to Wrath.

I don't linger in my frozen state, deciding it is better to get in and get out as fast as possible. I move towards the gas range stove and grab the kettle from its hook, refocusing on my task.

"I just wanted some tea," I say, lifting the kettle for evidence.

The two men behind me volley back and forth, sounding like chirping birds in the morning.

"Do you want tea?"

"I could go for some tea. Do *you* want tea?"

"I think I want tea. Nora, can you also make us some tea?"

"Gods, help me," I say under my breath. I don't bother answering their request, simply adding more water to the kettle.

The gas stove ticks on, a small flame flickering into existence. I plop the kettle down on top of it, then I open the cabinets, searching for mugs. They're all miss-matched, which is odd, given this is royal housing. Shouldn't Silas have this stocked with porcelain dishes and matching enchanted cups like his castle in the city?

I go to the pantry, pulling three bags of tea. I drop one cloth bag of bundled leaves into each mug, while the two men behind me—*boys, really*—whisper to each other. My ears twitch to make out their slurred words.

With nothing left to do but stare at the kettle and wait for it to boil, I turn around and face Silas and Wrath.

Their whispers stop. They both stare at me with strange expressions.

Silas speaks first, eyes flicking over me quickly.

"You're barefoot."

"And you're drunk."

A lazy smile dimples his cheek. "I think that's a matter of opinion."

"Well, I'd say my opinion is that you're smoked. Both of you."

My eyes cut to Wrath, and he bristles, crossing his arms over his chest with a pout.

"Are you judging us?" he says.

I laugh through my nose, shaking my head. "Not in the way you think."

"You're always so judgy," he grumbles under his breath.

"Oh-*kay*," I drawl.

So, Wrath is an honest drunk.

An awkward beat passes between the three of us where Wrath avoids my gaze, and Silas gets a devilish gleam in his eyes.

"We were celebrating today's achievement. But then, Robbie here made a bet that he could drink a half liter faster than me," Silas says, rolling his glass between his hands.

"*You* were the one who made that wager," Wrath says, seething. He points an accusing finger at Silas, so close that I think he's going to poke Silas's eye out. "I had to say yes otherwise you'd pull the king card on me—" He hiccups. "And don't call me that, *especially in front of her.*"

Silas turns to me with that *I told you so* smirk plastered across his face. "Robbie's very fun to rile up."

"I can see you enjoy doing that."

Another moment passes in awkward silence. The stove's heat sends warm waves up my back, which has finally cooled from my nightmares. I cross my arms over my chest, matching Wrath. His glare has lessened, but he's still visibly unhappy to have me interrupting.

"So, who won?" I ask.

"What?" Wrath says.

"*Who won?*" I raise my brows at the two, head tilting to the bottles.

They share a look, the one that Josie and I share often—the one where two friends have a conversation with nothing but their eyes and a tilt of their head.

And then they break out into laughter. It fills the air; the deep timbre of it matches the warmth of the room. The illustrious Unseelie King and the deadly militia leader, boiled down to giggling boys.

I wait, unblinking, waiting for their laughter to subside.

"Neither, unfortunately," Silas says on a wheezing breath. "I got a smidge animated and knocked our glasses over. They spilled, and we lost our place. We settled for a draw."

"Ah, so he's a cheat too?" I volley to Wrath.

His eyes narrow on me, suspicious, but I can see the agreeing smile twitch at the corner of his lips. I might not like the man, but I can see what Silas is trying to do here. He wants to break the vitriol between Wrath and I. But, to what end?

Isn't that always the question with Silas?

"Yeah, he is," Wrath relents.

"You wound me with such accusations," Silas croons, one hand spreading across his chest. "I'd never cheat."

"Uh-huh," Wrath mutters as he takes a swig straight from the bottle of liquor.

"Did you know Wrath was named after his father?" Silas asks, turning to me, wounded facade gone and replaced with foxlike cunning. "He hated his father. So, he prefers his formal title. Makes me use it even though we grew up together."

"Are you going to tell her my entire life story?" Wrath snaps.

Silas shrugs. "Why not? Don't you know hers?"

"You know my facts, Silas." I roll my eyes. "Not my story."

At least, not the whole one.

Thankfully, the kettle sings: a high-pitched whistle piercing the air.

I busy myself with filling the cups with hot water, watching it leech color from the tea bags and fill my nose with a sweet aroma. I don't bother trying to find sugar or cream; they can have theirs plain or not at all. I bob the tea bags in and out a few times for each mug until it's steeped evenly.

Grabbing two, I walk them to the men and place one in front of each. I get a murmured *thank you* from Wrath, and I shoot him a tight smile.

When I've got my hot mug tucked between my hands, the hot ceramic nearly burning my palms, I turn towards the door.

"Sit with us," Silas calls from behind me, and I freeze.

Pivoting, I eye Silas through the steam floating from my mug. He tilts his head to the side, motioning to the empty seat beside him and across from Wrath.

"Sit."

The word is devoid of the tipsy-humor I've come to expect from him tonight. I war with the command, weighing the consequences of disobedience that his tone warns against. Then I remember what I have waiting for me beyond the kitchen door—an empty bedroom with only my mind for company—and my decision is easily made.

Without a word, I pad over to the bench and sit, leaving about a foot's distance between me, the end of the bench, and Silas.

Now that I'm sitting with them, I notice their state of dress. Their suit jackets are strewn lazily over the bench at Wrath's side. Both their shirtsleeves are rolled to their elbows, and their collars are unbuttoned, revealing a sliver of dark hair on Wrath's chest and a peak of black tattoos on Silas's.

"So," Silas says, gently blowing on his tea. His rings clink as he taps his fingers on the ceramic mug. "You both killed your fathers. Maybe we could talk about that."

"*Adoptive* father," I correct.

Wrath groans, his head falling to the table with a *thunk*.

"Why are you groaning?" Silas says, voice pitching up an octave. "They were both assholes that the Court is better off without. I would have found a reason to get rid of them at some point, but you both beat me to it."

Wrath's hands run through his hair, tugging on the strands as his head lifts. He glares at Silas. Though it conveys more exhaustion than anger.

"Silas wants us to get along," I say to Wrath, taking a sip of my tea. It's too hot to taste and it burns my tongue until it tingles.

"Clearly," Wrath deadpans.

"Why?" I quirk a brow at Silas.

"Because we need to be a team if we want to kill Patience," Silas says, matter-of-fact.

"Are we not a team by nature of cooperating?" I ask.

Silas shakes his head. "I need you two to trust each other in case something goes awry."

"I trust in your desire to kill him and Wrath's desire to follow suit. Is that not enough?"

I place my mug on the table. I pause, and Silas purses his lips. His gaze slides down my arms to my hands, where my ungloved thumbs run small circles on the ceramic.

"I'd prefer it if there was a stronger bond than that," he says.

"Friendship doesn't come easily to me. And I imagine it doesn't for him either," I say. I meet Wrath's eye. "Though I am curious, why *don't* you like me? I understand why Envy doesn't care for me, but what have I ever done to you?"

Wrath sighs, cheek resting on his forearms. "I see you for what you are, Pride. Someone willing to sacrifice others to get what you want. As I did."

Silas hums over his tea. "That's very insightful, Robs."

"So, that's all? I remind you of yourself?"

"Unfortunately."

I mash my lips together, forming a tight-lipped smile to hold back my laughter. It's such a silly reason, but it gives me the sudden urge to mess with him.

"Well, I don't like you because you always have a frown on your face," I say, leaning forward. "And you seem like a big stick-in-the-mud."

Wrath frowns, deep lines marring each side of his mouth. Silas cackles, loud and uncontrolled. He gets the joke. Wrath doesn't.

"I don't frown that much," Wrath says.

"Yes, you do," Silas and I both say at the same time.

"And I can be fun!"

"He can be," Silas says. "He wasn't always so grumpy and responsible."

"I'll believe it when I see it," I say.

"Don't tease him with a good time," Wrath groans, head hitting the table again. At this rate, he's going to have a bruise blooming on his forehead. "The man loves a challenge."

Silas and I share a conspiratorial look, finding a strange kind of common ground in teasing Wrath.

"Unfortunately, Wrath," I say. "So do I."

"Here," Silas says, pushing the bottle of whiskey towards me. "You need to catch up. I have an idea."

We come to a stop at a large metal door, so simple compared to the intricately carved wooden ones around the rest of Mt. Bramble. The hinges squeak as Silas opens it, and freezing midnight air rushes past us, ruffling our hair.

He swings his arm out to let Wrath and me pass; I take a tentative step out and the boots I had grabbed from my room crunch on a dusting of snow. I tug my long wool coat tighter over my pajamas, thankful for the whiskey flush providing me an extra layer of warmth underneath it. The air is sharp and dry, and my tongue darts out to lick my lips against the chill.

It's dark, but the stars and moon are bright, casting us in soft, cool-toned light.

The door swings shut behind us, the boom of metal-on-metal echoes in the small valley we stand in. On either side, jagged rock juts up into the mountainside. It's a long, natural alleyway with snow-covered targets set up along the length of the gorge.

It's a makeshift target range.

"Is *this* when you kill me?" I ask, turning to Silas.

He barks a laugh, making his way to an overhang against the back wall of our little carved-out spot in the mountainside. Shadows curl in his hand, forming a key that he uses to unlock a tall and thin cabinet.

"You're known to be a good shot," he says.

"Yes." I stretch out the word with suspicion. "And?"

He pulls out two rifles, a wild grin stretched over his teeth as he holds them up.

"I'd like to make a bet," he says.

"A bet," I scoff, peering up at the mountains around us.

Wrath groans, raising his hand like a grade-school student. "Can I not participate? I want to go sleep."

"No, you having fun is the whole point," Silas says. "You and me versus Nora. The loser has to make the rest of us dinner tomorrow."

"What's the point of having a cook if you're just going to do it yourself?" I ask.

"Humor me."

Silas hits me with puppy-dog eyes so wide, they could convince the gods to open the gate to their realm.

I look to Wrath for help in turning Silas down, but he shakes his head in miserable solidarity.

"It's very hard to tell him no," Wrath says, taking a direct swig from the whiskey bottle he brought up for us. "He'll keep pushing until you cave."

"Hey—some would call that determination," Silas chirps.

I sigh.

Fuck it. We're already out here.

"Fine."

I walk forward and grab one of the rifles from Silas.

"Attagirl," he croons.

Rolling my eyes, I walk away, going through movements I know by heart. I check the gun for ammo, peer through the scope—rubbing it clean with my trousers since it's covered in dust—and unlock the safety.

Silas uses his shadows to clear off all the targets; the strange wisps of night dance along the valley in stark contrast to the snow, much like Silas's own visage.

We take our places at a low wall that divides the space,

settling over a faded marking on the ground. Wrath stands to my right and Silas sidles up to the other side of him.

I click my tongue at Wrath, holding out my hand.

"What?" he says.

I nod my head at the whiskey. "Gimme some of that. I'm fucking cold."

Wrath stares down at his hand, as if he forgot what he was holding.

"Oh."

He hands it over and I go to take a swig.

"Wait!"

I pause. "What?"

"Waterfall it."

"What?"

"Her spit won't kill you," Silas groans. Then he stiffens, curious concern slacking his features. "Wait, can it?"

"No," I say. "Are you stupid?"

"I don't like other people's germs," Wrath says, wincing. "Please waterfall it."

"Gods help me," I murmur, tipping the bottle back without it touching my lips. I don't pour too much down my throat, but it still makes me cough as I swallow it down. I hand the bottle back to Wrath and then wipe my mouth with the back of my hand. "Happy?"

He nods genuinely.

Asshole.

"Alright. Every round, we'll each get one shot. Start at the closer targets then move our way back. Best of five wins," Silas says. "You get the five on the left and we get the five on the right."

"You each get five, or are you sharing the five between both of you?"

"Each of us."

"So, your team gets ten shots? Hardly fair."

"I really don't have to participate," Wrath says, but we ignore him.

"Fine, we'll both shoot but only count the best of both of our shots."

"That's still not quite fair, but fine," I say. "No using your shadows to help guide your bullets."

"I wouldn't dare to cheat like that."

"Wrath would argue differently." I point at the man.

"I would," Wrath agrees with me.

"That's because I *would* cheat against him—it gets him all frustrated," Silas says.

"And you wouldn't cheat with me because?"

"I already make you frustrated by existing."

To that, I have no response. He is right.

"Fine. Let's do this."

I pull the gun to my shoulder and set my eye to the scope. Locking on the target, I take a steadying breath before pulling the trigger—the pop echoes through the small valley.

It's hard to see the target, but I know that I hit the bullseye.

I roll my shoulders back, tucking the gun at my side and cocking a brow at Silas.

"Your turn."

He chuckles, shaking his head as he brings his own rifle to his shoulder. His stance is stable, strong; he's familiar with a gun. It's not surprising, given most fae use modern weapons, though I'm off-put by his casual demeanor about it.

His shot rings out, echoing between the mountains.

I hope we don't cause an avalanche.

But no snow comes crashing down over us as we continue. Wrath holds his own, despite his drunk grumblings every time he pulls the gun to his shoulder. We go back and forth, taking our time, until Wrath and Silas's final shot rings out.

I smile when we make our way to each of the targets, tallying who got a closer shot for each round. It's close—closer than I would have liked. Three-two, with me coming out on top. And while I know I have the skill to beat them, I can't help but wonder if Silas went easy on me. As if he knew I needed a win.

"I hope you didn't let me win to be nice."

"Gods no," Silas scoffs, setting his gun down. He leans back on the wall, putting his arm around Wrath, who sits on top of it with the whiskey on his lap. Wrath winces when Silas jostles him. "I let you win so I could force you to socialize with us."

I huff a laugh, joining them on the ledge and letting my feet dangle. My soul feels playful in the moonlight, my body lighter than before, the lingering shadow of my nightmares nowhere to be found under the stars.

"The wager was that the loser had to cook. You didn't say anything about the winner needing to stay for the meal," I say.

Wrath cackles at my technical retort, the deep timbre filling the gorge.

"It seems I might win you over yet," I say, bumping my shoulder into Wrath's.

"Say that again when I'm of clearer mind."

"Yeah, I'm sure you'll be frowning at me again before sunrise," I say. "But that's okay. I'll still be a bitch in the morning too."

Silas gives us a suspicious side-eye while reaching into his jacket pocket. He pulls out a pack of smokes and a lighter, reaching over Wrath to offer me both. I pluck a cigarette from the pack, but shake my head at the lighter, pulling my own from where it lives in my jacket pocket. He shakes his head with amusement before sticking a cigarette between his lips.

"I didn't know you smoked," I say.

Clicking open the lighter, I ignite the flame and hold it

close, shielding it from the wind with my free hand. When it's back in my pocket, I shake out my hands, the cold having made the joints stiff and numb.

"It's a new habit," he says begrudgingly. "I recently found myself craving the taste of smoke on my tongue."

Smoke curls around us in silence, mixing with the cloudy puffs of our breath.

I close my eyes, letting the burning embers warm my face —such an honorable little war the cigarette rages against the chilly mountain air. It's unexpected, the stillness we linger in. It's what three friends would do, not three strangers-turned-colleagues-turned-co-conspirators.

It doesn't last more than a few minutes before the itch to leave twitches through me. The one that warns me that the quiet is getting too loud.

I flick the half-smoked cigarette onto the ground and stand, smashing it into the snow with my boot.

"Well. This has been less than pleasant, but better than terrible," I say, retreating towards the metal door. "Goodnight."

"Night," Wrath parrots back to me.

"Sweet dreams, Nora," Silas says to my back.

26

IMOGEN

The middle of the pencil is a bumpy mess where my teeth dig into it. I chew on the wood despite Josie telling me a hundred times that I'm going to get sick from the paint.

"What do you think about a fruit theme?" I say, releasing the pencil from my mouth. I jot down *fruit* with a few question marks after it onto my notepad. "And you can source us some unique human ones no one has heard of for signature cocktails."

"That could be fun," Josie says from the kitchen.

I asked her to come over to help ideate, given how amazing her collaboration was with Gluttony's restaurant, but we haven't gotten anywhere. My journal is full of crossed out thoughts and scribbled ideas that haven't gotten me any closer to finding the "it-factor" we need to make this new place special.

It needs *something*, otherwise it's a copy of the Den. Which, at this point, is probably better than any of the ideas I have.

I groan, flopping back on the couch and chucking my feet over the arm. The journal falls to the ground with a *thunk* when I fling my arm out, and the pencil rolls across the floor and under the coffee table. Blood rushes to my head as I lay, tilted back.

"All these ideas are terrible," I say.

"I don't think they're that bad," Josie says, coming back from the kitchen with the bottle of wine she uncorked and two glasses. I watch as an upside-down Josie sets them on the table and pours herself a glass, all the while smiling down at me and my dramatics. "But if it doesn't feel right, then it doesn't feel right. What kind of energy are you going for?"

"Energy?"

Josie curls up onto the armchair next to the couch, tucking her feet under her butt. She's dressed casually, in work overalls and a cotton button-down with the sleeves rolled up; I'm no different, wearing a plain polo and wool sport knickers.

Am I riding a horse any time tonight? No. But they are comfortable.

"The Den is alluring because it's dark and indulgent. You can get lost in anonymity on the dance floor or cozy up in a booth with friends," she says over the lip of her glass. "What do you want this one to be?"

I gaze up at the ceiling—the white slab of sheetrock is no different from my mind: blank.

"It's okay if you don't have an answer right now."

I roll my eyes. "Alright, miss mind-reader."

"It's not my fault you're easy to read," Josie snorts.

I twist, turning onto my stomach and propping my chin on my forearms.

"You think so?" I ask, genuinely curious.

Josie shrugs one shoulder. "Maybe not generally, but to me."

"Hm," I hum. "So, what am I thinking about right now?"

I narrow my eyes at her and think hard about cherries.

"That's not how it works," she laughs, tucking her short hair behind her ear.

"Lame."

"You don't want me rummaging around inside your head, searching for answers, trust me."

"Is said rummaging any different from what you've done with me before?"

"Eh, you already had everything you wanted to show me front and center. There wasn't much digging involved." She tilts her head back and forth. "Nora says it's a tickle in her brain when I search for something. Others don't even notice. So, I think it depends."

"Interesting." I push up into a sitting position and lean forward to pour myself some wine. "Speaking of Nora..." I drawl as I top off the glass. "I was thinking."

"You were? Wow, that's great."

"Oh, fuck off." I smack her knee, but she snickers. "I was thinking about getting Nora a special gift for Solstice."

"Yeah?"

"But I need your help to get it."

"Okay..." Josie quirks one thin brow, as if to say *go on*.

I take a gulp of my wine, and the refreshing notes of pear burst on my tongue. My smile is tight, knowing she isn't going to be happy with what I'm about to ask.

"Because it's on the other side of the Veil." I wince.

"What? Why?"

"I know how much she likes her guns, and I want to get her a personalized one," I say, tracing lazy circles around the lip of my glass. I smile when a crystal note emerges from the glass when I swipe *just* right. "There's this shop, apparently, that will engrave them."

Josie sets her glass down and plants both feet on the hardwood floor. She leans her forearms on her knees and levels me with narrowed eyes.

"How do you know about this?"

"*Well*," I start. "You know how you keep sending Wes to watch the bar despite me not needing a bodyguard? I refuse to let him stand there like a statue, so we got to talking."

"I'm going to murder that boy," Josie murmurs on a sigh.

"No, you won't."

"Of course, I won't," she levels. "Doesn't mean I won't scold him for inviting a civilian across the Veil."

"So, you will take me?" I say, excitement raising my voice a note. I push all the hope I can into my wide eyes and pouty, quivering lip.

"Mo, that's not—"

"Please, please, please, plea—"

She huffs a sigh, relenting. "Fine."

I squeal. "Thank you!"

"I might not murder Wes, but Nora's definitely going to murder *me* when she gets back and hears about this."

"No, she won't. I won't let her."

"And there's no way I can convince you to let me send one of the guys to do this for you?"

"Nope. I want to do it myself," I say with cheery confidence.

"Fine. But we're bringing the guys too. Human-side, you do need bodyguards. It's not only the Seelie out there we need to worry about."

"Wes said—" Josie hits me with one of her infamous reprimanding glares and my mouth snaps shut. "I can compromise."

We head across the Veil two days later.

My knee bumps up and down as Wes drives us through the streets of the human city. It's not terribly different from Anwynn, but the tall buildings are colder and the sky is grayer, as if the vibrancy of life has been drained from the air. We stop at an intersection, watching swaths of hat and scarf-clad pedestrians rush across the streets to work.

"I'm glad you took my recommendation, Lust," Wes says from the driver's seat. He meets my eye through the rearview mirror of the Cadillac, red cheeks plumped into a dimpled smile. "The owner's workmanship is excellent. You'd think he was fae. Trust me, you won't regret this."

"I've been looking forward to it," I say. "Thank you for accompanying us."

"When Boss says jump, you jump." He laughs awkwardly, eyes turning back to the road. "And who can say no to a Sin like you either?"

"You've got him quite chatty," Josie murmurs out of the side of her mouth, quiet enough for only me to hear as we sit huddled in the back seat together.

I lean my head towards her, whispering on a snicker, "Not my fault if he wants to please me."

"Uh-huh," she deadpans. "You and Leo aren't trying to snatch him for your House, are you?"

"I wouldn't do that."

She quirks a brow at me accusingly, but I haven't thought to poach the young talent for my House. There's not much value for those who can wield shadows in House Lust; empaths such as Josie, on the other hand, are a goldmine.

"Sin's honor," I add, fingers crossing over my chest.

Josie huffs a laugh, shaking her head as the car jerks to a stop.

"I'll let you two out here. Shop's right there." Wes points through the window across the street to an overhang with a tarnished metal sign shaped like a revolver dangling over the doorway. The shop window has *Sal's Gunsmith* painted in bold letters on the glass. "I will park the car and then stand guard outside."

Josie and I hurry out of the car, and I throw a quick thank you to Wes before shutting the door.

"This is exciting," I say as I pull Josie across the crosswalk, looking both ways before skipping across the white lines.

"Don't get your hopes up," Josie says. "The humans are tough bargainers. At least, the ones I deal with on a regular basis are."

I scoff as I twist the door handle to the shop; a bell chimes above my head as we enter, rushing out of the cold. I untie my scarf, letting it hang over my shoulders and down the front of my jacket.

"Josie, you should know better by now." I wink. "I always get the deal I want."

The distinct tang of metal and smoke fills my nostrils as I take in the rifles sitting upright on shelf-lined walls. In front of each rack are glass display cases, showing off revolvers and antique paraphernalia—little pieces of human history.

A bloody history, I think, then shake my head. *Nope. Don't think about the death part. Think about Nora's smile when she opens it on Solstice.*

"Now, what are two pretty young ladies like yourselves doing in here?" an ancient Yankee voice calls from the back of the shop.

The man pops out of a back door—likely where his workshop lives—and wipes his wrinkled hands off on a dirtied rag before tossing it behind the checkout counter. He shuffles forward, hands on his hips, where an oil-stained apron is tied around his waist.

I let my magic unfurl around me, projecting an amiable, compliant aura.

"I am in need of a gift for a special someone," I say. "And I was hoping you'd be able to help me with that."

Immediately, a gap-toothed smile spreads across his cheeks.

"Oh yeah? What are you thinking of?" He walks forward to the glass display cases. "Do they go upstate to hunt? Or are you looking for more of a collectible?"

I open my mouth, pausing, realizing that I don't know any of the proper terms.

I should have asked Wes more questions before this. I don't want Josie thinking I'm incompetent.

"I'm open to your suggestions," I say, leaning forward conspiratorially. "All I require is that it's somewhat small, and I can have something engraved on it."

"Ah," he croons. "Lovebirds." He rummages for keys in his pocket to unlock the case in front of us. "I've got just the thing."

It doesn't take long for the man to show me a few options and get my order placed. He's quite cute, the way he fusses over the guns, his knotted knuckles running over the metal with care as he explains what makes each unique.

Most of it goes over my head—but I nod and smile, nonetheless. When he pulled out the more modern model, with its sleek gray gunmetal and wooden inlay on the handle, I knew it belonged to Nora.

When he shuffles to the counter to write down the details,

I turn to find Josie staring at a shiny silver and gold western-looking revolver in a case.

I lean forward, my mouth near the shell of her ear.

"Do you want that one?"

Josie startles, jerking away from me. "You can't sneak up on me like that."

I snort. "Aren't you the one always telling the rest of us to be more aware of our surroundings, to be careful, to—"

"Alright, alright, I get it."

Leaning my hip against the glass display case, I nod my head at the revolver she was ogling.

"That catch your eye?"

Her lips twitch. "Yeah, but I don't need another—"

"Hey, Sal!" I call across the shop. "I want to add another to my order."

"You don't need to buy me—"

I tsk and place a steady hand on Josie's, cutting her off. Her cheeks pinken at the contact.

"Let me spoil you, Josie. Friends deserve good Solstice gifts too," I say. Then I shoot her a devious smile. "Plus, I got him to give me an *unbeatable* discount."

27
NORA

We find an odd but balanced rhythm by the end of my third week at Mt. Bramble.

Each morning, I take my breakfast alone in my room, savoring the calm loneliness provides before I brave the storm of my companions. Though, I'd be lying if I said watching the duo bicker wasn't growing on me. Silas was right; Wrath is extremely easy to rile up, and it's quite entertaining to poke fun at the grouch. Silas has taken to doing most of the poking, and while I egg him on from the sidelines wholeheartedly, Wrath doesn't shoot me anything more than exasperated sighs.

After that night on the mountaintop, we came to an unspoken understanding. It isn't a warm and fuzzy friendship. He's still a grump, and I'm still coarse, but there isn't that thrumming ire between us anymore.

By noon, we're killing time, going back up to the range for repeat contests—all of which I win, to their dismay—or finding our own spots within the mountain complex. Silas frequents the library, I tend to linger in the training room, and

Wrath sets off to his mysterious workshop. All of us wait for the clock to tick past our daily goalpost so I can release the tether of my magic on another soul.

We worked our way from one minute to thirty within the first twenty-four hours of adopting my newfound method. Pride had swelled in my chest the first time I tethered myself to one of the prisoners for more than a minute. But as we increased the goalpost, waiting for days with my magic stretching between me and the prisoners, we quickly realized how easily that connection could be broken.

Now, Silas has made it his mission to get me to crack. It's exhausting.

So exhausting that I don't want to get out of bed, despite the sunlight flowing into the room. It burns my eyes through my lids and I groan. Pulling the sheets up over my head, I remind myself what's waiting on the other side of this.

I think of Imogen.

Twinkling laughter fills the room, however muffled from my position under the covers. The bed dips with the weight of Imogen as she crawls to me. I lower the sheet, revealing the lazy smile that's plastered across my face.

She kneels in front of me, blocking the rays from the window and allowing me to bask in blessed shade. She's an angel, with a golden aura glowing around her. Her hair, loose and long, tumbles over one shoulder as she tilts her head at me.

"I'd normally be happy you're so willing to sleep in." Imogen's soft voice is a morning birdsong, rousing me from slumber. She runs a thumb over the dark circles forming under my eyes, gaze soft and teasing on me, and the gentleness of it all makes my heart stutter. "But I find myself a bit sad this morning."

"Maybe after this trip is over, I'll be more amenable to lazy mornings," I say, voice rough from sleep. "As a way to make up for being gone."

She laughs, and the sun brightens with her joy.

"I'll hold you to that," she says before leaning down.

Soft lips meld to mine. It's a languid kiss, and I marvel at how she tastes sweet as honey, even in the morning. I'm sure I taste stale, but she sucks my bottom lip between her teeth as if I'm made of nectar.

I shift and sit up, one hand keeping me upright behind me, and the other wandering to her knee. Her nightdress has ridden up her legs, exposing the smooth skin there. Lazily, my thumb strokes circles on her inner thigh, inching up and under the silky fabric.

Imogen pulls back on a hum, her forehead resting on mine. "Though I like where this is going, you only have an hour before you need to leave."

"Silas can wait," I murmur against her lips, leaning forward to capture them again.

She pulls back, one brow quirked up on her forehead; normally it would read as a sassy scolding, but the sparkle in her eye is missing, and her lips twitch like she's fighting a frown. I squeeze the ample flesh of her thigh.

"Trust me, for what I'm doing for him, he can wait an extra ten minutes," I say. And while it doesn't bring back the lightness in her eyes, her body melts at my words.

"I'm sure," she says, but I can hear by her tone that the moment has passed.

The sex has been electric since we made up, but in the weeks since our fight, I've realized that there are many other ways to share yourself with someone.

Just by existing alongside another, new layers reveal themselves.

Like how I've noticed that Imogen sighs wistfully anytime she gets a whiff of baked goods, as if she's been hit by a warm memory. Or learning that she loves the way my nails scratch at her scalp when I wash her hair. Or how neither of us want to get out of bed in the mornings; long gone are the days of me sneaking out at sunrise.

Small intimacies, I've discovered, paint a black-and-white life with color.

I pepper kisses across her cheek and to the hollow behind her ear.

"I could make you come for hours and still have energy to spare." I hum, running my nose down her neck and breathing in her delicious floral scent before pulling back to meet her flush-cheeked gaze. "You can hold me to that too."

"Okay," she whispers, lips parting into a smirk. But her eyes still aren't getting their sparkle back.

I trace her cheek with my thumb before anchoring my hand at the back of her neck, cradling her head.

"Are you okay?" I ask.

She blinks, a quick fluttering of her blond lashes. Her brows knit in confusion.

"Why wouldn't I be?"

I search her face for any tells of the opposite, finding no trace of untruth. But something still doesn't sit right.

I decide to let it go.

"No reason," I say, dropping a kiss to her forehead. "Meet me when I'm back, yeah?"

Silas eats as he watches me train. My hits against the hanging sandbag grow more intense with each bite he takes of his apple, the sound of his teeth crunching over the crisp flesh grates against my ears. My eye twitches as my frustration flares, straining the magical tether between me and the fae across the room.

I take a step back from the bag, my breaths coming heavy and sweat dripping down my back.

"Will you stop with that?" I growl.

"What?" Silas says, mouth full. He swallows. "You mean eating?"

"Yes. Can't you do that somewhere else?"

"Does it bother you?"

"*Clearly.*"

"Then no. I absolutely cannot stop doing it." His teeth snap through the apple's skin, a pursed-lip smile forming as he chews with full cheeks.

I mutter curses and go back to pummeling the sandbag. My knuckles start to ache under their bindings, signaling that either my form is slacking, or I'm hitting it too hard—probably both.

"Who taught you how to fight?" Silas asks a few minutes later.

"Pride encouraged it from a young age," I say between punches. "His Second took the job on when no one else would."

None of the other younglings, nor their parents, wanted to engage in hand-to-hand combat with me, and rightfully so. While I had gained control of my magic by ten, that didn't lessen people's fear of my touch. There weren't many options when it came to teachers, leaving me stuck with Pride himself for my magic and his Second at the time, Wes and Claude's father, for fighting and shooting.

He wasn't a good man, but he also wasn't afraid of me.

He should have been.

He realized too late that Pride was training me to replace him—things went south from there. By then, Josie and I were already eighteen, Pride's personal prized weapons lurking in the shadows. He learned that it's hard to get away with plotting a coup when your superior has a mind-reader and a soul-stealer at his disposal.

"Ah, yes. I remember him. Had ruddy-brown hair. Gruff exterior," Silas says. "Very sad, him dying in that automobile accident. Those older cars can be *quite* dangerous."

I give the sandbag a final hit and begin stripping my hands of their wrappings. The gauze and tape unravel onto the floor, curling into a pile of white.

"Yeah," I say, under Silas's watchful gaze. "Very sad."

He hums, before pulling out his silver pocket watch. The metal clinks against his rings as he flicks it open, reading the time.

"Oh, great," Silas says, perking up from his seat. "We're over time."

My attention turns to the bound fae shackled in the far corner. This was the second to last test before we hit the two-week mark Silas says we need to escape blame for Patience's inevitable death.

I make haste across the room, pushing past Silas.

I close my eyes and breathe deep, focusing on the two tethers of magic that linger within me. One leads to the fae before me and the other to one Wrath has in holding elsewhere in the complex.

Once I had studied up on tethering from the Seelie journals, our training went much smoother. It seems that with the right directions, I'm a natural.

Silas was both thrilled at how fast our situation has changed and jealous at how quickly I was able to grasp the new style of magic.

Training in on the correct tether, I call to my magic. It acts, swift and hungry, rushing through the man's heart and causing it to stall, before running back to me through the fading connection.

The fae shutters, then goes still.

Dead.

Satisfaction swells in my chest along with my magic. In two days, we can finish the last test.

"It is impressive," Silas says. I pivot to face him. "You are a quicker study than I gave you credit for."

"We've been at this for weeks. I don't see how that's a quick study."

He huffs, shaking his head in disbelief. His lips move, murmuring something under his breath that I can't hear.

"What you are doing is not easy. It should take you *months*, if not longer, to do this," he says.

"How would you know? Is there another soul-stealer you're training that I should know about?" I say, hands on my hips.

"Certainly not one like you."

My lips part at the strange answer, but before I can reply, there's a knock at the door. Wrath steps inside, quickly shutting the door behind him, drawing both my and Silas's attention.

He doesn't often interrupt our training.

"What is it?" Silas asks.

"There's been a wire," he says.

"*Okay*," Silas drawls.

There's a beat of silence where Wrath's jaw ticks. Finally, he looks at me, and there's pity in his eyes. Instantly, gooseflesh rises on my neck.

"Your Second sent a message. There was another attack."

28

IMOGEN

"I'm not a gun person, but I have to admit this is awesome, Sal."

"Can I see?" Josie tries to peek over my shoulder, but I shove her away.

"Nope. Not allowed."

The old man chuckles as he closes the small wooden boxes holding Nora and Josie's presents.

"Thank you, that's kind to say," Sal says. "Let me get your paperwork from the back, and we can get you on your way."

Sal shuffles through to the back room, leaving Josie and me alone. Wes is stationed out front like last time, keeping watch.

"You're in a good mood today," Josie observes, leaning back against a glass display case.

I play with the ends of my scarf. "I don't know. Life is looking up lately."

"I'm glad, Mo."

"Now, if only Nora would hurry up and come home…"

"I'm sure she'll be back soon."

"She hasn't sent any word yet?"

"No, not a peep," Josie says. "But she promised she'd tell us if it was going to be longer than—"

Josie's head whips to the front of the store, only a second before the glass explodes.

"Get down!"

Josie throws herself at me, but not before bullets and glass rain down on us. Pain erupts in my side as Josie tackles me to the ground, covering my body with hers.

"Shit," she growls. "We need to get out of here."

When the bullets stop whizzing above our heads, she pulls me up, dragging me through the emergency exit at the side of the store by my arm. She's already got her gun drawn. I stumble into the alley after her, clutching my side.

"Josie." Her name is shaky on my tongue.

Adrenaline rushes through me, numbing out my limbs and drawing the world into pin-point focus. There's a whooshing in my ears, an all-consuming ringing.

"Where the fuck is Wes?" Josie growls before pulling me further down the alley in the opposite direction of the shop's main entrance.

Gunshots sound from behind us and Josie's pace increases as we turn down different back streets, all of them somehow empty.

"Josie," I say again, fear striking through me. My fingers tremble as they clasp my side, coming away slick. Pain courses through my middle with every jolting step. "Josie, I can't run."

She whips around, giving me a once over and her eyes widen at whatever she sees. I can't look down—don't want to. I close my eyes, fighting the lightheadedness falling over me.

"Shit," she says. "Okay, we're going to—"

But she doesn't finish her sentence as she's ripped away

from me and thrown to the ground. I yelp as I'm pulled into a strong set of arms. Josie rolls, quickly recovering from whatever strike the attacker dealt. She's on one knee, gun poised and directed at us.

Freezing metal digs into my temple and my captor's arm bands across my chest. His hand grips the base of my neck.

A furious scowl is set across Josie's face. Her eyes dissect the situation with speed, calculating the chances of success if she were to pull the trigger.

"Ah, ah, ah," a cold voice scolds from behind me, addressing Josie's murderous glare. "Don't think I won't kill Miss Lust here as quick as you can pull that trigger."

My body stills.

He's fae. He's Seelie.

"Josie," I whisper.

"Let her go," Josie growls. "Or I will kill you."

My breathing catches on itself, my lungs hyperventilating as gray tints the edge of my vision. I close my eyes, tight, pushing away my panic and trying to channel calm.

Enough calm to at least connect to my magic.

I have to focus. I can do this. I've done it a thousand times.

Pain digs into my skull as the Seelie pushes the gun into my temple with more force.

Shit.

"Put the gun down," he says.

I flick my eyes open, locking gazes with Josie. I give her an imperceptible nod.

It's okay, I try to tell her with my mind.

She lowers her gun, tentatively, though she doesn't put it on the ground.

"On the ground," the man snarls.

Josie's jaw grinds as she places the gun at her feet and lifts her hands up in a placating gesture.

"Smart girl," the Seelie man coos, and my throat tightens with disgust. Then his mouth is next to my ear, hot breath making me gag. "Now, you're not going to give me trouble, are you, sugar? Let's move. Someone important wants to meet you."

Josie's warm brown eyes are still locked on mine, searching for a way out of the situation we've found ourselves in. But I close my eyes again, focusing on my magic, trying to pull it to the surface, past the fear and the pain and the light-headedness.

"*Imogen*," Josie warns, sensing what I am about to do.

I may not be a sharpshooter and my touch may not kill—I cannot walk between the shadows, nor mold them into weapons—but I have something else others don't.

Trust me.

I hope Josie can hear me as I push the words her way.

"Did you hear me? Let's go," the Seelie barks behind me.

He tries to back us up, but I squirm enough to get one arm free from his grasp. I slap my palm against the hand gripping the gun at my temple, calling my magic to my fingertips, pushing one word, one feeling into the Seelie—*compliance.*

"*Let go*," I command.

His body jerks, fighting the magic for all but a second before his arms drop to his sides. The gun falls from his grip, clattering on the ground.

I launch myself forward, my hands and knees scraping against the rough pavement. Just as quick, the gun is back in Josie's hand and she's releasing a round into the Seelie's gut.

He jolts with each bullet's impact, knees buckling and upper body twisting to face up as he hits the ground.

Surprisingly, he groans, not completely dead.

Josie and I watch as the wounds on his chest begin to heal.

One bullet at a time, they pop out of their bloodied wounds, revealing freshly healed scars.

But then the adrenaline in me crashes, and I fall face-first onto the cobblestone.

I hear Josie curse as she pulls me up, setting me against the side of a building. My vision blurs in and out, and I groan when her hands come to my side, pressing against my wound.

"*Shit.*" Josie repeats the curse over and over, and I let out a lackluster snort. "You're going to be fine. I've got you."

"I don't know if I've ever heard you curse so many times in a row."

She lets out a huff of terrified laughter. It's no time to laugh, but I guess that's just how we're both dealing with this.

Fuck. Am I going to die?

My side has gone slick and warm, and I tilt my head to the sky to avoid seeing all the red I know is pooling underneath me.

The sky is clear and blue.

How peaceful.

"Now's a good time to tell me I told you so," I groan as Josie rips part of her blouse and ties it around my middle.

"Not the time, Mo," Josie says. "Not the time."

"Isn't it though?" I squeak as Josie secures a too-tight knot over my wound.

"Nope," she says, suddenly sounding resolute. "You're going to be fine."

Footsteps sound at my left, rounding the corner of the alley.

"Get her back to Anwynn." Josie's voice has never sounded so powerful, so commanding. A shiver runs through me, whether from her voice or how cold it's gotten. "We have an emergency tonic in the drawer of my office. Get her there and make her drink it."

I crack an eye to see Wes standing, mouth agape at Josie's wrath.

"*Now!*" she yells, which gets him to move.

"Yes, Boss," he says, running to my side and lifting me into his arms.

As I'm whisked away into shadow—the last thing I see is Josie standing above our attacker, emptying another round into his stomach.

My lashes flutter open, and I wince, the already dim lighting in the room too much for my pounding head. I scan the dark wood frame and silk sheets, realizing that I'm in Nora's bedroom.

Someone shifts at my side, a rustling of cotton as they lean forward in the chair that's been pulled close to the bed.

My muscles ache, chills skitter over my skin, and my head throbs with every beat of my pulse.

"You're awake," Josie says, almost shocked. "How are you feeling?"

I turn my head, my cheek resting against the pillow. Josie's sporting a nasty bruise under one eye and a split lip, but otherwise she is unscathed.

"Like I could use a fucking drink," I huff.

Josie's head tilts to the ceiling. She rubs her weary eyes with an exasperated smile.

"I will get you a million drinks. But only after the doc clears you."

I try to sit up, but wince at a sharp ache in my side. Josie helps me into a sitting position with careful hands, and I realize I'm in a set of oversized button-up pajamas. Running my hand across my stomach, my fingers don't brush over any bandages, though there are some wrapped around my palms and one on my forehead. I tug up the shirt, revealing the pale expanse of my stomach, completely devoid of any wound or scar.

"What the hell happened?" I ask, pulling my shirt back down. "And please tell me you were the one to dress me."

Josie scoots the chair closer. "Wes got you the tonic fast enough, but you had already lost a lot of blood. It didn't heal everything, only the worst of it. You've been asleep for a couple of hours."

"Shit."

"Yeah," she says. "And yes, I was the one to change you. I gave you a spare set from my closet. I hope you don't mind."

My lips twist as I finger the soft striped cotton. "You wear men's pajamas?"

"They're more comfortable."

"I prefer silk to cotton," I say, pulling pink to Josie's cheeks.

"I can go to your apartment and pack you some of your clothes if you want," she offers. "Doc said you should stay on bed rest for a few days. Even if you look healed, your body needs time to recover."

I nod, looking down at my lap. Worrying my lip, I twist the extra fabric of the pajama sleeves around my fisted hand.

I don't know what it is about the texture of the cotton on my palm, but it makes me all too cognizant of the way it rubs against my body. I'm suddenly acutely aware of how heavy the sheets are and how clammy they are making my feet—of how my heart is beating too fast in my chest and how each one of my breaths doesn't fill my lungs as they should.

"Um, Josie?" I say.

"Yeah?"

"Why did this happen?" I ask. My throat constricts, emotion welling at the underside of my jaw as I try, with all my might, to hold back the impending spiral creeping on. "Why would someone attack us like that? I know the Seelie don't like us, and I know House Pride is having issues with the exiles but—"

"This isn't the exiles, Imogen," Josie says, a serious expression shuttering her expression. "This is Patience. *He* is why. He's tormenting Nora."

"But why?" I ask. "Because he killed her parents and she got away? She was a *child*." A frantic need to understand rolls over me. "Because she tried to buy tonics off the exiles? It doesn't make sense to me."

"Sometimes life doesn't make sense," Josie murmurs and I scoff.

Anger bubbles in my stomach, a churning boil at the unanswered questions.

I am Lust of the Unseelie; *I'm* the holder of people's secrets. *I'm* the one who should know all the answers. But right now, I feel like I've been given a test without having been taught the material. I'm trying to reason out my responses with only context clues.

My shoulders sag, that anger in my stomach overcome with self-doubt.

No, I'm barely a House leader, struggling like I am. I've known as much for a long while.

I never should have *been* Lust. Isn't that why I'm already half-way out the door? Handing over more responsibility to Leo with each day that passes?

I'm out of my depth here.

"First, this Virtue kills a family from your House, then burns one of your warehouses and leaves your supplier for dead. *Then*, they try to kill us?" I list, ticking off a finger with each event. "This feels bigger than retaliation for some petty revenge plot."

"That's because it is bigger than us, Imogen. It's because she's—" Josie cuts herself off with a frustrated groan—she sounds more irritated than I've ever heard her before. She scrubs both hands over her face. When she pulls them away, she levels me with a pained expression. "Because Nora's a *threat*."

My own anger fades in an instant, regret filling its place in my gut.

"Because she's a soul-stealer?" I ask.

Josie glances at the bedroom door, which stands open a crack, a small sliver of light filtering in from the living room.

"You should ask her yourself," Josie whispers.

A commotion sounds beyond the door, footsteps and shouts collide in the hall outside the bedroom, cutting off that sliver of light from the cracked door.

"Let me see her."

"She's in stable condition, but she will need rest, Pride. You should let her sleep and come back when—"

The door bursts open and there, with light haloed around her like an avenging god, Nora stands.

Her chest rises and falls with heavy breaths.

In a few frantic steps, she's at my side. Reaching out with a shaking hand, she pauses. She pulls her hand back. Her eyes are wide and wild as they scan over me; her searing gaze is tangible as it lands on my face. It burns a trail over my lips, cresting over my cheeks and up my nose until, finally, it meets mine.

"Hi," she says.

"Hi," I whisper.

Nora's hands flex at her sides. I reach out, my hand waiting for hers.

It's the sign she needs to move. Nora falls to her knees at my side and squeezes my hand. She lifts it to her mouth, turning it over and placing a gentle kiss to my pulse point.

"Are you okay?" she asks.

My throat is tight again, and I can't find it in me to speak, so I nod.

Her lips form a hard line, taking a deep breath through her nose.

"Good," she says, clearing her throat. "Good." Nora doesn't let go of my hand as she tilts her head to address Josie. Her voice spreads, as slow and cold as frost, through the room. "What were you thinking, taking her out there?"

"Nora, I—"

"I don't want to hear excuses," she snaps. "We talked about this before I left. You were supposed to watch her. *Protect* her. You, of all people, know better."

Josie doesn't respond. She turns her head to the wall, jaw feathering, and accepts the verbal lashing.

But what happened isn't Josie's fault. She doesn't deserve to be reprimanded for doing what I asked. We were lucky that she and Wes were unharmed, and it sounds like a miracle that I survived.

Nora should be focusing on the good. She should be *thanking* Josie for her quick action, not scolding her.

"How did they even know where you guys were? Hattie says you were at some shop in—"

"Nora," I cut her off. "Stop it."

The silence in the room is deafening. Nora's green eyes are a dark, churning sea when they slide back to me.

"It was my idea," I say.

"It doesn't matter if it was your idea—"

"Yes, it does." My voice is firm, my grip on Nora's hand firmer. "I pulled rank and made her take me." It wasn't the full truth, but I hoped that it convinced Nora to go easy on her best friend. "She took proper precautions, tried to talk me out of it too. But you know I can be as stubborn as you when I want to be."

I run my thumb over Nora's knuckles, realizing her fingers are bare. Pulses of anger bounce off her skin; it's one of few times in the past ten years that her inner turmoil has broken through her fortified mental shields.

"Your anger is misplaced," I say, easing my tone. "She *saved* me."

Nora heaves a great sigh, head falling back. Her eyes are screwed shut with crow's feet deep along the outer edges.

"You're right," she says, eyes still closed. She clears her throat. "I'm sorry, Josie."

"It's okay," Josie says, quiet.

Then, as quickly as she entered the room, Nora's standing and storming away.

"He's a dead man walking," she growls before she slams the bedroom door shut.

It takes a moment for me to register what happened. I'm stunned, silent and still, left staring at the closed door.

"She'll be back," Josie whispers.

"She better come back," I say, shaking my head. "I almost died, and she's storming off?"

"She needs to cool down. She has a right to be angry."

A war of emotions clash in my stomach. I could be angry too, but my body is tired.

My mind is tired too.

Josie sighs, crumbling against the armchair. "You really scared me, Mo."

"I know."

Her brown eyes are dark, like soaked soil after the rain. "Please don't try to convince me to take you across the Veil ever again."

I snort, though it lacks all humor. "I have no desire to go back there now."

"Also, before I forget," Josie says, reaching behind the armchair. She pulls out a solid wooden box and holds it out to me. "I hope it's not too soon. But I wanted you to know I grabbed it after I swept the building."

I take it, gently placing it on the covers of the bed. I tip the lip open, only enough to reveal a peak of the guns I bought for Nora and Josie.

An uncomfortable itch comes over me as I stare at the weapons. I ignore the feeling and close the box, putting it to the side.

A sad smile twitches my lips.

"Thank you," I whisper.

Tears well in my eyes, and my hands start to shake. Breathing becomes hard, my lungs taking staggered gulps of air that catch in my throat. I think the adrenaline in my blood has finally cleared, because my limbs ache, exhaustion clawing at them in tandem with the emotions swelling in my gut.

My cheeks are wet, and I swipe at them, but it doesn't help.

"Thank you, Josie," I repeat.

"Do you need a—"

I nod my head frantically. "Please."

The empath who can read minds silently reads mine; she lowers herself into the bed next to me, pulling me into a warm hug. I curl into her side, burrowing into her body heat as sobs rack my body.

"Did all that really happen?" I ask.

"Unfortunately."

My laugh is a sardonic bark between my sobs. "That's fucking crazy."

"Yeah, it is," she says. "But you're okay." Josie whispers platitudes and rubs soothing circles on my back until, finally, exhaustion succeeds in pulling me back into sleep. "We're okay."

29
NORA

"Take me to Bramble."

Silas jolts, straightening his back and shoulders from where he leans against the wall in my living room, one foot bent against the green wallpaper. He's focused, conveniently, on twiddling the silver rings he wears, pretending that he wasn't eavesdropping on our conversation.

I don't want him in my space—when Wrath told us about what happened, I had thought Silas would drop me off *outside* the building, but no, we landed right in my office. Then he followed me, like a second shadow, up to my rooms under the guise of *kingly duty*.

I hadn't the nerve to fight him. The urge to see Imogen safe was too strong.

"*Now*, Silas."

His brows raise to his hairline at my bark. He pushes off from the wall with grace, strutting over to me. My fingers twitch at my side, my entire body trembling with restless anger.

"Yes, ma'am," he taunts. He points to the green and black

wings mounted on the wall. "Nice decor, by the way. Very unique."

"If you don't want me to snap this last tether, you need to take me to Bramble right now," I snap.

Silas is shocked into seriousness. He nods, understanding shifting his features. He holds his hand out, and I go to take it but pause when I realize both our hands are bare.

Silas huffs a frustrated sigh. "I'm not afraid of you, Nora."

His hand quickly grabs mine. The world swirls around us, an inky swath of darkness that fills every space between us. It's weightless, traveling by shadow; the only sensation being that of who you are grounded to. In this case, that's the rough pads of Silas's fingertips and the cool metal of his rings on my palm.

I rip my hand free of his as soon as we step onto the white, snowy fields outside Mt. Bramble's entrance.

Flurries catch in my lashes as I storm to the cave, my heartbeat filling my ears. The thin strap of control I have on my rage snaps, and the world blurs around me as I fall into my feelings. It's always the same when I get triggered, as if I've jumped off a cliff, and the rush of air overwhelms my senses.

It's in the fall that I attempt to compartmentalize. I try to pack away the disappointment in myself—the shame of not doing something more to stop the bad things from happening to those I love.

I'm still not powerful enough to stop them.

Still not powerful enough to stop *him*.

A need churns my gut. It sets my limbs on fire, the restlessness.

I storm through the complex, taking the stairs two at a time and relishing the way it burns my thighs. Footsteps follow mine, Silas tracking me all the way to the roof.

Some would give me platitudes, try to reason with me— tell me that it wasn't *my* fault that this happened to Imogen.

She was right to say my anger was misplaced at Josie. The blame lies with me and Patience alone.

Others would try to fix the issue for me, try to problem solve and use action to cope—and while that should be the option for me, it doesn't help.

The past isn't something that can be *problem solved*. The future? Sure. But what's happened has happened. I cannot change the past, and that's the issue. The mistake has already been made.

I let Imogen fall into the hands of my enemy, and I almost lost her because of it.

Thankfully, Silas serves me neither platitudes nor solutions as he walks a pace behind me.

Does he understand my need for release?

When I finally burst through the metal door to the mountaintop, I scream.

I pull my gun from its holster at my side, and direct all that burning fire inside of me at the snow-covered targets. White puffs explode with each bullet, and far too soon, I'm pulling an empty trigger.

I throw the gun down, the hot metal melting the snow underneath it, and storm to the storage closet. I hold my hand out, staring at the little lock.

"Key, please," I grind out.

But instead of a physical key landing in my palm, shadows curl around the lock, breaking it. The pieces fall into the snow.

The jerking of the rifle into my shoulder each time I pull the trigger steadies my heart, gives it a rhythm to follow.

When there are no bullets left in the gun, and no ammunition left in me to keep going, I collapse in the snow. The cold wet seeps into my hair and my clothes, but I don't care. It's a salve on my burning soul.

Snow crunches next to me, and out of my periphery, Silas

copies me, making an angel in the white fluff. He lies there, unspeaking, both of us sinking deeper into the mountaintop.

If I stay here, let my body freeze in the snow, will time stop with my heart?

"I need to kill him, Silas," I say. "It's not a want anymore."

"You will," he promises.

"When?"

"I'm calling a meeting with the Sins in two days. Your doctor said Lust should be recovered by then," he answers me plainly, which I'm thankful for. "We'll get our revenge soon enough."

"Good."

The finality of the word echoes between the white-dusted cliffsides that tower around us. We lay there for who knows how long—until the clouds have finished their trek across the sky and our bones have gone numb from the cold.

"Tell me, Nora, when is a king not a king?"

My head turns to him, my cheek pressing into the icy ground. Silas stares off into the snowy peaks around us, searching for something we cannot see. My breath curls around me, floating into the sky.

"I don't know. When?"

"Even when he's dead, a king is still a king," he says. "But when he is alone, he is simply himself."

Silas's head turns to me.

I'm sucked into his eyes; the twin black holes are an endless abyss holding everything and nothing at the same time. In them, I find myself, something not completely whole, but not empty either—*a kindred spirit.*

"When I am here, I am just Silas. And it seems that when you are here, you are just Nora."

When I am with you, I am just Silas, the shadows that curl at our backs whisper.

His unrelenting gaze bores into me.

The hair on my neck stands on end, and my chest caves in on itself. Because I think the Unseelie King may be my friend.

I turn back to the sky.

"If you ever need this escape, it's here for you," Silas says. "But right now, you need to get back to your lover."

"Yeah," I say. "I do."

And when he reaches his hand out, I take it.

30
IMOGEN

Nora slinks into the living room well past sunset.

She pauses in the doorway, gaze tracking between Josie and me nursing our teas on the velvet lounger. Her throat bobs in the silence. Then she continues deeper into the room, dumping a medical kit onto the side table next to the loveseat.

Nora passes us, headed straight to the bar cart. Pouring herself a dram of whiskey, she throws it back, refilling the glass before bringing it—and the whole decanter—to the armchair next to us. She slouches into the leather, placing the bottle next to the med kit.

"Stop giving me that look," Nora snaps, and I realize she and Josie must be having another one of their silent conversations.

Josie stands with her mug, placing a gentle squeeze on my shoulder.

"I think it's time I head to bed," she says. She shoots me a soft smile. "Goodnight, Imogen."

"Goodnight," I murmur back over another sip of my tea.

It's lukewarm now, my sips too slow to catch the heat

when Josie first brought it up for me. She'd moved me to Nora's couch after my breakdown, both of us needing a change of scenery. A puzzle sits half-finished on the coffee table; we gave up thirty minutes ago, our brains too zapped from the day.

"Be nice," I hear Josie whisper to Nora as she leaves the room.

And then we're alone.

Nora doesn't meet my eye as she downs her second glass of liquor. She hisses and shakes her head as it goes down. Without saying a word, she discards her empty glass and takes the med kit into her lap. Opening the metal tin, she rifles through the materials, taking out gauze pads, bandage tape, a small pot of salve, and a bottle of antiseptic.

"Come here." She beckons me closer, still not quite meeting my eye.

The healing tonic Wes gave me only healed my bullet wound. The doctor said that it took all the magic in the tonic to repair whatever damage lingered from the blood loss, because I'm still covered in small scrapes on my face and hands. He already cleaned the wounds, pulled out shards of glass and washed the dirt from my palms, but I would need to change the bandages soon.

I slide across the couch, my knees bumping up against Nora's. I'd be lying if I said I didn't feel a pinch of relief that she doesn't shy away from the point of contact.

"Hands," she demands, holding out hers.

I place one in her grasp, and she carefully unravels the bandages there. The soft crackle of the fireplace fills the silence between us as Nora reveals the raw red scratches. She wets a piece of gauze with antiseptic.

"This may burn," she warns before pressing the damp gauze to my skin, pulling a hiss from between my teeth.

I bite down on my bottom lip as she quickly wipes off the

dried blood and puss the wound expelled. With gentle fingers, she applies a salve to the cuts. She covers it with a fresh gauze pad and tapes over the edges so there's a tight seal against the outside world.

She takes her time, is methodical in her care.

My eyes droop as she repeats her work on my other hand, and when she stops, my body mourns the loss of her touch.

"These shouldn't scar. But make sure to change the bandages and reapply a salve twice a day. I'll send you home with a jar and some extra gauze pads," she says, lithe hands quickly placing each item back into its rightful spot in the little metal tin.

I place a hand over hers, trapping it against her thigh.

"Why don't you keep it? That way I have an excuse to come over every day."

Nora finally looks up, and I'm struck by how sad her eyes are. The deep green has darkened to moss, dulled by guilt.

"You don't need an excuse to come over." She almost sounds defeated, a tone I've never heard from her before. She clears her throat. "I'm sorry. For tonight."

"For which part?" I ask. "For blowing up at Josie or storming out?"

"Both?" She grimaces.

"Why did you leave?" I ask, my throat tightening for the umpteenth time today. I try to swallow the reaction back. I'm tired of the emotional whiplash the past twelve hours have given me. "I needed you and you left me."

"Because I had nothing good to say, and I didn't know how to comfort you," Nora admits. "When I get like that..." She shakes her head, face contorting into a pained expression. "It's overwhelming. Like an avalanche inside my body that I can't stop. I need to let it run its course."

"And how did that go?"

"I ruined about five practice targets at a gun range, so," she huffs. "I know it probably doesn't make sense. It's hard to explain what goes on in here."

She points to her heart.

"You don't have to," I whisper. "I understand."

"Do you?" It's more of a plea than a question—a hope, a wish.

"I might not understand the mechanics of it, how it exactly feels inside of you. But I know what it's like to be scared."

She shakes her head, face shuttering. "I wasn't scared. I was furious."

"No, Nora. You were furious *because* you were scared."

The firewood pops, spitting red embers into the air.

"The thought of losing you…" She doesn't finish the sentence, but I know how it ends.

"I don't want to lose you either," I say. "But it sounds as if you're set on running headfirst into a conflict with this Virtue anyway."

"I can't be killed that easily."

I smack her arm, and Nora yelps, dropping the med kit onto the rug at our feet.

"Apparently, neither can I. But you are forgetting that neither of us is invincible. You might not be as fragile as a human, but you're not a god. Bullets can kill as easily as magic."

My hand goes to my side on instinct. While the wound has healed, phantom pains still shoot through me; the memory of the slick blood coating my skin lingers.

"You dish out hard truths, love," she says, and my heart skips a beat at the moniker.

"Promise you won't run away next time," I say. "I don't need to be protected from what goes on in here." I reach forward, placing a hand over her chest. Her heartbeat flows through my fingertips, in time with mine. "I just want *you*. Including the parts that are scared."

"I promise," she says. Nora stares down at my hand and I at her. Neither of us knows where to go from here, but neither of us is bold enough to break the connection thrumming between us. Then, as if she can hear my indecisive thoughts, she blinks from her stupor, pulling my hand from her chest. "We're both a mess. Let's get cleaned up."

I watch as she stands and saunters across the apartment, heading to the bathroom. I follow.

The light flicks on in the bathroom, fluorescent bulbs humming as they backlight Nora; her silhouette is a shadow dancing against the tile. The bathwater runs, and steam billows around the clawfoot tub. Lavender and eucalyptus salts fill the room with a calming perfume and cloud the water a pretty lilac.

I stand in the doorway, watching as Nora swirls the water with her fingertips, testing the temperature and adjusting the faucets accordingly.

"Can we cuddle tonight?" I ask.

The question comes to the tip of my tongue on instinct. Nora's brows are furrowed when she looks up from her perch on the porcelain tub.

"Of course," she says, her voice a brush of cashmere across my skin. "Tonight, I only want to take care of you, however you need me to."

I nod, warmth spreading through my chest.

"And we can stay in bed all morning?"

Her gaze melts. "Yes, Imogen, we can do that."

"Good," I say.

"Good," she says, a soft smile on her lips. "Now, come here. Before the bath runs cold."

We spend nearly two days in Nora's bed, not even doing anything; we simply exist. Together. And it's perfect.

She lets me snuggle against her as much as I want; when she gets fidgety from the constant contact, she tells me about it rather than pulling away. And then I tell her how much I appreciate her honesty and let her have some space.

We spend hours finishing the puzzle Josie and I started—getting frustrated when we lose a single piece to the ether. We play stupid card games, most of which I lose, and recall terrible stories of our youth over home-cooked meals that Wes's nan sends up for us.

When she found out what happened, she took it upon herself to aid in my recovery. She even whipped up a special dish that had Nora cursing the old lady for how infrequently she makes it; it was a bowl of minuscule pieces of pasta, creamy with butter and parmesan.

I let Nora have a spoonful and her resulting moan had us tumbling into bed, all thoughts of the outside world cast away.

There's soft laughter, and even softer touches, and by the time our little bubble of paradise pops—a single knock on the door calling Nora away until the Sins meeting—my heart is sufficiently full.

31
IMOGEN

"You didn't," Leo chokes on his laughter as he, Josie, and I step out of the elevator.

"We did," Josie says, a bashful smile on her face. It showcases an adorable little dimple on her right cheek. "Everyone at family dinner wondered why the sauce tasted strange. They were practically screaming it in their heads, but no one would say a word out loud. They didn't want to hurt Nan's feelings. Little did they know, it wasn't her fault the vodka sauce was more vodka than sauce."

"Did she ever find out?" I ask.

"Of course," Josie says, nose scrunching up. "Wes's nan finds out everything. We were on dish duty for a month."

I shake my head. "I'm going to scold Nora for keeping that one to herself."

"Good luck with that. She's still pissed we got caught." Josie snorts.

The three of us chuckle. We'd been laughing a lot lately.

Ever since the night Josie crashed on my couch, and even more so after the *incident* human-side, we've been spending more time together. I hadn't realized it at the time, but I missed her friendship. Josie needs the laughs more than ever, still holding onto a deep-rooted guilt that I want to rip from her soul. But I'm thankful I can still pull some laughter from her, even if it doesn't quite reach her eyes.

We come to a stop where the hallways fork—in one direction lies the Sins meeting room, and the other leads to where the Seconds wait.

"I'll see you after, Mo," Josie says, giving my shoulder a quick squeeze.

"See you," I say before she departs down the hall. I raise my brows at Leo, pointing towards the double doors I need to enter. "Are you sure you don't want to sit in for me?"

He shakes his head. "It isn't the right time."

A knowing smile curls my lips. "Don't tell me you're nervous."

Leo's smile is cautious. "I don't know what you're talking about. I am never nervous."

"Uh-huh."

"I speak the truth."

"Well, *I'm* nervous," I say, cocking my brow. "Silas doesn't often call mid-quarter meetings. It means something big or bad. Or both."

"And that's exactly why I don't want to sit in today." He pivots on his heel and gives me a wave. "See you after, Mo."

"Traitor," I murmur, but it doesn't have any bite.

"Heard that!" he calls from down the hall.

A little laugh escapes me and eases the tension in my shoulders.

When I enter the meeting room, it's empty. As I round the table, I shake out my arms, hoping that the action will shake off the rest of my anxiety.

It doesn't work.

"That some kind of new dance the younglings are doing nowadays?" Sloth's gruff voice calls from behind me, making me startle.

"You're even earlier than normal," I say, letting a warm smile spread across my face as I turn to the old man.

He grunts, gripping the head of his cane and tapping the thing on the floor as he hobbles past.

"My gut says this meeting will be important. There's something in the air, old magic stirring," he says.

"Is it?" I ask, humoring the old fae.

He sits with a groan.

"I'm getting too old for this," he says, resting his cane against the arm of his chair.

"Then retire," I quip, a smirk pulling at my lips as I take my own seat.

"Can't leave you younglings to yourself. It's chaos as it is," he says. "You'll see me retired when I hit the Fading and no sooner."

"You're fading?" Envy says, strolling into the room. "So soon? A pity."

"Hold your tongue, boy," Sloth replies.

I roll my eyes, letting the two banter back and forth. Envy loves to poke at everyone without a care for his own safety.

He thinks it makes him brave. I think it makes him stupid.

Envy is also clearly hungover; his mostly unbuttoned shirt is wrinkled, with the sleeves pushed to his elbows rather than rolled. His hair, that he keeps pushing back with one hand, falls in limp strands, lacking its usual volume and wave. And when he pulls his cup to his lips, it's water flowing over the rim, not alcohol.

He *never* has water at these meetings.

"Have a headache, Envy?" I ask.

He shoots me a glare. "And if I do?"

I shrug, my confidence waning.

"Just curious," I say.

My eyes drift across the room, landing on the doors. It's been ten minutes since I was with either Josie, Leo, or Nora. I haven't been without one of them since the accident. And while I'm not alone—Envy and Sloth's presence do little to quell the strange energy that fills me.

My hands are suddenly clammy, and when I rub them on my dress, the fabric itches my skin. I bite my bottom lip, my teeth worrying the skin there until I feel the metallic edge of it ripping open.

The doors open, and I suck in a relieved breath. Though disappointment strikes me.

Greed is on time, for once. He and Gluttony stride in side by side to take their seats. Gluttony is in a beaded white dress that falls to mid-calf; the crystal embroidery sends rainbow specks across the room. Meanwhile, Greed is in a simple black three-piece suit.

Then finally, Nora arrives, and my teeth stop gnawing at my lip.

But instead of walking through the door, she steps from a swirling mass of shadows with Wrath and Silas. Wrath strides through first, heading directly for his seat.

As Silas and Nora step through, he keeps his hand placed firmly on her lower back until the shadows fully dissipate. My eyes narrow at the contact point.

There's something in the way he touches her that sets me on edge. It's possessive. I know because Nora's touched me the same way.

A lazy, smug smile stretches across his face.

Nora, unaware—or simply unfazed—steps out of his hold

and walks to her seat with as much purpose as Wrath. She shucks off her jacket, not caring that snow falls off it and makes puddles at her feet. Draping it over the back of her chair, she sits.

Her hand finds my thigh under the table and squeezes.

"I missed you," she whispers.

"You've only been gone for twelve hours."

"More than enough time to miss you," she says. And while her comment makes butterflies flutter in my tummy, my smile must look forced, because her brows furrow. "Is everything okay?"

"Mhm," I hum.

"Clearly, there is something bothering you."

I don't mean to, but my attention strays to Silas, who now sits at the head of the table. He is whispering with Wrath as the rest of the Sins mingle.

When I turn back to Nora, I can tell that she knows.

I might be the empath, but she's skilled in reading a room. She clocks it for what it is: jealousy.

It's not a pretty emotion to have.

"Imogen," Nora scolds, as if she's the one who can read minds, not Josie. Her hand squeezes my thigh again under the table as she leans to my ear to speak, voice barely above a whisper. "Don't be a brat."

A thrill shoots through me, and I itch to play the game that she's set in front of us.

Silas clears his throat, calling the Sins' attention to the head of the table.

"I know it is unusual for me to call a meeting last minute, but I felt it important to tell you all in person," he says, his deep voice booming through the room. "In two weeks, for the first time in fifty years, we will join our sister Court in celebrating the Winter Solstice. Please prepare yourselves accordingly, as you are all required to attend with your Seconds." He points across the table, "Except for you, Sloth. You're to stay here to ensure all barriers and portals between realms stay intact in coordination with Wrath's Second and the Royal guard."

There is silence as he pauses to let the room process his unsugarcoated announcement.

"I'm sure you have questions. Now would be the time to ask them," he finishes.

The room erupts into chaos.

"Are you mad—"

"Why would we go to see the Seelie after so long—"

"This is insanity—"

"You know, I want to hear him out—"

"Enough!" Silas's voice booms. A burst of shadows spread from behind his back, the room vibrating with his frustration. At the resulting quiet, his magic retracts. "One at a time. You're all acting like children."

Nora snorts at my side, awfully quiet about the whole ordeal.

Is this what they've been working on? Some kind of plans for the Solstice trip?

"Did you know?" I ask, leaning into Nora's side.

"He only told me an hour ago," she responds.

"Do you have a question, Lust?" Silas says.

I plaster a smile on my face, swallowing all the questions that I do have, but wouldn't be asking him.

"No."

"Good. Now, who is next?"

Envy raises his hand, and you can practically hear the collective, yet silent, groan from the other Sins.

"Yes, Envy?" Silas says.

"What's the dress code?"

Silas smiles like a demon about to collect a soul. "My staff will send specific requirements to each House. But, please, dress to *kill*."

Nora's quiet as she enters her bedroom ahead of me, same as she was during the car ride here and in the slow rise of the elevator. It isn't an unpleasant kind of silence, but there is tension in her shoulders and laced through her sighs.

The rest of the Sins meeting went about as civil as it could have. Each Sin got their turn to question Silas's motives for resuming the tradition of spending the Solstice with the Seelie Court. To everyone's disappointment, Silas didn't give a very specific answer—simply, that it was time.

"*Time for what?*" Sloth had asked.

"*You'll see,*" Silas had replied.

Ominous and vague, forcing us to place our faith in him and his plans. Plans, it seemed, both Nora and Wrath were fully privy to. Part of me wants to know, while the other part of me itches to get as far away from the potential danger as I can.

I close the door, the small click of the lock engaging echoes through the room. When I turn, I lean back against the solid wood, letting my eyes trace over Nora's familiar frame.

Broad shoulders, tapered waist, and long legs—all sharp angles compared to my round edges. Where she is carved, I am shaped; I like to think we complement each other with our differences.

She faces away from me, head tilted to the side as she stretches her neck. Her arms raise above her head, her back cracking with the movement. And when she turns back to me, her eyes darken, drinking me in.

Gooseflesh spreads across my arms.

Nora stalks forward until I'm caged in against the door with one of her hands anchored next to my head. I swallow, my mouth suddenly going dry.

"Jealousy doesn't suit you, Imogen," she says, running a nail down my neck to my collarbone. She's slow, taking her time as she caresses my skin and hooks her finger under the strap of my dress. "That's Envy's schtick. Are you looking for a change in rank?"

She pushes the strap off my shoulder, her touch featherlight. Tracing back along my collarbone and up the center of my neck, she grips my chin between her thumb and forefinger, tilting my head up.

Our height difference has never felt so drastic.

"Use your words," she says, voice thick as honey.

"No," I say.

"No, what?"

"I'm not looking for a change in rank."

Nora hums. Her hand moves from pinching my chin to cupping my jaw, her long fingers tickling the back of my neck. Her thumb skates over my cheek, and with each stroke, she kindles a fire within me. There are inches between our bodies, but her heat, her energy, soaks into my skin.

"Then what's bothering you, love?"

Another swipe of her thumb over my cheek—another utterance of that damned moniker she's taken a liking to since my accident—and my lashes flutter.

"I don't like the way Silas is with you," I say. "It's too familiar."

The breath of her soft laughter brushes over my skin. Her fingers tighten against the nape of my neck, gripping the base of my hair and forcing me to meet her eyes.

They're burning.

"I'm going to ask you a few questions, and I need you to answer them honestly," Nora says.

I nod, brows knitting together on my forehead.

"Where do I spend my nights?" she asks.

"I don't understa—"

"Do I spend my nights in his bed?" Her tone is both gentle and demanding as she rephrases her question.

"No."

"Correct," she says, leaning down to peck my forehead. "And whose bed do I share when I'm not half-dead, napping at my desk?"

Her lips trail down my cheek, my jaw.

"Mine," I whisper. "Though it's technically been *your* bed recently..."

Nora nips at the tender skin where my jaw meets my neck, making me gasp.

"Don't be coy," she says. "Who do I dream about when they're not sleeping at my side?"

"Me?" My breath has become airy and light.

"That shouldn't sound so much like a question."

Nora kisses down my throat, sucking at the hollow where my neck meets my collarbone. There's a silent command to stay still radiating off her, to let her guide where this night will go.

I am all but putty in her hands, ready to submit to her whims, and yet, part of me is pushed to voice the rest of my worry.

"It's just that he is the *king*," I say. "He is manipulative at best and coercive at worst. And I don't trust him around you."

Nora's free hand slams into the door to my left, caging me in on both sides now. Our noses touch as she growls her frustration, the heat in her eyes a blazing wildfire.

"Don't be so insecure," she says. "While we were gone, we came to an understanding—we have a mutual goal. But believe me when I say he became a certified pain in my ass in the process."

She heaves a great breath, her eyes softening to the color of damp grass after rain.

"Do you understand?" she says.

Do you understand that there is only you? her eyes ask.

My head nods, fast and short little bobs as my throat swells with emotion.

"Yes," I rasp.

"Good," she whispers, forehead pressing into mine before her lips dip down to meet me.

The kiss is brief but demanding, and as she pulls back, she sucks my bottom lip between her teeth. The bite of pain mixes with the pleasure in my gut—a volatile combination. I'm a kettle ready to boil over, and she's barely touched me.

"Does it make you feel powerful, knowing I choose you?" she whispers, her lips grazing over mine as she speaks.

"Yes."

Her eyes are half-lidded and glazed over with restrained lust, and I know mine are a matching pair.

Soft lips resume their trail over my jaw, my neck, and lower, until they brush against the edge of my bodice. My hands finally find their courage and weave into Nora's hair. As she moves down my body, her kisses burn, despite the layer of fabric between us.

Nora kneels, her head pausing at my waist. Her head tilts up with a devious smirk. Her hands glide up my legs, gently lifting my skirt with them.

"Does it make you wet?" she asks, teasing fingers exploring my thighs. "Does it feel good knowing you've got me wrapped around your finger?"

"Yes," I repeat. The word is a whispered prayer as she glides over the lace trim at the apex of my thighs. Her thumb presses against my core, confirming how wet her words have made me.

"Good." Nora hums, continuing to rub with light enough pressure to work me into a frenzy.

It's a slow build, but she has me locked in a searing stare that increases my pleasure tenfold. But just as I crest the wave into ecstasy, she pulls away.

"I'm getting tired of you being a tease all the time," I hiss.

"Jealous brats don't get to come right away," she says with a smirk, rising, hands trailing back up my body.

Nora cuts off any protests I attempt by crashing her lips to mine, a fiery explosion of our need. Despite our weekend together as I recovered, she's been too gentle with me, and I haven't been fully satisfied.

Her body molds to mine, and our hands interlock in each other's hair. The sting of her grip shoots shivers down to my core. One of Nora's legs fits between mine, my dress riding up as I grind against the base of her thigh and top of her knee.

Groaning into her fevered lips, I silently beg for release.

She hears me, both hands gripping my hips and grinding me down harder on her leg. My eyes are screwed shut and my head hangs back, hitting the door as I whisper a curse.

It's heaven and hell, the way our bodies move together. Nora blesses me with torturous friction, slowly stoking that fire in my core. And when her lips find their way back to that spot on my neck, her teeth grazing and nipping, her tongue sliding over the sting, I come undone.

My hips stall and stutter, and my thighs strangle Nora's leg as I pulse against her, riding the waves of pleasure.

Nora smiles against my neck as we both come down from the high; our harried breaths turn soft and light. She rests her forehead against mine with a satisfied hum.

"You come so beautifully for me."

My core instinctively clenches against Nora's leg, and her smile brightens. I'm caught in its light, stunned.

Whether it be the orgasm fog or the way she beams so radiantly that gives me the confidence to speak—I don't know. Either way, I find myself uttering a string of words that could fuse us together or break us apart.

"I think I'm falling in love with you. Have been, for a long time," I say, breathless.

"Oh?" she says, one brow cocked.

"Yeah," I say. And when she doesn't say anything, the anxiety of the situation kicks in, making me ramble. "But it's okay if you don't—"

"I've never felt like this before, Mo. For anyone." Nora sighs. "It doesn't make sense to me. My need for you is irrational. But what else could it be, blooming between us?" Her brows furrow, as if she's ran the question through her head a thousand times already, always coming away without an answer. "I told you, I'm not good at this. But I want to make it work. I want to make it work for *you*."

"Yeah?" I bite my lip, trying, and failing, to suppress the beam of a smile that lights up my face.

"I thought I made it clear when I let you cuddle me for days," she says, plucking my lip from between my teeth with her thumb.

I lightly smack her shoulder. "It wasn't *days*."

"Hours then," she relents. A soft, teasing smile spreads across her cheeks. "Still the same sentiment."

I don't have any more words after that; the emotions in my throat have blocked them all.

"Kiss me again, please," I manage to squeeze out, leaning into her lips.

Nora laughs, deep and throaty, and it only makes me smile harder as she obliges.

"Only because you asked nicely."

32
NORA

I've discovered the heaven that humans love to preach about. It's Imogen, in my bed, golden locks shining in the gilded light of sunrise.

The sight used to make my body stiffen, and I wonder how that could have ever been; was I struck still by fear? Denial?

Waking up next to her has been my favorite part of the day for the past two weeks. My obsession with her body has only grown, and in turn, strange feelings have bloomed in my chest. Imogen helped me put a name to them the day she confessed to me.

She's mine.

It is a possessive, all-consuming thought. But one that pulls my lips into a smirk every time I think it. She was mine before, but the words mean something different now.

It's her turn to grumble and complain about waking up at the crack of dawn, a day of travel ahead of us. Her energy is low as she begrudgingly moves through the steps to get ready. Meanwhile mine is electric and thrumming under my skin.

Today we head to Casimir.

We have our plan. All we have to do is pull it off.

I toss the shadow gloves, courtesy of Silas, into my suitcase. We'd decided that given he was the stronger fae, we would use his shadows to craft them instead of Wrath's—though, oddly enough, I would have preferred Wrath's.

The idea of being coated in Silas's shadows raises the hair on my arms.

No less than an hour later, we're congregated at the roundabout outside of Silas's palace. A caravan of automobiles waits for us, exhaust pipes huffing a steady stream of steam into the chilled air.

We agreed driving was the best option, as not to drain any of Wrath, Silas, or Gluttony's power ferrying all of us back and forth. Greed isn't strong enough to shadow-walk long distances and Envy is an empath, so they aren't any help.

And so, here we are. Six Sins and their Seconds hauling suitcases as if we are headed off to a family holiday—which I guess it is, in a way.

Silas is Wrath's counterpart for this trip, and they stand side by side at the center of the hustle and bustle. Silas directs us all to our cars, a ringleader for the impending circus.

Gluttony, Greed, and their Seconds claim seats in one, while Silas pawns Wrath off to Envy and his Second.

"For gods' sake," he says, throwing his arms up. He points accusingly at Silas. "I refuse to be his babysitter when we get there."

"You'll do what I say regardless," Silas chirps.

Now that I've seen their dynamic up close and personal, I clock the joy sparkling in Silas's eyes with the command. I can also see the twitch of Wrath's lips trying to hide a smile at Silas's antics and can't help but silently chuckle. They continue to bicker as my attention moves to the first car of the caravan.

"I guess we get this one then," I say, pointing.

Imogen, Josie, and Leo follow me to the car, Leo whistling at the shiny chrome and sleek blue paint of the Cadillac as we approach. He rounds the back of the car, putting our bags in the trunk; I open the door to the backseat with a wide swipe of my arm.

"Ladies first," I say, playfully. Imogen snorts.

"Nora, you've gone from cute to downright sickening," Leo says over the hood, letting himself in on the other side.

I roll my eyes. "Watch your mouth, Leo."

It may be a threat, but he laughs it off, hopping into the car with a slam of the door. I place one hand on the roof of the car and lean down so I'm eye-level with Imogen.

"Put your seatbelt on."

Warmth blooms in my chest as her freckled cheeks bloom with pink.

"Yes, ma'am," she says.

"Josie, you want me to drive? You've always been better at reading maps and turning them into directions," I say.

"Sure." She shrugs.

"Actually, I'll be driving."

All our heads whip towards the voice; Silas stalks towards us with a smirk.

"Are you not taking your own?" I frown.

"Why would I use another car when there's enough room for all of us here?" he says, bypassing both Josie and me in our stunned silence.

I rip open the front passenger door, leaning in to talk to him. Silas pauses, already sitting, but reaching for the handle to close the door on his side.

"You can ride with Wrath and Envy," I say. "They have an extra seat."

"I don't want to listen to Envy babble the whole drive." Silas buckles his seat belt. He twists, turning to

Imogen and Leo in the backseat. "You two don't mind, right?"

Leo looks unsure; Imogen glares.

"Of course not," Imogen says, voice tight.

"See?" Silas says. "Now get in, both of you. We have a long journey ahead."

I huff, mumbling, "Fine."

"Can I still take the front?" Josie asks me.

I nod—she tends to get sick when she sits in the back.

"Of course," I say, holding the door open for her.

Imogen shifts to take the center seat in the back when I slide into the car; it is cramped but not uncomfortable, given we're three grown fae.

An awkward silence fills the car.

The car lurches forward, then jolts to a stop at the end of the driveway. I quickly band my hand over Imogen's waist so she doesn't fly forward.

"Respectfully, Your Majesty, could you brake a little smoother?" I say.

"You would be a backseat driver," Silas mutters. His eyes meet mine in the rearview mirror; they sparkle with the same mirth he gives Wrath.

I glare until he breaks our stare, attention moving back to the road ahead.

"This is going to be an interesting ride," Leo says under his breath.

It wasn't, really.

The five of us fall into a not unbearable quiet as Silas drives us from the city. We trade brownstones, skyscrapers, and pavement for dirt, rolling fields, and an empty skyline. Following alongside the river, the road runs north across the Unseelie Court.

Grass soon thickens into forest, imposing pines and spruce

surrounding us on every side. Imogen's head has long since landed on my shoulder, and her breath is even as she slumbers. Leo and Josie have followed suit; both will wake to indents on their foreheads from where they lean against the windows.

Silas and I are the only two awake, and I am thankful that he doesn't attempt conversation. I'd much rather let my mind run alongside the landscape that blurs past.

When the car eventually slows, and we pull into a small outcropping of trees—a dirt patch of a parking lot—I know our journey has ended.

"Are you ready?" Silas asks, not loud enough for the rest to wake.

It's a thousand questions in one, but my answer to all of them is clear.

"Yes," I say.

I am more than ready to rid the world of the scourge that is Patience.

I nudge Imogen at my side, and her lashes flutter open. She wakes quickly and silently takes in her surroundings. She, in turn, smacks Leo's chest, causing him to jolt awake with a snort. I do the same to Josie, poking her shoulder over the back of her seat until she rouses from sleep.

"I've got to be honest, this isn't what I was expecting," Leo says, popping open the car door. "It's a bit small for a castle."

"That's not Casimir," Silas huffs, turning off the ignition as we all exit the vehicle. He points to the remnants of a small cabin and stable that meet the clearing, long overgrown and unused. "That's where stable hands usually stayed when we traveled by horse."

"Ah, that makes a lot more sense." Leo scratches the stubble on his cheek. "I'll grab our bags."

Silas waves him off. "No need. The sprites will get them once I raise the bridge."

"Sprites?" I ask.

"Creepy little bastards that run the castle in our stead." Silas shivers before stalking towards a footpath next to the cabin. "Come. The others will follow."

I toss a glance back at the idling cars behind us. The other Sins and their Seconds are slow to get out, stretching and groaning from the ride. Wrath is the only one who is quick to leave his group. He strides after Silas with his signature pissed-off frown.

I jerk my head towards the path, a silent command to Josie and Leo. Grabbing Imogen's hand, I follow.

It's a short walk to the edge of the water. When we break through the tree line, then the thin shimmering shadow-veil, there's about twenty feet of rocky beach scattered with fallen logs and boulders. Waves crash against the shoreline, the sound peaceful.

My breath puffs around my face, and I know that if we dipped a toe in the lake, it would be freezing. The winter chill in the air is deeper here than in the city, being closer to the mountains. In the distance, I can barely make out snowy peaks below the clouds.

Silas stands before a white marble pillar, shaped into a lectern of sorts; it's out of place against the dark gray and brown-toned pebbles of the beach. Shadows weave through Silas's fingers, flattening into the familiar shape of a knife. We watch on as he pricks the pad of his thumb, blood welling to the surface, and swipes it across the top of the pillar.

His shadow knife dissipates, and the distinct tingling of magic shifts the air around us. The clouds above blow away in an unnatural breeze, and the water stills into a mirror-like pane. The earth trembles, rocking us, and Imogen's hand squeezes mine to steady herself.

The water parts, and a pristine marble bridge rises from

the depths. It leads across the lake, and there, a mile offshore, stands Casimir in all its mythical glory. A stunning castle that makes up the entirety of the island. Its name is interchangeable for the building and the land.

My mother had read me children's stories about it, but the memories are faded; more snapshots of her leaning over my bed with a book in hand than anything else. It wasn't until Silas told me his plan that I did more research into the ancient castle we'd be visiting.

It was the home of the first Fae Queen—the blood of whom runs partly through Silas and partly through the Seelie Queen. The first Fae Queen's children were the original sires of the Unseelie and Seelie lines. While they fought over who would rule over Faerie, cleaving the realm into two as a result, they always came together once a year to honor their mother on the Solstice. And thus started a tradition that has since become a bloody meeting between the Courts.

No one speaks as Silas steps onto the bridge and begins the trek across the water. He doesn't wave us on or command us to follow, leaving us to stare in our awestruck stupor.

"We aren't here to gawk. Stop staring and get moving," Wrath says, breaking our trance before following Silas across the bridge.

Imogen lets go of my hand as we cross the bridge. It's only wide enough to fit us single file, so I take the lead of the four of us.

Waves crash against the walls of the bridge as we walk, and about halfway across, the water turns from a winter gray to a summer blue. I unbutton my coat as sweat beads on my neck, the air turning thick and hot. The sun casts waves of heat on us, and soon we're all shucking off our jackets.

When we reach the end of the bridge, the beach is not the same pebbles and rocks and seaweed as on our side of the lake.

Instead, the castle sits on golden, red-speckled sand. Massive marble towers spiral above us. Swirling carvings serve as molding for the windows and archways, inlaid with pink stone that contrasts the white main structure. The architecture is detailed and precise, a masterpiece of stonemasonry.

There's only one door into the castle, which is already propped open—the aged mahogany reddish in hue, complimenting the pink carvings around it.

We step through the doorway and into a lush garden full of wildflowers and buzzing bees. Floral notes float through the air and ivy crawls up pillars that line the garden, hints of shaded hallways peeking between them.

Silas stops in the center of the brush; he stares up at the castle spires with his hands on his hips, quiet and contemplative.

It isn't lost on me that the last time he was here, he lost his parents.

Slowly he turns, a plotting grin plastered across his face.

"The land that bends season, gifting us a taste of spring in winter," he says. "Welcome to Casimir."

"I've assigned you all specific floors, but you can pick whichever rooms you wish for yourselves. Simply choose a room and the sprites will know where to bring your bags. The keys will appear when you open the door."

Silas drones on with directions on how to access the stairwells and other rules about the castle. Food will be delivered to our rooms, and tomorrow, we have a welcome luncheon with the Seelie. After that, an agenda will be issued listing out the rest of the weekend's festivities.

"Unfortunately, the sprites coordinate all the events, so don't blame me if you're unhappy. Tomorrow morning is a welcome luncheon, tomorrow night the Seelie host a revelry, and the day after that is the Solstice Ball," he says. "Now get some rest. And don't wander. The doors to the common areas will block entry to our sister Court's half of the castle, and vice versa, but this castle's magic has a mind of its own. Don't tempt it."

With that, Silas turns and strides into the castle, leaving us to our own devices. Where he's off to, I don't know, but Wrath follows him, a dutiful shadow. But with no reason for us to follow them, we make our way to our rooms.

It's not hard to navigate to the seventh level; each floor has a landing within the spiral staircase with the number carved into the marble archway. The pale stone is sunlit with rainbows that filter in from the stained-glass windows lining the curved walls.

When we reach the seventh landing, the staircase continues on, while we fork off down the single hall. Josie and Leo lead the pack while I linger towards the back, letting them choose first.

"I call the end cap," Leo calls, rushing to the farthest room, leaving us all in a puff of dust. "I don't want to hear them fucking. Sorry, Josie!"

His laughter dies out as the door at the end of the hall slams shut.

"I guess that means I'm this one."

Josie tentatively pushes open the second to last door lining the hall—each room sits to the left, while the right wall hosts a long windowpane overlooking the garden we came from.

Imogen's arm sneaks around my waist.

"Leo's being dramatic," Imogen says. "We aren't that loud."

Josie snorts, but then quickly tries to cover it with a cough that is obviously fake. Imogen pales beside me.

"Sorry," Josie says. "But that is decidedly false. You two are very loud."

Imogen licks her lips nervously. "All the way in your rooms, at Nora's place, you were able to hear us?"

"Mhm."

"Don't worry, we won't subject Josie to anything traumatizing this time around." I pull Imogen towards the closest door to the stairwell. "Come on, let's get settled."

"I'll see you both in the morning," Josie calls, and I hear the click of her door shutting.

Meanwhile, Imogen untangles herself from me and takes a sure step back, one arm extended in front of her as if she can keep me a safe distance away.

"Maybe we should take separate rooms?" she squeaks, a pink flush actively rising on her neck.

"Why so embarrassed, *Lust*?" I chide.

Her face sours at the use of her title rather than her name. "I'm not embarrassed. Maybe I need a break from the constant sex."

I stalk towards her, and she takes measured steps back until I've got her crowded against the windows. She does have a good point. I've been crazed over her body as of late, wringing more orgasms from her in the past week than I have in the previous month.

"I'm pretty sure you enjoy my debauchery. Encourage it even," I say.

She'd look delicious writhing under the stained-glass light, shards of color dancing over her smooth skin. I make a note to pull her into a side hall at some point.

Well, maybe after I kill Patience.

I wasn't letting her fall into his wrinkly, evil hands. Not ever again.

I was half tempted to leave her in Anwynn, but I couldn't stomach the thought of leaving her without my protection again.

I drop a kiss to her forehead. "Will you stay with Josie until I come back?"

"You're not coming to bed?"

"I thought you said you needed a break? Did you change your mind?" I tease, but then I get serious. "Do you think I'd be able to sleep without doing a sweep of what parts of the castle I can reach? I don't care about whatever wards Silas says are in place to keep the Seelie side sealed off."

"I'd hope you would be able to take a break like the rest of us," Imogen says. "But I know you can't."

"I promise to not cause trouble."

"Uh-huh," she says with a roll of her eyes. "Please be safe."

"I promise," I say. "I'll come get you when I'm back."

She kisses my cheek before quietly knocking on Josie's door. They exchange a few quiet words before Josie lets her in, nodding my way before shutting the door.

The apple of my cheek tingles where Imogen's lips left their mark as I veer onto the stairwell landing and climb the final steps up to the top floor.

The eighth landing is the same as the rest, though instead of a hall with multiple rooms, only a set of double doors stands beyond the archway. The dark wood still smells as if it was hewn and carved yesterday, the fresh musk of the wood filling the air. Golden handles line either side of the center and jut out from the wood, molded into an intricate design that resembles a tree.

The handles are tarnished at either end and shiny in the

middle, betraying the castle's old age. As my fingers brush the metal, the hair on my neck rises, a chill running down my spine.

I spin, unsheathing my gun from its rib holster and pointing it at the presence behind me—all to stare into an empty stairwell.

Walking down a flight to the seventh landing, I keep my gun poised and ready to strike if needed, all the while still feeling eyes on my back.

Minutes pass as I check each hall and the stairwell all the way down to the fifth floor. With not even a mouse to be seen, I re-holster my gun—though I can't shake the sensation of being watched.

Maybe it is the ancient magic running between the veins of marble setting me on edge.

Either way, the warm-and-fuzzies escape me as I continue my sweep of the castle. It is even larger on the inside than I could have gauged from our view walking on the bridge. I meander through the halls and peer into every sitting room. Each is decorated with an obscene amount of gold—curtains, couches, and fixtures all adorned and shining with the metal.

The castle is eerily quiet, as if the walls themselves have gone to sleep.

On the lower level of the castle, past the garden we entered from, is the last hall I've yet to map. But as I step towards it, a buzzing swoops past my ear.

I rip my gun from its holster for the second time tonight. Following the loud buzzing, I train my gun at the gray blur that circles me. It stops, and I find myself staring down the barrel at a bulbous little creature.

It's a beady little thing, about the size of my hand, with a large, round head that holds saucer-like eyes the color of the darkest shadow. The creature blinks at me, scratching its cheek with a taloned finger. Charcoal in color, with leathery skin that leads to the wings sprouting from its back, the creature cocks its head at me. It squeaks at me, clearly annoyed, and I can't help that my lips twitch upwards in laughter—which only spurs the creature on.

This must be one of the illusive sprites Silas mentioned. And the reason for why I've sensed eyes on me since I stepped off the seventh-floor landing.

I pull my finger off the trigger and tuck my gun away.

"Sorry, little one. You gave me a scare," I say.

Leaning forward with my hands on my knees, I get a closer look at the creature. It has worked itself into a fury, squawking at me. It surges forward, one taloned finger pointing at me, then the door at the end of the hall behind me, forcing me to take a few steps back.

I raise my hands by my shoulders, hoping to appease the creature.

"Alright, alright," I chuff. "What did I do to piss you off?"

I'm saved by a second buzzing—another sprite zooming by me. It moves so quick that it has my hair whipping around my face before stopping short before us.

This one is green and blue, iridescent like a dragonfly, with wings that move as fast as the insect—so it's as if they aren't moving at all. It assesses me, twitching up and down in the air. Then it turns around and squeaks in a higher pitch than the first sprite, berating its colleague.

It's all an incoherent language to me.

They fight in their little sprite language, forgetting that I'm even there. I silently inch my way down the hall until my hand grips the large doorknob at my back. I twist it, the internal lock disengaging and the door creaking open a sliver; the sprites freeze in their argument, two sets of beady eyes flicking to me.

I don't wait for them to berate me, slipping behind the door and quickly shutting it on them.

There's a stark difference between this part of the castle and the rest.

The air is thinner here, but no less thrumming with magic. I lean back against the door, my heart beating quickly as it works to pump oxygen to my brain. It takes a second for the room to register, for me to really take in all the detail, but it's just a sparsely decorated ballroom.

Across the room is a set of matching doors to the ones at my back. To the right is a large fireplace—surprisingly full of flames—and framed by another two sets of doors. Floor to ceiling windows line the left side of the room, draped with gold and silver curtains; moonlight now pours between the windowpanes, planting squares of cool-toned light on the tiled floor.

"Lost, little fae?" a voice calls.

I pan the room, searching for its owner.

The person must be sitting in one of the armchairs next to the fireplace, hidden by the tall chair back, because the distinct crinkle of leather fills the room. Not more than a second later does a mop of brown locks peek around the side of the chair.

While his face is half shrouded in shadow, I can make out a strong nose and jaw.

Seelie, my body screams, instinct causing the hair on my arms to stand on end. My magic perks, swirling in my belly, a keen predator searching for its next meal.

I step forward, my boot clacks reverberating through the room.

"I wouldn't consider myself *little*," I respond.

I round the chair and peer down at the fae. With chocolate-brown hair that is long on top and cropped on the sides, and tan skin that hasn't yet wrinkled around his eyes, he looks to be about my age. Though, that could mean he's anywhere from mid-twenties to one hundred. A folded book sits in his lap, a ripped piece of paper tucked between the open pages to mark his place.

One hand mindlessly moves up to twirl the curled edges of his mustache. His head tilts to the side, an action akin to the sprites, as he takes me in with keen eyes. They are darker than mine, a mossy shade of green rather than crystalline.

"No, certainly not little," he says. "Actually, you're on the tall side, I'd say."

"And I wouldn't claim to be lost. Being lost implies that I didn't intend to end up where I did," I say.

"Did you?" he asks. "Intend to be here?"

I shrug. "Does it matter?"

He hums knowingly, his cupids-bow lips curving under his mustache. The red glow of the crackling fire plays well with the undertones of his coloring, warmth bringing out warmth. It softens the sharp edges of his jaw and roman nose.

"Fair," he says, opening his book.

"This is one of the communal areas, no?" I ask, head tilting to the ceiling where intricate molding swirls around the base of each chandelier.

The Seelie grabs his crumpled bookmark and twirls it between his middle and forefinger.

"The doors to this area are supposed to be locked," I say.

"And?" He flips a page.

"I've been told the castle has rules. But clearly, it doesn't adhere to them. Bit hypocritical, if you ask me."

He throws his head back, laughter bellowing to the rafters. "I wasn't expecting you to be funny."

"You were expecting me?"

The fae replaces his bookmark and snaps the book shut.

"My father more than I, but I'd be fibbing if I said I wasn't intrigued to meet you. Been meaning to for a while, actually, but I couldn't snag the permits to visit the Human Realm." He states it all so casually, it's unnerving. "Rumors travel fast on our side of Faerie, and a soul-stealer taking on the mantle of Pride is *quite* a rumor."

"I'm not a rumor, though."

"No, not anymore. I'd say you've graduated to a cautionary tale for the younglings."

"And you are?" I ask, running my nail back and forth over the coarse fabric of the empty armchair at my side.

"Benevolence. But you can call me Bennie," he says with a blinding white smile.

"And your father?" I ask, though I suspect the answer.

His smile turns sour. "Someone you'll quickly learn to hate, if you don't already."

I tilt my head, scrutinizing the Seelie before me.

"Fair," I say, mimicking him from before.

"Now you're more than welcome to stay. The gods know I love company, but I would like to finish this chapter before I retire for the night," he says, pointing down to the clothbound book in his lap.

I snort at his forwardness, but I can't help but find myself impressed by it. There's a familiarity to his energy that whispers of homesickness. I almost think it would be a shame for me to have to kill him, if I learn he helped Patience in any way.

What a strange thought.

33
IMOGEN

I wake to a purring in my ear and a strange breeze tickling my nose.

Did I leave the window open last night?

I rub the crust from my eyes, blinking hard as I'm pulled from my dreams.

"Fucking gods!"

Scrambling to the headboard, with my heart nearly bursting from my chest, I gape at a creature floating mere inches from where I was sleeping. Its ears fold back against its head, the gray creature—*sprite*—wrings its sharp talons together, bashful.

"Hello," I say, as my heartbeat calms.

Its ears perk. Bulbous eyes stare at me, unblinking, little black voids. A single talon points to itself then to the wardrobe in the corner of the room.

"Were you the one who brought my travel case up?" I ask slowly.

It nods. Its wings flap harder, and it flies across the room to the wardrobe. With care, it pulls the doors open, and disappears inside the folds of fabric before emerging with a grip on one of the dresses I packed. It's one of the simpler ones, a green silk base with a starburst of black beading extending from the boat neckline and into beaded tassel sleeves.

Placing the dress on the edge of my bed, it points at it, then to me, squeaking a command before disappearing in a plume of shadow. A second later, it's dropping matching shoes from the wardrobe and a brush from the restroom vanity on top of the quilt.

My hand lifts to my lips to hide my smile.

"*Ah*," I croon. "So, you're my alarm clock then?"

Its head, round as a baseball and about the size of one too, tilts to the side, long pointed ears twitching in turn.

It's actually quite cute.

It still hasn't blinked though.

"It's been watching you sleep for nearly a half hour," Nora says, exiting the bathroom. "It clearly likes you more than me."

"Should I be worried by that?"

"No, everyone likes you more than me. Why should it be any different with the sprites?"

Nora deftly buttons the cuffs of her button-down, fastening a silver metal cufflink to the white fabric. She's already got on her vest and slacks, both impeccably tailored and colored a deep charcoal gray, the halfway point between her skin and hair.

I throw the covers off and pad to the end of the bed; picking up the brush, I huff a laugh.

"I'll tell you this, little sprite," I coo. "I'll need more than this to be presentable for today."

Nora snorts, righting her vest.

"How long do I have?" I ask.

"We don't have to be down for another hour," Nora says.

"Oh, then why are you dressed?"

"Because I thought I'd help you with your hair, and I can't do that if I still have to do my own." Hers is already set in perfect waves, one side pulled behind her ear, revealing the pointed tip dangling with a single dew-drop earring.

"I better get a move on then." I turn to the sprite. "Will you wait outside? I'll be out as quick as a jiffy."

It pouts, taking a second to consider, but then it nods, dissipating in a swirl of shadow.

"Huh." Nora frowns at the spot where it once floated, shadows curling in its place. "I asked it to leave five times."

"I guess I have a way with words," I tease.

Padding over to Nora, I stand on my tippy-toes, planting a small kiss on her nose.

"Let me get my dress on and then you can help me wrangle these waves."

Once I've washed up and gotten my dress on, Nora takes great care in curling my hair. She uses a heated iron—*who knew an ancient castle would be outfitted with electricity?*—to tenderly tame my hair into waves and gently pin them into a faux bob, while I dab makeup onto my cheeks. When she's done, she places a kiss atop my head.

"Good?" she asks.

I smile at her through the mirror. "Dare I say, very good?"

"*Very* good? That sounds better than pretty good."

"Exactly," I say, bouncing the bottom of my hair. "Because of this, I'm expanding the good scale. It goes from not bad, to good, to pretty good, and now *very* good."

Nora leans into my space, face fitting perfectly, like a puzzle piece, in the crook of my neck. Our eyes meet in the mirror, both of us admiring the other with soft smiles. Her hand trails over my shoulder, running through the beaded tassels and over the exposed skin at my collar. She brushes the hair back, placing a chaste kiss at my pulse.

"What can I do to add excellent to the list?"

She knows what she's doing, using that sultry tone that never fails in pulling gooseflesh to the surface of my skin.

"I can think of something," I murmur.

"I'm sure," she says. "But I'm going to have to take a rain check, or we'll be late."

Her electric touch leaves and I let loose a growl at how she edges me with such little effort. There's something about the way her body speaks to mine that has me melting into a pile of mush in her presence.

Nora wastes no time in pulling on her suit jacket and leather gloves while I add a final dab of blush to my cheeks. And then we're ready.

We're no less than two steps out of our room when the sprite flies at us, pulling our hands into its leathery grip. We're thrust into a shadow so thick I can hardly breathe. I stumble as we emerge, catching myself on the smooth marble wall. And as quick as it appeared, the sprite is gone, leaving us at a pair of double doors deeper in the castle.

"Creepy little buggers, aren't they?" Envy says, walking up behind us with his Second trailing behind. He fiddles with the black tie under his light gray suit, straying from his typical green garb.

"I think they're quite cute," I say, righting the skirt of my dress.

"You would," he snorts, sidling up next to me. He nods at Nora. No love lost between them in the past few weeks. "Pride."

"Envy," she deadpans back at him.

He pushes past us, pausing before the pair of massive double doors the sprite left us in front of. They reach the full height of the hall, a solid fifteen feet of carved wood. His warm brown hand stills on the massive brass handles.

"So, how do we think this is going to go?" Envy asks, his tone betraying his nerves. "I've never met one of them before."

Nora pushes Envy out of the way, sending him stumbling into his Second.

"Stick with Greed and Gluttony, and you should be fine. And don't let the faerie wine convince you it'd be a good idea to add a Seelie to the notches on your bedpost," she says, pulling the heavy door open. "No one will save you from that knife at your throat."

Envy's throat makes an awkward, choked sound, a singular strong hand coming up to brush the pulse point of his neck.

Nora enters the ballroom like she owns the place, and I follow, leaving Envy to fend for himself.

I don't stray far from Nora's side, but I take my time gawking at the room. To my left, golden curtains hang in billowing waves against floor to ceiling windowpanes; they let in the sunlight of this strange spring that Casimir is stuck in.

Odd, how we're about to celebrate Winter Solstice while bathed in warmth. Should we not be sitting, cozied up around a raging fire, drinking mulled cider?

My magic springs to life as I take stock of the bodies in the room, sensing some unease, a trickle of boredom, but no fear.

The room is far too large for the scattered groupings of two to three, even with the many sprites floating between the fae with trays of drinks and food. Some are akin to the one who woke me, but others are clearly their Seelie counterparts. They buzz through the air like worker bees, their wings refracting the sunlight onto the tiled floor.

The room is divided in half, with one side hosting a cluster of Seelie and the other the Unseelie.

"Did they bring civilians too? Or are those Seelie Royals?" I ask, snagging a glass off a sprite's passing tray.

I take a tentative sip, sparkling wine mixed with sharp orange bursts on my tongue.

"Silas said celebrations here used to amass hundreds, so probably a mix of both," Nora says, pulling me towards a grazing table at the center of the room.

Leo and Josie linger there; Leo points at different pastries, plate in hand, while Josie waves us over with a look that says *save me* over her orange drink.

"—it's dark like blackberry jam, but it could also be blueberry. What do you think, Joze?" Leo perks up when sees us. "Hey guys."

"Leo's very intrigued by all the Seelie food," Josie informs us.

Leo piles another few pastries and some fruit onto his plate. "I am viewing this whole trip as a way to experience a new culture. And what better way to do that than with their food?"

"I wouldn't eat any of it," Nora says. Her head swivels, scanning the room with her eyes narrowed. "Could be poisoned."

"I don't think it's poisoned, Nora," he says with a mouthful of flaky, buttery goodness. "Poison doesn't taste this good."

"You think the sprites would poison us?" I ask.

Nora's lips turn down at the corners. "No. But I wouldn't put it past the Seelie. Make sure you watch your drinks around them."

"So, basically like any other normal night out," I say.

"Stakes are a little bit higher this go-around, love," Nora says, placing a protective hand on the small of my back. "Remember what happened two weeks ago."

A pit forms in my stomach, my mood instantly souring. "I'm fully aware of the stakes, Nora."

"Here." Leo shoves his plate at me. "I already took bites out of all these, so they are pre-approved, no poison—"

The double doors at the opposite end of the ballroom burst open; the energy in the air instantly shifts as a wave of thrumming of power washes over us.

An entourage much larger than our six pairs of Sins and Seconds enters the hall: a peacocking group of men and women alike, dripping in gemstone fabrics and sparkling jewels. The gaggle of Seelie surrounds one woman, who is draped in a figure hugging, white frock. It shines like opals, reflecting rainbows as she passes under the beams of sunlight filtering through the window. A light tinkling rings through the now silent room when she moves—and I realize that the dress is *made* with shards of opalescent seashells.

The bodice wraps around her neck in a halter trimmed with pearl details. Her hair sits in waves of golden honey; cropped short, the edges curl around her ears and at the nape of her neck. She has a certain kind of beauty that the humans would describe as *fairy-like*. Her pinched features err on the side of youth and rosy, sun-kissed skin accentuates the apples of her cheeks.

Despite her small frame, which stands nearly a foot shorter than her companions, her power is great. It's familiar, this well of magic, though it is less suffocating than Silas's.

It's clear that this is the Seelie Queen.

Her entourage giggles and paws at her, stroking her bare arms as she struts towards us. One whispers in her ear, and she laughs. It rings through the hall, echoing off the vaulted ceilings.

She stops opposite us and inspects her options, tongue darting out to lick her lips, before plucking a single grape from the vine and popping it in her mouth. As she chews, her gaze lifts, meeting mine—ice-blue eyes clear as crystal freeze me where I stand.

Swallowing on a smile, she winks before turning back to her companions and flittering among the Seelie. The action reveals the open back of her dress. But where the smooth panes of shoulder blades should be, a set of wings hang down.

The thin film shimmers in a near-translucent rainbow, and like rivers on a map, white veins spread out from the midpoint between her shoulders. The wings are two-fold, the upper pair smaller than the lower, much like the insects that they mimic. The lower set drape to the ground, close, but not quite long enough to touch the tile. They curl at the end, the long tendrils twisting to a point.

"If you haven't already guessed, that's our dear Seelie Queen." I jump as Silas appears at our side. "She is a bit of a flirt, based on what I can remember. Do be careful," he warns, snagging a small cream-filled pastry from my plate and popping it into his mouth. He hums. "That's pretty good."

"Silas, darling!" The Seelie Queen's voice bellows through the room, a melodic siren's call. "Are you going to stand there all morning chit-chatting or are you going to introduce us to all the new meat?"

Silas sighs, muttering, "That's our cue."

He quickly pulls on a mask of cunning indifference, striding forward. With a casual crook of his hand above his shoulder, he pulls all six of the Sins across the room with him, while our Seconds stand back and watch on.

We line up, matching one-for-one the Seelie that step forward and bracket the queen.

"No wings?" The Seelie Queen pouts. But while her expression is animated, her blue eyes are keen, cutting across the seven of us.

"Not today," Silas says.

The queen stares at him, as if she is waiting for further explanation, of which she gets none.

That's when I notice that the Seelie Virtues all have their wings out, and although most are tucked tight and low like the queen's, some still poke out over their shoulders.

A shiver runs down my back, bracketing my spine, my own wings itching to be free.

"Maybe later, once the real festivities have begun." She winks. "I know it's all very new to the rest of you, but Solstice used to be a weeklong revelry meant to honor the first Queen."

"We may be younglings by your standards, but we are well aware of the history, Oonagh," Silas says, addressing the Seelie Queen by her given name. Trepidation trickles over the once light energy of the room. "Now, I'd like to introduce the next generation of Unseelie leaders. Over here we have Envy..."

Silas introduces us one by one, going down the line.

"...then this is Lust. Isn't she the spitting image of her mother? You must remember."

I smile and tilt my head graciously when Silas introduces me.

"And last, we have our newest Pride."

"*Your Majesty*," Nora greets, red-stained lips tilting up a fraction as she dips her head in respect.

Oonagh licks her lips, eyes rolling over Nora's frame.

"The infamous soul-stealer?" the queen coos to Silas. "Maybe you'll allow her to demonstrate the magic I've heard so many rumors about."

"Did you have someone specific in mind, or are we drawing sticks?" Nora asks.

The queen laughs—her entourage following suit—and the tension in the air lessens a fraction.

"You're a funny one, Pride," Oonagh says. She claps her hands excitedly, her dress tinkling with the movement. "Now our turn. Though not much has changed since you were here last, Silas."

She starts at my end first, with the two before Nora and me, Chastity and Charity. They are clearly sisters, with matching round faces, wide noses, and full lips framed by black braids that flow in straight lines over their shoulders. Their light brown skin shines warm against the cream-colored dresses they wear. They both look bored as their queen introduces them.

Next are Temperance and Diligence, two women who must be verging on the Fading, given their salt and pepper hair. One wears it long and wavy over her pale features. The other has it cropped short with finger waves; she's how I imagine Gluttony will look in a hundred years.

And then there are the men.

Humility doesn't have any wrinkles, but his rough beard, which is cropped short to his chiseled jaw, hints at a maturity only found with age.

Benevolence is dashing—a young man whose smile shines bright against his tanned skin. His wide smile, lined with a curved mustache, gives him an innocent air, but his mossy-green eyes spark with mischief. When the queen calls him out, he waves a hello.

Patience is last, the queen's right hand. As he is introduced, his energy flares with satisfaction. Running his hand over his coifed white hair, his lips quirk into a smug smile. Deep crow's feet bracket a set of emerald eyes.

On second glance, I note the similarities between him and Benevolence at his side; they have the same roman nose, sharp cheekbones, and tall-but-lean stature. While their coloring is different, Benevolence sporting a deep tan and Patience as pale as paper, they are clearly family.

When the Seelie Queen is finished, I turn over each of their titles, reconciling them with the fae before me. They feign innocence with their titles, cloaked in their white and cream fabrics. They tease dainty dispositions with their fragile wings, but lurking under the surface of each one of their gazes is a snake waiting for its moment to strike.

"Cheers to a beautiful Solstice, Silas darling," Oonagh croons, raising her glass and then downing it all in one go. Flirtatious eyes roam across the Sins. "I hope you all will join us tonight at the bacchanalia. It's a wonderful tradition to partake."

Silas shoots her a tight-lipped smile, making her no promises of our presence at the revelry tonight, and the group breaks. Most rush to the food, ravenous as they pile their plates with breakfast. A few linger, Silas, Nora, and I stand together, a united front opposite Patience and Benevolence.

Wrath, for some reason, has disappeared.

"It's a party, isn't it? Where's the music?" Oonagh calls as she scurries off to reprimand a green, beetle-wing colored sprite for the lack of background music.

Patience clears his throat, hands digging into the pockets of his trousers.

"I have some business to tend to today, but I hope that we can catch up during the ball tomorrow, Silas."

His voice has a deep and luring timbre, the male counterpart to Queen Oonagh's siren lilt. It's the kind of voice that sucks you in, only to drown you.

"And I hope you will spare me a moment, Pride. Your reputation precedes you," Patience says.

"I can't promise I'll live up to your expectations," Nora says.

"Not many do," he says. His attention then turns to me, piercing green eyes spearing my gut. My jaw tightens under his scrutiny. A slow smile spreads across his face, revealing teeth far too straight and far too white. "And Lust, you *are* the spitting image of your mother."

My cheeks ache from holding my own smile in place. "That I've been told."

The five of us lapse into silence; the air grows thick as the elder Seelie studies us.

"Tomorrow then," Patience says with a quick nod. He claps Benevolence on the back. "Stay out of trouble, son."

Patience strides from the room with as much self-importance as the Seelie Queen, and when the double doors close behind him, the room breathes a sigh of relief.

"My father is a bit intense," Benevolence says. His nose scrunches with boyish charm as he palms the back of his neck. "I don't plan on doing an ounce of work until the Solstice is over. I'd love to continue our conversation from last night if you're open, Pride. You can introduce me to your Second, who I've also heard lots about."

"I hope she is less of a cautionary tale than I am in the rumor mills?" Nora asks.

"I'd say she's just as scary to the Seelie younglings." He wriggles his fingers beside his head. "Mind control and all."

Nora mutters something about mind control not being possible, meanwhile I quirk a brow at her. I'm sure that she can read my silent *what the fuck?*

She shakes her head. "Later," she whispers.

Silas clears his throat, leveling Nora and me with a sharp glare.

"While I'd love to continue this little *hangout*, Wrath and I have business to tend to before the revelry tonight. Until then, explore, mingle, fuck—so long as it's not him," Silas says, pausing to jab a thumb at Benevolence. "I don't really care. Only that you make smart choices."

Then he's off, striding through the double doors to our side of the castle.

"He always like that?" Benevolence says.

"Overbearing and rude?" I murmur.

"He's got a lot of opinions and isn't afraid to share them," Nora says, a more politically correct answer.

"*Right*," Benevolence drawls. "I'm going to grab a drink and some food, but after, we can play cards in the courtyard?" The sentence trails off, the traces of hope palpable in his tone.

Nora shrugs. "Why not?"

"Great."

As Benevolence walks away, Nora places a firm hand on my waist. She leads me back to Leo and Josie, who wait patiently at a high table with a mountain of food in front of them.

"How do you already know one of them?" I whisper.

"My explorations last night led me to our new friend."

"And you want to hang out with Patience's son because...?"

"He intrigues me."

"Nora," I huff.

"I need to know if he is as guilty as Patience is." Her hand tightens on my waist, fingers digging into my flesh. "If he is, then he's going to be joining his father in an early grave."

34
NORA

Bennie slams down his cards, rattling the metal garden table.

Leo groans, head hanging back as he throws his cards to the table. They scatter across the poker chips, flipping over to reveal a handful of random numbers and houses.

"You lot are surprisingly shit at cards," Bennie says. He snickers as he collects his bounty of chips. "I thought empaths were supposed to be good at reading people?"

In just a few short hours, Bennie has developed a comfortable cockiness around us, as if we're old friends and not enemies.

Josie quirks a brow at me as if to say, *can you believe this guy?*

Leo snorts, cracking open one lid and side eyeing the Virtue. I suppress the smile threatening to break across my face. Leo is a master at cards, but today our goal isn't to win. Quite the opposite—it behooves us to lose.

Winners get comfortable. Comfortable fae get loose lips.

I gather the long since folded cards in front of Imogen and

me and pass them to Josie. Josie packs them back into their case with nimble fingers.

Silence settles over us.

Leo sighs, basking in the last rays of sun; it has finally begun its descent for the night, bidding us goodbye.

I check the watch in my pocket: twenty-eight past four. Strange how the sun still sets as it does in winter, yet the air is warm and riding the edge of humidity.

We set up shop in the center of the courtyard, taking over the long rectangle table and chairs. They're a set of green iron furniture, with unique twisting patterns and floral motifs. The metal was warm when we sat down, having baked in the sun all morning.

Not only was it too nice out to *not* enjoy the courtyard, but out here, we also have a semblance of privacy.

"They say Anwynn has exceptionally brisk winters. Is that true?" Bennie asks.

He stretches, reaching muscular arms up to the sky with a groan. Those of us in suits have abandoned our jackets, Bennie, Leo, and I all in various states of rolled up sleeves and unbuttoned collars to avoid overheating.

He's asked a slew of similar questions through the afternoon; some would say he's curious, but I know better.

I'd argue there's a carefully hidden reason why he wants to know so much about our lives.

Bennie's entertaining, but he's still a Virtue.

"It isn't much different from winters human-side," I say.

"Another reference to a place I've never been," Bennie says. "Are you trying to call my bluff?"

"Can you blame me?" I ask.

Leaning back in my seat, I cross one ankle over my knee and stretch an arm over the back of Imogen's chair. She shifts in her seat, scooting back enough that I can tease the base of her neck with my knuckle.

"Fair is fair." Bennie scratches his chin, tracing the sharp contour of his jawline. "When I was a youngling, I had a cousin who lived there with my aunt. I was a jealous little shit." The garden buzzes, bees fluttering between the overgrown wildflowers as his eyes sheen over with nostalgia. "I begged and begged my father to let me visit them, but I was always denied."

"Aren't the only Seelie who live human-side exiles?" Leo asks.

A shrewd smile spreads across Bennie's cheeks, revealing matching dimples that peek around the curved edge of his mustache.

"I didn't say they weren't exiles." Leo's face goes slack with understanding; Bennie raps his knuckles against the metal table to emphasize his point. "Now you see why I was denied. The family drama back in the day was intense." He shoots me a knowing wink. "Still is."

I lick my lips, ignoring the strange pit forming in my stomach. "So, I take it you never got to meet your cousin?"

"I had to focus on more important things, according to my father. Things like my magic." Bennie rolls his eyes. "I was an early bloomer, and was shipped off to train at age six. Patience —as I'm sure you could tell by looking at him—holds a tight leash on his assets. But I am happy to say I was able to meet her eventually, even though it was under less-than-ideal circumstances."

It's not lost on me that he refers to himself as an asset to Patience rather than a son. It's not unlike Pride's mindset on children, except instead of finding a partner to birth his legacy, he plucked me off the street.

"She turned out to be quite the impressive young woman," Bennie says.

"Is that so?" I murmur.

"And what kind of magic runs through your veins?" Imogen asks, changing the subject.

She leans forward in her seat, elbow resting on the woven metal and chin resting on the ball of her palm.

Bennie's attention is easily pulled toward Imogen, though his gaze lacks the desire that most hold when they look upon her. Instead, his mossy-green eyes shine with genuine interest in what she has to say.

So subtle, like a pheromone, her magic radiates feelings of calm, openness, and honesty. I've felt the brunt of her magic enough times to recognize the signs: getting lost in your thoughts, like you've taken one too many detours on a story you were trying to tell; a warmth that skitters all over your body; a blur at the edge of your vision, one that doesn't just blink away.

The Seelie may know how to develop mental shields, but I can guarantee they haven't been trained against the subtleties of her influence.

How could they? They don't have any empaths to train against.

Bennie matches Imogen's position, leaning close like they're sharing a secret.

"I always wanted to be a healer. We come from a long line of them that traces back millennia. Patience is the strongest of his generation, and, as the firstborn, I was expected to follow in his footsteps," he says. His expression darkens. "Unfortunately, I didn't get those genes. Someone else in the family tree inherited his supposed greatness."

"You sound bitter," I say.

"Actually, quite the opposite. It took a lot of pressure off me. Allowed me to explore my magic freely."

He lifts his free hand so that it is level between their noses. The world around us fades to background noise, the five of us all focused on the divot of his palm, where a miniature snow-storm swirls. Josie and I have seen Seelie magic in action before, but Leo and Imogen look on with open-mouthed stares as he blows the fake flurries around us. I touch one that sparkles near the tip of my nose and my finger passes through it, shattering the tiny illusion in a burst of rainbow light. The intangible snowflakes disappear as he closes his fist.

"It's hard, living up to your family's expectations. And then reconciling that with what you want," Imogen says.

"Few truer words have been spoken," he says. "Patience wanted me to be his Second despite the mismatched magic. But when the good old Benevolence before me kicked the bucket ..."

"In walked Bennie," I finish.

"You're so observant, Pride," Bennie say, sarcastically.

Josie clears her throat. "So, you truly haven't been to the other side of the Veil," she says, more a statement than a question.

A bee zooms past my head, its wings buzzing in my ear.

"For the eighth time, no. Not unless you count coming here."

Leo snorts. "She doesn't."

The bee flies between Imogen and me, lingering near the hair that cascades down her shoulder. I swat at it, and it flies away.

"Casimir isn't on the other side of capital-T, *The* Veil—the one that separates realms. So, it doesn't count," Josie says, ever the knowledgeable one. "It is, however, on the other side of *a* veil. There's ancient magic warding the castle. It's why we can shadow-walk within its confines, but not across the bridge."

"Look at miss smarty-pants over here with the technicalities," Bennie croons.

"I do my research," Josie says, a smug twist to her lips.

The bee zooms by my head again, this time evading my hand but staying persistent in its circling of my head.

"Maybe we should go back inside," I say. "I'm not a fan of bugs."

"Did you borrow one of Lust's perfumes?" Leo snickers. "We all know you don't have sweet enough blood to attract mosquitos."

"No," I say, rolling my eyes.

Bennie's eyes narrow on the bug.

"Hold on a second," he murmurs, standing and leaning forward with both hands planted on the table. Recognition flares in the form of a snarl. "Alexander."

Bennie throws his hand out, quicker than you'd think he could move with his bulk, snatching the bug straight from the air. He cups the insect between his hands and shakes. The four of us stare on, wide-eyed at the strange behavior.

He then chucks the bug; it hurtles through the air before transforming into a Seelie man.

The Seelie has the same coloring as Bennie, but is leaner in stature, his limbs gangly and uncoordinated, like he hasn't fully grown into manhood yet. Stumbling a few steps before righting himself, he runs a hand through his wavy brown hair, letting it fall messy over his brows.

"Anyone ever tell you eavesdropping isn't nice?" Bennie growls.

"Sorry, I couldn't help myself." He doesn't sound sorry at all. "Father had me doing paperwork back in our rooms, but I wanted to sneak a peek at the soul-stealer." Alexander cocks his head at me with pursed lips. "I pictured you smaller."

"You would have met her tomorrow at the banquet," Bennie grinds out between clenched teeth.

It strikes me that there's a clear divide between the brothers.

Maybe he isn't in league with his father.

"I'm flattered that my presence is in such high demand." I interrupt the brother's bickering. "But we *just* finished up our game of cards, otherwise I'd invite you to sit."

I spread back into my chair. Men always hate it when I take up more space than I need. But all I'm doing is mimicking them.

"Though, maybe that would be ill advised, considering it seems your family has a strange obsession with me." I turn to Imogen. "Lust, do you think I should be concerned?"

Imogen's lips quirk, sensing my playful show of dominance. "I don't think so—at least not for this one. What is he going to do? Shift back to a bee and sting you?"

"What else *can* you shift into, Alexander?" I ask. "I've always wanted to pet a dragon."

Alexander scoffs. "You can't shift into things that aren't *real.*"

He's young, hot-headed. I want to see what he'll do when provoked. Play along. I broadcast to Josie in my head. I trust that she's listening.

"Actually, I read once that a powerful Seelie, about two millennia ago, was able to transform himself into a wyvern. Little different from a dragon, but close enough," Josie adds, not missing a beat.

"It's okay if you're not that powerful," I say, waving a hand in the air nonchalantly.

Bennie snorts and Alexander glares at us all as he puffs out his chest.

"I'll have you know that—" Alexander yelps as Bennie flicks his forehead.

"You need to leave. Or I'll be telling father that you snuck out," Bennie says, all humor and snark gone from his tone. It's clear that this is him pulling rank on his brother. "*Now.*"

Alexander bristles but doesn't challenge his older brother.

As quickly as he appeared, he shifts in a flash of white light; a dragonfly hums where his body once stood. It pauses, hovering in the air, before zooming off towards an open window above us.

I click my tongue, standing from the table and pulling on my suit jacket.

"Nobody likes secrets, Bennie," I tut, buttoning the jacket over my vest. "Except for those that keep them."

Bennie scratches the back of his neck. "Alexander isn't so much a secret as he is a liability."

I hum.

Imogen, Josie, and Leo follow my lead as we extract ourselves from the table. The metal chairs scrape against the garden stone as we push them back into place.

Bennie's quiet as we clean up, but when I pass him, he grabs my arm, pulling me to a stop. My heart pounds in my chest at the contact, so strong that my pulse throbs all the way down to my fingertips.

"Come to the revelry tonight. My father never attends, and Alexander is too young, they won't let him in," he says in a rushed whisper. "I need to speak freely with you."

"Are you a fool? Don't touch me." I rip my arm from his grasp.

"It's important." His eyes beg me to heed him. They shine

with an all too familiar persistence. "You can trust me, Elenora."

My body goes still. The last time I heard my full name in use, it came from my mother's lips.

No. That's not true.

That honor was stolen by Patience the day he murdered her.

"You don't get to call me that," I snarl. "You can't tell us your little family sob stories and expect me to trust you. You're Seelie. And I only just met you."

"You and I both know that me being Seelie has nothing to do with your distrust for me," Benevolence says.

"It has everything to do with it," I snap. "Don't push your luck, *Bennie.*"

I storm off, boots pounding against the cobblestone.

"Come see me tonight," he calls at my back. "You'll want to hear what I have to say."

35
NORA

The springtime breeze that floats through the open window feels wrong on my skin. Casimir teases us with the rebirth of nature without allowing us to experience its death. The only reason the balminess of spring soothes us is because we fight off the sting of the winter wind before it.

Without that biting chill, I find myself at the mercy of my memory.

The nightmares love to harvest the field of my subconscious, plucking, like daisies, the worst moments of my life to replay while I slumber. Imogen lies tangled in the sheets next to me, chest rising soft and steady.

You can trust me, Elenora.

I stare at the ceiling.

You'll want to hear what I have to say.

Benevolence's words echo in my head, a record scratching on repeat.

What could he possibly tell me that I don't already know?

The ache in my gut hasn't eased since this morning, and it worsens now, pulling me from our bed. I tiptoe to the bathroom and lean against the porcelain sink, the cool surface icy against my palms. Staring into the mirror, I get lost within the tempest raging in my irises, a swirling mass of sea-storm green; I see myself, but I don't really *see* myself.

I see the past and the present, colliding with the severity of a bomb.

I see my father naively turning an enemy into a lover.

I see my mother betraying, and in turn being betrayed by, the older brother she once trusted.

I see both my parents trying to make a half-hidden life work for a daughter whom they loved, all to have that same child lure disaster to their doorstep.

I was deluded to think confronting my secrets would be easy. A niggling of regret worms its way between my ribs, the thought that maybe I shouldn't have come here. That I shouldn't have poked the bear that is Patience and instead kept my head down.

But then I take a deep breath and steel my shoulders.

No.

Nothing worthwhile in this life is easy.

I've been traumatized and abused. My mind's been invaded and combed through like it was a stack of paperwork. And my wings have been shorn from my back without a care for the pain it would cause.

I deserve to take every little piece of power I can back.

And that starts right here, right now.

With killing my cousin.

I somehow manage to sneak on a dress without waking Imogen, which is a blessing. The last thing I need is her asking questions, or worse, asking to come with me.

The halls are quiet as I stroll straight through the double doors of the shared ballroom and to the Seelie side of the castle.

It's no wonder the sprites were confused when I first explored the halls. They didn't know where I belonged. They stare at me now, with their heads cocked and their wide, curious eyes drinking me in. Each step I take towards the Seelie revelry feels like an act of rebellion under their scrutiny.

They're smart enough to let me pass, simply pointing me in the right direction with their taloned fingers.

Music grows louder as I climb the steps to a second level of the castle, a sultry cacophony of acoustic instruments. A deep drum holds a steady beat to which strings pluck a melody. Laughter floats alongside the music, a unique harmony.

When I crest the final bend of the spiral staircase, I'm met with a smoky den of debauchery.

You have to give them credit, the party is one out of a storybook.

Where the Unseelie have adapted to modern music, clothing, and social habits, the Seelie have doubled down, embracing more traditional versions of each. Half the dresses are sheer and flowing panels of fabric, draped and tied in a series of intricate designs unique to each wearer. The other half are in garb similar to the queen this morning, crafted with glittering shells, pearls, or beetle wings. The men are mostly shirtless—which makes my eyes roll internally—and sport outdated embroidered trousers.

I am sorely out of place in my simple black frock with beaded tassels that swish past my knees.

The room is decorated with fabrics draped across the ceiling in long strips; smoke curls up to the swaths, but it smells more of herb than tobacco. Some fae dance, some lounge, and some fuck in the darker corners of the room—all of them glowing under the floating Seelie fae-lights that bob across the room.

And of course, there are the wings. They are everywhere, glittering and fluttering and making my back itch with phantom pains.

I didn't have mine for long before Pride decided it was best to *"not take any chances"* and shear them. It was pure luck that House Pride used the barbaric practice as a test of loyalty; it made it all too easy to explain why a freshly turned sixteen-year-old had such horrid scars on her back.

It was the right decision, in the end.

How do you convince anyone you're Unseelie when you're sporting a pair of green and black butterfly wings?

The gods surely laughed when they gifted me those.

A tanned hand waves over the crowd of fae.

Benevolence.

My eyes narrow on the bare muscular arm that leads to the man. He's sat in the corner on a low chaise lounge with a gaggle of Seelie women draped across him—it's not hard to imagine why, with his dimpled smile and honeyed voice.

Seelie side-eye me as I walk to him, but when I shift my cutting glare their way, they quickly avert their gazes. The Seelie courtiers lack courage.

"Pride," Benevolence croons. "I'm glad you decided to come."

I cross my arms over my chest.

"You wanted to chat. So, let's chat."

His smile falters.

"Excuse me, ladies," he says, oozing with fake charm as he extracts himself from the lounger.

Benevolence leads me between the Seelie revelers, the scents of their sickeningly sweet perfume wafting into my nose as we pass. With his back to me, I'm able to appreciate his wings—there's no denying their beauty, despite what they represent.

They are tucked low, but the design on the four-pronged wings is clear. A deep swath of blue-black expands from between his toned shoulder blades, followed by a band of bright blue and a stripe of white dots. A lacelike pattern of black and white lines the edge of the wings.

As we walk through the side halls of the castle, I hike up my dress, pulling free my knife from its thigh strap. And when Benevolence opens the door to an empty room, I waste no time in kicking it shut behind me. I yank him by his brown locks and press the knife to his throat.

We're the same height, so my mouth fits perfectly against his ear to snarl my command.

"Talk."

"Well, you went to violence quicker than I thought you would." He winces when I dig the knife harder into his throat, pulling a trickle of blood from his veins. "Sorry, sorry. Jeeze, Elenora, they weren't kidding when they said you were ruthless."

"You throw my name and story around like you know me. You don't," I snap. Benevolence's ribs brush against my body in short bursts; his body betrays his panic. "You're stupid for admitting it out loud. At least before, you could feign ignorance, and I could look the other way. Now you're a loose end I have to clean up."

Benevolence raises his hands placatingly.

"Listen, *Pride*." His brittle smile falters as he pauses, gauging my reaction to the use of my title. "We were kids when everything with our parents went down. I have no ill will towards you. In fact, I want to *help* you."

Part of me wants to slide the knife across his perfect skin, let the floors stain red from his blood. The idea of Patience walking in and seeing his firstborn as a lifeless husk on the ground is more alluring than I thought it would be.

But the other part of me needs to know what he knows. What they *all* know.

And needs outweigh wants.

"I will kill you. Cousin or not," I snarl. "And I don't need magic to do it."

I pull the knife away and shove Benevolence forward. He stumbles a few paces but catches himself on the back of one of the armchairs in the room.

"Clearly," he says, rubbing at his neck with a grimace.

He pulls his fingers back, sticky with blood, and searches the room for something to wipe them off on. The room is devoid of anything but a few chairs around a fireplace and walls lined with bookshelves, so he opts to wipe them on his brown britches.

Silence lingers between us.

Benevolence twitches under my intense gaze.

"Why are you looking at me like that?" he finally asks.

"I'm waiting for you to explain yourself."

"Oh." His throat bobs. "Do you want to sit and talk?"

"No."

"I'd prefer to sit."

"*Benevolence*," I growl, taking a step towards him.

He backs up in turn, again raising his hands in front of him. He treats me like I'm a rabid dog.

He's not wrong to.

"Fine," he says. "Fine." He takes a breath, then on a whisper, he says: "I want you to remove him from power."

My eyes narrow. "Who?"

"Who do you think?" Benevolence runs a hand through his locks, tugging at them. "My father."

"You want me to kill your father?" I deadpan.

This has got to be some kind of twisted fucking joke.

His jaw feathers as he glances away, unable to meet my eye. "Yeah."

"Why can't you do it?"

"Because I *can't.*"

"That's not a real reason."

"I've already *tried,*" he admits, rushing forward but stopping a foot away from me. He ticks off his fingers with each example. "I've tried poisons: they don't affect him. I've tried hiring hitmen: they failed. He's extremely paranoid, and he's *really* fucking hard to kill."

"Then what makes you think that I can do it, or would even want to?" I shrug, twirling my knife in my hand.

"C'mon," he huffs. "Everyone wants to kill my father. I would think the niece he exiled and orphaned would be at the top of that list. And a soul-stealer? I don't know a single fae in history that could stop that magic."

I frown.

Benevolence's chest puffs with confidence, but his face shines with sincerity as he speaks.

"Look." He levels with me, licking his lips. "I was only a child back then. All I ever knew was that my aunt was taking a trip, and then I didn't see her for years. Then, one day, my dad came home angry as all hell, cursing her name. He was never a good father, but he was much worse from that day on."

He swallows, eyes glazing over with the memory; it's a look I know all too well. He reaches out. A shaking, tentative hand grips my shoulder. I let him, seeing the peace offering for what it is—his skin on mine, his life in my hand.

It's submission.

"It wasn't until he started grooming me for his position that he told me what happened. I wasn't lying when I said I was jealous of you guys. I didn't know what it meant for you to live out there. I thought it was the grandest thing, to be so free." Benevolence's lips tremble with bittersweet emotion. "You might have escaped him then, but he's been obsessed with you ever since."

"Then why has he waited so long to make his move against me? I've been working human-side for years for my House."

Benevolence's fluffy brows knit.

"He's embodied his title," Benevolence says. "He's not afraid to wait for a better opportunity."

He's dancing around his words, but I need him to cut the bullshit.

"Explain," I demand.

"Can I put my arm down?" he asks. "Was this a good enough trust exercise for you to at least hear me out?"

I bat his arms away.

"*Explain*," I repeat.

"He hasn't told me what he has planned. But there are far more fae here than usual," he says. "It feels off."

He runs his hand through his hair—that's twice now during this conversation, as if he can't help himself. Is it a nervous tick or one that shows he's lying?

I should have made Josie come with me.

"I only wanted to warn you. I don't think he deserves the element of surprise," he says. Then he grimaces. "*And* I wanted to put in that little request because I can't help but be a bit selfish."

"That's it?" I ask.

He marks an *X* over his heart. I shake my head.

This was fucking pointless.

"I will consider it," I say.

The grin that spreads across his face could blind a fae with one glimpse.

"Thank y—"

"But you need to answer one question," I cut him off. I stride to him, stopping when my face is inches from his, so that he cannot mistake how deadly serious I am. "Who else knows?"

His smile falls, leaving lips that quiver with pity.

"Nora, the only ones in Casimir who *don't* know who you are traveled here with you."

36
NORA

I leave Bennie alive. I may regret that later.

The rage that burned in my gut no less than an hour ago is gone, replaced by a deep-rooted emptiness.

Everyone knows.

The Seelie eyes on me feel different now, searing on my skin as I pass through the party to leave. On the way, I snatch a deserted bottle of liquor from one of the high-tops. Then I pilfer a pack of cigarettes off a Seelie who thought it was an excellent idea to try to flirt with *the infamous soul-stealer*.

I make it up to the seventh floor, taking a swig of liquor with every other step. It stings my throat, but the pain is good. And when the burn fades, the alcohol fills me with sweet numbness.

Everyone knows.

My mind is both eerily quiet yet entirely too loud; the static in my ears is overwhelming.

I pass the door where Imogen sleeps beyond—I can't gather the courage to wake her in this state.

She said she wants me when I'm scared, but that's a lie. She won't want me when she learns the truth.

I stop in front of Josie's door, but my hand pauses before I knock. Josie's always cleaning up my messes.

She shouldn't have to, but she does.

She knows the stakes—*has* known them ever since we were little and Pride made her sort through the trauma in my head. She's kept my secret and never judged me for it, which is more than I could have ever asked.

I can't ask her to catch me as I fall tonight.

Everyone knows.

My feet guide me from the seventh floor and up to the eighth, my body moving of its own accord. My mind is lost in itself until I'm jolted back into consciousness when my knuckles hit the door.

There's a moment where I don't think he'll answer, that this was a mistake, and I should turn around and find somewhere to pass these big feelings alone. But the door swings open, Silas rubbing the sleep from his eyes. His white hair is in a state of rumpled chaos, and when he runs a hand through it, it does nothing to tame the mess. He leans against the door, opening it enough to stick half his frame out; he's shirtless, only wearing long pajama pants, and my attention snags on the tattoo spread across his chest.

At the center sits a blackwork butterfly, framed by two birds that have their beaks aimed at it. The birds' wings are spread open and crest down his pectorals and over his shoulders.

"Nora?"

"You have a butterfly tattoo," I state.

His mouth parts, his tongue darting out to graze the bottom lip.

"Yes... I do," he drawls. He leans forward, head swiveling to see the hall behind me is empty. "It's the middle of the night."

I take a deep breath and do one of my least favorite things in the world.

I ask for help.

"You said any time I needed escape, it would be there for me," I say. "I'm calling that favor in."

Silas stalls, his white-knuckled hand gripping the doorframe before he steps back, waving me in with a wide sweep of his arm.

"Welcome to my humble abode."

His eyes track me as I enter the room; it's toasty, a healthy fire crackling in a fireplace. I don't waste time inspecting the rest of the room—I don't need to see his bed nor the bathroom —the fire is what I need.

I collapse onto the floor in front of the flames, the rug scratching against my shins. I fumble the smokes box one handed, but manage to get one out and cast the box aside. My cigarette doesn't take long to catch flame when I fit it through the grate of the fireplace. Pulling it to my lips, I take a deep drag, and let a different kind of burn work its way through me.

"I've always thought that was an archaic way of proving one's loyalty."

Smoke unfurls from my parted lips as I release my breath. I tilt my head over my shoulder—Silas stands above me, staring intently at my exposed back. At my scars.

Everyone knows.

I shift on my knees. My back falls against the coffee table and my legs stretch out in front of me; I turn the table into armor, defending my scars from curious eyes.

"The pain was worth the reward," I say.

"Was it?"

Those black eyes, so observant, make my skin itch.

I turn back to the fire.

"At the time," I say.

The only sound between us is the rustling of Silas's cotton pajamas as he sits next to me, back leaning against the coffee table like mine. He pulls his legs to his chest, arms banding around his shins. He lets a rosy cheek fall to his kneecap, the action squishing his mouth into a frown.

"What do you need escape from?" he asks.

"I had an enlightening conversation with Benevolence," I say through another drag of smoke.

"You went to the revelry?"

"I was invited," I say. I pause for another sip of alcohol. The liquid sloshes in the bottle when I place it between us on the rug. My vision starts to fuzz around the edges, giving me hope that I may be able to sleep tonight. "He thinks his father has nefarious plans for us on this trip."

Silas hums. "Wrath and I expected as much. Our own plan was never without risk."

"There's a *but* waiting at the end of that sentence."

"Of course, there is." Silas smiles. "*But* we're already here. If he pulls anything, I'll handle it."

"You'll *handle it?*"

"Mhm," he hums. "I'm the king. That's what I do. And I'm the one who brought us here. Everyone's safety is my responsibility."

"Fair," I say, but internally I scoff.

Will my safety matter to him past tomorrow?

My cigarette is on its last leg; I suck as much life from it as I can before flicking it above the grate and into the fire. The flames pop at the disruption. Embers float into the chimney like snow flurries.

"But all that wouldn't rattle the Pride I've come to know...

What else happened?" Silas asks, though he has the decency to have his eyes trained on the fire.

The flames are calming, an array of red, yellow, orange, and where it's hottest, blinding white.

"I can't tell you," I say.

"Okay," he says, reaching for the liquor. He takes a swing and coughs. "That's terrible."

"Yeah, it's pretty shit."

"So, why can't you tell me?"

I tug the bottle from his grasp. "You'll kill me."

"That bad a secret, huh?"

"Yeah."

"You should have a little more faith in me."

"Says the Unseelie King," I snort.

And when my eyes cut to his in my periphery, I'm frozen by the vulnerability in those night-like irises of his.

"I'd like to think of you as a friend," he says. "We're killing a man together, are we not?"

"Is that what constitutes friendship these days?"

"For us, maybe." He shrugs, then we both go back to staring at the fire.

The clock on the wall ticks sixty times before I speak again.

"Is it bad that I'm nervous to go back to my room?" I ask.

"To Lust?"

I nod, my lips twisting. "Why do you never call her by her name?"

"Do you want me to call her Imogen?" he asks in turn. "I don't think she'd want me to."

"I guess not, then. Forget I asked."

"But to your earlier point, I don't think that's the right question to ask." Then, he clarifies, "To ask if it's bad."

"Then what's the right question?"

"Do you love her?"

I huff a single, lifeless laugh. "What do you know about love anyway?"

"Far less than you."

I feel that giddy thread of energy flow through me, the alcohol finally settling in my bloodstream. I push onto my knees and turn to Silas, sitting back on my heels and quirking a brow at him.

"Weren't you the one who told me that I'd have to be in love to know if it's selfish? Or were you just posturing?"

"You caught me."

"You love Wrath, though."

His nose scrunches up. "Yes, but it's the same way you love your Second."

I hum.

"Were you right?" he asks.

"Hm?"

"Is love, at its core, selfish?"

"I think so, yes," I say. "I'm selfish to want her and my revenge too."

"I think you need to decide what's most important to you. You're *this* close. Will you regret it in fifty years if you turn away?"

Silas stands, taking the bottle of liquor with him.

"Hopefully I won't regret anything in fifty years," I say. Then I twist, leaning on the coffee table with my forearms. I track Silas as he paces deeper into the room, placing the bottle on the bedside table. "Also, that's a redundant question. You'd never let me leave here without completing our mission."

"I'm glad you're coming to terms with the inevitable," he laughs through a yawn, reaching up to the sky.

"We may be aligned in this, Silas, but you need to remember—" I stand, so I can level with him, the liquor that's running through my veins making me bold. "I'm never going to be a pawn for you to move around on a whim."

"You're not a pawn," he scoffs, then drops down onto the bed, his legs dangling off the edge.

"No?" I ask.

"If you were a chess piece, you'd be a queen, Nora." His hands splay in front of him, summoning shadows and molding them into floating chess pieces that crisscross in an imaginary game. "No rules. Moves wherever she wishes without consequence."

I roll my eyes because I, more than others, know there are *always* consequences.

Everyone knows.

My boot scuffs against the carpet as I shift in place. I got the distraction I needed. My mind has quieted enough that if I head back downstairs now, I know I'll be able to get at least a wink of sleep. And I'll need the rest if I'm going to kill my uncle.

A beat passes, the weight of morning pressing down on us. Then, I step towards the door.

"Nora?" Silas calls, stopping me in my tracks.

His tone is weary and laced with loneliness.

"Yes?"

He's staring up at the canopy of the four-poster bed, fingers laced and thumbs twiddling over his tattooed chest.

"Remember what bad people do to those their enemies love," he says.

"I could never forget, Silas."

Silas hums. Then he groans, sitting up in the bed. He squints at the clock on the wall. The hands tick past midnight.

A sad smile softens his features when he tilts his head back at me.

"Happy Solstice, Nora."

37
IMOGEN

Solstice was always my favorite holiday.

Solstice season warms the heart and the hearth—the fires rage from dawn to dusk and back to dawn, new wood thrown on the eternal flames each hour. My mother wasn't the most sentimental parent, but she always made sure my brother and I woke up to the smell of cinnamon buns and hot cocoa. We'd run downstairs, racing each other, only to tie, slipping on fallen pine needles from the tree that took up half our living room.

We don't have a tree here in Casimir, nor the chill of winter, but the distinct pitter patter of rain filters in through the cracked window.

At least we have each other's company and our presents to look forward to. I also may have bribed a sprite to make us some of the traditional baked goods for this morning...

A swirl of shadow forms across the room and one of the little buggers appears carrying a large tray of the tasty treats and a hot pot of coffee. Its wings flap loudly, and it squeaks at me, announcing its arrival. I scramble from the bed, shushing the thing and pulling the plate from its talons.

"Thank you," I say. Its wide eyes blink up at me expectantly. "You can go now."

I think it pouts as I wave it towards the bedroom door, but before I can open it, the sprite disappears in shadow with an outraged squeak.

Pulling the warm plate up to my nose, I inhale the decadent scent of cinnamon, sugar, and vanilla frosting.

Home.

That's what it smells like.

I place the tray on the coffee table before the fireplace with care, then crawl back into bed.

Nora's chest rises and falls with easy breaths; I nestle into her side, and she instinctively shifts to bring me closer, my curves slotting into place next to hers. I give her butterfly kisses in the crook of her neck before my lips double back and litter her skin with real ones—little pecks that have her stirring from her slumber.

"It's time to get up," I hum.

Nora's brows knit together, and her nose scrunches up as she groans, coming alive for the morning.

My hand snakes around her waist and tickles her side which has her eyes snapping open. Nora quickly snatches my hand and pulls me half on top of her.

"You're a menace, you know that?" Her voice is raspy and low.

"And you're a terrible morning person," I quip, leaning forward to brush my nose up against hers, back and forth. "Happy Solstice."

Nora hums, but it sounds sad. "Happy Solstice."

I lean forward, planting a lazy kiss on her lips. Immediately, I'm hit with the stale taste of liquor.

"You taste like day-old bourbon," I say. Pulling back so I can see her face fully, I quirk a brow. "Were you drinking last night?"

Nora yawns. "I couldn't sleep."

"Oh." I brush a stray lock of black hair from her forehead and behind her ear. "Why didn't you wake me? I would have stayed up with you, or at least tried to help get you tired enough to pass out."

She doesn't run with the innuendo like I hoped she would. Instead, Nora's head drops back onto the pillow and her eyes flutter closed.

"You sleep too peacefully," she says, pulling in another deep yawn. "I didn't want to ruin that."

I shift and straddle her, thighs bracketing her hips. My hands frame her head and my hair hangs in a sheet around us.

"It's not ruining anything," I say. "Is everything okay?"

"Yeah," she says, finally smiling up at me, though it doesn't reach her eyes. "Tired."

I twist my lips, holding back any other questions—Nora knows I want her to share her burdens with me. I have to trust her to do that in her own time, even if it's not as fast as I'd hope.

"That is an easy problem to fix. The sprites already dropped off a pot of liquid energy for you at my request."

"Hmm, they really do like you."

"I have my charms." I peck her forehead, then her nose, then her lips, avoiding the way they follow me when I pull back. "C'mon. Leo and Josie will be over soon."

Nora groans as I hop off the bed and I laugh.

Could every Solstice morning be this? I wonder with childlike hope.

An hour later, the four of us are huddled around the fire-place with bellies full of dough and espresso. Leo lounges across the couch, legs propped over Josie's lap; Nora takes up the armchair, and I sit on the floor between her legs, leaning back against her. We're all still in our pajamas, a colorful array of striped cotton and lace-lined silk.

The rain has gotten heavier, so we shut the window, but it has still caused the temperature to drop enough to warrant a fire.

I'm not complaining.

"Usually, I'd add some orange zest to the frosting," Josie says, licking her thumb. "But these were good."

"You're a little food aficionado, aren't you, Josie?" I say.

"Ehh," she drawls, tilting her head back and forth. "You could say that."

We laugh, the sound as cheery as wind chimes filling the room.

"Okay, present time." I clap, unable to hold back my giddiness any longer.

I hop up and scurry to my suitcase, pulling out the wrapped boxes for each of them.

"Wait, we're doing presents?" Nora asks. "Today? Right now?"

Leo laughs, a short singular "*ha*," then quickly covers his face with his hand.

I raise a brow in Nora's direction. "Yes... it's Solstice."

"I didn't bring them," she says, her pale face losing its color. "I swear I got you all gifts. But I didn't think we were going to do this while we were here."

"Hey, hey." I hurry back to Nora, placing my gifts on the coffee table. "I didn't explicitly tell you to bring them. It's not a big deal."

Nora turns to Josie, caught off guard. "You brought yours?"

Josie grimaces, reaching behind the couch and holding up a

small bag of presents. Nora groans, scrubbing her hands over her face.

"Shit," she says. "I'm sorry."

"The almighty Pride, brought to her knees in apology," Leo croons overdramatically. "I'd say that's enough of a gift for me, Nor."

"Ha-ha," Nora deadpans. Her hands still cover her cheeks, which are flushed pink.

I don't think I've ever seen her embarrassed. Or so amicable to Leo's jokes.

Is this the same woman who I went to bed with last night?

"It's fine," I say, rubbing my hand on her thigh. "Gives us an excuse to host a party when we get back."

Nora heaves a sigh.

"Okay," she says. "Alright. Who's first then?"

"I'm going last," I claim. I want mine to get the prime present spot.

"I'll go first," Josie says.

She tosses Leo a small box and passes me a similarly wrapped one. We both rip open the carefully wrapped presents.

"Aw..." Leo lifts up a gorgeous brown leather watch with a simple square clockface lined with gold.

"So you won't be late to any more meetings," Josie snickers.

Leo smacks her arm playfully. "That was one time!"

Josie laughs, but Leo adds a quick thank you before turning to me.

I sheepishly hold up the box I opened; a stately gold ring with a large amethyst set in its center sits in the plush black cushion. The gold is shaped into filigree detail around the stone, giving it an elegant daintiness that you wouldn't normally expect from a ring of this size.

"The stone is for protection and calming clarity," Josie explains. "Plus, I thought it looked nice."

"Thank you, it's such a thoughtful gift," I say, emotion aching in my throat. I slip it onto my fingers, seeing which it fits best on. Settling on my right middle finger, I leave it there, letting the weight comfort me. "What about for Nora?"

Josie shakes her head, a devious smile tugging at her lips. "We have our own traditions. No gifts."

"Oh?" Leo asks. "Tell us more about these traditions."

"You've recently been told about one," Josie teases.

I rack my brain for a moment before it clicks.

"The sauce prank on Wes's grandma?" I ask.

Josie's shy smile says it all.

"No." Leo sits up. "You did not do that to her *Solstice dinner*."

Nora snickers, but Josie has the decency to flush with embarrassment.

"We did, in fact, spike the sauce on Solstice," she relents with a wince.

"Best Solstice prank in my opinion," Nora murmurs behind me. "Still pissed we got caught."

"So, will we have a new funny story to add to the list of things to look forward to when we get home?"

"Depends. We've been too busy to plan it yet," Josie says.

Nora leans forward, whispering in my ear. "And who says you'll be spared from the prank this year, anyway?"

I bat Nora away with a laugh. "Evil. Both of you."

Leo clears his throat, throwing his feet off Josie's lap. He quickly grabs the brown paper bag he left by the door when he entered earlier; rummaging through it, he pulls out three small wrapped goodie bags of cookies.

"I will admit, I phoned it in this year. Ended up being a smidge busy," he says with a wink my way. He tosses each one of us our own bag. "However, I know for a fact that they taste delicious."

"You never bake anymore." I tug apart the ribbon holding the bag closed and sniff the cookies—rich chocolate fills my senses. "Oh my gods. Thank you, Leo. I am saving these for later."

Nora hums behind me, already nibbling into one. Her eyes meet mine and they hold the most joy they've had all morning, a purely devious glint residing in the emerald facets.

"Not bad," she says.

"Nora..." I chide, holding back my laughter. I know exactly what she's trying to do. I can't approve of it, but I also can't deny myself the pleasure of how they love to rile each other up.

"Not bad?" Leo repeats.

"Yeah, not bad," Nora shrugs.

Leo sputters, and the two of them launch into a heated argument about varying levels of cocoa powder and sugar. I chuckle to myself as I crawl over to the coffee table and grab my presents.

"Alright! My turn!" I cut off their argument and place a box in front of each of them. Josie whispers a sweet thank you as she takes the box from my hands, already knowing what's inside.

"Josie first," I say. "Because she's special and already knows what's inside."

She smirks at Nora's shocked mutter, ripping into the box. I perch myself on the edge of Nora's armchair, her hand snaking around my waist as we watch Josie ceremoniously reveal the old western pistol.

Sharp shocks of memory shoot through my side, but I ignore the pain, push it down.

This is the first step to moving past what happened that day. A way to reclaim the good that was stained.

Nora's thumb swipes back and forth over the bit of skin exposed between my pajama shirt and pants.

"I really do love it, Mo. Thank you," Josie says. She runs her hand over the detailed barrel, which is now sparkling since I had it cleaned. A quiet kind of gratitude exudes from her in the way she handles it so carefully, as if it might break if she drops it despite it already having survived a century of life across the Veil. "I'll have to see if I can shoot it while riding a horse like the humans used to."

Josie bites her tongue, poking into her cheek as she raises the gun away from the three of us, closes one eye, and pretends to aim and shoot.

"We'll have to figure out how to get you to a horse first," I laugh. "I'd love to see how it goes."

"What, you don't believe I can ride?" Josie teases.

"No, you'd definitely fare better than me," I say. I peer down at Nora. I knock my legs into hers. "Your turn."

Nora hums, eyes flicking between her box and Josie's, noting the similar wooden case. "I wonder what it could be."

"Open it already." I push at her shoulder.

Her hands still as they lift the lid; the room quiets, and we sit stagnant as we wait for her reaction. Then, one hand moves, fingers trailing over the more modern gun than Josie's; it's silver and sleek, a stripe down the center of the barrel engraved with an endless knot. It's supposed to symbolize unity and strength, and I was going to leave it at that before the attack. But after, it didn't feel like enough, so I found someone in town to add something extra.

Lower, burned along the wooden inlay of the handle, is a short message.

Scared pieces too.

My lips twist in on themselves, my nerves bubbling to the surface.

"It's okay if you don't—"

"I love it."

Nora looks up at me, eyes glistening with a mix of wonder and something *more*.

"You do?"

"Yeah. It's beautiful. Thank you."

"I didn't know what model to get, but I had Josie help me, and the old guy who ran the store, of course. His name was Sal, but—"

Her brows furrow, all that wonder gone with a blink and replaced with the curious beginnings of anger.

"Wait. *This* is why you were human-side?"

My mouth opens and closes, a seed of dread sprouting in my gut. "Yeah."

She glares back down at the gun, the air around her growing thick and tense. Then, she takes a single, slow breath; on the exhale, her features melt into something resembling guilt. She closes the case, flicking the golden latch shut with an audible click.

Her fingers intertwine with mine on my lap, and she pulls my hand to her lips, planting a gentle kiss to my pulse point on my wrist.

"Thank you," she whispers. "I'll wear it later."

"Later?" I ask.

"Mhm," she says. "I have a thigh strap that should work for it."

"I wanna see the gun," Leo whines, reaching out with grabby hands.

I roll my eyes. "Open your gift first. It's better."

"Fine," he groans. It takes him all of five seconds to rip open the terribly wrapped box and flick open the lid.

Leo stills, similar to Nora, fingers lingering an inch above the rusted metal key resting on a bed of fabric. His mouth falls agape, lower lip trembling from shock.

He shouldn't be *that* shocked. He's known this was coming.

"The key to the safe?" he whispers.

I nod, confidence steeling the movement. "It's officially yours."

"But—wait—you can't give this to me yet."

"Why not?" I ask, a sad smile spreading between my cheeks.

"Because I'm not—you're still—"

"No, Leo," I say. "You're in charge now. When we get back home, you are the keeper of the secrets. You own the key to the safe."

Leo gawks at the thing in his lap.

"*The* safe?" Nora asks, curious.

"You guys aren't stupid enough to keep the shit you blackmail Royals with in an actual, physical safe," Josie says, equal parts disbelief and concern falling over her features. "Right?"

Leo and I share a conspiratorial look.

"Right—" Leo says.

"Of course not. It's a metaphorical key."

"Right..." Josie drawls, seeing right through our terrible cover.

Nora squeezes my hand, pulling my attention back down to her.

"Imogen, what does giving him that key mean?" she asks tentatively, though by her serious gaze, I can tell she's already putting together the pieces.

Leo makes an outraged squeak. "You didn't tell her yet?"

"Mo..." Josie groans.

I wince, my lips curling over my teeth. "I meant to. But then I figured it would be easier to rip the bandage off like this."

"You're passing your title on to Leo?"

"Yeah," I say. I don't try to sugar coat it.

"Why?" Nora says, confusion marring her features.

I turn to Josie and Leo. "Do you guys mind if we end the morning now? Meet in the hall for the ball later?"

Josie and Leo are quick to gather their things. Josie gives me a small hug before leaving, whispering another thank you in my ear. Leo kisses my cheek, grumbling a stern *we're talking about this later* as he holds up the key, but there's no real bite behind the words.

He can't fight me on this. I made my decision.

And then it's the two of us, alone again.

Nora pulls me into her lap, both arms curling around, soft and warm. Her chin rests on my head and my ear presses against her chest; her heartbeat thumps in my ear, a beat off from mine, as if we're two different music tracks pressed into the same record. It's a confusing cacophony.

"Explain, please," she says.

"I'm tired of danger, Nora."

She sighs but doesn't say anything more. We breathe together, sharing a still moment as she processes the new reality that I've thrust upon her.

I break the silence.

"I started thinking about it after what happened with Silas," I say. "But with everything that's happened since... it's too much for me. It made me realize I don't *enjoy* being a Sin. Some of it, sure. But the constant posturing, the threats and deceit?" I shake my head, nose brushing against the silky camisole Nora wears. "I don't live for it like my mother and brother did. Like you do."

"But you're their leader," Nora says. "You can't abandon your House."

"Being a leader out of necessity is different from being one out of passion," I say, shaking my head. "And I'm not abandoning them. I'm leaving them in more than capable hands."

Nora's brows are knit, a divot of confusion forms between them.

"Leo wants it more than me, Nor. That's enough of a reason to pass on the title. But if you need more, then please understand when I say this: I've lived my life for other people for so long. First my mother while she was alive. Then my brother after he died. He's the reason I became a Sin. He wanted to bring our House to the level it's at now. But that was his dream, and I need to start living my life for me. And I don't want to live it as Lust."

"You just want to be Imogen."

Nora says it as a statement, not a question, my name sounding decadent on her tongue. I tilt my head back to meet her eyes, our noses grazing in the process.

"Yeah. Just Imogen. The kick-ass empath who runs the best bars in all of Anwynn."

"I can't say I understand fully. I would never give this up willingly," she says, eyes flicking to the fire.

"It's okay if you need time to process it. Took me long enough to realize for myself," I say.

"Does this mean I can finally steal you away to House Pride?"

Her hands trail mindless patterns on my back, sending shivers down my spine.

"No," I giggle.

"Give me a few weeks, and I'll change your mind."

Her arms band tighter around me and I shift, sitting up taller. Nora and I are nose to nose, flirty smiles on both our lips.

"Leo won't let you poach me to the dark side," I say.

"I can handle Leo," she huffs.

I tilt my head, allowing myself one moment to simply look

at her. My fingers trail over the sharp lines of her cheekbones and down the tip of her nose. When I graze over her bottom lip, she nips my finger. Her actions are playful and carefree, but the gleam behind her eyes is the opposite. A dark seriousness lines her irises, lashes hanging low as she regards me as deeply as I do her.

Nails dig into the flesh at my hip, pulling me flush against Nora.

"Can I give you an interim present?"

"Yeah?" I say. "And what would that be?"

"Lots and lots of orgasms."

"Lots and lots?" I tease.

Nora's hum of confirmation is a deep rumble in her chest. Then, she claims my lips like she's the desert and I'm the last drop of water on earth.

Hours later, my fingers run over the textured gold sequins on my dress as I wait in the hall.

The sprites had burst into our rooms two hours ago in a fury, primping and prodding at us until we were ready for the Solstice Ball. I had put up a fight—I can get ready myself—but ultimately succumbed to their strange little hands.

They were surprisingly good at taming my hair into glamorous waves that cascade over one shoulder, *and* they even painted on the perfect arched brow.

I play with the gold rings that line my fingers, twisting Josie's gift that sits at the center of them, around and around until my knuckles ache.

I jerk when the bare, light ocher skin of Josie's shoulder bumps into mine. Her normally straight hair is styled into waves that end below the jaw.

"You okay?" she asks, observant eyes boring into mine.

An exasperated laugh bursts from me. "As okay as I can be, I think."

"What you did earlier was hard. I'm proud of you for being honest with everyone," Josie says. Her gaze is a hot press of an iron over my body as she takes in my outfit. "You're beautiful, Mo."

"Thank you," I say, my cheeks running hot.

"Just the truth."

She shrugs, the silky jade colored shift-dress reflecting the low light with her movement. It's much less ornate than mine but suits her perfectly.

"You're not looking too bad yourself," I say. "You clean up nice."

"I don't get to doll myself up too often," she says. "It's nice."

"I may have to host some formal nights at the Den, so you can."

She barks a laugh. "Sure."

"I'm serious—you look gorgeous."

Now it's her turn to have pink rising on her cheeks. "Thank you."

Nora bursts from our room, shooing away a leathery winged sprite that keeps fussing with her hair. She gives us a wide-eyed glance, and I snort, covering my mouth to hide my laughter.

I had left her to their wrath once I was done. I knew if I stayed and watched her cursing at them while they did her makeup, I would cause more trouble than good.

After one last swipe at taming the flyaway hairs at Nora's

temple, the sprite finally deems its work complete and zooms off down the hall.

Nora murmurs expletives as she strides to us, heels clacking against the stone floor. Her dress is simple, a black silk satin bias-cut to fit her form and flutter around her ankles. The neckline is a sharp v that cuts into her decolletage. The exposed skin at her collarbone shimmers with glitter, giving her an ethereal glow. Matching gloves of pure night rise past her elbows, accentuating the toned muscles of her arms.

Warm lips press against my forehead. A shiver works down my spine.

"You left me with them," she murmurs into my forehead.

Josie snorts. "They're little menaces, aren't they?"

"Precisely." Nora cradles my waist, deft fingers skimming over the exposed skin there. Leaning forward, her lips crest the shell of my ear. "It's going to be exceptionally hard to keep my hands off you. We may have to sneak off to a side hallway."

Heat spreads across my neck, and I know that if I looked in a mirror, I'd see my skin flushed red as a strawberry. She places a kiss on the divot where my jaw meets my neck and the curve of her smile grazes my skin.

"I'm sure the sprites won't mind if we disrespect a hidden corner of their castle," she adds.

Three loud knocks booming through the hallways have me flinching away from Nora; we both turn to see Josie banging on Leo's door.

"Sorry." Josie cringes. "But we are going to be late if he doesn't hurry up."

I stifle my laughter as Leo throws open the door a second later. His shirt is still unbuttoned, and his tie is slung around his neck.

"I need five more minutes," he says, buttoning the shirt from the bottom up.

"Did they not send sprites to help you get ready?" I ask.

"Nope," he huffs and disappears back into his room, leaving the door open.

I snort before grabbing Nora's hand and squeezing it.

"I'm going to go help him. He's terrible at tying ties."

Her red lips curve into a soft smile. "Of course."

As I follow Leo into his room, I hear Josie's fading snicker. "Looking a little smitten there, Nor."

I bite my lip, reeling from the little bit of happiness curling in my belly. This morning gave me a small spark of hope, a small taste of a potential future where, if I'm lucky, we can all start a new phase of our lives, together.

38
NORA

"I need you to promise me right now that you won't leave Imogen's side tonight."

Leo and Imogen walk a few paces ahead of us, laughing and oh-so-oblivious to the looming threat that we head towards.

"Why?" Josie asks, quietly, as we curl down the spiral staircase.

"I met with Benevolence last night," I say.

Our eyes lock, and her magic pokes at my mental shields. I let her in, and she shifts through my memories, replaying the conversation with Benevolence.

It's faster—and safer—than me explaining everything out loud.

"Shit," she says when she's done. Her magic pulls away from me, and I shiver; she's rummaged through my mind a thousand times, but it never gets any more comfortable to feel the slimy prongs probing my mind. "Are you okay?"

"I've heard that question too many times this morning already."

"It's a valid one for me to ask."

"Yeah, well. I'm compartmentalizing," I huff.

"Not well," Josie says.

"Not at all," I concur. "But better than last night."

Josie is quiet as we step onto the ground floor, exiting the stairwell and filing into the grand hall. Her features are pinched, pensive, as we walk shoulder to shoulder.

"I'll protect her," she says, finally.

"Thank you."

Josie scoffs, betraying her carefully concealed frustration with me. "You don't need to thank me, Nor. I care about her too."

"Yes, I do," I double down.

Another tense beat passes between us.

"Are you sure you still want to do this?"

This. Killing Patience. Walking into that ballroom knowing every single pair of Seelie eyes sees right through my facade.

"I had my moment of weakness. It's passed," I say, steeling my shoulders. "I refuse to back down."

"Okay," Josie says. "Then I'm behind you."

I stop, Josie's steps stalling a moment after. Imogen and Leo continue down the hall, but we'll only be a minute behind. We'll catch up to them. I need to do this first because I don't know what will come after we walk through those double doors.

Rushing forward, I tug Josie into a tight hug. She hesitates, shocked at the overt affection, before her arms quickly wrap around me. My heart aches in my chest as our fingers dig into each other's flesh through layers of fabric.

"Thank you," I say, and I hope she understands that it's for more than just today.

"It's going to be okay," Josie whispers into my ear.

"You don't know that."

"I do. In the end, it will be." She somehow squeezes me tighter. "We always said the pain will be worth the reward. Why stop believing that now?"

The words soothe a part of me that I too often ignore.

The pain will be worth it in the end.

They're words I've muttered to myself a thousand times before. And a thousand times over to Josie.

Every time Pride lashed me with a belt.

When he sheared our wings.

Every time we cried into each other's arms over whatever fucked-up thing he had us do. Until the tears dried up, and there were no more left to cry.

She's right.

There's no reason to stop believing that now.

I release Josie, step back, and take a deep breath.

The sprites either have magic of their own, or they worked all night to transform the banquet hall into a winter dreamscape.

Icy blue drapes line the windows and bundles of evergreen zigzag across the ceiling, filling the room with the scent of the forest. Two long wooden farm tables bracket each side of the room, draped with gauzy white runners and pine garland. Fine crystal-white dishware, topped with a knotted forest-green napkin, make up the place settings for each of us.

Sprites of both Unseelie and Seelie nature flutter about the room carrying trays of hors d'oeuvres and drinks, though they've traded glasses of bubbly for festive cocktails. I grab one off a tray and sniff, cranberry filling my nose. I pass it off to Leo, who guzzles it down without a thought.

"Delicious," Leo says, smacking his lips.

He offers it to Imogen, who takes a tentative sip. Her eyes light up.

"Oh! That's not too different from..." they go back and forth about drink recipes, while my attention shifts to the stage at the center of the room.

Sprites pluck at a host of string instruments; a mix of iridescent green and leathery black wings blur with unnatural speed around the harp, violin, viola, and cello. A few Seelie already move at the stage's edge, swaying together in a graceful waltz that differs from the dancing done on our side of Faerie.

I tilt my head, studying a Seelie pair—who both have their translucent gold wings out—as they twirl at the center of the dancers.

I picture Imogen and me waltzing together, with one of my hands on her low back and one of hers on the nape of my neck. I'd pull her close and murmur inappropriate things in her ear that would have her giving in to my whims with ease.

"Do you want to dance?" she asks, curling around my arm and lacing our fingers together.

I smile down at her, softly. "I'd love that."

A rush of air flows through the room when the massive double doors behind us open.

Silas saunters through the archway, and my head snaps with a double take at the sight of his wings cresting over the back of his charcoal-gray suit. Pure white feathers bristle at his back, his wings flexing.

He's the only Unseelie with them out—a fact that does not go unnoticed. A wave of whispers roll through the room. With his matching white hair and dark eyes, he's a creature stepping out of a myth.

He is a man on a mission, the sea of fae parting for him without a word as he strides to Oonagh, the Seelie Queen. They exchange a few words, and she nods, grabbing a fork from a random place setting. Twisting the silver metal in her palm, she uses the dull end to tap against her cocktail glass. The sharp and repeated pings slice through the air, cutting off the band and any whispers of conversation.

The queen hands her drink and fork to a member of her entourage, stepping onto the stage and pushing the musician sprites out of the way. Her dress is similar to the one she wore at the luncheon, all opalescent beading, but today, it falls all the way to the floor and strands dangle off her shoulders. Silas follows her onto the raised platform, though he looks less than ecstatic to be there.

"Ah, thank you, thank you!" Oonagh beams as the Seelie applaud her. Just as the applause subsides, the room darkens. Beyond the windowpanes, dark gray clouds cover the sun as they journey across the sky, casting stormy shadows into the room. The queen scoffs. "We can't have that, even if it is the Winter Solstice!"

She throws her hands out and faerie lights burst from her fingertips; the orbs float to the vaulted ceilings and send sparkling rays of light across the room. Though her magic brings a visual warmth to the room, it cannot mask the tell-tale pitter-patter of rain beginning to pelt the glass windows.

Oonagh forces a smile and claps her hands.

"Much better!" Her entourage of fae laugh as if she told the best joke of the century; she shushes them and the room quiets. "Now, it's been fifty long years of celebration without the Unseelie. But I am *so* happy that our sister Court from across the river has found it in their hearts to embrace tradition again."

She pauses, and a beat passes before the Seelie get the hint and clap. Her smile is taut, not reaching her eyes, when she continues.

"Now, Silas, if you'll have a few words," she drawls, waving Silas forward.

He raises a drink-clad hand.

"Happy Solstice," he says. Then throws back the entirety of his drink.

The queen's lips curl over her teeth in what I would describe as more of a grimace than a smile as Silas stalks off the platform.

"Dinner will be served shortly!" She laughs nervously and snaps her fingers at the band. They start an upbeat tune, and she steps off the stage, swallowed by the throngs of Seelie on the dance floor.

All of them have their wings out; the fae-light filled room glitters with every flutter of their wings. Some are opalescent, like dragonflies, and others are more akin to butterflies and moths, with opaque patterns that mimic monarchs and swallowtails.

"That was... interesting," Josie says tentatively.

"Fucking awkward is what it is," I say, watching Silas stalk our way.

"It is the fiftieth anniversary of his parents' deaths. Maybe he isn't feeling chatty today?" Imogen offers.

"The man loves to hear himself talk," I say. "No. He's just being smart."

"Well, *smart* is headed right for us," Leo says over the rim of his glass.

Silas stops before our group, and the five of us stare at each other, unblinking.

"Happy Solstice?" Leo asks, breaking the silence.

Silas ignores Leo and raises a quizzical brow at me.

"Can we chat?" he asks.

"Sure." I give Imogen's hand a squeeze before letting it go. I lean into Imogen's ear. "Don't leave Josie's side, please."

She reads the seriousness in my tone and nods, pulling Josie and Leo away to go find some hors d'oeuvres.

I turn to Silas, finding his gaze locked on Imogen; there's a sadness that lingers there, but it's quickly shaken away as his kingly mask falls back into place.

"You're wearing your gloves," he says.

I tug at one, pulling it further up my arm, the silky shadow fibers slipping between my fingers.

"They are vital to our plan, no?"

"Yes, but it shocks me every time you listen to directions without putting up a fight."

"Funny," I deadpan.

He turns and we're shoulder to shoulder; the coarse fabric of his suit scratches the bare stretch of my upper arm. We watch the rest of the room like two hawks, ready to swoop down for our prey.

"Wrath is on standby in case anything goes sideways. He'll pull people out as fast as he can." Silas sips his drink. "I would have us develop some kind of signal, but a good shout will work just the same."

"Good to know."

I know Josie is watching Imogen, but it's an extra comfort knowing that Silas has an evacuation plan.

"What are the odds everything goes as planned?" I ask.

"They were never very good to begin with."

"But we're here anyway."

"We are here anyway."

Silas sighs at my side, shifting on his feet. His wings bristle with the movement, feathers brushing against my back. Immediately, I stiffen, all joints in my body locking as the soft plumes graze against the exposed tops of my scars.

"You seem calmer than last night," Silas murmurs softly, ignoring the way my body reacts to his.

"I—"

Any retort I might have uttered back to the Unseelie King is cut short by fanfare, a line of sprites carrying our first course to the dinner tables.

"That's our cue," Silas says. "Dance with me after dinner, yeah? Patience will take the bait."

He stalks off to the table, leaving me staring after him with phantom pains running down my scars.

Whoever made the seating chart was an idiot.

I glare at the sprites that flitter between each of us, making sure our drinks are topped off as we take our seats.

Benevolence shoots me a kind smile as he takes the seat across from me; the mousy woman to his right must be his second. To his left sits the Seelie Queen and across from her— meaning right next to me—is Silas.

Relief washes over me when his wings dissipate into shadow, revealing the smooth expanse of his suit jacket.

Magic works in strange ways, our fabrics enchanted to work around our wings when we wish—if we have wings.

My scars still haven't stopped itching.

To my left is Imogen, and I place a hand on her thigh. I squeeze it, the sensation of my fingers digging into her flesh is a lifeline, mooring me to shore. Josie and Leo are to her left, and the rest of the Sins spread out evenly on either side of Silas and I. On the other side of the table sit all the Seelie, at least, the important ones. The queen's courtiers are sat at the table on the other side of the room. Though, two important players are noticeably missing: Patience and Alexander.

A thrumming kind of energy shakes my leg, my heel tapping repeatedly against the marble floor. My magic perks, anticipating what's to come.

I just have to get through dinner.

The Seelie double doors finally swing open.

"Late," Silas scoffs to himself, but I'm close enough to hear it.

My thought exactly.

He *had* to make a dramatic entrance.

Patience is followed by his other son—my younger cousin—and they take the two empty seats directly to the left of the queen.

"Ah! Great, now we can start." Oonagh claps, the Seelie all digging into their plates after she stabs a piece of salad with her fork. "Patience, dear, this must be so nice for you. Your first Solstice with all your family in years."

My stomach instantly sours, any bit of appetite I had gone.

Patience laughs. "Yes, it's nice to have both of my sons here with me."

His cold eyes cut my way; a shark-like grin spreads across his cheeks that sets a storm rolling in my belly.

Benevolence clears his throat, addressing Silas. "This is my brother's first Solstice as Patience's Second."

"Is it?" Silas's brows flick to his forehead, vacant eyes landing on my younger cousin. His tone is unamused, lacking any actual interest.

An awkward beat passes, the only sound the scraping of

forks and knives against the ceramic plates. The air is tense, most eyes are firmly set on their food. But I know each set of ears is tuned to the conversation between the center seats.

"So sad about the late Pride," Oonagh croons my way. She speaks as she cuts, her knife scraping back and forth through a chunk of near-rare meat. Lifting one piece, her lips wrap around the fork and she hums, chewing and swallowing before continuing. "But he wasn't *really* your father."

Her lips curve into a devious smile, her questions spearing right through any pretense we were keeping between us; twice now, she's made jabs at my real heritage.

The queen thinks she's a cat and I'm a mouse.

She'll soon find out I'm a wolf in disguise.

"No." I clear my throat, dabbing the edge of my mouth with my napkin. "He took me in when I was a youngling."

Imogen's knee bumps mine under the table, the contact a steady comfort.

"Very kind of him," Oonagh says. "I don't remember him being a kind man."

"He wasn't."

"Yet he still took an orphan in to carry on his legacy?" The queen laughs, causing the rest of the Seelie at the table to chuckle. Patience joins in, a smug smile plastered across his face. "Seems like a silly thing to do."

"You could say I offered him more than a child born of his own blood would have," I say.

"She is quite talented," Silas quips.

"As we've heard," the queen croons. "We thought it would be good entertainment for tonight."

Silas's knife pauses halfway through his piece of chicken.

"Oh?" he says, putting both utensils down. Now they've hooked him.

The queen is absolutely delighted, having his attention.

She leans across the table, spearing us both with a conspiratorial look.

"I want to see it in person, if you will humor me," Oonagh says. Then she turns her head towards her Virtues. "Charity, dear, will you bring in our sacrifice for the night?"

"Sacrifice?" Imogen whispers at my side. Her hand has meandered to my knee, where her nails dig into my flesh through the fabric.

"Oh, don't worry, darling. We don't make it a habit of sacrificing people on Solstice." Oonagh waves away our worry. "You don't mind, do you, Pride?"

I think loud and clear for Josie to calm Imogen down, as all eyes are on me and I can't do it myself. Out of my periphery I see Josie lean in, whispering in Imogen's ear, and I feel Imogen's nails retreat from my leg. All the while, I shoot Oonagh a smile.

"Of course not," I say.

"See? She doesn't mind," Oonagh says to Silas, who is pitting her with a glare.

Then the Seelie doors burst open again, two guards dragging a disgruntled fae between them. His wrists are chained in iron, not unlike how we had our prisoners restrained at Mt. Bramble. The only difference being that this one is Seelie, and we don't know if his crimes justify the punishment.

I look to Silas for guidance.

He doesn't seem happy about it, but he nods anyway. Approval to play along.

The Seelie guards stop at the center of the dance floor, forcing the prisoner to his knees. His sobs fill the room, a somber sight for a day that's supposed to be a celebration.

I stand, pushing in my chair after myself. I make a show of pulling off my gloves, placing them in Silas's outstretched hand. I hope he can read the thank you in my eyes before I turn and walk to the prisoner. My heels are a rhythmic beat behind the melody of his sobs.

I don't waste any time.

My magic is already waiting and hungry at my fingertips.

I simply graze his forehead, his clammy skin brushing against mine. My magic rushes forward, clogging his veins and overloading his heart.

The Seelie crumbles to the ground and silence echoes in the space.

I pivot and hold my hands out, mimicking a magician who has performed a trick.

"There," I say, my own cunning grin plastered across my face. "Not very climactic, is it?"

That knocks people from their entranced stupor. The queen claps, her people following suit enthusiastically.

"That is unreal," she laughs. "Quite a talent indeed."

I take my seat, and Silas hands me my gloves. I pull them on carefully and quietly as the table assumes a state close to normalcy —however normal our two Courts can act with each other.

It's not until dinner is cleared and the sprites are playing a slow, somber tune that the energy shifts.

It's time.

Silas stands, offering me his hand.

"Dance?"

I hesitate; I know Patience won't approach me if I'm dancing with Silas. No, my uncle will wait until I'm dancing with the person who I care about most in the room. The one he knows I want to protect.

I push past the twinge of fear in my heart—he won't hurt her right now; I'll hand her off to Josie when he comes, and then it'll be okay.

And selfishly, I want this dance with her.

I grab her hand.

"Ask me again after I'm done with this one," I say to Silas, pulling Imogen from her seat.

"Dance with me?" I ask, mocking the question she would ask me every night I frequented the Den just to see her.

"Don't I always?" she chides, quoting my usual response.

She giggles as I draw her close to me on the dance floor; her arms circle around my neck, and my hands sit low on her back. We sway among the Seelie, no others from our Court having taken the opportunity to dance.

Too many eyes burn holes in my back, but I ignore them, my focus set wholly on Imogen. Resting my forehead against hers, I bask in her warmth.

"You're acting strange today," she whispers.

"*Shhh*, I want to enjoy a dance with you."

Imogen hums suspiciously. "Okay."

I twirl her; she laughs.

We sway, wrapped around each other.

We don't talk, at least not with our mouths. I hope my eyes communicate all that I want to say.

Something heavy passes between us.

Her blond brows scrunch over those molten amber eyes. I graze my thumb over her freckled cheek.

It feels like a goodbye.

I hope that it isn't—that it's all in my head—but it's hard to ignore the all too familiar sinking of my gut.

"Nor—"

There's a tap on Imogen's shoulder. She pulls back, startled, breaking the intimate moment.

"Sorry, but could I have the next dance?" Benevolence stands there with an impish grin, his hand scratching the back of his neck.

Imogen looks like she wants to refuse, but I reassure her. "It's okay. Go to Josie."

Imogen's soft gaze flits between me and Benevolence before she nods, scurrying over to our friends who stand by the Unseelie doors.

Josie's smart, staying close to the exits.

My gaze lands on Silas next, who sits in his assigned chair next to Wrath, nursing another glass of liquor. He's not looking at me though—his glare is trained on Benevolence.

Benevolence clears his throat, brows shooting to the top of his forehead in question.

I sigh, holding back an eye roll as I offer my hands to my cousin.

He pulls me into a waltz, the sprites playing the room into more formal dances.

"Are you having a good night?" Benevolence asks.

This time I don't hold back my eye roll. "Yes, I loved being the queen's entertainment for tonight."

"It was unnerving to see death up close, if I'm honest." His body shivers against mine.

We spin on light feet, following the couple next to us as we circle the center stage.

"Have you not killed anyone before?" I ask.

"Does indirectly count?"

"If you have to ask, then you already know it doesn't."

"So, how will the murdering go, with these things on?" Benevolence wiggles his fingers against the back of my hand, pressing into my gloves.

"Who said I was going to act on your favor tonight?"

"If you don't, I may have to retract my assumption of you being smart," he mutters. "If you aren't, then you should never have come tonight."

The music comes to a slow end, Benevolence hinging

forward at his waist in a formal bow to end our dance. He doesn't say another word before he walks away, leaving me partnerless on the dance floor.

"You are quite the commodity tonight," the deep voice that haunts my memory calls from behind me.

I turn, unsurprised. He did take his time, though.

"Can you blame them for liking me?"

Patience smiles, and it has the hair standing up on my arms. "I can, though I do understand the allure."

He holds out a hand. I take it.

My magic giggles under my skin, giddy for its next victim. It quickly passes between me and my gloves, seeping into Patience's skin.

Satisfaction rolls through me as the tether of my magic take root.

And then, we dance.

"You look very much like your mother," Patience says after a few steps.

"From what I can remember of her, I'd agree."

"Though you inherited your father's dark hair."

"You say that as if it's a bad thing."

Patience's nostrils flare with displeasure. Our movements are stiff as we spin between the couples on the dance floor.

"She wasn't supposed to fall in love with him," he seethes.

"Clearly."

There's a pause, a strange and awkward beat where our words, the music, and our feet gliding along the ballroom floor lose their synchronicity.

"Do you not have questions about them?" he asks.

"Who? My parents?" I huff. "Not for you. I know their story well enough."

My uncle spins me, and I'm caught by another Seelie man's

arms. We step for eight counts before he spins me back to Patience.

"You got upset because my mother didn't play her part as spy to your liking. She didn't get close enough to the *right people*. And then, she made the mistake of falling in love with her mark and falling pregnant with me," I recall with venom. "You exiled her. Then you chased us across the Human Realm when you learned what I could do. As if you had any right to claim me as family after how you treated her." I scoff. "I may have been a child, but she told me everything in so many words."

"You might resemble your parents in looks, but your personality is much closer to mine." Patience chuckles. "I always wanted a daughter, you know."

Bile curls in my throat.

I focus on the tether of magic between us, the reminder that I have my reward at my fingertips. All I have to do is pull the trigger when it's time.

"I'm surprised you didn't shoot me on-sight yesterday," he adds.

"I'm not planning on killing you today."

"Oh?"

"I want to savor it," I say. And for the first time as we dance, I meet his gaze.

We have the same eyes. A green so bright and clear, it's a wonder no one has called out the similarity.

Patience hums. "Even so, I got what I wanted in the end, didn't I?"

"How so?"

Our feet hop along with the music, the beat shifting to something faster, more primal, all plucky string and scaling notes.

"You're all here, the Unseelie Court's isolation broken. And I got my spy."

"I'm not a spy for you," I seethe.

Patience chuckles again, and the embers of rage stoke in my stomach.

"No, you're not. You're my unknowing Trojan horse," he surmises. "But that doesn't mean I don't also have a spy. How else would I have known where your little lover was going to be weeks ago?"

Those sparking embers roar into full flames at the mention of Imogen. And a spy who knew where she'd be? Only Josie and Wes knew before the attack... The fire in my veins is doused, frozen over with realization.

Josie would never. Which means he got Wes to talk. How the *fuck* did he get Wes to talk?

"How?" is all I ask.

"You shouldn't be bringing such fresh blood into the field without them properly marking their loyalty, Pride," Patience says. He makes a mockery of my title every time he says it with those sneering lips. "He was shocked to learn that daddy-dearest was slain by the people he's supposed to trust most. And that you're a half-breed? The poor boy was beside himself."

I burrow into my rage, breathing deeply and trying to keep it from exploding around us. Focusing on the tether, the boon of my pain, I keep it firm and strong between us.

I can't lose this.

"And what do you think is going to happen when your king learns who you are? What about your lover? Will lust be enough to keep you together after this?"

Patience drones on, and I attempt to tune him out.

Just make it to the end of the song. Why is this song so fucking long?

I glare at the sprites plucking away at their instruments over Patience's shoulder. The music is building, louder and louder. We have to be coming to the end soon.

Patience's hot breath spreads over my ear. "How many years have you spent wondering what would happen if they found out? You were so desperate to hide who you are that you clipped your own wings. It's a shame."

"There wasn't much of a choice in the matter," I growl.

"I could heal them, you know," he says, casually.

His hand runs up from my mid-back, brushing over the exposed tips of my scars. Prickles of pain flare along the mottled flesh, and I gasp, shoving Patience away. The music crescendos into a cacophony of sound and I stumble backwards into the Seelie dancers, not having realized how crowded the dance floor has become.

Patience laughs, a booming cackle, and dread fills my veins.

I turn, trying to push through the crowd, but they won't part for me. The prickles have turned into stabs at my back, the pain growing worse. I shove drunk Seelie down, and they harrumph at me for being rude, but I don't care.

I need to get away from this man.

I need to get out of here.

My instinct flares; alarm bells sound in the back of my mind.

I'm half tempted to start dropping Seelie right then and there to get past them. But then the double doors on our side of the castle open, letting in chaos.

The rest of my Court's backs are turned to them, because why wouldn't they be? That's supposed to be *our* part of the castle.

The Seelie aren't *supposed* to be on that side.

My throat constricts.

I had thought I could go to both sides because I was both

Unseelie and Seelie—but maybe I was wrong. Maybe the castle never cared who went where. And we were supposed to trust each other.

We were fools, then.

Seelie guards enter the room, armed with semi-automatics that I'm all too familiar with.

I yell, pushing all the breath from my lungs into this one cry. Silas's name unfurls from my mouth while Josie's name screams forth from my mind.

The world moves in slow motion as I break past the last of the Seelie courtiers, who are unaware of their Virtue's plan to massacre this entire ballroom. Guns like those aren't used for accuracy, they're designed to cause the most damage as quickly as possible. As many Seelie will be caught in this crossfire as Unseelie.

White hair whips towards me, black eyes meeting mine before disappearing into shadowy wisps. My gloves dissipate too, leaving me without any barriers.

Flashes of shadow and light spark across the room. Those that can, magic away, leaving the rest of us to fend for ourselves.

The Seelie guards unleash their weapons.

It's a hailstorm of bullets and screams.

I stride forward without fear, wincing at the discomfort at my back. I whip my head from side to side, hunting for Josie, Imogen, and Leo.

Flickers of Wrath appear, pulling the Unseelie one-by-one from the room. Meanwhile, Silas is taking out Seelie guards. He's a swirling mass of shadow, a black hole sucking in the guards and spitting their lifeless bodies out with speed and accuracy.

Finally, I spot them, Josie standing in front of Imogen and Leo in the corner of the room. Josie's got her gun out, shooting at Seelie as they slowly inch their way toward the windows. The Unseelie doors now the center of the worst violence; she's smart to lead them away from—

A hand smacks between my shoulder blades. A searing agony spears through my back.

It's all-consuming. White-hot, like being burned from the inside out.

I feel it this time, his magic, swirling beside mine; it rearranges the cells of my body, building new tissue and cutting through muscle. I fall to my knees, screaming through the pain.

My core splits open. It's a reawakening of something I had lost a decade ago.

Wings. They sprout from my back, reborn.

An ache lingers in my bones as the agony subsides and I push up from the floor. The world tilts on its axis as emerald meets amber; Imogen's face is stricken white across the room. Her hand covers her parted lips, devastation racking her features as she takes in the impossibility unfurling from my back.

And then she's gone, Wrath's shadows engulf her.

And I'm left with my rage.

I turn and unleash it on my uncle.

I don't care about plans. I don't care about Silas. All I care about is killing him. Right *fucking* now. In the most violent way possible.

Patience laughs as I launch at him. He laughs as I tackle him to the ground. And he laughs as I punch his stupid face bloody.

Any bit of restraint I had breaks. I grip his suit lapel, hauling his face into the air, only to punch it back into the marble floors. With all the reckoning of an avenging god, I rain down on him the violence of a hurricane.

"You're going to regret leaving me alive that day. When I'm done with you, you will wish you could die so easily." Spit flies from my mouth as I speak. My fist meets his face on every word, bone crunching under my knuckles. He laughs through the pain, his bloody teeth curled into a smile.

Bullets whiz past me. It's a miracle that I haven't been hit yet.

Patience's face heals as fast as my blows are dealt, his flesh stitching back together every time my knuckles rip it apart. I lose myself completely to my fury. My magic roils and cheers in my belly, pushing me closer to using it in its full might, but I hold tight to that tether. I make it strong, weaving it with the iron thread of my will.

I will not let it break.

But I *will* savor his death.

This pain will be worth this reward.

Patience's eyes flick beyond my shoulder, but I'm too slow to catch it, the back of my head blooming with pain as I'm knocked onto my back.

My vision is blurry, but I can still make out the curled mustache of my cousin standing above me.

"I'm sorry." I hear.

The world goes white around me. I'm thrust into the heart of a star, burned whole.

39
IMOGEN

We stumble out of Wrath's shadows, Leo falling to the ground with the momentum. He mutters a curse, pushing up from the sand and brushing off his hands. The wet specks of red seashell and crumbled white sand stick to his skin—the ones that do fall away leave behind little indents on his palms.

Rain mists down on us, dampening our gowns and flattening our curls.

My body is taught and pulsing, my blood thrashing through my veins. The edges of my vision cloud, and I blink hard, trying to push the haze away. My chest heaves; the air is too thin, and it doesn't fill my lungs.

Pain lances my side, but when I press my hand to the stretch of abdomen there, it runs over unscathed fabric. There's blood on my hands, but it's not mine.

There are voices shouting around me and somebody pushes me past the stormy edge of the lake. We cross the stone bridge. Waves slosh against the stone and splash over the edge, soaking our shoes.

Josie ushers me and Leo away from Casimir with a firm hand on my back. I peer over my shoulder, my hair whipping around my face with the wind. The hard set of Josie's jaw betrays her worry, despite the resolve in her tone. The words she speaks are garbled and slurred together through the rain, but I somehow get the meaning.

Get to safety.

Gun shots echo from the castle and through the lakeside valley. With each resounding *pop,* I jerk. Leo's hand finds mine, and I realize I'm shaking. Not from the cold, though as we get farther from the walls of Casimir the chill deepens, but from the rush of adrenaline and memory.

This can't be happening again.

My head whips from side to side, searching for the thick swath of Nora's black hair.

Where is she?

"Wrath went back for her. She'll be fine." Josie's voice is strong and steady. She's navigated these situations before, and not only with me. "But she won't be if we don't get you two across this bridge."

We stumble through the ancient magical barrier that surrounds the lake, and then through the extra thin film of the shadow-veil. Leo and the others fall to the soil in varied states of respite, but true relief evades me. Gluttony and her Second heave with their backs against a pine and Envy paces in circles, wildly pulling at strands of his hair.

"What the fuck just happened?" Leo says, staring at the castle in the distance in disbelief.

"I knew there was something wrong with that bitch," Envy seethes. He turns to me, rushing forward with an accusing finger pointed my way. "Did you know she was Seelie? She sold us out!"

Josie steps in his path, a strong hand shoving at his chest.

"Watch yourself, Envy. This is bigger than you," she says.

They have a silent standoff, the tension thick in the air between them. But Josie's the one with a gun, and the audible click of the safety has Envy backing off. He scoffs, a sneer marring his features.

"You're just as much a traitor if you knew." His disdain quickly falls away, a twist of deep-rooted fear and knee-buckling sadness taking over. "And if you didn't, well, then we're all screwed." He falls to his knees, fingers weaving back through his hair, clutching tightly. "Fucking gods. They killed my Second."

"Josie," Leo calls. "Is what we saw true? Those were—" His throat catches on his words. "Those were Seelie wings."

The image of the bright green and black wings flash in my mind.

When Nora's scream rang through the hall, Josie had sprung into action, pulling Leo and me away from the onslaught of bullets. It all happened in a matter of seconds— the shout, the shots, the way I searched for her in the crowd. When I found her, the overwhelming terror I felt as Patience gripped her from behind had the blood draining from my face.

I didn't want her to die. She screamed, and I felt her pain, my magic reaching out to her. It was vast and unyielding, like my soul was burning on the inside and bursting out of my back. I'd never felt anything like it before.

Then the wings unfurled around her, a dark halo. I'd seen those wings before. On the mantel in her living room.

Her wings.

Josie releases a slow sigh. She doesn't deny it. Can't anymore, I realize.

Nora is Seelie.

"Gluttony, start getting everyone back to Anwynn. I'm going back to help Wrath," Josie says, ignoring the question.

"Don't bother with the cars. Shadow-walk everyone now that we're past the wards. You should have enough power for that."

"What?" I say. My voice is rough and scratchy. "No. No, you can't go back there. They will kill you."

I grab the hand that doesn't hold her gun. Our fingers slip together, mine trembling and hers steady. The rain is now a deluge falling down on us. Water runs down my face, masking the tear-tracks that I know are on my cheeks.

My eyes sting.

Josie's dark brown hair is slicked and sticking to her skin, darkened to almost black with the water and the clouded light of the storm.

"Don't leave me," I beg.

It's a selfish thing to say, but I say it anyway. I want to save Nora, but I don't want Josie to go either.

Does that make me a terrible person?

The stubborn fight leaves her. I see it in the way her shoulders fall at my request. Her jaw feathers, and her lips mash together.

My heart starts to ache.

"Mo—" She doesn't get to finish whatever she was going to say because the other Sins rush into the clearing.

Greed carries with him the limp body of his Second. Wrath does the same, but carrying Envy's Second. Silas strides behind them, a dark god, shadows already whirling around his feet and curling towards each of us.

"It's time to go," Silas says. His voice echoes between the trees like thunder.

Shadows wrap around my ankles—*what the hell is happening?*

I search for Nora behind him, but she's not there.

"Where is she?" I ask.

No one answers me. The rest of the Sins slowly disappear

into shadows. I step around Josie and towards the Unseelie King, my soaked and muddied heels spearing through the inky tendrils of darkness swirling at our calves. My teeth chatter, the icy chill of the winter rain finally seeping into my bones.

"Where is Nora?" I demand. "You can't just leave her!"

"They took her, and there's too many to fight right now without reinforcements. We need time to regroup and make a plan," Silas says.

"They won't kill her, Mo," Josie says behind me.

I whip around, realizing it's only the three of us left, standing at the center of the storm and Silas's shadows.

"No, they won't," Silas says at my back.

"So, you knew?" Josie asks Silas over my shoulder. A huff of sardonic laughter shakes her head. "Who am I kidding? Of course, you knew. It's the only thing that makes any sense in hindsight."

"Knew what? That Nora's Seelie?" I ask.

Josie steps forward, wrapping me in her arms. I'm stuck in place, trembling in her strong embrace.

"You need to calm down, Imogen," she says, tucking my head into the warm crook of her neck. "You're going into shock."

"Why wouldn't they kill her? They tried to kill all of us! They—they shot me!" My teeth are chattering. My legs are weak and wobbly, and I'm sure I'd be on the ground if it weren't for Josie holding me. My breaths are coming too fast, and darkness creeps at the edge of my vision—*or is that Silas's shadows crawling over me?* "Wh—why are you all being so calm about this?"

"Mo, you need to calm down or you're going to pass out," Josie whispers in my ear.

"Nora's reputation may be wounded, but her life is safe for now. Patience surely has bigger plans for her," Silas says.

I manage to crack open my eyes, seeing him standing beside us with a look of pure rage twisting his features. There's something there, in the way his eyes soften, that I recognize. My chest heaves in uncontrollable bursts and my lids grow heavy again.

Josie's magic worms its way past my shattered mental barriers, attempting to quell my panic. But before the darkness of sleep or Silas's shadows overtake me, I'm left with a promise from the Unseelie King.

"I'll get her back."

40
NORA

LATER

I wake from suffocating darkness in the water-logged bowels of Casimir.

There's no natural light. Only a single torch burns on the wall outside the iron bars of my cell, casting everything in an eerie glow.

I lick my dry, cracked lips, wincing as my tongue swipes over a raw and bloodied crack at the center. I lean my head back against the cold stone, the spot at my crown still aching.

I'm still wearing my dress from Solstice, even though weeks have passed—at least, I assume it's been that long. Without the sun, I would count the passing hours by the meals the Seelie brought me. The food resembled something like breakfasts and dinners at first, but then I got my hands on their delivery boy.

It didn't end well for him.

They haven't sent down a meal since.

Fae can live without sustenance for a month. But it isn't a pleasant experience.

My stomach is long past the point of rumbling its frustrations; it wails on about the constant ache that I try to ignore.

The stone wall is cold as ice at my back, but at least it makes me feel something other than numb. I close my eyes and focus on the one thing holding my sanity together: the tether of magic still linking Patience and me.

It's the only thing to do in the dungeons of Casimir.

I'm tempted to snap it every time I wake from my nightmares. But I wasn't lying to him when I said I wanted to savor his death. It's more than a want now.

I *need* to see the life drain from his eyes, feel his pulse stop under my fingertips. Simply snapping this tether isn't good enough anymore.

Still, the tether is a fail-safe, so long as I maintain it. I build it up, slow and steady, siphoning all the magic I can into fortifying the connection.

Either way, his fate is sealed. In that alone, our plan worked.

The image of Imogen, shock and desperation stricken across her face, flashes across my mind. I wince at the onslaught of memories. They strike me without warning, sharp and to the heart, more often than I'd like. The way betrayal burned in those amber eyes before she was consumed by darkness replays in my head over and over again.

It's a new ghost, haunting me the same way the memory of Patience once did.

This is worse, I think.

All I can hope is that she is safe. That Josie and Leo are safe. And that they can take better care of her than I did.

I palm my thigh, where the gun Imogen gifted me still rests, strapped to my flesh. I'm keeping it safe.

In my fantasies, I shoot Patience between the eyes with it.

Hours or days pass; I'm too tired to count the minutes.

But then the air shifts with a strange breeze, the shadows in the corner of the dungeon swirling in a familiar pattern. I know it's him before he even steps through.

It's not a relief, like it should be, because I'm not Pride anymore. How could I be?

Silas's nose scrunches at the dank smell of the cellar. He is all casual nonchalance as he stands on the other side of my iron cage, fresh blood splattered on his shirt and white hair glowing red under the torchlight.

He frowns.

"I owe Wrath fifty dollars," he mutters. "They really kept you down here this whole time?"

No "*Hello.*"

No "*How are you?*"

No "*You traitorous bitch.*"

My throat is rough from disuse and dehydration, but it still holds the same snippy spark I reserve for the Unseelie King.

"Yeah, well, I don't think they trust me enough to keep me in Avalon."

A silence passes between us where we study each other. Silas tilts his head as he takes in the damp dungeon and my state of appearance. Any wounds I sustained from the altercation in the ballroom are long healed, but the fact remains that I haven't bathed or looked in a mirror since before the ball.

"So," I say.

"So?" Silas mirrors. He leans back against the stone wall, crossing his feet and shoving his hands in his pockets.

I roll my eyes. *Even now, he has to be a pain?*

"Are you going to kill me now? Because if you're going to do that, I'd love to get on with it."

Silas laughs, a full-bodied chuckle, as if *I'm* the crazy one for asking such a question.

I think it's a valid one.

"Nora," he says, wiping away a stray tear. "I'm not here to kill you."

"What?"

"I already knew."

Shock reverberates through my body, down to my soul.

"No." I shake my head. "No one knew." I sit up on my knees, crawling to the iron bars and gripping them in my hands. "*How did you know?*"

We must have been too loud because a metal latch slides, echoing down the stairwell. Steps sound, a quick patter of boots on stone. I watch as Silas watches me, all with a quirked brow, like he's challenging me to tell him to leave.

He doesn't move as the Seelie guard rounds the bottom of the stairs.

"Hey, you can't be down here—"

Silas simply touches the Seelie guard, and the body crumples to the ground, unmoving.

Dead.

Dead *by touch*.

My brain processes the information, then tries to cross-reference every memory of Silas to see if I missed *something*—a hint that he was more than he let on. But there are none.

"You're a soul-stealer?" I whisper.

"Shadow-walker, empath, soul-stealer—a king can be many things." Silas levels with me, crouching on his heels and folding his palms together. "You must have noticed in your guided research at Mt. Bramble that soul-stealers haven't emerged outside Royal bloodlines since before the split of Faerie. So, imagine my surprise when Pride revealed you to society."

"Is it wrong of me to have pretended I was special?"

"You are special. Just not in that specific way." Silas rubs the day-old stubble growing on his chin. "Pride kept your magic well disguised and kept you well hidden from my spies. I always had suspicions, of course, but it wasn't until I saw your magic up close that I realized what you are."

His tongue darts out and licks his lip.

"Something different entirely. The magic of a healer twisted in such a way that instead of life, you gift death." He huffs a short laugh, an awe-filled smile dimpling his cheeks. The way his black eyes roam over me has gooseflesh rising across my skin. "I wasn't lying back then, in your office, when I said I couldn't get a good picture of you."

"Is it clear now?" I ask. "The picture of me?"

"I see you clearer now than I've seen anything."

My throat is tight as I swallow. My eyes drift away from Silas and to the darkness at the edge of my cell.

"Why doesn't anyone know about you?"

"Because I don't want them to."

"But you want me to know?"

"You and Wrath." He shrugs. "It's not nearly as fun a power as yours. There's no pain with me. No finesse. No control. It's just, *poof.*"

On the last word, his eyes widen, and his fingers stretch out in front of him, a mimed explosion.

"So, you really aren't here to kill me?"

"No, Nora."

A tense beat passes between us. My hands fall from the bars to my thighs, my fingers digging into my flesh through the dirtied fabric of my gown. Then I let myself ask the question I'm yearning to know the answer to.

"Are they okay?" I ask.

I don't have to specify who. He knows.

"Yes. All three of them."

Relief cuts through me, the release of a deep-rooted ache inside my chest.

"Greed and Envy lost their Seconds though. And Envy was grazed by a bullet. He's being a big baby about it, if I'm being frank," Silas adds, but his humor is lost on me.

"Are you telling me the truth right now, Silas?" My voice cracks; I have to tamper down the sudden flux of emotion rolling through me.

"Do I have a reason to lie?"

"Answer the question," I snap.

"I've only ever told you the truth when you've asked." Silas smirks, quoting the words I'd so perfectly crafted for him months ago.

"So only lies by omission, then?"

"Of course," he says.

I nod. I can live with that.

"What happens now?" I ask.

His resulting grin chills my blood.

Silas stands with a groan, and leans forward against the iron bars. I sit back on my heels, peering up as his head pokes between two bars, his forearms stretched above him.

"The past few weeks have been... frustrating. I've officially pardoned you, but the Sins are split on whether they want you back," he says. "Your House is also unsure if they should stand by you. Seems there's a faction growing behind a young man giving your Second a hard time. It's all unwanted chaos, given the war that's brewing. Patience has Oonagh's ear, and he's practically foaming at the mouth for bloodshed. But I'm sure you expected as much."

"I think we've established I expected to be dead by now."

"You need to have more faith in your friends, Nora," Silas chuckles. "We came back for you, after all."

"We?"

"Wrath is upstairs," Silas says.

To that, I have no response. Instead, I watch as tendrils of shadow wrap around his hand and snake down to the padlock on the cage door. It takes only a second for his shadows to pick the lock.

It falls with a *clank* to the floor.

My tongue darts out, tasting freedom in the air as Silas pulls open the cell door.

"C'mon. Your lover is worried," he says. "And we still have a Virtue to kill."

He holds his ungloved hand out to me.

It's an offering. A claim. A statement of unquestionable trust. I didn't understand it before, but I get it now.

We're the same.

I take his hand.

WHAT'S NEXT?

Nora and Imogen's story continues in Sins & Virtues Book Two, coming in 2025!

In the meantime, gain access to bonus content (*like Silas and Wrath fulfilling their end of the bet at Mt. Bramble*) and stay up to date with G.B. Bancroft's releases by joining her newsletter!

https://authorgbbancroft.beehiiv.com/subscribe

ACKNOWLEDGMENTS

You would think writing the acknowledgments section for your book would be easier than writing the damn book… but somehow it isn't. So, please, bear with me as I ramble on about all the amazing people that made this book happen.

First, thank you, Reader. (I've always wanted to write that.) Now that it's out of my head, this story lives on because of *you*. Imogen's half of this book is a love letter to those of you who might feel lost, or those who trudge forward on a path set before them without questioning why they're walking and then suddenly find themselves living a life they didn't want, or don't like. You can always choose yourself, no matter how far you've strayed from where you want to be. Nora's half of this book is an ode to female rage. To women who are ambitious, capable, and stubborn—us girls who refuse to change for anyone. I hope you feel seen in some way by these characters.

Thank you to my cover designer, Maria Spada (@mspremades) for creating the perfect debut cover. And thank you to my proofreader and formatter Kay (@kmortonedits) for polishing this manuscript until it was shiny as hell.

Thank you to my editor, Maddi (@end_of_my_trope). Your insights and talent were instrumental in refining this story. Your in-line comments had me giggling and gave me the confidence to keep pushing forward.

To my alpha reader, Hana: I'm lowkey embarrassed with how vastly different the final product is from the raw, second draft you read. Thank you for sticking by my side from day one and giving me the feedback I needed to turn it from an ok story to a great one.

To my betas, Nicole, Valentina, Charity, Sam, Sarah, and Jenna: you all are the best. I cannot express the gratitude I have for each one of you and your feedback. You fueled my fire when I was burning on embers. Sharing my story with you all was the most rewarding experience. And to the few of you who I know are writing their own stories… I can't wait for the day I get to read your books.

To the rest of my insta-fam: you know who you are. Every like, reply, comment, share… it means more than you realize to a baby author just getting started. Thank you.

To the college lads: Brigid, Chris, John, and Nicole. You guys were on the receiving end of every anxious freak out and every excited squeal. You've cheered me on for years and I am so thankful for your friendship and support.

To my bestie, Erin. My day one. My ride-or-die. My go-to soundboard. You've been a part of this journey from the start. Without our late-night phone calls, I never could have figured my (or Imogen's) shit out. I hope you know that the reason I can write such realistic friendships is because of you. Love you babe.

To my in-laws: siblings, parents, and extended family alike, thank you for always asking about my book and cheering me on from the sidelines.

To my fam-bam…

Nana, thank you for helping cultivate my artistic passions from a young age. I love thinking back on the days we spent painting, sewing, and baking together, they are some of my fondest memories.

Grammie, you are always there when I need you. I am so thankful I have you in my corner. Your facetimes make my day and your texts make me smile. I don't think I could have gotten where I am today without your never-ending support.

Dill & Zach—I really am the luckiest older sister. You put up with my bullshit and we've always got each other's backs. I couldn't have asked for better little bros.

Mom & Dad—I don't think I can ever repay you for everything you've done for me. You've supported me wholeheartedly and enthusiastically, and always encouraged me to follow my passion. That's not something I take lightly. I'm literally crying as I write this (oops) because I truly have the best parents in the world. I love you guys.

To Miso, you can't read, but you are the best co-worker on the planet, even if you are kind of a bitch sometimes. I love being your cat-mom.

And finally, to my husband. You're the gamer-boy to my bookish-girl. Every day with you is a dream, even when we're both stressed as fuck. You never once doubted me when I said I wanted to publish a book and you always made sure to remind me not to put so much pressure on myself. You are my comfort and my relief. Also, I secretly love that this will be the first book you read since college English classes. I love you, I love you, I love you.

ABOUT THE AUTHOR

G.B. Bancroft, *aka Gabs*, is an events producer for global sports teams by day and a baby author by night. She loves all things magical, gritty, and romantic, and is a voracious mood reader. Originally from New York, she's currently enjoying a few-year stint in sunny California with her husband and her grumpy orange tabby, Miso. *A Sin So Pure* is her debut novel.

You can find her @authorgbbancroft on Instagram, Threads, and TikTok. You can also add her on Goodreads and Amazon.